JASON ANSPACH   NICK COLE

REMAINS

SEASON 2   BOOK 4

GALAXY'S EDGE

Paperback ISBN: 978-1-949731-67-5
Hardcover ISBN: 978-1-949731-68-2

Edited by David Gatewood
Published by Galaxy's Edge Press

Cover Art: Tommaso Renieri
Cover Design & Formatting: Kevin G. Summers

Website: www.GalaxysEdge.us
Facebook: facebook.com/atgalaxysedge
Newsletter (get a free short story): www.InTheLegion.com

EXPLORE ALL PRODUCTS AT

GALAXYSEDGE.US

WHO'S WHO...

What follows is a summary of some of the characters found in this book, and their stories up to this point. More characters will appear in this volume but listing them up front would kind of spoil things. If you find yourself lost, consider joining one of the Galaxy's Edge fan groups listed at the end of the book. There is no shortage of fellow leejes who love talking about the story of Galaxy's Edge (and speculating and theorizing about what comes next).

Aeson Ford – See Aeson Keel.

Aeson Keel – See Wraith.

Andien Broxin – A Nether Ops operative who worked closely with Legion Dark Ops (*Kill Team*). Broxin's military career began as a Republic Marine (*Forget Nothing*). She was selected for an experimental Legion training program (*Forget Nothing II*). Presumed dead at the hands of the Cybar (*Message for the Dead*), Broxin was saved by a dissenting Cybar named Praxus and is currently working with him.

Archimedes – The head of a peculiar Savage mini-hulk that gathers lost star-farers and pits them against combat simulations. Archimedes made a deal with an ad hoc alliance composed of Prisma, Ravi, and members of Goth

Sullus's elite strike force, allowing them to leave the ship if they would restore control to Archimedes. He awaits a final solution to a high-value scenario... one that requires the help of Wraith.

Bear – Dark Ops captain who oversees Kill Team Victory. No longer regularly involved in direct action due to injuries suffered in the Second Battle for Utopion (*Retribution*), he fills the role once held by Major Owens.

Crometheus – A Savage marine who lived in a simulation on the edge of madness (*Gods & Legionnaires*). Part of the Savage tribe known as the Uplifted, he was presumed deactivated. The reasons for his reappearance and the subsequent change of his reality are currently unknown.

Cybar – A species of mechanical, non-biological life. Created by unknown causes in one of the Temples of the Ancients (*Legacies*). Discovered by the Republic and recovered by Kill Team Ice (*Legacies*, again). Given the planet Khan Sakh (*Legionnaire*) as a home world, while also used to construct a doomsday fleet (*Message for the Dead*).

Donal Makaffie – Eccentric, existential genius. The inventor of H8. An expert on many things Savage, possesses an ability to intuitively comprehend what they're attempting. A member of Kill Team Ice and veteran of the Savage Wars.

Garret – A technical wizard and savant. Was a former slave of Lao Pak, "liberated" by Aeson Keel, and now serves as a crewmember on the *Indelible IV*.

J316 – A very old "missionary" bot meant to evangelize and/or proselytize humanoid species. Programmed in multiple faiths, J316 has been receiving "new revelations" concerning the worship of Oba.

Kill Team Ice – Early in the Savage Wars it became apparent that the post-human Savages had an advantage over the humans they sought to destroy: long lifespans. Savages were content to attack, disappear, and re-attack when many of the tactical lessons learned had been forgotten. Tyrus Rechs and Admiral Sulla took volunteers from the best of the Legion who agreed to remain in cryo-stasis until a military application arose that required their unique talents. Members of Kill Team Ice served throughout the Savage Wars. Some opted to resume life in the decades after the wars' official ending point.

Kill Team Victory – Dark Ops kill team founded shortly after the Battle of Kublar. Active team members: Bombassa, Pina, Neck, Nix, Nobes, "Toots," Wello.

Lao Pak – He pirate king.

Leenah – Endurian "princess." Exceptionally skilled mechanic. Former MCR rebel. Keel's main squeeze. A surrogate mother to Prisma for a time.

Masters – Quite possibly the sexiest man in the galaxy. Definitely the best abs in the galaxy. Screenwriter. Heartthrob. Dark Ops legionnaire. Currently evading hostile zhee while navigating the blighted and desolate areas of the planet Kima.

Nilo – A genius-level intellect who controls a vast corporate empire. His shadowy past involves parents who were apparently lost to Gomarii slavers, though he believes his father is alive and trapped somewhere beyond galaxy's edge. He is desperately seeking as much Savage technology as possible, despite it being illegal to possess such artifacts.

Praxus – A member of the Cybar collective who dissented from the directives of MAGNUS and CRONUS. He was the lone Cybar to oppose aligning with those discovered beyond galaxy's edge. He accepted exile in order to save the life of Andien Broxin, who he saw as the next evolutionary step for the Cybar—the perfect blend of machine and humanity.

Prisma Maydoon – Juvenile girl whose father, Kael Maydoon, was murdered by Goth Sullus. She hired Tyrus Rechs to seek her revenge and found herself swept up in the rise of the Cybar and the fall of the Republic. Has a preternatural ability to use what Goth Sullus called "the Crux."

Ravi – One of the Ancients, left behind to help humanity resist the destruction coming from beyond galaxy's edge... if such is even possible. See also *Urmo*.

Reina – A Savage prisoner who helped free Tyrus Rechs and Casper Sullivan (*Imperator*). She later disappeared, though she seems to have had some communication with Casper before the man became Goth Sullus (*Gods & Legionnaires*). Trained in what Goth Sullus called "the Crux," she has returned to the galaxy, revealing to Prisma Maydoon that she is her mother.

Skrizz – Wobanki smuggler who briefly co-piloted for Tyrus Rechs (*Galactic Outlaws*) before joining the crew of the *Indelible VI*. "Tamed" by Prisma, Skrizz sought the girl out on his own before turning to piracy. He was enticed by Donal Makaffie into resuming the hunt for Prisma, this time by leading Makaffie to Aeson Keel.

Tyrus Rechs – The founder of the Legion (Savage Wars trilogy). Given immortality by Savages while their prisoner (*Imperator*), Rechs escaped and dedicated his life to destroying them. Rechs lived multiple lives, primarily serving as a soldier on the galactic stage. When the House of Reason sought to assassinate him (*Legionnaire*, Epilogue), Rechs went underground, living a new life as a bounty hunter (Contracts & Terminations series, *Galactic Outlaws*). Plagued by a degenerating memory, Rechs was killed by Goth Sullus and Kill Team Ice.

Urmo – Urmo. Urmo Urmo. Urmo! (*Imperator*)

Wild Man – A tortured soul and exceptional sniper. Savage Wars veteran and member of Kill Team Ice (Savage Wars trilogy).

Wraith – Former legionnaire turned Dark Ops deep cover operative who developed a fearsome reputation as a bounty hunter and mercenary. Former member of Kill Team Ice. We'd talk about what happens in Savage Wars, too, but if you haven't read it... spoilers.

X – A Nether Ops department head whose machinations led to the wholesale slaughter of friend and foe alike. A man accustomed to playing all sides, he ultimately aligned with Goth Sullus and the Black Fleet's imperial takeover of the Republic. He was killed by the legionnaire Exo (*Retribution*). While deceased, his plans are still being carried out by a deep state network of operatives.

Zora – The bounty hunter daughter of former Dark Ops legionnaire Doc. She was brought in by Doc to help train Aeson Ford to better serve in deep cover. Hired by Nilo to convince Keel to work for his corporation, Black Leaf.

PROLOGUE

United Worlds Frigate *Montague*
Savage Wars, 1500 Years Ago

"I'm not saying we can't do it, Admiral." Marine Colonel Hartswick walked alongside Admiral Sulla. The marine's mechanical legs came down heavily on the deck to issue deep thuds that contrasted with the softer, clicking footsteps of his counterpart. "I'm just saying it would be nice if some of those legionnaires who just got off Hardrock could be along to help."

Admiral Sulla nodded. It *would* be nice to have legionnaires—even new ones—for this mission. But the only way to make that happen involved waiting. This couldn't wait.

"Unfortunately, that class is spoken for," he said as they passed bulkheads and inlaid overhead lights that washed the corridor of the "borrowed" United Worlds ship in a clean, antiseptic white glow. "General Rechs—excuse me, General *Marks*—made it clear they were to report directly to Enduran given the situation there." Sulla stopped and smiled. "It's his Legion, Colonel."

"Sure. Which is why we have to remember to call him Marks instead of Rechs. Because it's his Legion."

Sulla smiled anew at the colonel's cheekiness and then continued to move. "We're on the brink of something big, Colonel. You know that. A unified federation—a Galactic Republic—it's going to happen. But not if we treat the rumors of Tyrus Rechs somehow being involved in the creation of the Legion as anything but that: a rumor."

Hartswick nodded silently.

After a few moments of walking quietly side by side, Sulla said, "I wouldn't ask this of you or your marines if it couldn't be avoided. But this could be the last shot we'll ever get at finding out whatever this *Strand* thing is."

The Strand had started as one of Makaffie's theories. It was a communication device capable of immediate connectivity without regard for distance, interference, or anything. It was purported to be impossible to spoof. And though every Savage tribe that Sulla had had the misfortune of coming across was aware of it, none seemed to have ever possessed it.

Until now.

A Savage ship had emerged from the dark, its tribe seeming totally separate from any of the recently encountered Savage tribes. Their hulk was a different ship design, and they had sent no calls for help from Savage allies. Sulla's best guess was that they were an independent tribe who'd left Earth a long time ago and were coming up for air only now. But they *had* sent off a signal—one that Sulla and Makaffie had identified as a potential match for whatever this Strand communication technology was.

No incoming signal had been returned.

For all the Savages' apparent unification, which had culminated in New Vega a few years ago, there were still plenty of independent Savage tribes floating around; Enduran had made that plain enough. The Savages there were nothing like the Savage marines the Legion had taken down at its formation. And so far, Sulla hadn't again seen the type of Savages he'd encountered while a slave with Rechs and Reina. Although some—a multi-headed abomination that had howled for Sulla's death came to mind—came awfully close. The point was, the Savages were at once both overlapping and unique. They were allying and fiercely independent. In truth, there was no telling what to expect until you cracked open a Savage hulk or made planetfall on a Savage world. Only then would you find out exactly what you were dealing with.

Colonel Hartswick stopped as they arrived at their destination. All that was left was for him and his officers and senior NCOs to hear the admiral's briefing. "Show us the can you want breached, and we'll bust it open, Admiral."

"The good news, Colonel, is that I've already figured out how to get your marines inside. I just need them to fight their way through."

"My hullbusters will be ready, sir."

The Savage hulk was a two-and-a-half-kilometer-long tube with a blunt nose and no discernable bridge or portals. It was a deep gray that swam through the stars like a black hole, blocking out the shining lights it silently moved in front of. Impossibly thick hulls kept it protected from the natural damage of stars and cosmic rays and also more than a few run-ins with Coalition warships.

What Sulla hoped would become a united Republic had first spotted the ship as it shot through space under the power of a single rear super-engine that glowed a faint blue as it propelled the dark monolith toward a storm nebula so fierce that most in the navy dismissed the ship as a derelict drifting helplessly. If anyone was left alive aboard, they were witnessing a slow burn toward suicide.

If not for its hull. The Coalition had found out the hard way that this hulk could take every pounding they could dish out. It didn't cut and run, it just kept going. Its projectiles and archaic energy weapons fired back ploddingly until eventually the pursuing Coalition ships were limping and the big monster hulk continued along no worse for wear.

That was why Sulla knew that the ship hadn't been on a trajectory for death, but on the final leg of a surfacing. When a Savage ship revealed itself, one of two things was usually true. It was about to carry out some long-planned crime against humanity, or it had poked its head out to acquire the salvage and resources needed to keep its inhabitants alive during the long planning phase of a future crime against humanity.

Like many Savage hulks—ships once called lighthuggers—this one was capable of cruising at near light speed once it really got going. But Sulla's target had slowed considerably, lured by a planted cargo frigate loaded top to bottom with ores and other raw materials and pinging a steady distress signal.

A light year away, a tech sat inside the command cockpit of Assault Shuttle *Junkyard One*. He watched a video feed, grainy and a monochromatic gray, of the Savage hulk as it moved to eclipse the freighter.

"Amazing how quickly that thing slowed down," the tech murmured.

Admiral Sulla stood next to the tech and shared the view of the screen. "They're sniffing the bait." He spoke louder, to also address the two pilots in the cockpit. "Last chance to place your bets: where the hell is the docking bay on this thing?"

"Maybe they don't have one," the tech offered.

Sulla looked back at the screen. The Savage hulk dwarfed the mammoth cargo frigate. Even with a docking-to-hull ratio cut in half from what had become standard, it should be able to swallow the lure whole.

"My only fear is that they have too large a docking bay," Sulla replied. "I'm counting on this thing getting stuck in its throat."

"We're about to find out, Admiral," the tech said. "Bay is located just beneath the main propulsion engine."

Sulla looked past the man's outstretched index finger to the screen. The Savage hulk had come to a stop just ahead of the freighter, and a previously hidden seam on its aft end was now levering open like a cargo ramp or set of jaws to swallow up the freighter.

The tech spoke eagerly. "*T-H* is moving. No sign of cables. Must have a tractor array."

T-H, or *Trash Heap*, was the designation given to the bait. And the Savage hulk was now pulling it in. The prow of the big ship was already entering the Savage docking bay.

"Sir?" the tech asked, and everyone in the cockpit knew exactly what the one-word question meant.

"Not yet," Sulla answered, staring intensely at the display. "A little farther in..." He waited. Waited...

"Now!"

The tech's fingers danced over his console, and micro-thrusters came alive on board the *Trash Heap*, driving it hard into the deck of the docking bay, half-in and half-out of the ship.

"Pilot," Sulla said. "Get us inside that thing. Execute."

"*Junkyard One* to Junkyard Wing," the pilot said. "Jump on my mark. Mark!"

The stars elongated and then shrank back to normal size in the brief moment it took *Junkyard One,* along with its team of assault shuttles collectively called Junkyard Wing, to cross the single light year standing between their ambush point and the Savage hulk. Thrusters then flashed behind the assault shuttles as they raced in an arc up toward the hulk's docking bay.

It didn't take long for the Savage hulk to identify the incomers and initiate its defenses. There were no telltale flashes of laser fire, but screaming warnings from the instrument panels alerted the cockpit to incoming rounds.

"Long-range projectiles," the second pilot hissed. "All Junkyard elements: evasive maneuvers."

The shuttles began to slide from side to side as though on a pendulum, not letting up on speed as they pushed toward the opening. Whatever Savages were on board the hulk realized the enemy's objective and began to close up the docking bay.

Sulla watched as the powerful solid bay doors began to close back up, attempting to shear in half a freighter so large it was unable to fly in any gravity greater than four meters per second squared. Fearsome as the hulk was, its docking bay doors weren't up to the task of chomping through the snack the admiral had put there.

Now the Junkyard assault shuttles needed only to arrive and unload their marines.

Sulla re-checked his atmospheric suit. Like the hull-busters, he was ready for zero-g, no-atmosphere movement. "Time to target?"

"ETA ninety seconds, Admiral," the pilot answered.

Sulla could only wait as the distance was covered. The co-pilot called out in alarm over a near-miss that flashed invisibly past them. One of the other shuttles ahead, visible in the forward cockpit viewscreen, erupted without flame. A gust of vapor poured through two holes: a small, fist-sized entry and a massive crater on the other end.

Junkyard One raced past the destroyed shuttle, and Sulla whipped around as if he could observe the damage in his rearview. He turned his attention to the ship's external cams and got a view of marines and debris pouring out of the opening. The spot was marked for rescue, but the reserve elements wouldn't jump in until the Savage hulk was disabled, to prevent more casualties.

"Final approach," the pilot shouted, waiting until the last possible moment to reduce speed. "Hang on!"

As the Savage docking bay door ground and sparked around the carcass of the freighter, the small shuttle raced through and into the docking bay. It came to a hard landing as quickly as possible—and then the cabin filled with red lights to alert the marines in the back that their time to shine had come.

"Let's move, hullbusters!"

Colonel Hartswick wanted every marine he had on that deck, and he wanted it done yesterday. Readings and visuals all showed an empty bay. Sometimes that meant a trap, sometimes it meant abandoned ship. Hartswick had seen both, plus a whole lot more in between.

You could never count on the Savages to be predictable. Couldn't even count on them to make sense. Each encounter was a new day and a fresh way to get killed by the bastards. But if any of Hartswick's marines were going to get iced, it wasn't gonna be because their buddies were still sittin' strapped in aboard the assault shuttle.

"Get this bay secure, let's go, let's go!"

Marines poured out of the first assault shuttles as others from the wing shot into the docking bay and set down to let out their own hullbusters. Hartswick buzzed about the bay, personally inspecting the work of his men and women, reminding them to be ready to take lives, and watching for some sign of Savage life or activity. But none came.

"Someone tell the admiral. Deck is secure. We're good to go hunting."

Three rooms into the Savage hulk and things began to feel tight in the armor. Readings were constant in two regards: there were no signs of life, noise, or movement apart from the marines; and the atmosphere was warm and breathable.

The confines made moving in the heavy zero-g suits impractical, and Hartswick gave the order for his marines to forgo them. "Shed your shells and let's move. Light and lethal."

The marines stripped out of their heavy, cumbersome zero-g armor down to the light flak jackets and fatigues underneath. They removed their helmets from the full-faced enclosure and set them loosely atop their heads. Targeting reticules were pulled down in front of their dominant eye.

"Gunny," Hartswick said to his senior-most NCO to have safely arrived on the Savage hulk, "post someone to watch the gear. This doubles as our CCP until we move further in."

"Yes, sir." The gunnery sergeant barked out orders at the end of knife-hand chops and soon had things the way Hartswick wanted.

Sulla gave a slight smile. The colonel was more like Tyrus Rechs than most men he'd met. At some point, he'd have to learn to work through his own chain of command. Something Hartswick surely had known to do before he lost his legs while serving with the UW Marines. But Tyrus Rechs—or General Marks—had a way of rubbing off on those around him. Hartswick now ran the hullbuster show and led from the front. Just like Tyrus and his legionnaires.

Ahead at the blast doors leading to the next chamber, one of the marines called out, "Gunny, come take a look at this."

"I ain't your call girl so don't bark at me tellin' me what to come and do." The hard-nosed sergeant nevertheless marched forward to see. He stooped over and grunted. "Hm." The gunnery sergeant then waved Colonel Hartswick over. "Sir, you might want to have a look at this."

Hartswick plodded forward with Sulla at his heels. "What is it, Gunny?"

"Don't know. Ain't seen nothin' like it before."

Sulla and the colonel bent over to inspect what looked like a spill that had seeped from beneath the blast doors. It looked shiny beneath the bright white overhead light strips.

"Looks wet," said Hartswick. He moved his gloved hand toward the slick.

"Careful, sir," interrupted the gunnery sergeant. "Can't trust anythin' Savvie." He unsheathed his knife and prodded the peculiarity. The tip of the blade didn't penetrate. "Huh. Solid as impervisteel."

"What kind of readings are you getting?" Sulla asked Hartswick.

"On the ship? Nothing. No life forms, at least. Slight increase in temperature on the other side of this door."

"Let's find out why."

"Rah," mumbled the gunnery sergeant, who organized the marines to stack up and prepare to move forward, leaving Sulla and Hartswick with a rearguard, the last to go through.

The corridor beyond the doors led to a dark chamber that billowed with a low, white mist. It spilled into the hall where the marines stood before evaporating into hooded vents that steadily circulated the ship's air. The comfortable environment of the bay now felt chill when compared to the humid warmth that pulsated from the open door, and a musty odor of jungle and wet moss greeted each man's nose.

"Nothing on bioscans," announced one of the hullbusters.

"Keep going," Hartswick ordered after getting a nod from the admiral.

Two by two, the marines moved into the room with the mists.

"Sure as hell looks alive," one of them said as his eyes shifted to take in the oozing, uneven architecture contained in the new chamber.

Sulla felt the wave of humidity hit him as he stepped forward. Moisture gathered at his collar and the small of his back. Sweat began to trickle down his temples and sideburns. The chamber had an oppressiveness that made him long for a cool breeze.

"Seen anything like this before?" Hartswick asked.

Sulla shook his head. "No."

The shape of the chamber matched what Sulla expected to see, as did its size. But the architecture was completely different. It looked as though something had poured or secreted more of that dark, shining matter over everything, sending it dripping down the walls to create alcoves and pockets. It pooled on the floors near the bulkheads.

Ahead, a marine stumbled over the uneven ground and had to be held up by his buddy. He cursed his step and drew grins from his fellow hullbusters.

"Gotta pick those clown shoes up higher," one of the marines teased before getting a withering look sent in his direction by the gunny.

The mist and the strange material, which Sulla imagined to be organic despite how hard it seemed, both gave off a faint green glow. The white lights of before seemed filtered here somehow. Perhaps the choice was intentional. Savages had their reasons.

The marines worked their way farther through the ship, twisting and turning through corridors and chambers. They rolled up their sleeves against the heat, their arms and faces slick with sweat and glistening in the green light as the mist swirled around their ankles. Despite the oddity of their surroundings, they moved swiftly, holding their rifles at the ready.

They encountered no one. If the ship was empty, all the better. That would give Sulla time to find the Strand and determine whether it was even possible to move it.

But something sat heavy in his stomach. This ship had taken the bait. Maybe that was an automated system at work, but thus far, no such system had revealed itself. Not even in defense of the hulk's secrets.

Sulla could count on one hand the number of hulks he'd encountered that were completely toothless. All were primitive, among the first that had left Earth. In every instance the Savages had killed one another and left nothing functioning to deal with those who found their stellar graves.

But here? No bodies. No signs of struggle. Nothing but the queer walls, ceiling, and floors. And the white mist and green pallor all around them.

"Still no readings?" Sulla asked. He knew Hartswick would have told him if it weren't so, but asking made him feel like he was doing something. It reminded him to stay alert if nothing else.

"Negative, Admiral." Hartswick's eyes were fixed on a battle board. He held it out for Sulla to see as well. "Bioscanners are only reading my hullbusters."

"We're being spoofed."

Hartswick stared at the man for a beat. "I'd be inclined to agree. Except I'm getting a solid read on us. How do you spoof a system and only make half of it work?"

"Savages find a way, Colonel Hartswick."

Sulla looked beyond the battle board and saw that the marines had come to a halt. He squinted to the far end of the corridor and saw the marines on point stacked outside an open bulkhead that let out into absolute blackness. Marines farther back leaned against the walls, their rifles aimed at whatever might be on the other side.

Sulla expected to hear from the gunnery sergeant so much that his breath left him. But no calls came. Just silence.

"Let's move up," Sulla said as he advanced with Hartswick. "Whether it's working or not, something is preventing your scouts from moving any further."

"Gunny," Hartswick called. "What's going on ahead?"

"Fellas up front got their minds playin' tricks on 'em, Colonel. Saw somethin', only the NV says nothin's there. Heard somethin', but the more we listen, the more we don't hear sket. I'll get 'em moving, sir."

Sulla held up a hand. "Perhaps we should—"

A sudden flurry of blaster fire erupted from the end of the corridor as the marines opened fire with shouts of "Contact!"

Sulla stepped back despite himself as dark, man-sized creatures with smooth black skin that shone in the light, appearing almost wet, just like the oozing ground and walls, leapt at the marines. The creatures had long, knife-like claws that shredded the hullbusters' fatigues and light armor, eliciting screams of pain and terror.

"Seal that door!" Hartswick shouted, but the fight was up, and if any of the marines heard the order, they weren't in a position to follow it through.

The mists seemed to rise. A marine was skewered by the dark, skeletal hand of one of the creatures and pulled down by the claws until you could only see the man's arms and legs flailing as he screamed for rescue from his buddies.

Hullbusters did their best to save their downed comrade. They sent careful shots into the creatures, evoking primal screams of pain that rattled eardrums above the bursting fire of the blaster rifles. And when the creatures were hit, the effect was spectacular. Large holes were punched through them, sending clotted gouts of black blood dripping down the walls and splattering across the chests and faces of the marines. The creatures in their death throes thrashed about wildly underfoot, causing as much damage there as they had above as they sliced open boots and drew blood from legs. There was no telling how many there were... but they could be killed.

"We need to put them down and push past them," Sulla told Hartswick.

"Yes, sir." The colonel was adding his own weapon to the fight before he gathered two hullbusters and reoriented them. "Watch our backs! Watch our backs!"

The marines nodded and focused on the sector assigned to them.

Ahead, the hullbusters were grouping and making use of the distance they managed to put between themselves and the creatures. The nightmarish Savages streaked low in the mists, creating sharp rises in the swirling fog like the wakes of fin-fish on the hunt, but were put down by carefully aimed shots. They kept coming, but not so fast that they threatened to again overwhelm the marines.

Sulla counted heads. At least a quarter of the marines he had for this mission now lay somewhere beneath the mist, dead or wounded. There was a point where he would have to call it. Where the loss of life was too much or the risk of total defeat too likely. This kind of decision-making was something that Tyrus could do in an instant. Sulla wasn't so sure.

"Contact!" called the rearguard and then opened fire.

Sulla whirled around and saw a fresh onslaught racing for their position. He fired his sidearm, in his hand since the fighting began but now given an opportunity to be used. There were a lot of the creatures before him, and only two marines; the risk of friendly fire from this angle went down drastically.

The admiral squeezed off several rounds and found that the slug-thrower was as effective against the creatures as the hullbusters' blaster rifles were. Large gaping holes were ripped into the monsters, sending black volcanic splatter flying. Each gut punch was punctuated by a high-pitched shriek that made Sulla's eye twitch.

He fired repeatedly. Colonel Hartswick appeared at his side and brought his own weapon into the fight. Behind them, the marines continued to deal with the original assault.

For a time the creatures dropped...

...and then they were on them.

Dark man-beasts pushed into the melee, slashing and biting and clawing at the two marines posted to the rear. One man was tackled by the full weight of one of the things and went down beneath it in the mist. The other had his midsection gouged and then his throat torn out as he tried to keep his insides in.

Sulla felt a gash at his pant leg and whirled away from the strike, firing at the devil that had caused it and blowing a hole in its rounded skull. Colonel Hartswick used his powerful mechanical legs to punt another one across the corridor, where two of his marines lit up the squirming monster until it stopped moving apart from the dark blood that poured out of it.

This wasn't an endless wave. It was diminishing. But... so were the hullbusters.

Sulla looked to his left and right, gently hopping on the balls of his feet, his pistol up and ready to take action as he tried to take in the situation. Marines fought up close using secondary weapons—shotguns that blew off large chunks of the creatures in explosive spasms of gore, rifles swung like clubs. The creatures were trying to herd them into a last stand in the middle. But their numbers had diminished considerably.

The admiral took a step and stumbled on something he couldn't see beneath the mist. A body; the dead. And still the marines were dishing it out worse than they were taking it. But how long could that continue? How many more Savages might there be? Finishing this fight might cost him every man he had.

He looked to Hartswick and saw that the colonel knew it, too. This fight, if left unchecked, would go to the last man. And if it went to the Savages, and they took the ships in the bay and discovered the hyperdrive technology inside of them... what then?

They were so close...

"Colonel!" Sulla shouted. "We're falling back!"

The running fight back the way they'd come, harried and pursued, cost more marines' lives. The creatures stayed back like cautious predators, only surging forward when they had a chance to grab a wounded straggler and carry him back into death and darkness. Sulla could hear the screams fading each time they pulled back another victim. He could see the looks in the other marines' eyes. Looks of terror, but also hatred. Of the things, of Sulla, and of themselves. They both wanted and loathed the thought of going back for those pulled to their death.

But that wasn't going to happen. The few who tried it were taken and killed as easily as the wounded who'd been snatched.

Colonel Hartswick had positioned his reserves to take over the fight once the battered main element reached their cache of armor. Those hullbusters made a line and laid down hate on the creatures, which never charged the ranks a single time.

Sulla wondered if the Savages were beaten and this was all a show. A token chase done in the desperate hope that it would convince the invaders that they were right to retreat. If he rallied here and pushed everything left, armored up with extra protection against those claws... if he did that, would they achieve the Strand?

He watched as bloody marines were helped into their armor. A young man coughed just as his face enclosure was sealed, sending rivulets of blood and spittle onto the transparent armor-glass.

Sulla couldn't send those boys back into the hell they'd just escaped from.

He couldn't.

They fell back to their shuttles and left the Savage hulk, defeated.

The hulk dislodged the bait from its docking bay, sealed itself, and fired until the shuttles jumped away. Then it slipped into the soul-crushing gravity well it had been angling for to nurse its wounds. Along the way it transmitted a log of the events—sent over the Strand, of course—to the designated Savage reclaimer for the sector. The marines had come dangerously close to overwhelming its defenses, and the reclaimer would be able to determine how much more the defenses could have withstood. Adjustments would then be made for next time.

The hullbusters had no idea how close they'd come to achieving mission success.

Later, when Sulla gave a briefing to General Marks during a lull on the fighting on Enduran, he tried to communicate the responsibility he felt to the marines he'd taken on that god-forsaken horror show. Sulla admitted to his friend that he'd felt they were close. But...

"I couldn't let all those men die on a hunch, Tyrus."

Though volcanic eruptions roared in the distance behind him, a sooty-faced Tyrus Rechs managed to look icy as he stared into the display at his friend. "Sometimes, Cas, you have to."

01

Republic Frigate *Defiance of Reason*
Now

Aeson Keel approached the band of Dark Ops legionnaires that had congregated near the ruined remains of
the freighter Keel had flown into the mutinous Republic
frigate *Defiance of Reason*. Plans had been made on the
fly to jump to the planet Kima to look for Masters, who
was missing in action following a surprise takeover of the
Republic world by a resurgent Mid-Core Rebellion.

Those plans were now rapidly changing.

"This is an odd little bot," the operator called Nobes
remarked as Keel approached. The legionnaire looked in-
tently at the little gunnery bot who had been sitting capti-
vated for the better part of an hour listening to the current
members of Kill Team Victory swap stories. "My signica
isn't all that great, so I'm pretty sure I've missed some of
his questions, but as long as we talk war stories, it's like
he's entranced."

Keel gave a lopsided smile that faded all too quickly.
"Probably trying to pick up a few pointers."

"Somethin' wrong?" asked Bear, the biggest by far of
the men and also the most-senior ranked.

Keel gave a fractional nod. There was no sense putting off what was coming. "Yeah. Change of plans. I'm not
going to Kima."

The other legionnaires exchanged looks while Bear tried unsuccessfully to read the reason for this from Keel's face. "How come? I thought the plan was we all get there and find Masters before the sket really hits."

"You're still going, but I can't. Sorry, pal."

Bear looked back at his Victory men. Keel could remember several of their names—Neck, Pina, Nix, Nobes... there were others on the tip of his tongue. He had run an op with them and found them capable, but they were strangers. Other than Bombassa and Bear, Kill Team Victory was so far from familiar to Keel that it felt completely foreign. Like visiting an old friend who'd started a family to find that the man you once knew no longer existed. Not really.

"Hey," Bear said, his voice low but still finding a way to echo in the hangar as liberated navy spacers and a maintenance bay's worth of bots cleaned the mess that Keel had made. "Let me in on what's happening, will you?"

Keel tossed his head to tell Bear to follow him. The pair walked away from the group, leaving Death, Destroyer of Worlds to chirp in delight about an old Dark Ops story that was now legend, about an operator named Kel who dropped an asteroid on an advancing line of tanks... or something like that.

"You want to find Masters," Keel said softly. "So do I. But he's not the only person I've been looking for."

"C'mon," Bear whispered. "Masters is... he's *Masters*. You two go all the way back to Kublar."

"I know. That's why I need you to find him while I do this."

"What's 'this'?"

Keel frowned. "This is me trying to tell you how to make it work. Step one involves not asking questions, because what you don't know can't be used against you. Step two is turning off your comm until you've got Masters or you're past the point of no return."

Bear looked down at the micro-comm sticking out like a miniature stud from near his neck armor, to be used while his helmet was off.

"Shut it off," Keel urged, sounding like the veteran, savvy rule-breaker showing the new, regular Legion boot how to get around fresh out of selection.

Bear did. "Okay. But you've got a ship and we need to make Kima."

"I've got a meeting. No can do."

"But we need a ship."

Keel waved his arms. "This hangar is full of them. That's how you got here, isn't it? Take one."

Bear looked around, unsure. He was out of his element. Bombassa had managed to go undercover to infiltrate Black Leaf as a no-nonsense mercenary called Lashley, but for Bassa, that wasn't exactly a stretch. For Bear to behave like... well, like Aeson Keel... that wasn't even remotely plausible.

"Bear," Keel said, refocusing the big man's attention, "look at you. Which one of these spacers is going to stop you?"

The mammoth operator let out a gruff laugh, drawing a smirk from Keel.

"Here, take this." Keel handed over a thin black card. "It'll get you just about anything you need with the right people. You're gonna need to talk to folks in the night markets to get leads on our friend. You understand what I'm saying, right?"

Bear slid the card into a pouch on his utility belt. "Yeah. I get it."

"Good." Keel nodded at the tall legionnaire approaching behind them. "Here comes Bombassa. Get him in on the plan before it's too late, because you only get one shot to pretend you don't know what's going on. Trust me."

"Captain," Bombassa said as he joined the circle. "General Chhun has been trying to reach you, sir."

Keel made a slicing motion across his neck.

Bear sighed. "He, uh, wants me to call him back, Top?"

"Negative. He told me to tell you that Kill Team Victory is being recalled to the super-destroyer *Centurion* to develop an insertion plan for the liberation of Kima. We should go, sir."

Bear frowned. He switched his comm back on. "Yeah. I'll get him on comms in a few. Thanks, Top."

Bombassa looked to Keel. "He also wants to talk with you, but can't raise your comm."

Keel shrugged. "I left the ship a half hour ago and didn't say where I was going."

He patted both men on their armored shoulders.

First Bombassa. "Good luck on Kima. KTF."

Then Bear. "Try to find Masters. I'll get there when I can."

Keel was nowhere near as big or intimidating-looking as Bear, but none of the spacers challenged his commandeering of a small service shuttle for the trip back to the bay where the *Obsidian Crow* was docked.

Death, Destroyer of Worlds was unable to fit into the single-man cockpit, and chirped questions at "New

Boss" from the other side of the open partition while Keel brought the shuttle down to the planet.

"I mean, he's not a big killer exactly," Keel answered. "Nothing like Tyrus Rechs."

DDOW chirped flattery.

"No, or like me either. Or you, come to think of it, you little psychopath."

Now it was Death's turn to feel flattered. Its optical sensor lights flashed through a rainbow of colors.

"But he's done his fair share," Keel continued, "mostly in the pirate wars. Slimy and strange as the guy can be, he's still dangerous if you don't know how to handle him."

The little bot beeped another question.

"Of course I can handle him. The point is, when he calls, it tends to be legitimate. Usually he's the only one who will benefit from whatever scheme he's running, but he's also usually telling the truth."

The bot asked why he hadn't pinged Keel back on the comms yet in that case.

"Because he's a little twerp who can't pass up an opportunity to make himself feel important. Trust me, he gets a thrill up his leather pants making me wait."

Death asked if that meant New Boss would kill him, or at least severely beat him.

"Only if he's lying." The comm chimed. "Here he is. I'll put him on speaker so you can listen in. Go for Keel."

A familiar, boasting, grating, presumptuous voice filled the shuttle's cabin. "That how you answer? No. I call again. You answer, 'Go for best friend Keel.'"

The comm went dead. The little Nubarian gunnery bot beeped its thoughts.

"Not yet," Keel replied. "But believe me, I'm tempted."

The comm chimed again. "Go for Keel... Lao Pak's *best friend.*"

"You not my best friend, Keel. You dumb guy who need Lao Pak, because Lao Pak is Keel's best friend."

"I'm going to pay my best friend a visit if he's not careful."

Lao Pak scoffed. "Keel, you so stupid. You have to do that anyway if you want information. I not give it for free. I should charge you so many credits for what I already tell you. You owe Lao Pak lots of money."

"But it's Prisma?" Keel asked. "You're sure that's the name this new contact of yours used?"

"How hard it to remember name? Yes. Prisma May— Mazy-something. It her!"

Keel brought the ship down through the priority automated docking sequence afforded to him by virtue of the shuttle belonging to the Republic Navy. As he glided down through the atmosphere, an errant repulsor sled traveling higher than it was rated for stunted and stuttered across his path, eliciting a warning chirp from Death, Destroyer of Worlds.

"Yeah, I see it." Keel banked the shuttle to the left to put distance between himself and the sled, and then swung back into position to resume his landing pattern.

"You there, Keel? Don't try to trick Lao Pak. I too smart for that."

"Yes, I'm here. Tell me about the guy."

"Oh, I tell you about him." There was a hint of mirth in Lao Pak's voice. "He crazy. Say he know you, but he not know anything about you. He say you war hero and brilliant tactician, use so many big words but they all lies. I not believe he know you at all. I say, 'You try to get bounty for Keel' but I not turn you in to some bounty hunter. If Lao Pak need money, I turn you in myself."

"You'd try."

"I do it. I rich pirate king. No one say no to Lao Pak."

"Yeah, yeah," Keel mumbled beneath his breath. "But you told him you'd pass the word on to me, huh? Because of the—"

"Wobanki," Lao Pak finished for Keel. "Sharp claw. Big muscle. Long tail. He say he know you too."

Keel nodded. "I *do* know a wobanki named Skrizz, yeah."

"Skrizz. That what he say his name is."

"I know. The only reason I'm taking this seriously is because of that. What did he look like?"

"I just tell you!"

"No you didn't. What you said fits every wobanki in existence. That's like me describing a pirate king by saying dirty fingernails, bad breath, greasy hair."

"That not describe me, Keel! I have new coat that cost fifty thousand credits!"

Keel brought the shuttle down for an easy landing on the assigned docking pad. "Well, do you have a holopic of him or something?"

"Why I take his picture? He not pretty girl or dead body." Lao Pak started to laugh. "Remember that time we take picture together?"

"How could I forget?" Keel deadpanned. "Sounds like I've got a meeting to take. Where and when?"

"Okay!" Lao Pak could be heard clapping his hands together. "I set it up already. They waiting for you. I send you coordinate now."

"What do you mean you set it up?"

"I get paid to set up, I set up."

"How can you set up a meeting if I didn't even agree to go until now, Lao Pak?"

"Wobanki pay me already. He pirate. *Lesser* pirate. He give me his crew and ship for meeting with you. No one else know where you are. He say you change your commkey. But you not change commkey for best friend."

"What do you mean 'gave you his crew'?"

"What else it mean? Only one definition! The pirates work for wobanki, now they work for Lao Pak. Ship is junk. Worse than your ship that got blowed up. Not as ugly, though. They happy to work for *real* pirate king. Make more credits. Good for me so I take it. I not stupid like you, Keel."

Both Keel and the shuttle let out sighs as the landing cycle continued winding down. "All right. Just... give me the coordinates."

"I do that after you send me credits for payment."

"You just said you got a crewed ship for this meeting. You're paid."

"Not from you, Keel!"

Keel threw his hands in the air. He looked back at his gunnery bot and held his thumb and forefinger an inch apart for DDOW to see. "I'm about this close to following your advice."

To Lao Pak, he said, "How about this, Lao Pak? You tell me the coordinates and I go to the meeting. You don't and I skip the meeting and you can explain to the wobanki and his pal that you double-crossed them. Skrizz is the kind of guy who kills a moktaar and then feeds it to his friends."

"That true story?"

"Cross my heart."

There was a pause over the comm.

Then... "I just kidding, Keel. You not have to pay. But... after meeting, you tell wobanki he can work for pirate king. I make lot of money if I have wobanki like that cooking up people who double-cross Lao Pak. Tell him I very dangerous, too. Wobanki and Hool both respect dangerous people."

"First thing I'll mention," Keel said as he leaned forward to flip the comm off. "But if this meeting is legit, I don't think you'll be hearing from either one of us for a while. Keel out."

02

It *was* Skrizz. Keel could see that immediately as he entered the small diner that Lao Pak had indicated as the meeting place—after a ten-hour jump aboard the *Obsidian Crow* that had provided just enough time to get some sleep and second-guess every decision he'd made since setting down on Ackabar with Garret what seemed like ages ago.

Neither the wobanki nor the rail-thin man dressed in a miner's duster with hair tucked behind his ears and down to his shoulders took any notice of Keel when he walked in. Nothing loud and conspicuous. They both worked at their meals—Skrizz's a thick cut of raw meat and the human's a plate of either noodles or worms, depending on if he went in for Hool food.

But it was definitely Skrizz. And the wobanki recognized Keel as well; he gave off an excited twitch of his tail and then coolly let it drop to the floor where it undulated back and forth slowly as if nothing had ever happened.

"One?" asked a bot dressed up in a dress, meant to look humanoid and feminine. She looked tired and grimy instead, the uniform spotted with grease stains and spills, never washed because it wasn't really needed and this was the sort of place where nothing was ever done unless it couldn't be avoided.

Keel grabbed the menu card from the bot's hand and walked past it to find his own seat. The robotic hostess let out a programmed sigh and then wheeled its way toward the kitchen pass-through to grab a tray of something that smelled of crushed peppers and oily fish for a table of sooty humans wearing thick mining boots, their coveralls rolled down to the waist to expose white tank tops turned gray, still sticking to chests with a glue of sweat and grime caused by their recent shift in the shafts.

"Hey, off-worlder—no trouble." The voice belonged to a human cook, shirtless from the heat of the makeshift grills and sweating, calling through the window as the bot moved off.

"No trouble," Keel repeated as he waved the menu card in greeting. The card flashed from a list of entrees and prices to an advertisement for dancing and drinking later in the week. Cheap liquor. Live music. Standing room only.

Probably coincided with whenever the miners were paid.

Keel looked around at the tables and chairs. They were fitted with miniature repulsors so they could be easily pushed clear. At the center of the diner was a stage that housed a few crates of supplies waiting to be stocked. Next to it were Skrizz and the man, both with their backs to the wall, leaving Keel to have to expose his own back to the front door should he sit with them.

Skrizz or not, that wasn't going to happen.

Keel stopped at the table and stood tall over the two humanoids seated before him. Skrizz's tail swished again as he gnawed at a thick bone, cracking it open between terrifyingly sharp and long teeth and then licking at the marrow. But the man, who wore some kind of smart spectacles and dangling necklace with a symbol Keel didn't recognize, looked up and smiled. "Sergeant Fast."

When Keel didn't answer, the man laughed. He gestured at the table. "Sit down. I'll buy your lunch."

Keel grabbed hold of the edge of the table and activated its micro-repulsors with the toe of his boot. He pulled the table away from Skrizz and the man, pulled it to another spot nearby, then sat with his back against the wall. "Join me."

The man gave another tittering laugh and covered his mouth with his fingers. He scooted his chair toward the newly relocated table, sending echoing scuffs resounding across the diner. Skrizz stood, carried his chair, and sat down before what was left of his slab of raw meat.

"*Yo jabba tenchu paki tu ma,*" Skrizz yammered.

"I wouldn't have except for you," Keel answered.

He leaned in close, careful not to let his tone sound accusatory. Skrizz had saved Keel's life in the past, but Keel had been through enough lately to be wary of another trap. This meeting didn't seem out of sorts, but then, neither had Ackabar until right before the shooting started. Either way, he wanted to avoid insulting the wobanki.

It rarely was in one's interest to insult a wobanki.

"Where is she?" he asked.

Skrizz purred at the word "she" and then yipped and yowled that he didn't know... exactly. "*Matcha hampa nay... Priz-mah.*"

Keel shifted his gaze to the stranger, who evidently knew the girl's location. "Where is she?" he repeated.

The man gave a big, toothy smile and seemed on the verge of laughing again. He held it together, but didn't answer the question. Not directly at any rate. "Straight and to the point. You always were that way. I liked it except all the times I didn't like it. But that's really how it goes with anything. You hate some things until you miss them, and you love some things until you learn to hate them. And the things... they never change. It's just..." The man placed an index finger on either side of his head against the temples like a psychic barker from Rubagah 10's Avenue of Oracles. "It's your perception that changes, man."

Keel furrowed his brow. He didn't like the way this man acted like he knew him, though he was sure they'd never met. That wasn't uncommon; people always angled for some kind of advantage, and one way to do that was by acting as if they knew something you didn't. Keel could tolerate wise guys who carried on like they could read everyone's thoughts before you could even think them. But he couldn't tolerate the sudden sinking feeling that this man, who looked like a recovering H8 junkie given how scrawny he was, was wasting his time.

"Can you perceive that I think you're wasting my time right now?" Keel asked.

"Actually, that fact eluded me. But it is rather plain now that you've put it out there. I am not, however, wasting your time. And you won't be wasting my time unless you decide that my wobanki acquaintance was, shall we say... *incorrect.*"

"About what?"

"About the fact that you would help me out of a certain bind I find myself in with your stellar skill set... in exchange for *definitive* information as to the whereabouts of one Prisma Maydoon, her war bot Crash, and... her mother."

"Her mother?" Keel blurted out.

"See, now that surprised me too," the man said. "But Prisma was very insistent, and who was I to argue? I didn't know a thing about that girl or even what she looked like until the hour I met her, let alone her mother, father, grandparents, or anyone else in the Maydoon family tree.

Although I do recall having met a Maydoon at least once before. But then, you meet a lot of people should you ever avail yourself of the opportunity to leave your planet of birth. Why, I myself have met Tyrus Rechs. Did you know that?"

Keel could see that the man was studying him. "Why would I?"

The man shrugged. "Not many people have met Tyrus Rechs and lived to tell the tale."

"Maybe more than you think." Keel rapped his knuckles softly against the tabletop. "Skrizz. You believe this guy? Lao Pak says you gave up an awful lot to make this meeting happen."

The wobanki was resolute in his affirmation that yes, he believed the man, whom he called Makaffie, and that the crew and the ship, and everything else that Skrizz owned, was always second to finding the girl.

Skrizz said all this in a few clipped words. A single sentence in fact. But something about the way he said it, especially the second part, made Keel believe that he'd tried hard to make it not be so. Prisma had done something to Skrizz that didn't seem to be going away.

"How'd you find me, Makaffie?" Keel asked, still not ready to trust the man.

"Makaffie." The slim man opened his eyes wide. "That doesn't bring forth any memories?"

"No."

"Well, that is something of a shame, Aeson. It really is."

"Don't act like you know me."

"I do know you."

"No, you don't."

"I do. I'd venture to say I know you better than you know yourself right about now. For what it's worth. And

I see you rolling your eyes in that rakish, devil-may-care attitude that I'm sure works on the girls and might work on me if I were trying to play some confidence game to get what I was after. But I'm not. And I *do* know you."

"How'd you find me?" Keel asked again, frustrated by the odd little man sitting before him.

Makaffie nodded to the wobanki. "Skrizz."

"*Collectively*," Keel said, letting some of his frustration out through sarcasm. "I've been keeping a low profile."

Makaffie waved a hand as if that part were simple. "Oh. Well, Skrizz found that you changed your commkey. But he still had..." Makaffie snapped his fingers. "What was his name, Skrizz?"

"*Garr-ott.*"

"That's right, Garret. He had Garret's commkey. So he called Garret and they got along fine and he told him all about me and Prisma and that we needed you. But it seems you weren't answering any calls from him or someone named Zora, whose name I *do* remember because she was rather unpleasant toward me, though I think that was just redirected anger owed to you." Makaffie shook his head and clucked his tongue. "You have created a considerable amount of enmity in your relationship at this point, if you weren't aware."

"I had a hunch, thanks."

"Your funeral. Zora suggested that I call a pirate on Pellek named Lao Pak, who knew how to contact you but was unwilling to do so previously on Zora's behalf because she was unwilling to pay his fee. I believe it involved holopics of her, if you take my meaning."

Keel nodded. "Sounds like him."

"Personally, I think Lao Pak would have taken credits, but Zora... well, my communications with her were limited to a single conversation, but she seems like the sort who would thwart her own goals if she didn't like the way they were going to be met."

"Sounds like her, too."

At that point the bot running the store rolled up. "You want somethin'? You gotta order somethin' if you're gonna sit."

Keel looked up to see the cook watching him through the little window, sweat drenched across his sagging breasts and rolling across an expansive belly.

"I'll pay," Makaffie offered. "This is the kind of establishment where everyone is expected to place an order."

"Tugg rum," Keel said. The bot whirled off and returned with a bottle of beer that it set down before departing without a word.

"Out here," Makaffie said, as Keel stared at the green bottle, "it all falls under two categories: beer or whiskey."

Keel shot the man a glare. "I'm so glad you're here to tell me these things, Professor." He pushed the beer away. "Not even a good beer."

Skrizz asked when they thought they would be leaving and how long it might be to reach Prisma. He crunched a bone between his teeth as Makaffie made a show of thinking about the answer, rubbing his chin and pondering the ceiling lights.

"Well now, I suppose that depends on our friend Sergeant Fast here."

"You keep calling me that. It's not my name."

"Are you so sure of that? Because I'm sure it is. When I was growing up, I had a dog. You like dogs? Doesn't matter. The point is, I had this dog. Called him Roscoe. Now Roscoe, he did what he wanted. Sometimes he wanted to come over and get his belly rubbed and sometimes he wanted to slip the leash and disappear for a few days. I only had him for a year before he ran away and didn't come back." Makaffie fluttered his fingers. "Our story progresses and I see Roscoe again. He's older, I'm older, but it's him all right. He had this diamond pattern over his eyes, you see. So I call him, and he pays no mind. Not in the way he paid no mind when he was just ignoring me. Pays no mind in the same way you pay me no mind when I call you Sergeant Fast."

Makaffie folded his arms and leaned back in his seat. He turned toward the bot running the diner and called, "I'm done with this."

The bot rolled up and collected the plate and dinnerware and departed.

"You're wasting my time," Keel said. He stood. "Skrizz... I don't know what this guy sold you on, but he's a spanner short of a full kit."

"Kill Team Ice," Makaffie said at last.

Keel froze. "What did you say?"

"You heard what I said." Makaffie stood as well. "We all got something the other wants. The girl. The Strand... and the key to what you don't remember about your past." Moving around behind Keel, Makaffie patted the smuggler on the back. "And the best thing is, I can fill you in on that last part on the jump there."

03

Orange dust swirled through the street outside the diner as Keel and the others exited. The duracrete road, laid two centuries before when the colony was first established, was marked with holes and uneven cracks from normal settling and the ravages of seismic activity, and each little nook and cranny served as a catch that accumulated the sand into miniature dunes and drifts along the road. A few miners wrapped scarves around their mouths and fixed goggles over however many eyes they possessed as they ran from building to building.

It wasn't as bad as it was capable of getting on the little co-op consortium world. A rough place where everyone had a stake and a purpose, and wages were paid out accordingly each week. Off-worlders were allowed on planet partly because it was a free world inside Republic space, but mostly because they infused fresh credits into what was otherwise a closed economy.

Keel could feel the eyes of the miners watching him as their heavy boots tramped across the road to duck into squat apartment buildings or low-roofed bars and entertainment houses. This was a place where those who'd spent their lives on the planet knew instinctively when something was out of place. And so when the eyes of the miners shifted from Keel and his two companions to something obscured behind a corner amid the swirling sands, the smuggler's alarm bells started to ring.

He grabbed the blaster strapped to his hip. Should the dust storm pick up, it would be much less likely to misfire than the slug thrower he wore on the opposite side. "You aren't thinking to double-cross me, are you Makaffie?"

"That would defeat every purpose and intent I have in play," the scrawny man answered. "Also, you may not remember me, but I remember quite well what you're capable of, Fast. So, in a word... why, of course not."

Skrizz yammered that he wouldn't do that to Keel either and then sniffed the air for a moment before quickly sealing his nostrils and sneezing at the fine dust particles that drifted their way in. He shook his head, as much saying that he couldn't smell anything as trying to clear his nose.

"This way." Keel kept his hand close to his blaster. He had to squint against the wind. It wasn't a true sandstorm; he could still see. But it was enough to make his eyes water and force him to tilt his head down.

Overhead, a yellow sun that should have been in its final bout of glory before setting now glowed orange to match the particles in the clouds swirling out beyond the colony. The light lacked intensity and gave the street an eerie glow that draped everything not directly touched by the weak rays in shadow.

As Keel led his companions down the street, the memory of being ambushed on Ackabar replayed in his head. Surely Lao Pak would have told him if another sizeable bounty had been placed on his head... right?

Wrong, thought Keel as a line of humanoids stepped out from the corner the miners had eyed and into the street. With the sun behind them, they were little more than back-lit shadows. Since none of them had hands on pieces, Keel kept his blaster holstered as well.

"Captain Keel... it's us!"

Keel squinted at the voice, then tied the sound to the thin shadowed form it came from. "Garret? That you, kid?"

The thin figure stepped forward until Keel could make out Garret's features. "Yeah! I can't believe we actually found you. We've been trying to reach you almost since you left and—"

Keel held up a hand. "Not now, kid. Who else is with you?"

"Oh! Well, there's—"

Two more figures started toward Keel, but one stopped when the other power-walked straight for the smuggler.

"Hey, Zora," Keel began, before letting out a *whuff* of air as she punched him in the stomach.

"You've got some nerve, jump jockey!"

A sudden burst of angry beeps in alphanumerica trilled into the street as Death, Destroyer of Worlds rolled into sight from his hiding place in the alcove where Keel had left him before entering the diner. The little bot carried a small repeating blaster over its head and moved menacingly toward Zora, who jumped back and put her hands up.

"It's all right," Keel said to the gunnery bot. "She's just violent. You'd like her."

Death let Keel know that he didn't like anyone who laid hands on New Boss.

"Thanks," Keel said, smoothing out his shirt where he was punched.

"That thing is with you?" Zora asked.

"Yeah."

"So you just armed a bot with a blaster. Made your own little war bot."

"Pretty much," Keel admitted.

"That's fantastic!" Garret called. "Can I meet him?"

"Death," Keel called to the bot. "Go say hi to Garret. He taught missiles how to think and kill better once. Blew up an entire shipyard. Oh, and he also blew up an entire capital ship once during the war."

With an impressed and interested whistle, the little bot rolled toward the code slicer, but not before jabbing its blaster toward Zora once more.

"Charming," she said. "You make the kid sound like a killer."

"Only when I need him to be." Keel patted his stomach and glared at Zora. "What're you so upset about, anyway?" He started toward Garret and DDOW, and motioned for Makaffie and Skrizz to follow.

Zora stayed with him, her anger still up. "You blocked my comm. Didn't return a single message." She lowered her voice. "You left me looking like an idiot in front of Mr. Nilo." She tossed her gaze toward the other person in her party, who was now standing with Garret.

"That's Nilo?" Keel asked, following her eyes.

"Yes, and—"

Zora was cut off by a shout coming from around the corner the group had first emerged from. "Aeson!"

Keel again froze. This time he was well and truly stunned. "Leenah?"

And there she was again, rounding the corner and running toward him, her pink, hair-like tendrils bouncing up and down with each stride. Her smile glowed, a bright star that shamed the soft orange sun overhead and made Keel feel as though all the air had escaped his lungs.

Confused but utterly absorbed by the sight, Keel could only stand there as she ran toward him. Another man jogged lightly behind her as though he had been attempting to chase her down and gave it up once she broke free.

He joined Nilo and Garret, who rocked back and forth on the balls of his feet, smiling.

Keel's bewilderment was cut short by a swift slap to the back of his head. His hand went to the sting and he once again glowered at Zora. "Hey!"

The bounty hunter pointed. "*That's* the other thing we wanted to tell you about, jump jockey."

And then Leenah was on him. She jumped into his arms and wrapped her legs around his waist, fastening herself to him as she pressed her cheek against his and locked her arms around his neck in an embrace.

Feeling tears stream down Leenah's face and against his own, Keel had the wherewithal to wrap one arm around her waist while the other held her back. He was in shock. Garret had never stopped believing that, somehow, she was alive... but Keel had never allowed himself the hope that she was anything but dead. And so, to him, she was.

And now she wasn't.

He could think of nothing to say or do but to squeeze her tightly in his arms until she laughed and wriggled herself free of his grip and back to the ground. Keel looked down at her smiling face, staring dumbly until he broke into a smile of his own. "How—how did you...?"

Leenah's smile softened—from unbridled jubilance to a contented warmth. "It's a long story. I'll tell you about it on board the *Six*."

"The *Six*?" Keel blurted. "I thought for sure both you and it were..."

"Sorry about that," called the man who had been chasing Leenah.

"Jack," Keel surmised. He looked back at Leenah, locking eyes with her, even as he replied to Jack. "No need to say you're sorry. I'm not."

"Happy to bring about the reunion that much sooner then," said Jack. "You, uh, seem to be short one Tennar."

"She didn't make it," Keel confessed. "But it turned out the way you wanted it in the end."

Death beeped proudly and Jack nodded once before looking to Nilo. It occurred to Keel that Jack, Zora, and to a lesser extent Leenah and Garret, were all watching the man—the liberator of Kublar.

"We should go," Zora said. She grabbed Keel's elbow and attempted to pull him toward Nilo.

Skrizz gave a warning growl and Keel shook her elbow off. "Watch your hands, sweetheart." He looked back at Leenah, who despite obviously feeling joyfully relieved at being reunited with Keel, still harbored a look that said she agreed with Zora.

"What do you mean about the *Six*?" Keel asked her. "Garret said there was no trace of it left."

"Oh. It was a total loss. But Mr. Nilo had Garret and me piece it back together. You *have* to see it, Aeson. It's better than before. It's amazing."

Keel nodded slowly. This was almost too much to keep up with. Almost too much to believe.

And then Makaffie walked up beside the pair. "You two, uh, know each other?"

Keel didn't smile. He nodded to Leenah. "This is Makaffie. He says he knows where Prisma is."

"I know," Leenah said. "He made contact with Garret through Skrizz. But we really should go and see—"

The wobanki took the mention of his name as an invitation to come over and wrap Leenah in a furry hug. Keel took the opportunity to study Nilo. He might have been smiling at the reunion, though it was hard to tell as the dust continued to fly on the breeze.

Makaffie cleared his throat. "Fast—I mean *Keel*—how many of these people, and I realize that this question might sound insensitive given the nature of what is obviously the reunion of two lovers separated across the stars by some heretofore unfortunate circumstances, but the question does need to be asked so I will, indeed, ask it... How many of these people do you require with you? Because I just made a count and my ship won't fit them all. It's a sleek affair, you understand, and while there *are* lots of ships where we're going, and so logistically it's not really a problem, it is a problem because I don't know these people and I didn't ask for them to come here. So if we could get down to the bare minimum of who you need with you for what we're set to do next, I'd appreciate that."

Keel turned to face Makaffie fully. "Who said we'd be taking your ship? We're taking *my* ship. One of them, anyway."

Zora rolled her eyes. "Time for all your decisions to catch up with you, jump jockey. There's no chance I'm letting you out of my sights again. We have unfinished business with Mr. Nilo." She lowered her voice. "And you're being rude making him wait over there."

Makaffie giggled and then addressed Keel, completely ignoring Zora's comments. "You can be the one to *fly* my ship if you want, I don't care, Fast. But my particular vessel has the only nose to sniff out where we're going, you understand? And we need to get going now. I have a man stationed alone on a place that hasn't historically been too friendly to wayward star farers. You know him, by the way. Kill Team Ice and all that."

Keel clenched his jaw, annoyed at the way the man dropped the name of this unit that was, to Keel, still very much a mystery. A mystery that he'd put off since hearing it from his... his... he was so unsure of it all that he no longer knew how to describe the woman's relationship to him or the man he still thought of as his father.

It was then that Arkaddy Nilo stepped forward, prompting Garret and Jack, and Death, to follow. "I hope you'll forgive my intrusion here, but I have a stake in what happens next. A larger one than you might imagine."

Nilo shook Keel's hand and officially introduced himself. The Black Leaf magnate was only as tall as Keel's shoulders, but he had a presence that spoke of supreme self-confidence. His eyes were studied and keen, taking in the surroundings. Ready for a fight. Ready for things to go sideways. And not just from Keel or Skrizz being unpredictable. He appeared a man ready for anything.

"I appreciate that you had business to attend to," Nilo began before nodding at Leenah, "and as you've seen and heard, we've also been attending to business on your behalf."

Keel looked at Leenah and then back to Nilo. She seemed to like him an awful lot, but Keel wasn't sure what to make of the man and hadn't expected to see him until *after* he'd gotten a solid lead on Prisma's whereabouts. "Yeah. Thanks."

"You can thank Garret for it, mostly. He has a talent that... well, a talent I haven't seen in a long time. Maybe ever."

Keel didn't think Nilo could be more than five years older than the kid, but he didn't disagree, either. "He's something else." Keel looked around. "Let's find someplace other than the street to talk, though."

Zora scowled at Keel calling for the very thing she'd been trying to do earlier. He winked at her but was spared another attack due to how close her boss was.

Nilo seemed not to notice. He nodded graciously. "My shuttle can take all of us up to my cruiser. It will be far more comfortable than anything available on the colony."

Makaffie interjected, waving his hands. "Oh, no-no-no-no. 'Captain Keel' does have a ship to get on, but it's mine. And we have to go now. No time for chit-chat except on the way. And the way we're going, young man, doesn't include you."

Nilo smiled, and behind him another man wearing a suit and holding a briefcase emerged from around the same corner. He was flanked by two armed men with tan slacks, polo shirts, and some kind of N-4 rifle variant.

"Friends of yours?" Keel asked drily.

Nilo looked behind him. "Yes. Jack's job was to keep an eye on Leenah. Keep her safe. Their job was to keep an eye on me. I've stepped out of their view, and that makes them uncomfortable."

"What, specifically, were you trying to keep an old friend of my old friend safe from?" asked Makaffie, using far more words than Keel would have used to ask the same question had he had the opportunity.

Nilo addressed Makaffie, never for a moment showing anything but patience and grace. "Safe from the risk of there being a misunderstanding. A man who's gone through what Captain Keel has may be suspicious. Despite Zora's and Garret's insistence that he wouldn't start shooting without cause, I thought it better to keep Leenah out of sight so as not to give the impression that she was our captive and we had come to bargain." Nilo looked to Keel. "I hope you understand."

"I'm fine," Leenah said, placing her hand against Keel's chest. "And these are good people, Aeson. You need to hear what they have to say."

Makaffie crossed his arms. "Well. I'm not leaving my shuttle. And Fast—"

"Stop calling me Fast."

"Okay... *Aeson.* Time is of the essence. Not just for Prisma but for my friend. Who, even though you don't know it, is your friend too. So we need to go."

"I agree," Nilo said. "And my team needs to be going with you. You're talking about a Savage reclaimer mini-hulk. Ten are known to have ever existed. Eight were confirmed destroyed. And all have something on them that I very much need in order to complete my life's work."

"How did you..." Makaffie began, and then quickly figured it out. "You were listening in. On our conversation in that diner. How? I swept the place."

Nilo smiled. "That was Garret's doing."

Keel frowned. "Kid?"

"Sorry!" Garret said. "I only did it because it was important. When Mr. Skrizz said he was going to meet with you, I uploaded a backdoor on his comm so I could listen in on it without him knowing because the model he uses is a FinMark and you really shouldn't use those because they're so easy to preload with backdoors like Mr. Skrizz's and once we heard about the uh, the situation and what that meant we couldn't risk letting you off world again, Captain, which we couldn't risk before either but now we really can't risk it and I'm really sorry for spying on you Captain Keel and Mr. Skrizz."

"What do you mean, couldn't risk?" Keel was now beyond frustrated at the way everyone but his bot seemed to be hiding something just out of his field of vision.

"This matters to all of us," Zora added. "To the entire galaxy. We need you on this, Keel, and we need you on it right now."

Leenah nodded. "Listen to Zora."

Keel looked from one woman to the other. "Really piling it on, aren't you?"

Nilo took a step forward. "Only because I've filled them in on everything I believe to have happened—everything that has happened."

"I was taken by slavers," Leenah said. "Gomarii. And they—"

Nilo cut her off. "Not here."

"Gomarii slavers," muttered Makaffie. "And they didn't happen to be..."

"A modified hulk, yes," Nilo finished.

Makaffie looked down. "Sket."

"Hey." Keel snapped his fingers. "Someone want to fill me in on what in the nine hells is going on?"

"I would like nothing more," Nilo said. He turned to Makaffie. "And I invite you to come along."

"Well, I appreciate that invitation. But, as I've stated multiple times, I'm not leaving without my ship, and I'm not letting our mutual friend here out of my sight."

From the back line, one of the men whom Keel assumed were Nilo's bodyguards called out, "Is there a problem, sir?"

"Only a logistical one, Surber," Nilo answered.

The name sent a jolt through Keel's mind. He looked around again, feeling like he was being closed in on. But... he knew most of these people. Trusted them with his life just as they had entrusted him with theirs.

Surber had been the name given to him by Mallet Kline. But nobody ever had a name all to themselves. And if it was Nilo who wanted him dead, he had an odd way of going about it. Keel decided he would watch the man, continue on mission for Chhun, but all with eyes open. Same as it always was. Same as it always needed to be.

"How big is your ship?" Keel asked Nilo.

"Little smaller than a corvette."

Keel nodded. "I think I've got something that can get us all where we're going together. You ever hear of the *Battle Phoenix?*"

04

Kill Team Victory
The Planet Kima

The display of ferns, vines, and brush faded into the background as a targeting reticle overlaid itself onto the Dark Ops legionnaires' HUDs. A competing chorus of battlespace information washed across both sides of the screen, projected directly onto the soldiers' retinas. Distance, direction, and wind speed vied for attention with humidity and elevation until the spot being observed came back into sharp focus.

A six-man MCR patrol moved from the top of the trail to the base of the rocky overhang. The patrol leader pointed hurriedly to a spot just in the shade. A lone Kimbrin followed the order to step around the crag.

"That was fast," commented Barret "Toots" Utz over the private channel he shared in Kill Team Victory's L-comm.

"Probably looking to see who's trying to lick the icing off their birthday cake," quipped the Dark Ops weapons sergeant, Dupres Pina. He adjusted the scope on the Greis Telemetrics N-18 anti-materiel blaster rifle. Barely moving his hand from the stock, Pina adjusted the view so that his perception of the far roving squad was near perfect in the pre-dawn hours.

"Would you look at that? They actually sent out a *squad* to check the sensor we smooshed." Toots adjusted the feed from his NS-151 spotting scope to a wide view and scanned the surrounding area for anything that would make what came next more difficult.

"Smoosh. Don't use that word," Pina said. He shifted his L-comm to the command channel to grab Bombassa's attention. "Hey, Top. Spikers just moved a squad into position to check that sensor."

A control module populated one of the windows with a variety of command prompts. The sniper and spotter team had used a mixture of elbow grease and a little robotic assistance to rig the nearby trees with security measures. These were programmed with complex algorithms able to tell the difference between cretins and creatures in the event either got too close to their hide.

"Understood. Support units?" Bombassa asked in his usual all-business style. Most of the guys on Kill Team Victory could count the number of words he said during an operation on their digits without needing to remove their boots. They could also count on him to have their backs whenever things went pear-shaped.

"Negative on support. Just six little mid rats praying there ain't wobankis in the trees."

"Remain in place for overwatch. Bombassa out."

The moment the team sergeant ended the transmission, Toots launched a series of operations windows into his HUD. This was where the perks of being a Dark Ops leej truly showed themselves. Dark Ops got to play with the new toys before anyone else.

Toots and Pina both wore the latest in Dark Ops body armor. Their gear had mimetic functions that automatically blended into any environment they were a part of. Still, in true Legion fashion, the two operators also used an actual ghillie tarp to further conceal themselves.

Newly acquired defense contracts ensured the fabric was layered with the same mimetic tech as their armor.

"Overwatch," Toots said.

"You got something else to do?" Pina countered.

"Thinking about going for a drink."

Pina pulled up the feed from the security cams. Toots had refocused them to look at their hide. Even with enhanced optics and exact knowledge of their location, Pina could barely make out their position. "New buckets still have drinking tubes."

Instead of some witty rejoinder, Toots called out, "Hey. Heads up. It's go time."

The men cleared the other screens from their HUDs, leaving just a single display with a waveform signature passing before it. Somewhere down below, their squad mate Nix was working a targeting mic to capture the conversation between their newly arrived Kimbrin friends.

"Tasco!" shouted a Kimbrin checking the camera. "This one's out of position. Probably bumped by a lugahr going after something."

The patrol leader responded. "Check it for damage and reorient it back toward the path. I'll call it in."

He produced an old-style hand radio that looked like it belonged on the furthest reaches of galaxy's edge. An old colonial model. The thing was made of hard plasteen, light enough to carry and strong enough to survive being trampled by a bullitar. Old tech like this had worked wonders for the MCR as they sought to build up their forces out of view of the native planetary army, the Republic Army, and elements of the Legion prior to the catastrophic civil war. The results of which the rest of the Legion was now en route to clean up.

But first, Kill Team Victory had a job to do. And it wasn't the job they'd hoped to be assigned to: finding their friend and squad mate Aldon Masters. Instead they'd gotten intercepted by the man with the plan and were put into action on behalf of the 131st.

And then there was Keel. Bear and Bombassa seemed to revere the man, but to the rest of the squad, he came off as flighty. Deadly, capable, knowledgeable, sure. But one minute he's coming to get Masters, and the next...

"Got the frequency," Nix whispered over L-comm.

The buckets filled with MCR radio traffic. "Rascha Base, Rascha Base, this is Seventy-One Seven on the south ridge past Waypoint Aputah Four, over."

"Roger, Seventy-One Seven. We have you on our scope," came the reply from the radio. "Stay put for a second while we roll in a sweeper."

"That sucks," Toots said in a private message to Pina.

Sweepers, sometimes called sniffers or catchers, were often used by Republic worlds that funded their own militaries. They were diminutive bots with slaved AI packages designed to look for errant signals across an operations area in the event the native force was being observed by their enemies. The sniffers could suss out any non-aligned broadcasts in their maximum effective range, isolate it, and trace it back to the source to be verified by the targeted patrol. The bots' sensor packages were extremely sensitive, making remote long-range reconnaissance difficult for Republic forces. But unfortunately for the members of Seventy-One-Seven, the one thing the sniffers couldn't track was an L-comm.

"This is Bombassa. All units hunker down. They'll probably keep it on station until the patrol moves on."

The waveform fluttered in their HUDs again as Kimbrin patrol leader Tasco called over one of his NCOs. "Hey Sergeant, go tighten up that patrol halt and tell those morassas to stop chewing those seeds and spitting out the kernels. Did these guys sleep during the patrol brief?"

"Guy knows his stuff," Pina whispered. "Probably an RA defector."

"What's the big deal?" the Kimbrin sergeant asked.

"Big deal is that any time now, we're going to have to prove how bad we want this," Tasco admonished. "That means having a fistfight with the Legion. We already heard in the staff meetings that the House of Laughability authorized Legion force. We don't want to make it easy for them to figure out what our patrol routes are."

"I'll straighten them out," the sergeant said on his way to adjust his soldiers.

The MCR patrol leader looked to the soldier inspecting the holocams. "How much longer, Rip?"

The Kimbrin rebel adjusted a sensor and closed the lid. "I'm done. But something serious knocked this around. Look at these claw marks. This was no lugahr. If I had to guess, it was probably a tigorrah."

Tasco came out from the tree cover to investigate the device himself. He wore old Repub Army fatigues with the camo pattern changed to tiger stripe, and light recon armor. As he strode from the cover of the canopy to the stony crag, his rifle was held at the patrol ready.

He drove his fingers into marked-up tree bark. "Tigorrah leaves a much bigger dig than this. And look here—these marks are slashes that carved up the tree instead of poking the nails in for grip and occasionally prying loose some wood as it climbed."

"Maybe someone wanted us to *think* it was a tigorrah."

"Maybe. Is the camera set?"

The Kimbrin nodded enthusiastically. "Yes, sir."

"All right. Then let's get out of here. Sergeant, roll us back home." Tasco circled his hand above his head to let the team know they were leaving.

As they picked up from their security halt, the MCR sniffer bot flashed overhead, rotating in slow arcs along its hover. The squad made their way from the engagement area, disappearing back the way they came, with the bot in tow.

Nobes was the first to broadcast. "I have good capture on that signal. Translating the freq-hop now."

The waveform reappeared in everyone's HUD. Tasco had switched channels and was talking to a group on his radio. "Falcon Bravo, this is Seventy-One Seven, we have potential signs of intrusion at Waypoint Aputah Four."

"Roger out," was the curt MCR reply over the comms before they went dead.

Nix broadcast into the team channel. "Top, we have eyes on these guys moving back through the ridge. I think they're going to hump it out."

Pina activated his own L-comm. "Top, I have them at the lip. They're not going to hump it out. He's working on the drone. Probably going to kick in new crypto."

Nobes was quick with a suggestion. "Let him load the next set of codes so we can slice those assets before they get out of the AO."

"Agreed," Bombassa said. "Toots, Pina, you're further than we are, but you can skirt the lip of the ridge to avoid detection if you hurry."

"On it, Top." Pina slapped Toots on the arm. "We're going to get our workout in today after all."

"I'll cache and tag so we can move out," Toots said, climbing from under the tarp. "Too bad we've gotta run. Ground had just perfectly conformed to me."

"Beats waiting in the weeds for something else to happen," Pina said. He slid from under the tarp himself and rotated the barrel from the N-18 to drop it into the carry case. After slapping the rest of the frame in beside it, he latched the box with a snap that would have made both of them cringe if they weren't in such a hurry.

The duo raced into the thick foliage behind them in the event there were more observation bots along the route from the ridge. Bombassa didn't need to tell them what to do next. Kill Team Victory had worked together for months and were dialed into the operational protocols that not only kept them alive but let them continue to ask for forgiveness instead of permission on more than a few of their outings.

The Kimbrin sergeant Tasco had demonstrated that he had a working knowledge of the AO as well as a willingness to sound the alarm if something didn't meet his approval. This was a resource they needed to tap. But the window for doing so was about to be slammed on their fingers.

Alert soldiers were difficult to surprise and counter. The *stay alert, stay alive* mantra had obviously found its way into whoever had trained the patrol leader, and it was now serving as the primer that required an early morning run through triple canopy for a pair of legionnaires. It would be interesting to capture the trooper and find out if he was the rule or the exception.

The invasion force would benefit from knowing what they'd be up against.

The two legionnaires raced along the terrain, sometimes hopping, sometimes crawling over obstacles in an all-out rush that would mark an easy trail to follow should these MCR guerrillas have any reconnaissance training. It wasn't their neatest work, but judging by how fast the MCR patrol had entered the AO—likely from following an old animal trail—they needed to hurry. Otherwise the group would be gone, and so would the opportunity to get into their network with minimal exposure to the team.

Toots nearly got clotheslined by a vine that hung heavily in their path. Pina caught his fellow leej before he struck the wet jungle floor. Years of obstacle courses and buddy-team terrain negotiation training made the near costly mistake only a hiccup in the forward momentum of the fire team. Toots hissed an expletive-laced vow at having to go so quickly. Moving through the terrain like this was not the way Dark Ops preferred to conduct their business. This was how you moved during a firefight, not when you were trying to play the role of the raptor silently diving toward its prey.

The pair reached the edge of the ridge line and slowed their pace, nearly crawling to the point where the jungle gave way to an open expanse of green woods and plains between the towering verdant hills leading toward Fort Blake.

"How many motion sensors do you think we tripped?" Toots asked Pina.

"All of them."

"They're coming out over there," Toots observed. He tore open a kit strapped to his leg and removed a folding tripod and something that looked like a blaster mean enough to punch holes in battleships. The contraption was assembled and waiting in under a minute.

Pina pulled his own kit and set up the power supply and CPU for his partner. "Nobes, this is Pina. We're set."

"Make sure to aim the collector at Tasco," Nobes indicated. "It's better if he's broadcasting, but I'll take what I can get. Copy the transmission to me so my slicer-mod can crack the new code and get us into their network. If you get eyes on the drone covering them, try to capture that too."

As if on cue, the flying mini-bot exited the trees for a sweeping arc around the basin where the jungle forest terminated into the lowlands leading to Fort Blake. It swept back and forth with an undulating tick while it searched for signals belonging to anyone but its controllers.

"Got a problem," Pina said into his bucket. "The signal strength from our collector isn't strong enough to push the code to Nobes without tipping that thing off. Gotta see if I can get what we need to burst through L-comm."

"Work it," Toots answered. "You got about two minutes to lock it in."

Pina began to cycle through his bucket's features.

"Pina! We're coming up on your six, running clean-up and checking for tripped sensors. We think you're good but—"

"Nobes!" Pina interrupted. "The signal tap can't make a connection. You're out too far and I don't want to risk alerting that collector. I'm trying to broadcast through the L-comm in my bucket."

"Make it happen, Leej," Nobes called back. "Let me know if you need a walkthrough on how to sync them."

"I got it..."

Words appeared in his HUD.

SIGNAL CONNECTION ESTABLISHED.

"Receiving," Nobes said into the link. "It looks like Toots is nabbing the radio chatter as well."

"Good," Pina said, feeling relief over having successfully cut off the MCR patrol and captured the signals. "Back trail?"

"Bombassa's recovering your gear, and the rest are trying to hide the canyon you blazed through the canopy."

"We didn't have a lot of time to be subtle."

Nobes chuckled. "Top thinks they only wired the trails they use for the patrols because no one is stupid enough to run through the jungle like an agro-bear. I mean, did you see the size of the big jungle cat back there?"

"No, and don't tell me," Pina said. He waited for a few of the leejes to come near before getting to his feet. "C'mon, T."

Toots rose and followed, the operation a success. When one of the oncoming troopers extended a hand to acknowledge the run, Pina punched the man in the part of his armor where the plates fold for flexibility. Carbon-fiber knuckles clacked against the force-mitigating effects of the armor, producing just enough impact to send his target back a step.

"Hey! What's your damage, kelhorn?" shouted Sergeant "Neck" Kenecni through the team channel.

"You were supposed to rough up the tree a little, not make it look like it almost got taken down by a Cybar Titan. The damn scout leader nearly searched the woods for us."

"Listen, crowbait. I roughed up the tree. How was I supposed to know the MCR had some kind of wild animal scratching expert? I ain't fixin' to be the zoology expert when the only thing I've wrangled is pigasaurs, man."

"Enough," Bombassa said as he trotted up. "Nobes?"

"Yeah, Top," the Dark Ops intel sergeant said. "We're locked in. We can listen to their radio chatter and we'll get updated crypto for the day through the worm Pina and Toots just planted. If they continue to fly that sweeper, we might get a read on troop movement and time hacks."

Bombassa nodded in that way he did that let everyone in the vicinity know he was done talking about this or anything else, most likely for the day. "Let's get to work."

05

"You know that's why Bear doesn't come play with us, right?" Nobes asked Bombassa. "You keep stuffing us in these little cubbyholes that the Spikers barely fit in."

Bombassa dragged his rifle from behind him so he could fit his large frame through the portal. "The Yawds built them this way for precisely that reason."

A squat Kimbrin from the Yawd tribe was kneeling by the entrance into the tunnel complex. "Welcome back, friends."

"It's good to see you, Colonel Novo," Nobes said. "What's the good word?"

"My men are receiving the signal you stole from the MCR. We are very grateful for your efforts."

"*Stole* is such a strong word," said Sergeant Nix as he tumbled from the narrow crawlspace. "I prefer *requisitioned for the greater good.*"

Bombassa removed his helmet and let his nostrils drink in the smell of the damp wet earth all around them. The room they were in was a hollowed-out space, not unlike the deep mines of his home world where his people sometimes worked to enrich the robber barons of the now-toppled old Republic. While he hadn't worked in the mines, he knew plenty who had come home at the end of a long, miserable day smelling very much like this place. And worse.

The Dark Ops first sergeant stood from the exit to slap one of the many support timbers holding the roof and sides in their proper place. While they were no more than a few meters from the surface at any time and their armor would protect them, it would be a bad day for their allies if the pillars gave way. Rock, dirt, and vegetation collapsing all at once into a tunnel had a habit of ruining one's day. The big guilds had all sorts of technology to protect miners, but the smaller mining corps couldn't afford modern safety protocols. Out on the edge, mining disasters were common, and in the old Republic such a tragedy was inevitably seized on by senators and delegates alike as a chance to pop in for a somber and caring photo op. Consoling the little people with promises they only barely meant to keep while on camera became an art form among the social elite of the House of Reason, and a wonderful opportunity to enrich a public figure's career.

Here in the jungles of Kima, the Kimbrin, and especially the Yawds, didn't rate such safety equipment either. When Colonel Novo and his forces from the Second Free Rifles Regiment had reached out to the legitimate government for aid, they'd received nothing by way of an answer. But Kill Team Victory had materialized out of the trees, as though they'd been there the whole time just waiting for someone to reach out to the gods for help.

The colonel pointed to Nix. "You're starting to sound like those MCR recruiters with that 'greater good' stuff."

"Sir, that's just the polite way to say we took something without permission," Nix replied. "To the MCR, 'greater good' means filling a few graveyards."

The Yawd commander smiled and gestured them into the tunnel. In addition to the combination of support beams and sewer piping that kept the structure intact beneath the spongy ground above them, vines and occasional tree roots scraped the legionnaires' buckets, the jungle doing what it could to reclaim ground typically reserved for worms.

The crew exited the passage into a chamber barely bigger than the inside of a freighter cockpit. A gathering of Kimbrin Yawds and a few humans turned suddenly to regard the leejes entering the space, but when they saw the colonel enter beside the new arrivals, they returned to their tables and datapads.

A stout Yawd, with some sort of mascara or eye tattoos that extended his eye line, walked up to clack forearms with the colonel.

"Gentlemen," said the colonel, "this is Jinaar, my XO. She's running the operations here, outside of Blake and Kam Dho City. She's newly arrived."

"Pleasure to meet you, Major," said Bombassa.

"Likewise," Jinaar replied. She accepted his hand, though this was a human tradition and not a Kimbrin one.

Nobes offered his hand as well. "We heard you were down in Kam Dho when the takeover went down. Good to see you made it out."

"Thank you, Sergeant. Yes, I was gathering as much of First Battalion from the city as I could. Unlike the active-duty planetary security forces, the militia is very spread out and only meets occasionally for training as a major force."

Pina shook the last bits inside of a water bottle after dropping it from his mouth. "Did you get everyone?"

Jinaar's head dipped. The shadows and scant glow from the track lights placed above them highlighted her eye makeup, giving her the first hints of her species' femininity—and her regrets.

"We got half," she said. "And those we recovered had to be vetted afterward so as not to pull in any MCR plants. I was forced to shoot a few that I'd served with for fifteen years."

"There is little loyalty to be had in the Kayum," the colonel said. He turned to Bombassa. "Those are the ones who have given up the Yawd ways. They are also what the galaxy thinks of as Kimbrin—much to Kima's shame."

"I'm sorry to hear that, Major," Nobes said. "But if you don't mind, given what you've gone through, I'd like to go over some of the intel on Kam Dho."

As Nobes pulled the regimental leadership aside, the rest of the Kill Team Victory slithered through a side passage to the antechamber they'd been given. The leejes had constructed a heavy timber partition with a matching door carved with a koob skull and lightning bolts. After the fall of Victory Company to the deprivations of the House of Reason, Chhun and his crew had taken to Dark Ops. The koob skull served as a reminder of all those they had lost—those who now demanded honor by the living, one fragger at a time.

The door slammed shut on the spartan hole in the ground that had served as the kill team's lair for the last few weeks. A central table gave everyone a place to work and sometimes even eat as the hostile takeover of the planet by the Mid-Core Rebellion raged over their heads. Using support rigging and pylons, the men hooked their hammocks so that they could be rigged or stowed in short order. Bombassa stowed two of them in the rafters to make room as he signaled the leejes who owned them.

"I know what you're going to say, Top," Neck said, holding his hands up in surrender.

Bombassa held up his own hand to command silence. He looked from one to the other and back again. Then he folded his arms and sighed, a noise like the huff of a bull ready to charge. "What's the problem?"

Pina spoke first. "Hey, man," he said to Neck. "We spent that whole time setting this up and it almost went stupid. I got twisted after all that sprinting. My bad."

"I get that," said Neck. "And I get that there could have been any number of IEDs out there. But how was I to know they had a freakin' tigorrah expert on hand? Or that you hit like a girl?"

"If I hit like a Drusic girl, I'm okay with that."

Bombassa shoved them both into the wall, nearly tangling the duo into the dangling hammock lines. "Enough."

He turned his attention to the table where he'd dropped his datapad. Calling forth the holographic keyboards and displays, the big legionnaire began the process of outlining their next hop for the approval of the team commander.

"I don't like it when he yells at us like that," Neck whispered to Pina.

Pina went about the delicate process of re-rigging his hammock. "Borderline abuse is what that is."

Nobes leaned on the table beside the team sergeant. "How long till we have to separate them again?"

Not looking up from his work, Bombassa said, "I give it five minutes after Neck gets that case of swamp gas he suffers from those ration bars."

Nobes laughed, nearly choking on the kaff he'd poured from the plasteen bottle in the center of the table. "Gotta admit I was tempted to give him to the MCR the last time. Aside from Neck's gastro-troubles, where are we?"

Bombassa cast one of the holographic screens toward him. Nobes waited for his datapad's curt beep, indicating it had scooped the info from the tidal pool of information swirling over the table, then sifted through the information.

"These guys talk on the radio a lot," he said. "That's different from prior intel. Seems like our retrans is working too. All this data is going orbital to the Old Man's new ride. Speaking of which, have you seen that thing?"

Bombassa's attention drifted from his map only long enough to shrug his shoulders at the comment.

"Yeah I know, if you've seen one starship you've seen 'em all, but damn if that thing ain't a beast." Nobes studied his screen and then rapped his knuckles on the table. "Okay, that worm we loaded is definitely doing its job. We're getting radio chatter and that sweeper drone is still doing its thing. Hasn't docked yet though, so we won't know until later if we got into their network or not."

Bombassa pointed to the table, directing Nobes's attention to the holographic map. Just outside Fort Blake and away from Kam Dho were three dots in various spots around the valley. "See that?" Bombassa tapped one of the dots, which spawned a dialog box floating over the position.

"Torrid. Those lockboxes look prime," Nobes said. He flashed his team sergeant a thumbs-up. "I'll get on it."

Nobes left the confines of the kill team alcove to find the command element for the Second Rifles. He had to sift through a network of tunnels and personnel before finally coming upon the colonel and XO speaking with some haggard-looking militia.

"Sorry to interrupt, but we have some actionable intel that might get our boys on the ground a lot faster."

Jinaar motioned to the Kimbrin she was speaking to. "This is the Kalo company commander, Captain Reevee."

Reevee looked much older than the other two Kimbrin, and had a scar that ran from the top of his scalp, across his left eye, and down his face onto his neck. Whatever trauma had ripped up the man's face had also sheared off several of the trademark Kimbrin spines from his brow line and jaw.

Nobes struck his forearm against the captain's in the typical greeting of the Kimbrin military. "A pleasure, Captain."

"Captain Reevee just returned from a raid in Kam Dho," Colonel Novo said. "They've been doing good work there since this affair began. He was just telling us of his mission to pull medicines from one of the hospitals."

Listening to Reevee's voice was like listening to a two-pack-a-day stim-stick user trying to sing a lullaby. "We got into the city well enough. We played the part of low-tech herders bringing in animals for the butcher. MCR patrols are everywhere, and a lot of them look the same as planetary army. Some even look like Repub Army. Nhal went in for the meds. We have a contact at the hospital. She came out, and the next thing we knew our contact was being dragged out by these."

Reevee's datapad wasn't as new or shiny as the models carried by the kill team. A hairline crack ran the length of the lower left side, and there appeared to be a layer of slime in the crease between the composite border and the screen. Nobes took the machine from the captain and saw something he didn't expect to see. A Yawd—man or woman he couldn't tell due to the monomorphic nature of the species—was being led away from the hospital by a pack of Hools.

Nobes knew there was an old Hool colony some-where in the jungle, but he wouldn't have guessed that they were involved. Making out details of the troop on the scratched-up screen was a little difficult, but not so much that they didn't trip Nobes's internal *that's-not-right* sen-sor. The Hools favored cunning and cruelty more than ac-tual tactics. Yet the team on the screen was moving in a coordinated squad escort of a prisoner.

"Can I copy this?" Nobes asked.

The colonel nodded. "Of course, Sergeant. This same force chased the militia from the city, trying to capture or kill them. We lost a few good men to these monsters."

"That's what I'm hoping to prevent, sir. We have in-tel that these points here"—he highlighted the spots in question—"may be functional security boxes outside the camp."

The military leaders were unreadable. They showed no change of expression as they patiently waited for the narrative to continue.

"Um… so, when a Republic military base goes up, the Legion comes in behind the construction and builds a se-ries of cache sites that we call lockboxes. The boxes have Legion-grade encryption so they can't be used against us, but basically, each one contains a data log and input to the network running inside the camp, sort of like the black box on a starship. It's a protocol for big bases that was installed after the Battle of Kublar. Anyway, getting to one of those sites would give us access to the system. From there we could learn how they managed to overrun us—since we don't have anyone left alive to tell us what happened."

Reevee raised his hand as though he was about to hand in his book report. "Sergeant, wouldn't the MCR have sent people to shut down or destroy these boxes?"

Nobes shook his head. "They're not common knowledge. And only Dark Ops would know where they are."

"Does this give us a way into the camp?" Jinaar asked eagerly.

"I'm not sure. Each site is different. The only way to tell for sure would be to recover a box and see what else is there."

Reevee stood ramrod straight at attention, facing the colonel. "I want this mission, sir."

Nobes looked on, careful to hide his skepticism for fear that it would be interpreted as Dark Ops trying to take over the show. The Second Rifles were spread thin as it was, and they were already engaged in consolidation ops that had them running all over the countryside looking for their people. The MCR takeover had been so swift, the only thing the militia could do was flee the cities and regroup later. It was the defiant Yawds in the hinterlands who were putting up the stiffest resistance, at least on this continent.

Then again, as motivated as the Yawds were at killing MCR, it didn't make sense to turn down the help.

The colonel considered. "Moving a company, even through the jungle, will not go unnoticed."

Reevee tried another tack. "I can assign a rifle platoon with assets. That should get the legionnaires to the box and provide any support they might need along the way."

Nobes nodded. "I would appreciate the help, sir."

"This is our home, Legionnaire," Reevee said. "We can't have you fight the whole battle for us. It is our duty to help you."

"That's settled then," Novo said. "Please inform your commanders of the plan. Only we three from the command staff will know of your mission. The less eyes and ears that see you, the better."

06

Legion Super-Destroyer *Centurion*
Classified Staging Area

The overly damp mop slapped on the deck with a wet sucking noise. It had been six months since Kildane had been sentenced to an endless dance of bar codes and zombie mops running across the floor. The chief had decided on day one that he was *persona no nada*, and since he was one of a handful of unrated spacers on board, he was getting crap details that were made up just to punish.

"We got bots for this," Kildane muttered beneath his breath as he dragged the sopping wet mop across the deck. "Had 'em for thousands o' karkin' years already."

Last night had been insane as the flurry of spacers, marines, and more than a few legionnaires came into the commissary to get their loads of snacks, energy drinks, and stims. This morning it was as quiet as a waller. Only a few people had wandered over to the kaff shop to grab a quick bite away from the galley, and one scarred-up legionnaire had come into the shop looking for ice cream, of all things.

The super-destroyer *Centurion* had been built just after the toppling of the House of Reason and the rise— or restoration, depending on whom you asked—of the House of Liberty. At the request of the Legion commander, some holo-star who'd managed to not get his bucket split during the A-19 war, the *Centurion* was built as the flagship representing what the Legion once was and would be again.

That all sounded like garbage to Kildane. A bunch of fuss about nothing. He'd seen plenty of legionnaires come planetside on his home world to enforce some tax restriction, only to get blown away by gangbangers that had been former army or marines. Bullets and blaster bolts don't care how many push-ups you can do. They only care about going through whatever's in their way. More than a few of those discos—what his people used to call the Legion in the shiny armor—got spent in some back alley by a banger with a better grip on the terrain.

Still, the holo-channels always had stories about these guys. Back in the day, they were first-rate killers of the highest order. Kildane had seen some documentary that went into detail about the unity of the organization— their most secretive handshake or some such and how their motto, KTF, was a play on how they treated their enemies. If that was ever true of the Legion, it was no longer, not after the House of Reason was done with them. There was no kill in the legionnaires Kildane had seen up close; they were mere bullies used for political purposes. A glorified police force led by fools who didn't know enough to stop them from getting flaxed by the gangs, pirates, and mercs who fought tooth and nail for everything.

Dogs don't stay wild on the leash.

"The vaunted Legion," Kildane mumbled. He dropped the mop into the wringer at the top of the bucket and wrenched the lever back to squeeze the excess water out. "Oba, I hate my life."

"Mopping the deck like that, I would say so."

Kildane whipped around and saw the legionnaire watching him. The one who'd come in with a fresh sheen over his drenched PT uniform and very politely asked if the StarEx, one of the three Star Port Exchange shops on board the ship, had any ice cream. He'd taken a seat in the palladium, the food-court-like center where Kildane found himself most days, to savor the treat. The palladium was typically visited by those coming off rotations in their various ratings, looking for a snack or just something with more flavor or variety than what was served in the galley. Kildane hadn't found the need to spend his own credits here; the food in the galley was plenty good enough for him. Ten times better than what he ate in basic training and a hundred times better than anything he would have eaten back home. The vets on the ship had just gotten soft about chow.

The leej, still holding the end of an ice-cream cone between two fingers, stepped into Kildane's personal space. That set off alarms in Kildane's mind, honed by his time growing up rough.

"Good reflexes there, SNR-2 Kildane," the legionnaire said.

Kildane kept the derision from his face. He'd been good at that since they dropped him into basic. Hide the snarl. Hide the hate. Do what you can to get through this until you're out. Two years. You could do anything for two years.

"Sorry, sir. I didn't mean to spin on you like that."

The leej snatched the mop from Kildane's hands in a swift motion that deposited it into the masher for a squeeze-dry. "Not enough cleaner, way too much water on the deck, and damn if you don't look like you've been forced into a life of slavery instead of volunteering for the fleet."

"I... um... sorry, sir."

The mop slapped the floor with the legionnaire's hands gripping the top of the handle. Unlike the lazy *plop* Kildane produced on the deck each time, the legionnaire's was more of a *snap*. He swiped across a section in front of the StarEx, back and forth in practiced motions until the water was barely a sheen. Then the mop was flung into the press again and Kildane swore he heard the strain of a handle ready to break from the legionnaire exerting way more force than the mop was rated for. In another series of motions, the dry mop sopped up most of the water until the decking in front of the shop was nearly dry.

"Tell you what, SNR-2 Kildane. You fetch us each another one of those cones, I'll finish this like it was my chosen profession."

"I shouldn't. I'm on duty, sir."

"I have it good with the chief. I can square it if anyone says anything."

Kildane hesitated for a moment as the legionnaire sent the mop for another round at the floor. Then he drifted back into the shop and returned with ice-cream cones and napkins for the both of them. They unwrapped their treats, and without asking, the motivated floor washer took both wrappers to deposit in the trash bin on the side of the bulkhead.

Kildane closed his eyes at the first taste of the dessert. It was creamy and cold past anything he'd had in months—the scrambled eggs in the galley being the one possible exception. This was truly a pleasure.

"Thank you for the break, sir," Kildane said. "I... I'm not used to people giving me a fair shake, much less taking the time to show me anything worthwhile."

"No worries. I needed the break myself. Plus, it's been a few years since I had ice cream. I saw it on the window sticker and thought I might as well splurge before things get busy." The legionnaire took a bite off the top of his cone. "Wasn't planning on two, though. How'd you come to StarEx duty?"

Kildane shrugged one shoulder. "The spacer that normally runs the shop is getting fire suppression training for the next week. Since I'm the chief's favorite dog, this is where my leash is tied for the moment. That's the life of an unrated."

"You mentioned that no one shows you anything of value."

Kildane shrugged again. "Honestly, they just stick me somewhere and tell me to do something until I get it wrong. I appreciated the little lesson from today on how to properly mop a floor to get on Chief's good side. The bigger lesson was that legionnaire clinch, followed by a hook to the body, a hook to the head, and the throw to the ground you did on the mop."

The legionnaire stopped chewing and swallowed the rest of the ice cream. "You saw all of those motions in me working the mop?"

"Yes, sir. One of the guys that took care of me when I was a kid, he used to fight for money so we could eat. He'd say a good hook was all body, no arm. I didn't know what he meant until now, watching you. All the motions were there. You weren't mopping, you were training."

"Yes, he was!" said another voice.

For the second time in the last few minutes Kildane whipped around, moving so fast that he caught the approaching man—another legionnaire—off guard. He cheeked the last bit of his ice cream like a Sinasian water squirrel before snapping to parade rest. In his peripheral vision he saw the first leej, the one who'd been helping out, lean on the mop and observe.

"Stand easy, Ace," said the new man to Kildane, then turned to the other legionnaire. "Now what do we have going on here? I got a whole fleet o' hurt outside this dunk-n-go hut readying for war, and here's a leej and a spacer trading time on my very advanced battleship. Don't mean to be pushy like it's my job or anything, sir, but where are you supposed to be?"

"PT first, Sergeant Major, followed by a breakfast of champions and some impromptu training with my new friend here, SNR-2 Kildane, with just enough time for the three S's before my meeting."

"I get it, sir. Legion doesn't issue you friends so you go make a few of your own?" The sergeant major shook his head. "I have to chase you down to sit you in the right chairs. That's probably why I ain't retired right now in the arms of a zhee mare and her colts."

Kildane let slip a look of shock and horror at the statement, prompting the sergeant major to respond.

"Don't look at me like that, kid. Back in the day on Ankalor—I'm talkin' one of the first times, not the *last* time—probably before your old man climbed whatever petri dish he dropped his seed into, I was the only one left on my kill team. Shot, alone, and cold. But that lady donk took me into her house and hid me from the tribe until my boys came to get me out. Hell, you could even be my baby boy. You half donk, kid?"

The helpful Legion officer—what else could he be given that the sergeant major was calling him "sir"—buried his head in the crook of his arm as he held the top of the mop handle, his shoulders bouncing up and down as he struggled to contain his laughter. Kildane took it as a sign that if he just rode this out quietly, he might survive. The feeling disappeared as quickly as it had arrived with the oncoming clack of hard-soled boots sounding their way across the deck. The chief had arrived.

"Morning, sir. Sergeant Major MakRaven," said the chief. "Is this kelhorned reject giving you any trouble, sir?"

"No, Chief, he isn't," the officer answered. "But I'd like to know what his deal is."

"Aw, hell no, sir," barked the sergeant major, rolling his eyes, neck, and head all at once. "I done read your memoirs and learnt all about that Kags fella. You like to gather up the strays. We ain't doin' that again."

The officer shrugged. "Maybe I see Legion where other people don't."

The chief politely took the mop from the officer and then looked over the floor in admiration. "If I'm picking up what the both of you are laying down, sir... do you aim to hold on to SNR-2 Darius Kildane during your stay?"

Kildane felt like he was watching a seamball match. He was looking from one guy to the next as he heard everyone have a say in his fate but him. This was just like how he'd ended up here in the first place.

The chief apparently saw this as an opportunity to air all of Kildane's dirty laundry for the two legionnaires to inspect. "Mr. Kildane was part of a crew on Utopion scooping up sleds after the removal of Goth Sullus," he said with a sneer. "Seems they were jailbreaking the few sleds that made it through the destruction, most likely because all the fighting had dusted their original owners. And rather than allowing the vehicles to be sent back to a loved one, these skets decided to take it upon themselves to unburden those next of kin from having to deal with such expensive pieces of property. They loaded them onto heavy freighters and sold them for prices that would make a junk-pirate shake his head."

The two legionnaires joined the chief in taking a long look at Kildane. The spacer held their gaze.

"Judge musta saw something in him when he wouldn't roll on the rest of his crew," the chief said with a shrug. "Plus there was the matter of him kicking all his money to some poverty-stricken kelhorn. So he got a choice: fleet or jail."

"That true?" the Legion officer asked Kildane.

Kildane nodded.

"Who were you sending the credits to?"

"We take care of our own, sir," Kildane said, his pride evident in his voice.

The sergeant major let out a sigh. "Well, I've seen worse in the Legion. Points, for starters. Chief, you might as well put a bow on him." He looked to the Legion officer. "Unless...?"

The Legion officer gave a nod.

"Aw, the nine hells." The sergeant major held out a hand, and Kildane shook it. The leej had the grip of a tyrannasquid. "I'm Sergeant Major MakRaven. This here's General Chhun. Formerly *Legion Commander* Chhun."

Chhun never dropped his smile. He leveled a two-finger salute into a finger-point toward the stunned spacer. "Boosting sleds, huh? Can you drive?"

"Yes, sir," Kildane said through his amazement.

"No, spacer. Can you *drive*?"

A hint of fire crept into the young man's mouth. "Like it was my chosen profession, sir."

07

Chhun fought the urge to squirm as he and MakRaven walked the passage toward the squadron briefing room. He'd never really been comfortable with this part, especially coming up as a Mustang officer. Watching uniformed men and women fling themselves at both sides of a passage on a starship to make way for him was still a little unnerving. For most of his career *he'd* been the one to do the jumping out of the way thing—and there were days he wanted to go back to it. Return to the time when you received orders just to carry them out with discipline and professionalism. Know the standard, do the standard, and be the standard.

Rising through the ranks as he had didn't mean those days were entirely over, though. Now that he was no longer Legion commander, he still received orders; those orders just came from much higher up the ladder. Now it was his job to inform all the officers of those orders, who would in turn pass them to the men under their commands.

Still, days like today made him miss the simplicity of the trigger. That was where his heart truly lay: the point between an N4 trigger at rest and the break, when the world erupted into violence just long enough for him to put it in check.

"You got that look on your face, sir," said MakRaven. "You gettin' buyer's remorse on the sled thief? I can drive him out to some edge world and leave him there. He won't know how to follow us back home."

Chhun tapped his temple. "Bigger dunns to hunt, Sergeant Major. But to answer your question, negative. Some of the basics we got on the stick are fresh out of training. That kid ran some of the tightest streets on Utopion, which isn't Ankalor, but it was rough. He doesn't need to be *my* driver, but I would like him behind the wheel to show those regs what's up."

MakRaven eyed the general. "Sir, you been hanging with your old V-Co buddies? You're startin' to sound like a leej company CO rather than a combined forces commander about to thunder-slap a planet into submission."

"Maybe a little bit of both," Chhun said. "Took this job after researching some of my options."

Chhun had wondered how it was that certain men like Pappy managed to stay put seemingly forever in one place. Or how some generals managed to get themselves in the thick of things without the Legion commander coming down on top of them. The answer was traced all the way back to General Rex. The famous legionnaire had regularly fought on the line during the Savage Wars. Afterwards, he had shifted to direct action missions with Dark Ops.

Because of Rex, the Legion made exceptions for leaders who excelled at both planning and executing on the battlefield, and Chhun used that to his advantage. While he could have swung his way into Dark Ops and overseen his own hand-picked operations, that wasn't his choice. No, the only way he could see his vision for the Legion fulfilled was to command the 131st. That meant less involvement in the fight than he would like, but it also meant selecting the best legionnaires for mission success—like

Sergeant Major MakRaven, who had built up a storied reputation of his own.

The duo exited the tight confines of the passage into one much wider and more akin to a corridor. The foot traffic here was amazing in contrast to most of the ships Chhun had been on. Cramped destroyers and battleships with every ounce of space accounted for to maximize the ship's potential while minimizing waste. Not so the super-destroyer. There was so much room in this corridor that spacers drove in opposite directions in specially marked repulsor cart lanes, whisking by as flashing yellow lights cast their glow against the walls.

One of the carts pulled to a stop alongside Chhun and MakRaven. "Sir!" called the driver. "You looking for a lift, sir?"

MakRaven took stock of the spacer driving the cart. He had a square jaw and the hiked-up sleeves on his fleet combat shirt displayed arms that looked like they would give a Drusic a run for its credits in an arm-wrestling match. He wore a plate carrier and was also under arms.

"That your daily driver, M.A. Matsuoko?" MakRaven asked.

"No, Sergeant Major," Master-at-Arms Matsuoko replied. He set the safety brake and rose out of the vehicle at the position of attention to address the pair. "Had to run a bunch of shapes and sizes up to the SBR. Don't know why they needed an armed escort for that aboard the ship, but we got it done and I'm just returning the cart. If you need a lift though, I'll be happy to go full Legion on this passage for you. Not every day you get to drive the two top rates from your organization."

Chhun was enjoying this NCO's bravado. "Full Legion. Haven't heard that particular fleet term before."

"It's catchin' on, Legion Commander."

"Former," Chhun corrected. "I'm just a general officer, now. And thank you, but we'll keep going on foot."

"One other thing," MakRaven said. "General here is poachin' spacers. You ever think of going Legion with those arms?"

Matsuoko nearly laughed himself out of his armor. "No, Sergeant Major. You guys spend too much time in the drift and not enough time in port chasing the local talent. I've gotten more than my share on a trigger in the fleet. We had to chase pirates on the edge after Article Nineteen. They had themselves a war or somethin' out there to see who was top scumsack."

That elicited a chuckle from MakRaven. "Between that and everything else goin' on, you've been busy in the fleet."

"Livin' the dream, Sergeant Major."

Chhun shook the master-at-arms's hand. It was always a welcome change to meet a warrior, whether they were wrapped in the Legion's armor or not. These past few months before stepping down, he'd been forced to shake hands or tap limbs with members of the House of Liberty and the full assortment of hangers-on that went with that environment. A handshake from such people was often as limp as they were. Master-at-Arms Matsuoko seemed hard as nails but had the easygoing demeanor of someone with nothing to prove.

"Good to meet you," Chhun said.

Matsuoko nodded and sat back down behind the controls. "Have a good day, gentlemen." The master-at-arms hurried away along the cart lane, his warning lights flashing amber over the crew moving on foot in the middle thoroughfare.

MakRaven and Chhun rejoined the normal flow of people heading amidships. "That's twice now you've been impressed with the crew on this boat," MakRaven said. "Did you think Deynolds was going to staff the thing with yo-yo balls or something, sir?"

"No, Sergeant Major. Just remembering what it was like before. Leejes usually worked with competent crew, but damn if we didn't run into buckets of stupid here and there."

"Yes, sir. I remember it about as well as I do my third wife's cooking—too bad to ever forget. S'pose this is what happens once we burn all the points out of every branch."

"My thoughts exactly, Sergeant Major."

"That's why I got the job." MakRaven thrust his hand toward a door guarded by a Republic marine. "After you, Your Highness."

Chhun stepped through the hatch to a booming "Group! Atten-HUH!"

"Thank you, Chief," Chhun said before casting his eyes to the rest of the room. "As you were." He made his way around the holotable where the rest of the officers aboard the super-destroyer *Centurion* waited for him. At his insistence, they all resumed their seats, prepping to stand at any moment for someone senior to him to arrive. They didn't wait long.

"Don't bother getting up," Admiral Deynolds said on her way through the room like a tornado. "I'm sure you've all played enough officer aerobics to not mind keeping your seats. General, if you'd care to begin?"

Taking his cue from the admiral, Chhun selected the interface on his battle board to dim the lights. A colossal hologram of the planet Kima hung suspended in the middle of the room. "None of you are in need of a recap of the events that have led us here. We've all read the SITRO from Republic Intel on MCR taking control of the planet. Republic and indigenous forces fell in a matter of hours around the majority population centers and within days in outlying areas. Currently we have pockets of resistance mostly in rural communities. And make no mistake, it's the Yawd mountain dwellers who are driving that repulsor."

The hologram whirled inside the room, dropping into a topographic map of a heavily forested area just north of the equator. "The epicenter of Republic military presence on the planet was here in Kam Dho City, some seventeen hundred kilometers north of the equator. And then Fort Blake was completely overrun and all combat outposts in the area wiped off the board. Currently, Kill Team Victory is on the ground in combat support operations for the Second Free Rifles militia regiment. Again, these are primarily Yawds, augmented by trusted Kimbrin who left the Yawd tribes for military vocations, both Republic and planetary alike. This team will spearhead our retaking the planet, call sign *Operation Atlas Wake*."

Chhun ran his hand over a smaller holographic display on his datapad, causing the big display to zoom into the high peaks containing a city-sized operating base. "Stage one, Kill Team Victory, working with indigenous forces, gains us access to Fort Blake. It is imperative we take this position with as minimal damage as possible. Blake will provide us with mission staging and support, control of the artillery, and protection of Kam Dho City. First Bat, you're up."

The First Battalion commander, a legionnaire who looked composed of equal parts aggression and hate, stood from the assembly. "Major Carden will deploy

Victory Company in support of Kill Team Victory and the Second Rifles to retake Fort Blake. Before we hit it, Repub Intel pulled the following clips from co-opted observation bots in the AO. We're going to need digits on these."

The holo shifted to an aerial view of the jungles giving way to the hilly plains and fields leading to Kam Dho City. The video halted as a heavy construction rig used its shovel to drop a load of muck onto the wet plain. A naval intel officer rose to her feet beside the First Battalion commander, who nodded his approval for her to proceed.

"We put this footage through every algorithm we have and ran it past some of our best sets of eyes. Based on the outline and this raised portion here, we believe we're looking at a Mekkasaw 381. That's a long-range artillery piece." The officer touched the table and drew up a schematic of a six-legged mechanized crab with a giant gun barrel mounted on its back. She took the hologram and deposited it on a hill just outside of the Kam Dho City map. "From this elevated position, the L-RAP's maximum line of fire is thirty-seven kilometers."

The First Bat commander shifted a toothpick from one side of his mouth to the other in a gesture of annoyance. "How did the MCR get 381s on planet without us knowing?"

The intel officer had an answer for that. "Planetary militia helped us unseat the MCR militants our last time on Kima assisting the Legion to win over MCR assets in the town of Khal Rho. Our sources on the ground are saying the militia from that area flipped when a new command element came into play. The L-RAPs are theirs."

Chhun looked to the battalion commander. "Colonel, deploy Venom Company to those target points to secure the 381s. We're in contact with the team on the ground.

They've got Second Rifle scouts out looking for them and they're confident they'll have them tagged once we make orbit."

The colonel nodded and took his seat, ceding the room back to Chhun.

"Stage Two will encompass Second Battalion making a mass-tac airborne operation over the following cities in a coordinated assault to regain control and protect the populace," Chhun said. "Flying escort will be Captain Danns and the Star Reapers. For those on the ground, this is going to be what we've been training for over the past few months. A knock-down, drag-out fistfight going house to house."

The members of Second Battalion's command staff whispered under their breath. There were knuckle knocks and quiet slaps on shoulders as their CO, Colonel Scholtes, rapped his fist on the table in anticipation. Off to the side, Dax Danns and his crew looked on impassively. The Star Reapers had seen some of the most intense starfighter combat in the wars against the Black Fleet, Cybar, and House of Reason. If the pilots all acted like they'd been there before, it was only because they had.

Chhun continued. "Third Batt has the hard part: pest control. You'll come in behind the main bodies and sweep the hills and holes for any MCR that slipped the noose. You find command rats, you roll them up and slide them to intel. Anyone that resists, you back off and we level a grid square.

"Commanders, OPORD is on your boards with all available assets and time hacks. The citizens of Kima prayed to Oba for a miracle, and the MCR prayed for the Republic to send the same old Legion. Both are going to see what happens when you pray for angels but get demons. Good hunting."

As the officers and their senior leaders poured from the SBR, Deynolds hovered beside MakRaven. "You know," she said, "I've witnessed more than a few briefings like that where you couldn't keep a roof on the room. But these men stepped off quiet as the grave. I could practically taste the violence building but not a sound on their way out. You weren't kidding when you said they aren't old Legion, were you?"

"That's just it, ma'am," the sergeant major replied. "That's precisely what we've been doing all this time since Nineteen went down. We've rebuilt the Legion, but not just any Legion. What we have here is the version of the Legion that won the Savage Wars. At least, that's what we've got here in the 131st. And now those MCR kelhorns are gonna choke on it."

08

MCR Patrol
The Jungles of Kima

Drom checked his GPS for the third time. Hardly an easy task as the blistering heat playing off the canopy was enough to cover the screen in the misty condensation littering the downslope. Kima had been his home for all his life, but certain parts of the planet still pissed him off.

The six-man patrol halted along the hill, finding whatever cover they could against the possibility that something was out there waiting for them. Tasco had drilled this awareness into them from the moment Drom had been brought in. Apparently Tasco had been some big deal out on the edge at one of the bigger merc companies, part of that fleeting bit of glory the MCR had before things went to hell.

But that hell had also been fleeting. Now the MCR was back, and no one—not the duplicitous Republic, not the Cybar, not some loon of an emperor—could stop them. The Legion would try, but this wasn't Ankalor. Kima was ready to forge its own path. The native population who couldn't see that just needed to get out of their own way.

In fact, that was what Drom and his team *should* be doing: convincing the population to stand united against the invasion that was sure to come, the same way the

Kublarens had reclaimed their own world. But Tasco had other ideas.

A younger Kimbrin, Krell, knelt behind a boulder jutting out of the hillside, dutifully scanning the terrain. Drom liked the kid, and not only because Krell was fascinated by Drom's stories of fighting the Legion with the MCR at Khal Rho. Krell was a good fighter, and the kid most likely would have joined the Republic military if not for a genetic defect that kept him from seeing different shades of red. At the time, the House of Reason would only fix such maladies if you were already enlisted; defective species need not apply. Drom didn't know what the House of Liberty's position on such things was, and he didn't care. He was just glad things had worked out so that he had the kid's attention and could rely on him to do the lion's share of the work. If the kid was that motivated to do it, why not let him?

"This is the spot where the obs-bot caught sight of that flash, whatever it was," Drom said. "But I don't see anything. Do you?"

The assembled Kimbrin fighters rocked their heads from shoulder to shoulder in the native signal for a negative. The only one that didn't move was Krell.

"There's something out there, sir," the young fighter reckoned. "Hey, sir. Drop your lens."

Drom released a slight sigh. It was just loud enough to make himself feel better but not so loud as to discourage the kid. Every minute they lingered here was a minute they wouldn't have back at the Republic chow hall at Blake. Ever since Tasco and his boss had gotten the local supply lines back up, the victorious MCR had been enjoying the best food in forever. Drom didn't want to get waylaid on this little sneak-and-peek mission to where he had nothing but scraps to come home to. If the chow hall was cleared out they'd probably get stuck with army ration packs, and no one wanted those.

After counting to five to soothe his nerves, he dropped the combat information lens from his helmet and handed it to Krell. The younger soldier secured it in place, then thumbed the designator on his rifle. Drom knew that a beam was now being sent from the rifle into the expansive jungle, though it was only visible through the monocle or to those using enhanced vision. But its presence was evident in the fact that some of the wildlife, sensitive to the light frequency, went silent. Their stillness then spread to other animals like a contagion, and the jungle went quiet.

"Sir, I think there's something in that nest over there," Krell said. "About a hundred meters." He pointed to a gnarled overhang of branches coming off a rock-strewn basin and cascading down the hill in a tangle of vines.

"Animal?" Drom asked, suddenly losing his appetite.

"Not sure. I feel like something in there is watching us, though. I just can't see it."

The kid's tone bothered Drom. Out here in the jungle, a little bit of premonition could save a life. The chow could wait.

"Everyone move by twos back over the hill," Drom said in a low voice. "I don't want to risk us getting s'suffad. For all we know, what the bot saw was simply a lure to get us out here."

"I think I have a bead on whatever it is," Krell said. "I'll move last, sir."

"Good. First two, up and over."

As the initial moves of the bounding overwatch maneuver took place, Drum used the time hunkered into some palm fronds to make a call. "Rascha Base, this is

Sixty-Three Sixty. We have potential contact at Waypoint Aputah Four. Deploy sweeper to my location for perimeter scan. How copy, over?"

"Sixty-Three Sixty, this is Rascha Base. Can you identify threat? Over."

Drom angrily keyed the push-to-talk switch mounted to the top of his armor. "Negative, Rascha Base. That's why we need the sweeper, over."

A click sounded on the net, and the squelch was interrupted by an unknown voice. "Rascha Base, this is Sixty-Three Sixty, we have eyes on the disturbance. Looks like something dragged off a bit of shrapnel from when we took the camp. We'll conduct a quick scan and RTB."

"Good copy, Sixty-Three Sixty. Rascha Base out."

"What the—I didn't say that," Drom commented breathlessly.

Just as he was about to scream for his men to take cover, the voice came over the radio again.

"Sergeant Drom, tap the side of your helmet twice if you can hear this."

The sergeant froze—and then did as requested. He looked slowly to each side to see if his men were having similar experiences.

"Good. Now take that targeting monocle back from your soldier and look through it."

"Krell," Drom hissed. "Bring me that combat scope."

The young trooper did as commanded. "What is it, sir?"

Drom took the scope and ignored the question. "Move up and join the team." He put the scope up to his eye.

"I'm going to upload an overlay for that monocle you're looking through," the mysterious voice said over the net. "Click yes to accept when it comes through."

Drom did as instructed while his troops settled themselves into the top of the hill. The overlay he'd accepted cast everything in a grayish-blue pallor, allowing him to see some kind of targeting laser aimed at the back of Krell's head as he bounded along.

"We're now shifting that beam to your position," the voice said.

Drom watched as the beam disappeared from view. He swallowed and felt a trickle of sweat gather on one of the horns on his jawline.

"This targeting laser is now set on you, Drom. If you move, or break the link, it will assume you're a loaded vehicle leaving your position. What'll come your way will be enough to blow every bolt off a tank."

"What do you want from me?"

"Just sit tight."

Drom waited a moment before keying the mic. "For how long?"

"However long it takes your buddies to find and disable the trap."

The transmission ended.

"Last calling station, this is Rascha Base. Say again, last transmission, over."

Drom felt more drops of sweat drip from his horns. "Rascha Base, Rascha Base, this is Sixty-Three Sixty. Disregard my last. Deploy QRF to my location ASAP and send someone who can defuse a laser tripwire!"

For twenty minutes, only Krell dared venture near the team sergeant. The younger soldier kept Drom from drifting out of position and potentially setting off the trap. Finally, a SLIC arrived and hovered in the distance. An MCR team that included a few humans roped down through the canopy and moved carefully to the patrol leader, approaching from the down side of the hill for fear of interrupting the beam centered on his torso.

A second SLIC put down a squad wearing full combat armor. These soldiers plummeted along the drop lines and then took to the jungle, showing off a level of training uncommon to much of the Mid-Core Rebellion. The troopers slithered under the foliage, buffeted by the assault of the repulsors keeping the SLIC overhead. They took up positions by Drom as the techs moved forward toward the laser's projection point.

"Long day at the office?" Tasco asked through the digital grit of his mask.

Drom nodded in appreciation. "Good to see the rebellion remembers its friends."

"Of course. Where would the MCR be without the dedicated men and women of the Kimbrin people? Make no mistake about that. I understand Raptor COC heard you calling out to someone on the radio."

"Whoever set us up, they had our frequency."

"Not unexpected, but also not the news I was hoping to hear."

Drom sneered dismissively. "I'm surprised the Yawds could even figure out how to turn one of our radios on."

Tasco gave a fractional shake of his head. "They could have broadcast a tight beam to you. Or... it could be Legion."

Drom widened his eyes for a moment and then compressed them into slits. "We haven't had any word that those shinies have deployed yet."

Tasco waved his hand. "One rarely does when the advance teams infiltrate a planet."

A chime sounded.

"That'll be the techs," Tasco said. He patted Drom on the shoulder, careful to keep out of the beam. "Not much longer, I'm sure."

Tasco took the incoming transmission.

"Hey Tasco, it's Dekar. Found an old MKS-3 rocket grenade launcher, and it's set up like they said. Nothing special except someone put a laser trip activator on the trigger, so I think we're good to disable it. You'll want to get everyone clear of the target just in case."

"Stand by. I'd like to have my team take a look over the hill."

Tasco motioned for Krell to follow him over the hill. The two took long-legged strides toward the crest, and when the kid was settled in with the rest of Drom's squad, Tasco directed the rest of his own squad to fan out, looking for clues as to who might be behind this.

"Dekar, it's Tasco. That laser trigger. Is it Legion issue?"

"Negative, sir. This stuff was fairly common during the initial MCR uprising here on Kima. Likely surplus."

"Yawds?" Tasco asked.

"Out here, I'd think so. I can take the laser down at your word. Simple setup. Five seconds."

Tasco looked back at where Drom sat, perfectly still and alone. "Do it."

"Laser down. We should have the scene clear for you within minutes."

Tasco cut the connection and switched over to the next in a series of protocol transfers that led him to a net that only he had access to. Or so he hoped. "Sigma 21 reporting on incident four thirty-two on Waypoint Aputah Four. IED discovered with Yawd indicators. Unknown if a Legion advance party is involved. This could also be the work of Legion survivors from the takeover. Further update to follow. Sigma 21 out."

Tasco retracted the overlay from his HUD, returning him to the regular network. Down below, one of the techs was informing Drom that he was free to move. The pot-bellied Kimbrin gained his feet and stretched his limbs.

The net chimed with another incoming signal. "Hey, sir. It's going to be another minute. I have some sort of interface down here hidden among the vines. It should be—"

A shock wave of force detonated all around them, sending gravity and rational thought into a tailspin. The firestorm of white light, pressure, and heat washed over the hill in a tremendous wave of destruction as everything around the teams was sent up from the ground toward the sky. Bodies flew in all directions, fusing with the landscape in a cacophony of searing light and pain. When the rampant rush of energy was expended, broken men and Kimbrin followed the bits of landscape to thump into the formerly wet ground.

Tasco stumbled to his feet, scrambling for handholds to right himself. Everything he touched was either on fire, turning to ash, or ash. His head was spinning uncontrollably. His armor, complete with full-faced helmet, and his distance from the detonation, were the only reasons he was alive. Even so he tasted blood in his mouth and felt it dripping from his nose.

Unable to find anything by which to pull himself upright, he rolled onto his back to assess how severely he was hurt. The sky came into view, still spinning. He rolled his head to the right and saw the body of the kid lying in the muck and ash. The young soldier looked dead, so when the kid moved and started coughing, Tasco had a start. The Kimbrin patrol weren't wearing fully enclosed helmets like Tasco and his team, and he wouldn't have expected a single one of them to have survived that devastating blast.

"You alive?" Tasco said.

"No, sir," Krell rasped out.

The kid had a pair of comm-cans over his ears. The units weren't common kit among the MCR patrols, but the protection provided by the device—and the sheer good luck of having been positioned in a saddle facing away from the blast—must have saved the kid's life.

It was a good sign that the kid was already joking. He would more than likely make it through this; Tasco had seen it before. And now he was going to need every scrap of information the kid could give them. Besides which, the kid would make an excellent replacement for the former patrol leader, Drom, who was now in more pieces than Tasco was willing to count.

"What in the nine hells hit us, sir?" Krell asked.

The spinning had subsided a bit. Tasco lifted his head and found that the movement didn't bring on a new flux of dizziness. "If I had to guess, trooper, it was some sort of air-fuel explosive. Must've been small and well-hidden because those techs we brought out are good at their jobs. Excuse me, those techs *were* good at their jobs." Tasco grunted as he rolled onto his knees. "Losing them is gonna hurt like hell if the Legion shows up."

As he looked around, Tasco couldn't decide whether he was more horrified or impressed by the level of devastation. The forest around them was completely razed to the ground, leaving only the barest stubs of tree trunks. The formerly wet soil beneath them was now dry and caked, like mud that had spent too long under the sun's heat. Smoke and the remnants of what had once been humanoids were spread over a fifty-meter radius. And everything around them was smoldering, including the survivors. Those in armor were covered in ash that wafted smoke behind them whenever they moved—which wasn't very far—and men without armor, like Krell, had either rolled the flames out in the muck or lay dead and burning.

There were far more dead than alive. Those that weren't lucky to be in just the right spots were broken and twisted. They looked more like animals than humanoids now, at least to Tasco's eye. And even those who were still alive didn't look like they would be for long.

"From what I'm seeing, kid," Tasco said after a thorough scan, "we're the only two who are still gonna be breathing in the next few minutes."

"What about the ones that went down to disarm the IED? Did they make it?"

Tasco almost laughed at the naivete of the question. The optimism of youth. "Pretty sure that's where the bomb went off."

"My radio's dead, but I can go look and confirm."

Tasco waved away the kid's thought. "Armor protected my radio, and it shows no one local as capable of responding. Gonna call this in."

He forced himself to concentrate as he navigated the delicate encryption in his most private communications system. "It's Sigma 21. I need you to send the SLIC to pick us up. The IED strike at Waypoint Aputah Four was us. We lost everyone except me and one of the Kimbrin scouts. If I had to guess, I believe we were drawn out to make this look like an attrition hit by a light, mobile, raiding force. The more I sit here with my armor smoking, the more I think this was all staged to hide something. I'll report in when I know more. Sigma 21 out."

Tasco turned to face the kid. "Okay."

"Sir, what do we do now?" Krell asked.

"We wait for our ride, my friend. And then we plot our revenge on whoever did this to us."

09

Kill Team Victory
Kam Dho Valley

Bombassa toggled the flashing message indicator in his L-comm, and Bear's face blinked onto the display. But Bear's focus was on something other than the holocam, and he was speaking to someone Bombassa couldn't see.

"Just set it up over there. Yeah, that's good."

"Boss."

Bear didn't jump, but said, "Bombassa. You damn near scared me out of my skin."

"You called me."

The team commander harrumphed at his team sergeant. "We made it to Kam Dho City. The MCR is really doing a number on people coming and going. I was flash-scanned twice when the Kimbrin security for the city saw that I wasn't one of them."

"Credentials holding?" Bombassa asked.

"Seem to be. The last checkpoint got a bit dicey though. There were humans mixed in with the Kimbrin troops. They were very thorough. I swear one guy wanted to cavity search me and ask for my number."

Bombassa ignored the levity. Despite being a bionically enhanced legionnaire the size of a wobanki with a steroid habit, Bear always seemed on the edge of a good mood.

"How is the setup?" Bombassa asked. "We have the lockbox from outside Fort Blake, and the faster we can transmit, the sooner we can get the info to the general."

Bear nodded in agreement. "Data cores are set up. We're rigging the last of the broadcast unit now. Should be a few more minutes. Until then, I'm bouncing you a grid and a FRAGO. I need you to make your way there on the quick. Once we get that box decoded, the general is going to greenlight Atlas Wake. That means we need to control the ODPs on the ground."

"What about the orbital defense platforms in orbit?" Bombassa asked.

Bear waved his hand in front of the cam. "We have that part figured. It's not going to be easy, but we have a plan."

"Then I'll have to get with Colonel Novo and work out a plan for the two ODPs in my hemisphere. It won't do to take out a single defense platform when they can use the others to shoot our friends out of orbit."

"I just sent you an image from Repub Intel. They pulled a bunch of goodies from your slice."

Bombassa enlarged the grainy image. "Those are mobile artillery pieces."

"I trust those would come in handy?" Bear grinned like his namesake watching fish in a stream.

"If the enemy was so kind to place them close by, who am I to refuse such a gift?"

"Antenna is up. I'll bounce you back when it's done. Bear out."

Bombassa looked out at Kill Team Victory. They had found a relief at the top of one of the mountains that bordered Kam Dho Valley. Everyone was dug in and camouflaged on the side of the peak facing the city. From this distance, only the occasional smoke plume gave any indication that anything was wrong down there, but the Yawds and some of their city-dwelling cousins could tell a different story. MCR forces had completely overwhelmed the city police, both from without and within, in a matter of hours. Military forces loyal to the Republic fell almost as quickly, as insurgents situated within the different commands used their access to confuse defense forces on the ground while allowing access to the incoming enemy.

Public access broadcasts spread propaganda like Hool venom. *The MCR isn't here to oppress you, but to free you from the yoke of high taxes and the never-ending demands of the Senate and the House of Lies. Kima doesn't need the Republic; it's the other way around. Kimbrin are now liberated thanks to the roving MCR patrols, curfews, and a newly installed government that will provide the secure democracy the Republic could not. The time for planets to rule themselves is here. Violence and bloodshed are a thing of the past... unless the Republic forces it upon the Kimbrin once more.*

Bombassa used the time waiting for Bear's follow-up transmission to alter one of the many target packages he aimed to push onto the Second Free Rifles, changing it into an ad hoc fragmentary order. The plan was simple, and with the 2-FR spread throughout the Kam Dho basin, it wouldn't take them long to get into position to support Kill Team Victory.

"Got a ping from Bear," Nobes said. "We're live. Time to upchuck is eight mikes."

"Push it," Bombassa answered.

Eight minutes was a long time to broadcast a data burst this big. Huge swaths of information through a secure L-comm encrypted network would be impossible to slice by the MCR but could still give off a signature to anyone who had the right tools and knew what to look for. Bombassa had watched these MCR honchos since they'd landed dirtside; some of these men had training, and if they suspected the Legion, they might be on the lookout for an advance-party kill team feeding the force with intel.

"Romeo Actual, this is Victory Seven, over," Bombassa called into the Yawd network.

Colonel Novo answered. "Go for Romeo Actual."

"I am sending you assignments for the Romeo elements. Assess, direct resources, and wait for jump. How copy, over."

"Roger out," came Novo's simple reply. Just the way Bombassa liked it.

The big legionnaire checked for the confirmation code on the file he'd transmitted to Novo. With the black box going out over Nobes's comm gear, he'd had to send the burst direct to the colonel through his own gear. Unfortunately for the Yawds, they had no access to the L-comm, so everything had to play over their own secure network. While this presented a better chance for the MCR to catch and possibly decrypt their communications, the system the Second Rifles used was so old as to make it highly unlikely the rebellion techs even had machines capable of pulling in the signal. For now, anyway. If the MCR continued to field troop commanders like the ones they'd blown sky-high at the lockbox pickup site, then it was only a matter of time before they discovered the Yawds' transmissions and hacked them.

"Boss," Wello called back from his position higher up the slope. "We got sweepers swinging toward us. Probably to see what music we like."

Nobes turned to catch Bombassa's glare. "Two minutes, Top."

"That's going to be close," Wello added.

Nobes circled his hand over his head. "Everyone un-ass the hill. I'll stay with Neck and cut wires if they get too close."

"If they get too close it will cause trouble," Bombassa noted. "I'd like to get this out quietly."

The kill team scattered about the hill and moved through the trees toward the summit. They stopped and set in place, waiting for Nobes and Neck to withdraw to them under cover should the need arise. Farther down the mountainside, two arrow-shaped observation bots were gliding toward their position. One descended from high altitude while the other swept toward the base of the hill and rose to meet its mate.

"Top, everyone's under cover, except for them." Pina pointed to Nobes and Neck. The duo carried equipment bags with dangling wires.

"Keep an eye on those drones," Bombassa said. "Wello, see if you can plug in and get us some back chan-nel on what they came up here for."

Minutes ticked by as Wello and Pina found a spot be-low the main team to dig in against the scrutiny of the aerial bots. Once settled, they looked no different than any other bit of vine-covered landscape found across the mountain. Their concealment, complete with a ghillie tarp equipped with anti-spectrum and auditory dampening technology, would be undetectable to anything other than a scout stepping right on them. They just weren't there.

The drones surveyed the area where Kill Team Victory had been moments before, plying their detection soft-ware across a myriad of sensor methods and algorithms in an attempt to source the nature of the disturbance.

"Boss, I'm in," Wello said. "Bots were deployed via Fort Blake to search for any non-MCR ancillary movement outside of the blast area. That included signal. Probably caught a whiff of that non-friendly connected traffic we were bursting and came to see what it was."

"Sit tight, everyone."

Bombassa stayed stock-still, blending into the terrain with the rest of his men and trusting the combination of signal-defeating hex-coat and mimetic camouflage technology in their armor to hide them from the enemy machines. Nearly ten minutes passed before the bots assumed a joint flight pattern and circled on for the next mountain in the chain.

"They're moving on," Wello announced. "Some new commotion deeper in the jungle to check out."

The kill team assembled and slithered like serrapines through the forest. That ten minutes they'd been forced to stay hidden wasn't a mission killer, but it would make everything tighter until they reached the valley floor. The legionnaires disregarded loose footing, clinging vines, and obstructing timber to break trail faster than the jungle wanted them to, relying on their armor and their physical conditioning to move quickly while not cutting a major path, though occasionally Bombassa and Nix did break out their machetes to clear some stubborn bit of brush or vines. While they could have boxed these obstacles using the navigation software in their buckets, they didn't want to lose too much time. Besides, it didn't hurt that it also gave Bombassa something to bash in, keeping his mind on the mission at hand.

He had already sent a full workup to the colonel regarding what had to happen with the orbital defense platforms. All the pieces needed to be in place so their plan could kick off all at once. With so many moving parts—not to mention this new, very competent MCR looking at every shadow for signs of the Legion—Kill Team Victory was cutting it close if they were going to give the 131st an entry window into Kima.

The team made it to the valley floor with a few minutes to spare. As they rounded a bend they took in the sight of the massive gun barrel rising out of the mountainside. The ODP structure looked like a ball with a stick coming out from it—essentially a tremendous cannon on a rotating housing set into a massive basin that allowed it to rotate to affect different strike profiles against ships orbiting this hemisphere. When combined with the orbital weapons systems, it made attaining orbit over a mid-core world like Kima a near impossibility for capital-class ships.

Which was why these platforms, along with air defense artillery and a host of other Republic military-installed features, had to be dealt with if the approaching elements of Operation Atlas Wake were going to approach the planet and effect landfall.

To execute this part of the mission, they'd first have to negotiate the Yawd village just shy of the facility entrance cut into the mountain. From their vantage point across the river, they could see the small settlement going through the motions of their day, the elders in the camp lazily kicking their feet off the dock while they cast fishing lines and chatted about the events of the day. They didn't care that the MCR had taken the facility above them, and the MCR didn't care about them either, so long as they continued to provide a buffer from the jungle—and supply food to the rebels inside.

Meet the new boss. Same as the old boss.

Nix pushed an overlay to Bombassa displaying a single dot moving down the center of the river, with two more dots trailing on either side. "Top, we got Dave waiting for us down in the drink. Harry and Henry are right behind and ready to deploy."

"Put Dave under that dock. Have Harry and Henry split and come at the village from the flanks."

"On it, Top."

Bombassa linked his L-comm to Bear. "We're in position across from the ODP. Novo is moving his forces for a hot takedown on the others while Kalo Company takes two of the mobile weapons platforms."

"That was fast," Bear said, nodding his approval into the camera. "Hey, what the hell is a kalo, anyway?"

"Big, black-feathered local bird," Bombassa said.

"The more you know. Any sign of Masters out there?"

"None. But I wouldn't expect there to be even if he's still alive."

"He's still alive."

Bombassa wasn't so sure, but he held his peace. He knew the two men were close, despite how adversarially they talked when in the same room. Bombassa could respect that. He'd felt the same way about Exo, once upon a time.

The good guys don't always make it.

"I'm getting a ping from the Kalo CO," Bombassa said. "They have a platoon at our backs ready to roll in when we're set."

"You know my feelings on the matter, Top. Hit me up when you get to the other side."

"Roger out," Bombassa acknowledged. He keyed the L-comm to send three flashing blips into the corner of the kill team's HUDs. On the third blink, the team moved as a single unit. They fractured into teams of two, navigating through the much lower underbrush on their way to the water's edge. As one, they slipped into the drink, quietly disappearing into the water as though they'd been born into it.

10

Jurn walked closer to the water's edge from his position on the back of the hut. This was stupid. Just because the rebellion leaders were afraid of the Republic sending the Legion, they'd doubled security next to every single defense station. He should be on the army bunk they'd promised him right now, watching the latest and best entertainment holos. Instead he was guarding the only dock in the village from behind a house made of bamboo.

He activated a stim stick and reveled in the tingle carried to his lungs by the chemical-laced smoke. Jurn let the stick dangle from the corner of his mouth, much like Matteo Morelli, one of his favorite actors. Granted, Matteo was a human, and not as good-looking as the ugliest Kimbrin, but he'd gotten the Kimbrin mindset down when he played the role of the getaway pilot in *Three for the Credits*. Of course, a guy like Matteo wouldn't be caught dead out here guarding a river slip unless there was a holocam crew involved, but imitating the swagger the man showed in his films made Jurn feel important and tough— if only just for a moment.

The surface of the slow-moving river gurgled and splashed. The fishermen on the dock paid it no mind. They were content to just toss the lines in over and over while smoking their long, slender pipes and talking about who'd been able to catch the bigger fish twenty years ago.

Jurn stepped from the cabin to better survey the water. The river had some strange-colored bottom-dwellers that liked to come up and jump into the air for bugs. They didn't usually come out at this time of day, but if they did, so much the better. The lighting was good now and maybe Jurn could get a good holo. Something to send to Murneera, that cutie back home with the second row of thin head spikes that drove him crazy.

After shuffling down to the lazy river, Jurn tossed a few seed-petals onto the surface in the hopes that the fish would take notice and jump. He's seen it a few times now, and even in the usual low light their scales shimmered in a way that might impress Murneera. She seemed to like biology back in school, didn't she?

But as Jurn watched and waited, his hopes of capturing a Murneera-impressing fish holo dwindled. Nothing surfaced. The splash he'd heard must have been a single errant fish swimming by, or maybe even some kid throwing a rock in the water. It wasn't like these backward Yawd settlements had anything else to do out here in the middle of nowhere.

Jurn resumed his position back at the side of the house and activated another stim stick. He really should ration them—the stim sticks were the highlight of his boring existence, and he still had two hours to go watching this stupid slip. Sometimes it was longer. His patrol leader, Griel, had learned from some veteran mids that a rotating guard schedule of different times and durations would keep an enemy from timing it just right to slip into the village undetected. Like that would ever happen out here. If there was glory to be won in the revolution, it sure as hell wasn't going to be found here, in this nowhere village. Even if some disloyal Kimbrin or the Republic or whoever thought this village was a threat, they'd just bomb it. No one would take the time to invade a settlement of farmers and fishermen. Who cared?

As Jurn leaned against the wall of the hut, he felt a sharp pain in the side of his neck. He slapped his hand to the spot, and hot blood poured over his fingers. The feeling of choking, as though something was pressing on his windpipe from the wrong side of his neck, caused him to gag, but just for a moment. The sound was cut short when a gloved hand gripped the top of his head and the pressure on his windpipe increased. His deep, wracking gasps gave way to soft, choking gurgles as the combat knife exited the front of his throat.

Jurn's head turned, not by his own volition, and he beheld the face of a dark helmet with a hexagonal-patterned visor in deep crimson. He reached for the ghastly figure with his blood-soaked fingers, only to have his weakening hands knocked aside. The feeling left his legs, and the needle-like pain of blood seeping into his lungs lessened as the seizing gags diminished. His vision went in and out of focus and then shifted into a complete haze just as his world drifted into the horizontal.

He was vaguely aware of the branches and stones scratching through his clothes to his skin as he was dragged across the jungle floor. His body's small spasms didn't seem to bother his attacker as the last bit of Jurn's blood left his neck in trickling spurts. He felt the heat of a pool warming his rapidly cooling skin, and he surrendered to the dark murk, sinking to the bottom to nourish whatever awaited him in his watery grave.

As the last moments of his life faded away, someone moving through the water next to him said, "Tango down, Top. We're good to go."

11

As the six-wheeled utility vehicle sputtered through the town, meal boxes covered in peeling olive-drab paint bounced around in the back of its hitched trailer. It made its way down the village's primary road—little more than a dirt lane—and trundled up to the gate for the orbital defense center.

Stepping out from a checkpoint beneath twin guard towers, an MCR Kimbrin sergeant approached the vehicle with his hand up. Two of his guards moved to flank the utility vehicle holding their rifles at the patrol ready position. A quick snap would seat the rile stock into the pit of the shoulder to give them a stable shot at the four Kimbrin in the cart.

"Increased security today," observed the old Kimbrin driving the vehicle, grinning wide enough to show a mouth missing more than a few teeth. He absently scratched the space where a facial spine should have been and waited for the sergeant to answer. In the rear of the vehicle, one of three Kimbrin villagers wrapped in serapes snored beneath a wide-brimmed hat meant to provide shade from the oppressive sun while working in the fields.

"Had an attack last night," the sergeant replied, his eyes darting left and right as though the attackers might be lurking at the edge of the road. "An entire patrol from Zidar Company got s'*suffad*, plus some from central command. Increased security is therefore required. I need to see inside all the boxes. And your vehicle, too."

"Of course," the old Kimbrin said. He climbed from the driver's seat and waddled slowly around to the trailer holding the boxes. After popping open all the lids, one by one, to expose steaming hot foods, warm breads, and ice-cold drinks, all kept at their proper temperatures by the segmented internals of the meal cases, he snagged a flatbread and split it into four pieces using a set of tongs. "Everything look in order?"

The sergeant happily received the food and handed the excess to his subordinates. "Make sure Dael gets one." He looked back to the old man. "Any Sprigg eggs?"

"Not today. Sorry."

The sergeant was not quite able to hide the disappointment on his face. He passed around the back of the trailer and opened a mirror on an extending rod. He ran the device under the trailer to see if there were any unwanted surprises hiding in the undercarriage, then repeated the procedure on the utility vehicle, only closing the mirror when he was satisfied.

"Thanks for the snack, old-timer. Latch them back up and get this inside."

The old man did as he was told and drove beyond the chain-link fence that spanned the space between the two guard towers. The fire control center, a stone structure with two additional guard towers, appeared ahead of them. The building's windows were little more than slits, and if the sills were any indicators, they were cut out of more than a meter of duracrete. The building's big main doors parted to allow the vehicle and trailer inside, where it came to a sputtering stop.

A security squad of Kimbrin MCR regulars wearing khaki shirts over olive-drab fatigues approached the vehicle carrying surplus MiiF7 blasters interspersed with the older variant of the Legion N-4, the PK-9. While still capable of punching a person's ticket, the models in the hands of the MCR looked as though they had been sitting on a shelf for a while. Improperly maintained blasters of these types were notorious for having charge and cycling problems as internals wore out, yet this fact seemed to have been overlooked by the Kimbrin rebels.

The old-timer swung from his seat, prompting the three villagers in the back to follow suit. He handed each of the security element a wooden dish for them to partake of the meals he'd brought.

"Hold up, old-timer," the patrol sergeant barked. "We're the security element here to check your stuff."

The old Kimbrin looked over his shoulder in the direction of the previous checkpoint. "They just did."

"Today you're getting checked again. And take these plates back. Security team doesn't eat until we're relieved."

As the others soldiers still held their plates and made no move to return them, the old Kimbrin muttered a single sound. "Huh."

His three compatriots suddenly pulled heavy pistols from under their serapes. The back of each weapon spat out a collapsing stock that affixed to their shoulders, and rapid-fire taps, barely louder than someone snapping their fingers, sounded. The patrol sergeant's seven-man security team was dead in a matter of heartbeats.

The sergeant dropped his plate and attempted to recover his weapon hanging on its sling when the old Kimbrin drove a knife-handed chop into the man's throat.

Moving far too spryly for his age, the Kimbrin reversed direction into a sweeping kick that brought the rebel sergeant to the hard slate floor with a crack that echoed off the entrance bay walls.

Bombassa, Toots, and Pina pulled their wide, conical farmer's hats from their heads and yanked their Kimbrin serapes from their shoulders, exposing Legion light reconnaissance plate carriers beneath. Toots reached behind the spare tire affixed to the utility vehicle to recover a bucket, then recovered two more by reaching under the wheel well and peeling off the tac-tape that kept the buckets secure.

"Thank you for your assistance," Bombassa said to the old-timer.

The old man gave a hard stare and then nodded. "You want to thank me? After you're done clearing out these *rappa,* do the same to the Republic."

Bombassa took note of the man's expression. He was a warrior who clearly hadn't forgotten the fight. The old lycanlore still had a few teeth left.

"I already have the right man lined up for that job," Bombassa said.

The rebel sergeant was dragged to his feet, prompting a coughing fit. He managed to spit out a curse between coughs. "Humans. You're all dead men."

"Shut him up," Bombassa ordered.

Pina pushed the man against the vehicle and made sure the sergeant could see the barrel of his blaster rifle out of the corner of his eye. "Everybody's gotta go sometime. Say the word."

The defeated security leader watched the legionnaires peel the enviro-covers from their buckets. These had fooled the mirrors at the checkpoint, and for a moment they fooled the sergeant as well by obscuring the design underneath. He seemed to think that these intruders were mercenaries—until they placed the revealed buckets on their heads to become the nightmares of every enemy of the Republic.

The sergeant's face flushed, his mouth dropping open just enough to whisper the word, "No."

Bombassa looked down on the Kimbrin, who despite being a member of the taller species, came only to the legionnaire's chin. "How many more are left in the facility? How long until the facility is reported as compromised and we can expect a counter-assault force?"

"You'll get nothing from me, Legionnaire." The word was a curse in the sergeant's mouth. *Legionnaire.*

Bombassa spoke to the man as if he were an old friend. He reached out and took the sergeant's hand and shook it. "Thank you for your help in getting us in here. We could not have done it without you. The Republic owes you a tremendous debt of gratitude."

"Got it," Toots said, his words a signal that allowed Bombassa to change the pose he'd been holding, as though a holopic director had just shouted *Cut!* "Uploading the holo to the Mal Kidaam Network and the Strato-Net now."

"Wait! What?" the sergeant shouted as Pina turned him around and slammed him against the vehicle to apply ener-chains. "You uploaded that to the MCR's news nets? You're going to get me killed!"

"That's the idea," Pina said, whirling the man back around. "Or you could tell us what we want to know. Talk fast enough and maybe we can purge it from the net before anyone has time to do a facial scan and add you to a kill list."

The Kimbrin's shoulders slumped nearly enough to brush his jaw spines. "Twelve more men in the facility. Two roving patrols outside. Each with twelve men."

"Now was that so hard?" Toots asked, turning the man over to the villager.

The older Kimbrin took the younger by the arm with the practiced ease of a soldier who'd handled prisoners before. He set the man into one of the seats of the utility vehicle before snapping his neck with no more concern than if he'd done it to a chicken.

"Damn!" Toots said in surprise.

"KTF, Leej," the old-timer said in response before giving a toothy smile.

Bombassa nodded and then keyed into the Yawd militia's net. "Kalo Actual, this is Victory Seven. Go for green. How copy, over?"

"This is Kalo Actual. I copy green, out."

The leejes reloaded their weapons. The shoulder-braced sidearms came up in a snap as the three men formed a wedge to take the center door on their way to the command-and-control center. The doors of the food trailer behind them swung open as two more legionnaires in full battle armor pushed their way out from behind the food trays and containers. The newcomers positioned the utility vehicle to block the doors and took up space behind it.

"Set," Nix called into the L-comm.

"Taking center hall as direct path to the C&C," Bombassa said. "Watch side passages for squirters."

"On it, Top," Wello acknowledged.

The central doors slid open, revealing a Kimbrin walking toward them holding a datapad. At the sight of three legionnaire helmets advancing on her, she dropped the device and groped for her sidearm. A shot from Pina slapped her between the eyes before the tablet hit the floor. She slumped against the wall as the life drained from her.

Bombassa used the augmented reality of the enhanced buckets to mark a side door in the passage ahead. Toots moved forward to point toward the door's activation plate. Powered sliding doors positioned along a main passage like this one were typically installed without a motion sensor so as not to slide open at every passerby. Pina nodded as Toots gripped his shoulder in their mini stack outside the portal. Bombassa took a position on the opposite side of the hall, just offset from the door to watch the hall, and Pina hit the plate only when Toots slapped his shoulder.

They rushed into the room with Pina hooking inside to take the first wall. Toots entered next and continued along the opposite wall. Five Kimbrin working around a holotable looked up just as the first rounds dusted two of them. Another two shots perforated the skulls of two more, leaving the last MCR rebel enough time to draw his sidearm from its holster.

Toots slammed the rail stock on his GK-21 Scorpion Variable Capability Pistol, causing it to close as he committed himself to a break-fall toward the floor. He landed on his side as the Kimbrin's weapon came up to his line of sight. Two quick blaster bolts to the rebel's chest threw the weapon offline, discharging a single blaster bolt into the opposing wall. A third round punched the Kimbrin center skull, and the humanoid collapsed under his own weight.

"Clear," Toots and Pina both sent over the L-comm.

"Boss, you get sound of that shot outside?" Pina asked.

"Barely," Bombassa confirmed. "The door closed as you went in."

"Coming out," Pina reported.

The two exited the room, and the Legion weapons sergeant turned to draw a big circle with what looked like spikes on the door. The marker ink was only visible to a legionnaire with his bucket settings keyed to that spectrum; anyone else passing the door would be none the wiser. Toots then pulled a piece of stripping from a pouch, removed the adhesive backing, and stuck it to the floor just inside the door. He plugged in a wire from a laser sensor he clipped right beside it. Anyone trying to enter the room without disabling the sensor or stepping over the laser was in for a bit of time off their feet.

The group moved on to the next door, which stood at the center of a T-intersection. If this facility held to spec, one side would lead to the barracks entrance, arms room, and washrooms, while the other went to the chow hall and kitchen. None of the legionnaires were concerned with being snuck up on from behind; they'd just cleared this hallway's only side exit and Nix and Wello were at the entry door to deal with any strays. But before they could take the control center, they'd have to ensure the two side passages were rigged to prevent anyone walking in on them during their takedown of the controls.

While Bombassa knelt behind the intersection and watched the door, Toots handed Pina a bundle containing a tray of six studded metal balls. Pina took the first three balls, each marked with a green stripe, and flung them at different points along the ceiling. They stuck into the stonework with a soft yet satisfying *kathunk*, indicating they had a firm set into the structure. The remaining three balls each had a red stripe. He threw two of them at the opposite side of the ceiling from the greens. The third he placed at knee level on the wall about halfway down the hall.

Pina and Toots rejoined their team leader across from the main door. "Micro-APs set. Three fraggers, three bangers set for det," Toots reported.

"Good. This door has a card reader on it." Bombassa motioned with his rifle at the device.

Toots was in the process of removing a slicer kit from his armor when the door flew open. A Kimbrin was walking out backwards holding four cups of kaff by their handles, two per hand.

The legionnaires remained out of the direct line of sight of anyone within the control center.

"Anyone else want anything from the galley?" the Kimbrin asked.

Varied negatives called back above the hum of computers and holo-displays that cast their glow through the open portal. The rebel tech shrugged as the door shut.

He turned directly into Bombassa's waiting knife—which plunged up through his throat into his skull. A twisting snap cut out the light in his eyes and silenced any gurgling that might otherwise have taken place. Toots and Pina were quick to snatch the cups from his hands before they could clatter to the floor, then guided the body into one of the side passages.

Bombassa unclipped the ID card hanging from a retractable lanyard on the Kimbrin's chest pocket and stood beside the door, waiting for his team to stack up. The legionnaire refreshed their charge packs, and after a nod from Pina, who was first in the stack, Bombassa set the countdown and held the card-key up to the door's terminal.

Three circles appeared on the display. The first circle flashed green once before becoming a solid dot, then the second did the same. When the third followed suit, a chime sounded and the door slid open.

"What'd you forget—" began one of the techs inside as the legionnaires rushed the room.

Three technicians went down at their stations with head shots that showered Kimbrin blood and brain matter through their ghostly holodisplays. A pair of security guards whirled from watching the screens to face the door, only to be cut down by the suppressed GK-21s, which diminished the destructive report of high-density, low-velocity blaster bolts shattering skulls and rending flesh.

Bombassa was last into the room. The big legionnaire sent a single round into one more technician before slamming his knife into the shoulder of the last tech, a human female, pinning her to the wall. The impact of the weapon punching through her clavicle stopped her arm from reaching a toggle switch on her opposite shoulder. Bombassa twisted the weapon to grind the cleaver against her broken shoulder, prying the flesh apart in blood-soaked agony. Before her surprised grunt could turn into an all-out scream, he struck her jaw, leaving her to hang unconscious on the end of his blade.

MCR humans had a tendency to be more useful in doling out information than their alien compatriots. Bombassa wanted this one alive. For now.

The legionnaires hadn't even had a chance to call clear before a series of explosions rocked the C&C. Bombassa motioned the other two leejes to take position across the room to maximize their cover of the door, creating a fatal funnel across the portal, then he heaved the woman up from her impromptu meat hook, leaving the blade in her shoulder in the event he'd clipped any major blood vessels on the way in. The Legion N9 Combat Survival Knife had a tremendous gut hook on the nose of its blade, and removing it without Doc Chance around to help would probably turn her inside out.

"Which one was it?" Bombassa asked.

"Kitchen side," Toots answered.

"Holocams are showing three dead in that hallway," Pina added. "Got a couple more heads popping out from the D-FAC, but no one is brave enough to take on the hallway. They're staying put."

"Other hall?" Bombassa asked.

"Looks like they're talking to the ones on the D-FAC side. They're squirting out the back toward Nix and Wello."

"That won't end well," Toots said. "Hey boss, I have comms jammed on our side. Nothing is getting in or out of here unless it's on L-comm."

"Good. You two roll out the D-FAC. I'll get this thing working in our favor."

"On it, Top." Pina chin-checked Toots and the two slipped out into the hallway.

Bombassa reached into his survival kit for a small ampule and cracked it between his fingers so he could run the fumes under the captive woman's nose. She awoke with a start, only to have her screams cut short by the burly team sergeant clamping his armored glove over her mouth.

"I do not wish to continue to hurt you, but I will if I have to. Agree to keep silent and I'll give you something for the pain."

The woman nodded, the action sending tears down multiple paths across her cheeks. As Bombassa's glove levitated above her mouth, she heaved in gasping breaths against the pain of a seven-and-a-half-inch blade protruding from her body. But she didn't scream.

"Have you installed any other codes into the network requiring a data key to operate?" Bombassa asked. He pressed an injector to the woman's shoulder that pushed drugs into her system with an audible hiss.

She instantly relaxed and her breathing became more regular as the meds kicked in. "We have... an apocalypse key, but I didn't have time to... install it. It's... on a feather... chip in my pocket."

"Good," Bombassa grunted. He fished the chip from her pocket and melded it to his datapad. When the machine confirmed it was what the tech had said it was, he stashed the destructive little thing into a pouch on his belt. "I have a medical sergeant on my team. He'll be here shortly to deal with your injuries. In the meantime, I'm going to bind you. Remain still and cause no trouble, and he will attend to you. Try to impede my mission, and you will join your friends in death."

He knew that the deep rumble of his voice through the speakers in his bucket—especially when combined with the haze of the drugs he'd given her—sounded like something out of a grim faerie tale. A mysterious creature who would be true to its word, especially where violence was concerned.

"I'll be... no trouble, Legionnaire," she assured him.

Bombassa switched from the external speakers to his internal comms. "Kalo Actual, this is Victory Seven. Sitrep, over."

The radio crackled with the static of the older system used by the Second Free Rifles. "Victory Seven, this is Kalo

Actual. We have two in custody. Plotting now. Twenty-seven red, four blue. How copy, over?"

While the Second Free Rifles' radio net was secured through a host of measures, it was no L-comm. And seeing as the network had already been up for the better part of the day, it was prudent to speak in code and sign as much as possible in the event the enemy had found a way to tap in. Going from a system where they could simply talk as though they were standing next to the caller to a radio channel with the potential for being sliced was jarring. Still, Bombassa was heartened to hear the report, even as he cursed inwardly at the little encoded detail at the end, which soured what was otherwise an overwhelming success.

The Yawds of Kalo Company had taken down twenty-seven men in the MCR forces controlling the Mechasaga-381 long-range artillery pieces. But they'd suffered a loss of four Yawds in doing so.

This was only the opening salvo. They were now prepped and ready to ruin the other orbital defense platforms so the Legion, resuscitated and revitalized after Article Nineteen, could descend on the planet to flex its muscles, prying Kima out of the hands of the MCR and delivering it back to the people. But they needed to continue to hold the line prior to the 131st's arrival, and every Kimbrin that they could leverage toward the mission, Yawd or otherwise, was crucial to that objective.

Bombassa finished ener-chaining the MCR tech to the chair so that her arms and legs were locked into position, then he keyed Bear's icon in the L-comm.

"Sir, Task Force Victory is phase two," he said. "Send the Harvester."

12

Kam Dho City

Bear dodged what had to be the fourth pedicab repulsor-cycle that had tried to drive into him while he was crossing the busy street. He used to think the intersections on Utopion or the Sinasian planets were busy, but here it felt like every vehicle in the city was out on the road and trying to drive in every direction at once. The streets remained clear from accidents thanks to the usual AI driving guidance—Kima was mid-core, not an edge world—but moving around Kam Dho City was an example of one of the classic laws of the universe.

If you know, you know.

He made it to the other side of the street before a cutthrough caught his eye. He slipped into the alley, cats scurrying out of his way, laundry dripping overhead on lines hung between buildings. The ground was slick beneath his feet thanks to littered bits of cardboard now reduced to little more than gritmeal, but his legs' hyper-attenuation motors and gyroscopic sensors mitigated the slippery mess.

The big powerhouse of a legionnaire had gotten used to this latest set of legs, making what would otherwise have been a treacherous trek little more than an annoyance. Smart stabilizers in the cybernetics were constantly working to make sure he didn't fall over. In fact, the

Legion docs had made a game of how hard it was for him to trip over himself now that he had them. Anything short of a deliberate attempt to throw himself on the ground would be counter-balanced by the stable artificial limbs.

Bear tried not to think about the day of his injury, but it was always in the back of his mind. The tank. The fighting. Wondering if he would ever feel whole again.

And Masters, who saved his life that day. Masters was still out there, needing someone to return the favor. Because he had to be. How could a guy like Masters die?

The thoughts were only there for a minute before the scent of urine and rot brought him back to the here and now. It didn't matter how many different worlds he'd been to, populated by how many different species: if there was an unwatched corner in a city, someone was going to pee on it.

He exited the alley into a market bazaar full of life and color. If the MCR's ousting of the planetary government and then murdering Republic supporters on live holo-casts had had any effect on the merchants of the street, they weren't showing it. The first stand off to his left sold some kind of local nut, freshly toasted over a real fire. The scent was amazing and immediately covered the squalor of the adjoining alley.

"Gimme two of those," Bear told the merchant, speaking stilted, heavily accented Kimbrin.

The merchant nodded to him, showing an appreciation for the effort. In Standard, he said, "Thank you for your business."

Bear didn't ask if the vendor accepted Republic credits, he simply dropped the chit into the man's hand and received a wispy plastic bag with two paper bundles of smoky, sweet-smelling nuts. The merchant didn't even bother to check the chit.

Even though Kam Dho was one of the larger cities on the planet, it still somehow managed to hold on to a rural attitude; the residents here paid close attention to what was happening in their neighborhood. Bear could sense the other vendors picking him out of the crowd—a simple enough task given his size.

But as he turned on his heel, he realized he'd miscalculated just who it was that was watching him. He found himself in a meter-wide ring of space, cordoned off by a small gang of Kimbrin with PK-9 blaster rifles. They wore green baggy pants—not quite fatigues—and loose black shirts with bandoliers over their chests that held spare charge packs for their weapons.

One of the Kimbrin stepped forth, eager to make some things known to the grotesquely large human. "I'm patrol captain for these men. Who are you? Republic?"

Bear looked around before centering back on the captain. "Who says I'm not here because I'm just as tired of the Republic as you are? Last I heard, the MCR was for all the galaxy's species. Besides, everybody knows Kam Dho has the best nuts."

The captain pulled his head out of the way when Bear waved the steaming bag too close to his head. The men that surrounded them laughed, some nervously and some seeming to be genuinely entertained by this large human's antics.

"You have papers to be here." The captain growled out the suggestion, seeming reluctant now to question the big man.

"Didn't come with the Republic, so no, I don't got papers. That didn't seem to matter not that long ago. Look,

I came here to make a few credits. That's all." Bear didn't break eye contact with the Kimbrin as he tossed a handful of nuts into his mouth.

The captain stepped toward him, pushing the bag out of the way to prevent Bear from eating any more. "You have papers or you have problems."

Bear loomed over the man, growling deep enough to scare the gaggle of fighters back a step. "I'm here to talk to a Kimbrin named Grelin, and I had to pay a bunch to do it. Now you're in the way of my meeting *and* my snack. I don't appreciate losing money or a meal. Keep hassling me and I swear to Oba I'll beat you in front of everyone on the street and take your rifles. Grelin'll give me an extra five minutes of his time in return for them, and you can go explain how you lost them to whatever kelhorn sent you to bother me."

The enraged little patrol captain looked nervously toward either side of the street. "Grelin is a good Kimbrin. He pays all the right people. We wouldn't want to upset him. But don't do anything else stupid or maybe Grelin won't protect you."

The patrol leader stormed off through the crowd, knocking a junk vendor over on his way and sending his wares to the ground.

Bear watched the men go and then exited to the street and into the dusky confines of a tea shop. The place featured sparsely occupied tables where the few patrons sent exhaled hookah smoke up to be distributed by spinning ceiling fans. One particularly elderly Kimbrin rested against a batch of pillows on the floor with a group of varied species from across the galaxy. He puffed on his pipe while watching Bear cross the shop to deposit himself into an empty seat.

A young Kimbrin girl came out to take his order. She slid a piece of paper from under a napkin to him.

"Tap-Bo. Cold," Bear ordered.

The girl nodded and disappeared to prepare the drink. When she was out of sight, Bear looked at the note. It was written in a Yawd cipher that said:

Wait until they leave and then join me.

Bear dropped his bag of nuts on the table and began to crunch them. They tasted every bit as good as they smelled. They were mostly smoky with a sweet aftertaste of cinnamon to make them more palatable. No processed bits. No preservatives. No roofed-up price due to the inclusion of some nanites promising to fix something broken inside of him. Just a bunch of natural crunch going down like Oba intended.

He cast his eyes over to Grelin, the old Kimbrin smoking the hookah among the assortment of aliens. Several Endurians, a Ridoran, and a Tennar all took their leave from the enigmatic old Kimbrin, who continued to puff on his pipe. Bear waited until his server returned with his order before he crossed the space to join his host.

"*Zeen kho*, Grelin," Bear said.

"*Zeen kho*, Barlo. Please join me."

An ache from where Bear's knees should have been traced its way up his legs to his spine. He knew it was mental, and the doctors had told him to expect it. Eventually, they'd said, he wouldn't be able to tell where the old legs ended and the new ones began. There was no fixed timetable for that, and Bear often found himself wishing his body would hurry it up already.

"I was glad to get your call, Barlo." Grelin puffed out a smoke ring from the hookah. "It's not every day I get a call from a doctor."

"Virologist," Bear corrected. "I've found that moving about the Republic chasing this disease or that makes people remarkably willing to open their borders. Whatever it takes to keep them free of boils or coughing to death."

"You believe I am looking for a smuggler."

Grelin's sharp blue eyes, surrounded by a deep yellow sclera, bored into Bear in an attempt to assess the truth of this statement. The only thing he received for his effort was a relaxed expression from Bear as he slurped on the wet concoction of green noodles that went with his tea.

"Not quite. The Republic is willing to pay for traffic in and out of Kima—namely any citizens trapped on this side of the clouds when the hammer fell, if you take my meaning."

"We are *all* Republic citizens, Barlo. Kima may be a mid-core world, but we have been part of the Republic longer than most of the core worlds." A coy smile crossed Grelin's face. "Until recently."

"Yeah, but not everyone wants to get off-planet. Some do, and they need help to do it. Now me, I don't want to leave the place. I like that it's mostly quiet. I like that it's only inhabited in a few key spots so I can spread out and enjoy myself without being hassled by some planetary tax hat looking to shake me down for credits every time I switch a time zone."

Bear slurped more of the jelly-like noodles, and Grelin smiled. "Do you even know what you're eating?"

"Yeah. Seaweed with a spicy paste loaded with pepper and honey. To me it tastes a bit like a sweet relish. I like it."

"You're a strange one, Barlo. Now tell me. What does any of this have to do with me?"

Bear set down the empty bowl to free up his hands to recover the accompanying cup of cold tea. He offered some to his host, who gestured his preference for the pipe. After a sip to wash down his latest snack, Bear said, "Word around the street is that you have it good with the people still running Kima. You know the game and all the players. I have an opportunity to make a lot of credits if I ferry Republic citizens, who the MCR ultimately don't want here anyway, off Kima and back to Republic space. I'll give you twenty-five percent of what the Republic offers me to get them off-planet."

Several wafts of smoke left the pipe before Grelin spoke. "I don't know you. I took this meeting as a favor to an old friend, who is apparently your old friend. Why should I trust you?"

"You can trust me because so far my credits have been good. If what the Repub is offering for safe passage is legit, even twenty-five percent will make you a rich man."

"I'm already rich," Grelin said with a twinkle in his eye. "So the Republic's bravado about activating the Legion—a ruse? They simply want to evacuate those who wish to remain citizens and leave what's left to the Kimbrin now in power?" He scoffed.

Bear shrugged. "They must have forgotten to include me in those meetings. Now, you say you're rich. Well there's rich, and then there's *rich*. If my ears are good, then you've already got the goods it takes to buy an election or get yourself a seat in the new government or whatever. But the credits I'm talking about are the kind that buy you those core-world longevity treatments like those old House of Reason delegates got. Like Kima's old senators got. No disrespect, but the way I see it, the only thing you haven't been able to buy out here is more time."

The twinkle in the man's eyes was replaced with something else. Hunger. "And you could secure those treatments."

"I could make it happen, yeah. Easily. I'm a doctor, remember? I just need someone in a position to open the doors I need opened."

"Things are difficult for us right now," Grelin said, chewing on the end of his pipe stem. "Despite what you say, the Legion is expected to show up any minute. We all saw the vote from Spilursa. War is coming. Those in power are busy setting up their supply chains to keep them ready to repel Republic interference with whatever form the next government takes. Not to mention there's also the need to move forces around the jungles after the takeover. Not all the Republic military they went after during the takeover are accounted for."

"What do you mean, accounted for?" Bear asked.

"Ah, there." Grelin pointed the stem of his hookah at Bear. "That is something a spy would ask me to gain more intelligence for his masters." The old Kimbrin smiled, and smoke vented from his teeth.

"Of course I'm interested," said Bear. "If there are organized Repub citizens I can pull out in one swoop, why wouldn't I be? So don't go pointing at me like I'm the spy. *You* brought it up. Does that mean that you're a Republic spy trying to gauge what I'm doing here?"

In his first display of aggression, Grelin slammed the table. Patrons at once got up and left their snacks, hookahs, and tea, no matter how deep into their orders they were. Once the tea house was empty, the Kimbrin criminal facilitator leaned back into his cushions.

"Mind your tongue," he said. "To even suggest such a thing could get a man killed. Even me." He paused to take a long draw from his pipe and a longer exhalation of smoke toward the rafters. Finally he looked Bear in the eye. His gaze intense. All business. "I like you, Barlo. You're peculiar for a human. But give me one good reason I should trust you with my reputation."

Bear could almost feel the gun barrels at his back. He slowly reached into the breast pocket of his shirt to produce a paper-thin plasteen card. He tossed it on the table between Grelin and himself.

The Kimbrin took another pull from his hookah, letting the smoke drift out of his nostrils while he looked at the midnight-black card. He tapped the center of it and recoiled when an image appeared on the surface. It lingered for only a moment before disappearing back into the obsidian card.

"How do you have this?" Grelin asked as though he'd been stabbed in the soul.

Bear took note of the fear in the man's expression and his tone. "He approached me when I was in a tight spot. Offered me a chance to get more than the bargain-basement cybernetics the military was offering when I lost my legs. In return, I was supposed to be open to certain business opportunities. Did you hear about the thing that happened on Rakka?"

Grelin nodded, clearly enthralled, not even bothering to remove the pipe stem from his mouth.

"Well," continued Bear, "he's looking to make up some of the credits lost from that little trip. And if these military members that are unaccounted for happen to be alive, some of them might just be the sons and daughters of those willing to pay through the nose for their return. That's less hassle for the MCR *and* more credits in everyone's wallets."

Grelin rubbed his chin, recovering his composure. "That's actually not a bad idea. Maybe something I can sell to the generals. Tell me though, were the soldiers the people you were originally hoping to extract?"

Bear finished the tea in his cup. "No. Some big-time business execs didn't want to leave things to the 'savages' when the takeover began. Big money to pull them out."

Grelin motioned to someone in the kitchen. "Barlo, I had every intention of killing you until you put down that card. Too many spies. Too many things to go wrong at this stage. But that card bought you that commodity you spoke of earlier."

"Trust?"

"*Time.* I'll make some calls. But if this is a trick, the MCR will kill us both."

"Grelin," he said, "if this is a trick, the MCR won't have anything left to shoot. The Wraith will kill us both."

13

Bear walked through grimy side streets toward the safe house. He was envious of Bombassa running through the jungles causing trouble while he played the part of the face man for the team.

It had been the idea of a navy intelligence officer for Bear to work as a "disease control contact manager." Agent Jaela had even gone so far as to provide Bear with an aerosol irritant that the Kimbrin were highly allergic to in order to bolster the need for him to be on planet. It was a clever idea, even if it did ultimately require that an un-caring kelhorn infect a major population center with skin lesions and a sore throat just to sell a cover. Sometimes Bear thought these Repub INSEC types the navy was filled with were as bad as the Nether, though in truth he knew they had miles of amoral deviousness to dig through for them to even approach Nether's level. And he'd required their help. They had proven to be the hyper track to finding the connections and resources Bear needed in order to get the team linked up with Colonel Novo.

Now Agent Jaela appeared from the shadows and smoothly fell into step beside him, garnering a few looks from the locals. She was a Zaan, a Kimbrin from a region west of here, and the Kimbrin on this particular continent weren't generally fond of her kind. She wore a braid-ed headdress resembling a hood that draped from the crown of her head down behind her ears. With her diminutive frame, she almost crossed over into the realm of what human males would find attractive. In fact, Masters would have been all over her if only to prove his little theory of the universe. But Masters was somewhere out in the jungles Bombassa now roamed.

Dodging a wave of Kimbrin foot and motor traffic, Bear used the HUD in his sunglasses to sift through details for the legionnaire combat outpost where Masters went missing.

Jaela noticed his distraction. "If you don't pay attention, you're going to get your pocket picked."

Bear shrugged. "The Kimbrin here all think you're a witch. They won't come near you for fear of getting the Nano Plague or whatever. Might've helped if you had gone into that meeting with me. Grelin seems like the type to be scared by witches."

"Then who would have had you covered from across the street?"

Bear almost got clipped by a motorized pedicab, and he took his partner's advice, giving his attention to his surroundings. "It still kills me that somewhere under that dress is a rifle."

Jaela winked at him. "Among other things. What did you get from Grelin?"

"A lot, once I convinced him to talk. Apparently there's an entire dark net for the Kimbrin underworld that the MCR heads are clued into out of respect. That's a new one on me, but I'll run with it. So the rebel factions that swatted Fort Blake and the leej COP uploaded a ton of video and images. It's a gold mine, but it'll take me a minute to sift. Unless you have something that could run it?"

Jaela laughed. "Why, Captain. Are you asking for my help?"

"Don't make me regret it."

Bear gestured to a back alley, another cut-through they used not only because it was a direct route without any prying eyes but because it provided many exits onto the avenues into the city. Its only drawback was the stench—of trash and much worse. It was so bad and so enduring that any windows in the facades on either side had long ago been sealed over.

As they neared their destination, Bear linked via micro-comm with the personnel on the inside of the safe house. "Brit, it's Bear. How are we looking?"

"Clear to walk in the house, Captain. Don't forget to wipe your feet."

Bear removed a brick from one of the walls, exposing a black panel. The proximity of his link triggered an automatic response from the panel, which appeared in his sunglasses HUD in the form of a rotating checkmark. Anyone else looking at the panel would assume the opaque slate, and the home it kept locked up, was without power.

The wall pulled back and slid aside to allow entry. Bear checked the alley one last time before following Jaela into the gloom. They moved through a maze of tight passages made of corrugated sheets framed over rough plank flooring until they reached another door. This one slid open at their approach.

"Wipe your feet," came the call from one of the techs swarming over the holotable in the center of the room. The holodisplays provided the only light save for a single strip of track lighting somewhere in the nether parts of the ceiling.

"Don't gimme any grief," Bear retorted. "This place is one giant mold spore. I should wipe my feet on the way *out*. We're trying to save Kima, right?"

Brit, a human, turned her head. Her pixie haircut made her earpiece visible, along with the wired connection that disappeared into her collar. "You ready for the news?"

"Yeah. What do we got?" Bear said as he watched Jaela walk up the stairs to the apartments above.

Brit keyed a wave-form diagram in the center of the holos. "We just got this back from First Sergeant Bombassa."

The legionnaire's voice came from the holo. *"Sir, Task Force Victory is phase two. Send the Harvester."*

"Let's bounce them a link for some uploads," Bear told the tech. "See if you can trace them to source so we can monitor uploads and geo-location markers in real time."

Brit raised an eyebrow. "Captain, do I tell you how to do your job?" she asked with more than a bit of snark.

"You do tell me to wipe my feet all the time," he reminded her. Tapping into their broadcast array, he pushed a note into the L-comm. "Harvester, this is Victory. Phase line two."

Bear had just turned to follow Jaela upstairs when Brit tapped him on the hip. "Hey, you might want to see this, big guy."

She flipped a holo onto the main hard screen. The recording started with someone running through the jungle and speaking in the local Kimbrin dialect. They tumbled and the microphone made awful noises until the device was recovered and pointed into a basin above the highlands near Kam Dho City. MCR fighters were being slaughtered in droves as a small detachment of Yawds and legionnaires fought like lions to dust their incoming enemies.

After a moment, the holo spliced in a new recording, this one showing the MCR fighters pursuing the same leejes. In a matter of seconds, the defending legionnaires were caught in a deluge of long-range ballistic fire courtesy of the artillery batteries atop Fort Blake. When the smoke cleared, the better part of a grid square had been vaporized.

As the holo continued, it went back to the prior moments and zoomed in for a close-up replay. In slow motion, it showed a lone legionnaire jumping from the rock face just as an artillery shell destroyed everything behind him. The recording stopped on a freeze frame, and a circle appeared around the jumping trooper, along with words written in Kimbrin:

Could this Legion Devil be alive? Fifty thousand Cr for capture. Ten for kill.

Bear felt a numbness in the spot where his knees should be. "Masters, you are the luckiest unlucky kelhorn I know."

14

Super-Destroyer *Centurion*
Flight Hangar

The klaxons reverberating through the launch bay were at once terrifying and thrilling. This particular bay, larger even than a seamball stadium, was one of several readying to deploy a massive engagement force bent to a single will—that of Task Force Commander Cohen Chhun.

"Three minutes to transition," MakRaven said beside the general as they dodged the flurry of cargo trams, personnel, and troopers. "And it's dawning on me that you really did talk me into doin' this again, sir. I could be on a Pthalos knockoff world right now, drinkin' beer and smokin' stim sticks."

Off to their left, a Republic marine unit, Bravo Company, Second SOAR, all snapped to attention at the command of their battalion commander. He spun on his heel, leveling a salute to Chhun. Returning the gesture with the precision of a laser scalpel, Chhun rendered and dropped the salute in her direction.

"Board it!" Chhun roared.

Rising to almost deafening levels inside the bay at being saluted by a Legion general, the marines shouted back, "Breach it!"

"How many mottos them hullbusters have, anyway?" MakRaven commented. "And how'd you manage to secure them SOAR Peregrines for this? Probably the scari-est bunch of hullbusters in the Marines."

"I told the Legion commander that if Asa Berlin want-ed every Legion finger on the trigger, this was going to be a task force op." Chhun pointed to an assault lander. "This is us."

The crew chief snapped to attention at their approach. Only the bottom part of her jaw was visible beneath her flight helmet, its mirrored visor lowered so she could take in direction from both flight control ops and the pilot through her HUD. "Welcome aboard, General."

MakRaven peered inside the lander and saw it packed with legionnaires. "Damn, lady. Don't look like there's enough room left in there for me, let alone a crew."

"Sar'nt Major, this bird is rated for a complement of one hundred and twenty trigger-happy death dealers to shoot out the back and ruin whatever kelhorn was stupid enough to bring us all the way out here's day. If I have to, I'll ride on the roof."

"What's your name, petty officer?" Chhun asked.

"Damiano, sir. My friends call me Domino. Now if you don't mind, gentlemen, I need you to board my aircraft and lock in before we transit. I ain't takin' the blame if we come to a hard stop and one of you takes a trip into the bulkhead."

She snapped a crisp salute, which Chhun returned.

MakRaven nodded at the approach of another Legion officer. "Sir, Major Riggs."

The man looked like the kind of guy you dropped into a back alley full of Gomarii with no more than a pair of PT shorts and a spoon, only to have him come out the other end dressed to the nines and the only one left alive. Chhun had heard about the man's reputation as a platoon leader across several battle zones, which was what made him the perfect company commander for Victory Company. He was relentless.

"Riggs, good to see you," Chhun said, knocking his fist into the man's armor.

The two moved to the open seats reserved for them. Chhun sat against the bulkhead and the colonel sat down next to him.

"We got a problem here, sir," MakRaven said gravely. "You're in my spot, Major."

Riggs looked at the sergeant major with a smirk, causing MakRaven to wag his finger at the man.

"I don't care what rank you are, sir. You try taking my seat next to the old man, we're having it out right here."

Riggs and MakRaven erupted into laughter that devolved into a match of slapping hugs. The Victory Company CO shook his head as he rose from the seat. "I'll just take my place at the back of the shuttle, then," Riggs said. "I just hope my old fourth point of contact doesn't get shot. That's how you got your last Purple Heart, wasn't it Mak?"

MakRaven chuckled. "Been shot there so many times that I got more assholes than elbows. Don't expect nothin' less this time."

With the officers on board, the ramp closed and the leejes all stopped their cross chatter and various happenings to secure themselves into the jump seating for the drop. Domino raised her hands over her head and clasped them together, indicating to her flight crew that the ramp was locked in place.

A warning message was overlaid onto each legionnaire's HUD:

TRANSITION TO REAL SPACE IN 3... 2... 1...

Everyone's insides felt a little more on their outsides as *Centurion* exited to real space. When the feeling settled, MakRaven said, "Hey sir, I hope you had breakfast, 'cause I don't plan on stopping 'til we hit that cafe on Sadoa Street in Kam Dho City."

**Super-Destroyer *Centurion*
Combat Information Center**

"Captain Aguiar, transition complete. *Centurion* is in real space over Kima at targeted designation. All fleet IDs report real space. The fleet is green." After the announcement, the combat information officer went back to the assortment of crew under her command, controlling the various screens distributed about the CIC.

Admiral Deynolds nodded at the CIO across the deck from her post, then leaned into Captain Aguiar standing beside her. "Bring us into high orbit and have the other capital ships above us at the Lagrange point. Move the destroyers and battleships into position just beyond the moon and ready them for any ships attempting to escape the system."

"Yes, Admiral," Aguiar said. The Endurian turned to relay the orders from his superior.

The information officer announced an additional update. "Admiral, Victory One is receiving our comm burst. He has the orbital defense platforms on the ground."

"Did we time it right?" Deynolds asked.

"Yes, ma'am. Orbital Defense Station Alpha One-Two-Four is in line with controlled ODP."

"Take it."

The CIO nodded. "Victory One, this is Centurion Fox One. You are cleared to engage."

Kill Team Victory
MCR Orbital Defense Station
Outskirts of Kam Dho City

Bombassa keyed into the Kalo Company channel. "This is Victory Seven to Kalo Actual. Execute Zeus. I say again, Execute Zeus."

After toggling a viewer window from a holocam being worn by the Kalo company commander, Bombassa watched as their newly acquired mobile artillery platforms thundered out their chorus of violence on an unsuspecting target zone. He switched again to the sliced communications from their initial operations and listened to the cries for help from the other two orbital defense platforms as they were decimated by the long-range munitions of the co-opted L-RAPs.

He then activated several controls in the command center of his own orbital defense platform, causing a tremendous rattling hum as the power plant for the building-sized artillery piece revved to max power. Interfacing the command console with his bucket allowed him to select targets rapidly as the combat AI in his HUD worked the various algorithms and formulae necessary to align the gun. Atmospheric conditions, orbital drift, and anomalies in gravity all had to be factored in to ensure an accurate shot, but the bucket handled it all with the same ease as the specialized gunnery helmets that now lay spattered in blood next to their deceased owners.

Bombassa confirmed his selection of the unsuspecting target.

The scream of the energy buildup reached a crescendo, and holograms notified Bombassa that the gun was ready to get barking. When the targeting selection key locked on target, he gave the command to fire.

Long-settled dust from the ceiling of the fire control center shook loose from the overhead panels in response to the weapon's tremendous blast. Up above the gargantuan barrel rocked back in its globular housing from the force of its shot, while vents opened to enable rapid induction airflow systems to cool the housing and weapon system and allow for additional shots spaced a minute apart should the need arise. As he monitored the outer gun cam, Bombassa took the briefest of moments to marvel at the beauty of the sparkling aftershock coming off the cannon. Unlike the other two ODPs in this hemisphere, the one they'd captured was a massive ion cannon. Each shot was actually a wave of ionized particles bonded together in a cohesion field that detonated on impact, shorting out any powered system. It was a favorite among planetary defense corps—as long as they could afford the massive upkeep.

"Victory Seven, this is Kalo Actual," Captain Reeve blared over Bombassa's headset. "First strike package complete. First and Second Platoon have control of the two 381s. We're moving them to Waypoint Rufus.

Third Platoon is moving to blocking position as counter-assault."

"Good copy, Kalo Actual. Stand by for follow-on mission. Bombassa out."

Bombassa had already witnessed the destruction on his holos. Now that Captain Reeve and his Yawd commandos from Kalo Company had used the two L-RAPs to destroy the two other planetary defense guns, Bombassa's captured ODP was the only ground-to-orbital weapon remaining. The timing had been crucial, because if the MCR had time to figure out what was going on, the rebels holding Fort Blake could still shell Bombassa's ODP, destroying the village and potentially killing Bombassa's men. The hope was that the MCR command team wouldn't put it all together until *Centurion* was in place.

Regardless, it was prudent to have Reeve move the L-RAPs so as not to suffer a swat from the long guns at Blake.

Bombassa rotated through the myriad of holograms floating in his HUD. The trail cams they'd placed around the village outside became of particular interest to him, as the two squads patrolling outside the village were rapidly approaching.

"Nobes, it's Bombassa. Deploy Harry and Henry to deal with the incoming MCR patrols. Also, pull Dave from the water and get those jammers working."

"On it, Top."

Super-Destroyer *Centurion*
Hangar Bay Seven

"Gunnie!" shouted Captain Mazzara. "Load 'em on the line."

"Aye, sir," Gunnery Sergeant Losey barked. "Falcons on the roost!"

The assembled members of Bravo Company, Second SOAR slammed their feet along the yellow-and-black warning line painted on the floor of the hangar bay. They were only a few feet from the bay shielding that kept atmosphere and gravity on the inside. Wrapped in Hammer Void Combat Armor, they looked like super cyborgs out of a hologame. Rifles and assorted kit cases were magnetically locked to their backs to keep their hands free to latch on to whatever hull had offended the gods of the stars that day.

"We're lined up with the target, Marines!" Mazzara growled. "Board it!"

Before anyone could shout out the standard reply to someone shouting that to a SOAR marine, the company element sprinted for the shield, and a last-minute push off the line sent them sailing into the vacuum of space toward their target.

The moment they cleared the lip of the hangar, the hullbusters lit their angling thrusters en masse, angry rockets flashing in the blackness of space. The rocket-propelled boost launched them away from the super-destroyer toward a towering spire in high orbit around the planet. The planetary defense station was a nearly kilometer-long obelisk that boasted a habitat ring on one side. The station slowly rotated as it glinted the first hints of the sun cascading off its hull. Point defense cannons were leveling an epic level of hate toward the cyclopean frame of *Centurion*, but had little effect against the ship's powerful shields.

The station had thus far fired its maneuver thrusters twice in an effort to line up its main gun barrel with the super-destroyer. Both times, the massive capital ship's helmsman—who had the advantage of jumping into system at the worst possible angle for the defensive platform—had shifted position to leave the less agile platform to fend for itself with only minor rail guns. Normally, the planetary ion defense cannon would have been brought into the battle to keep a ship this size still. Instead, it was the orbiting facility that found itself targeted by the ion gun that was currently under the control of First Sergeant Bombassa. A series of ion blasts pummeled the orbiting defense platform, rendering inoperable everything from plasma casters to ion defense grids—and, of course, the platform's main gun.

Making matters worse for the MCR who'd taken the station from the Republic, their techs lacked the ability to repair the main gun—at least, not with any haste. The best they could do was re-route shielded emergency power to feed the only weapons that wouldn't blow the grid: a few anti-boarding rail guns that could only manage sporadic fire. Against a lone destroyer, or even a small attack group, maybe even a battleship, those weapons *might* have dealt sufficient damage to slow the attack. But *Centurion*'s shields drew energy from a state-of-the-art reactor compound capable of powering a small moon, meaning there was almost no end to the energy it could supply. So whatever damage the defense platform dished out, it was quickly absorbed.

The MCR might as well be throwing spitballs at the super-destroyer.

SOAR marines flew through the occasional hail of magnetically fired rounds. Hyper-energized projectiles periodically lit the dark silent vacuum, highlighting the swarm of hullbusters descending to their target zone. Some unlucky marines met their end as the weapons found them in the dark while trying to strike the much bigger *Centurion*.

When Mazzara had received the warning order for the breach, he'd suggested what the SOAR called a puddle jump. The incoming larger craft would jump in a few kilometers away from the target and the marines would jump for it, using their combat thrusters like angling jets to guide them in. The small profile of the hullbusters juxtaposed against the massive *Centurion* would make them all but invisible to those on the station looking to repel them.

The marines closed the last of the distance and flipped their feet toward the skin of the space station rushing up toward them. Quick pops of their jets brought them into an easy glide toward the hull, and magnetic soles in their boots locked them onto the exterior, making for a momentary respite as squad leaders made their ACE reports to higher echelons. Several members of the company rapidly switched to catch-and-recover detail in order to retrieve what was left of the bodies of fallen comrades who had not made it through the jump. No hullbuster would be left to burn up on re-entry. They'd receive the rights due to the fallen.

"Breacher One, up!" Captain Mazzara called out.

Gunnery Sergeant Losey relayed the order and moved aside as a breach unit from the squads made its way to the maintenance hatch near the midpoint of the station. They traced the exterior of the hatch with high-explosive breaching tape as another squad moved into position behind them. With the explosives set, the breach team backed off, trailing a command wire from the charge some ten meters away from the emergency hatch. The second squad dropped a metallic ring around the breach point, rigging more wires to a power supply hub on the exterior of the station. A quick flip of a switch deployed a polycarbonate fabric shell that hardened on contact with the power vented from the outlet. This would serve to form an immediate seal around the breach, giving them their own door to use to get inside without venting the station and triggering emergency countermeasures that would slow them down.

The squad leader relayed his progress across their battlenet. "Breach point set. Chapel is set."

"Blow it," Losey ordered.

The magnetic fields holding their boots to the hull shuddered as the shaped charge blew the outer casing of the door. Two marines entered the shell the squad leader had called the chapel to remove the door from the airlock. They pulled the door out of the chapel opening and magnetically sealed it to the hull for later recovery.

"Power up the chapel and give me the key," Losey growled into the net.

Another marine with his battle board plugged into an access port leveled a thumbs-up at the gunnery sergeant. At the signal, an entire platoon ready to breach the doorway clacked their way across the outer hull and stacked up outside the chapel. The first man's visor acted like a mirror from the open doorway to the shell, which set an energized field over the breach—a smaller version of the shielding that kept docking bays from venting their artificial atmosphere. A trooper could pass back and forth through the shield as easily as Republic Raptors coming in and out of the *Centurion*.

"Breach!" called Losey.

The platoon pushed into the airlock by twos, rifles locked into shoulders, and the first fire team swung from the airlock to cover both sides of the passage. The marines covering shouted clear, ushering forth another gush of hullbusters. Hard soles thumped across the rubberized decking as warriors poured into the station to form up into squads ready to take control of the platform.

"Negative atmosphere on that side of the airlock. They must have vented it to keep us in our armor, sir," Losey said to Mazzara.

"Cry me a river, Gunnie. Have First Platoon move to room thirty-one. I want it taken for our command and control. Restore atmo so we can advance through the station. Tell my slicers I want control of the network yesterday."

As Losey was about to answer in the affirmative, a blaster bolt slammed into the side of Captain Mazzara's helmet, scorching the outer frame and turning him into a floating corpse magnetically locked to the frame of the station.

Marines still outside the station sent a furious wave of blaster fire into the oncoming advance of MCR outfitted in vac suits. Squad automatic blasters came to life, talking across a skirmish line forming with the SOAR taking up positions behind spots of cover along the station. One marine jumped to a gantry and locked himself to it, fighting upside down in the zero-gravity environment.

A squad leapt from the station hull in the direction of *Centurion*, using their jump jets to maneuver to the underside of the rotating station. Apparently the MCR had the same idea, as the moment the squad traversed to their location they came under fire from an MCR squad attempting to slip past the skirmish line away from the marine line of sight. The hullbusters rushed for cover and concealment among the many protrusions along the hull, and then made short work of the skulking MCR squad. Their foes' unarmored suits were no match for the Republic marines' firepower. Even glancing blows were enough to vac the person inside to an early grave.

On the top side, Losey and his crew fired and maneuvered, holding down the enemy squads with suppressing fire until their swing elements could move into position to catch them from the flank. While the Legion were the lords on most fields of battle, the Republic Marine Special Orbital Assault Regiment were the masters of zero-gravity combat. So much so that it wasn't uncommon for legionnaires to train with the SOAR elements in order to obtain better proficiency in zero-g tactics.

Fighting on a moving starship while trying to blow a hole in the hull without destroying the entire ship wasn't just a mission, it was a way of life.

The last of the MCR security team threw his rifle into the void and launched his hands toward his head in surrender. Several marines corralled the enemy combatant, who now seemed all too happy to comply as he looked into the faceless visors of his hulking aggressors. The marines checked the prisoner for explosives or any other weapons before standing him up and removing his safety line from the hull.

Losey turned away from the impromptu arrest, and that was all the permission the hullbusters were going to ask for. Releasing the man's line, they kicked him off the hull, waving goodbye as the rebel flew into space.

One of the kickers turned to face Losey. "Hey Gunnie. Old man still with us?"

"Negative, but nothin's changed. Get the rest of the of 'em inside."

Losey paused to watch waves of assault landing craft fly out of *Centurion*'s hangars. Ships of varied size and description, some carrying soldiers, others carrying vehicles and equipment, flew from the flight deck like a cloud of necro-bats from a cave at sundown.

"Go get 'em, Leejes."

15

Harvester Command Element
Heavy Drop Shuttle *Bulldog Four*

Chhun rattled in the drop seat beside his legionnaires as the ship catapulted from the main hangar bay of *Centurion*. Info from the various battle-nets flew across his HUD, detailing the unfolding missions as they progressed. Kalo Company's Yawds had blown up two orbital defense guns on the planet by sacking them with stolen robot artillery vehicles. Bombassa had hijacked the remaining orbital defense platform on that side of the planet to put a truckload of ion blasts into the station in orbit over the planet. So far, everything had gone surprisingly well despite some losses to the Yawd militia.

These were the opening strikes of what was sure to be one of the bigger fights the Legion had ever had with the MCR. The rumblings of this conflict had been there for some time. No one believed that the ideologues and power brokers in the upper echelons had lost their taste for the fight when Goth Sullus was declared emperor by the House of Reason. If anything, the MCR being called upon by the House of Reason to help fight the Legion had only laid down the tracks for the rebels to do what they had, for the moment, done on Kima—achieve a complete planetary takeover.

Chhun had been keeping tabs on the MCR since the events following the execution of Article Nineteen. Many of the rebel ships and troop elements, rearmed and supplied by the Republic itself under Goth Sullus, had gone rogue and fled into the shadows at the turning of the tide against the empire. Dark Ops did a stellar job of hunting down both the Rogue mids and the defiant House of Reason loyalists. The two groups—MCR and loyalists—tended to work together toward a common goal. But it was a game of numbers, and the MCR had them in spades.

The early indicators post-empire were that the MCR and the loyalists would coordinate an attack on Sinasia. That system had the most extreme ire from the loyalists. Yet it was Kublar that blew up first, seemingly out of nowhere, and to Chhun and the Republic's surprise, the MCR wasn't even involved, and the loyalists on the planet were crushed by a corporate-backed uprising. Chhun was hoping he could finally get a sense of what was truly going on there now that Ford was—finally—emplaced.

As it turned out, Kima was the only thing the MCR ever had in play. The planet's fall was meant to be a statement to refresh and revitalize the group, potentially spurring action on other planets once sympathetic to their cause. That had worked after Kublar.

But this time, Chhun was in charge.

He had worked tirelessly to position the Legion as the necessarily premier fighting force in the Republic while the horrors of Sullus and his Cybar were still fresh in everyone's mind. No more appointed officers. No more interference from the House of Reason. Chhun had spent months reminding everyone why the Legion had to exist outside of the normal chain of command. Why they had to be the Republic's Praetorian Guard. Their autonomy granted them the ability to craft the most lethal fighting force for the people's protection. It was also an assurance that if the government ever got out of control again, the Legion would be there to cut out its still-beating heart like they'd done to the House of Reason—far, far too late.

After taking the reins of the Legion, Chhun had reverted to the old ways of doing things. He'd studied the old leejes from before Psydon and pored over the campaigns against the last Savage remnants crushed by General Rex. Took in the various accounts of the birth of the Legion and the Hundred... although how much of General Marks's story was fact and how much was legend was anyone's guess. Recordkeeping isn't as precise as future historians might hope when a galaxy is desperately fighting just to survive.

Chhun hunted down every bit of leej lore he could find in order to map out the best way to train a legionnaire. In the end, the training wasn't all that dissimilar from what Legion instructors were already doing; it still came down to the hammer and the anvil. One man acting as the hammer to pound the potential recruit against the anvil of the training regimen. Think of an enemy so brutal it keeps you awake at night, and then train to become whatever that thing is afraid of.

And that was what the House of Liberty had unleashed on Kima. An old, throwback Legion come to reclaim its crown of glory on the galactic stage. Let the planners, shadow players, and brokers who set up this takeover be damned.

There was no planning for the Legion.

Chhun looked at the men in the seats across from him. These men had met the hammer and anvil and had begged for another hit. More stress, more fire, more steel.

They wore newly minted MK-150 combat armor with mimetic camouflage, augmented impact dispersion, and the best in NBC—nuclear, biological, and chemical—defeat technology in case the MCR wanted to fight dirty. Outside the armor, magnetic attachment systems with loop hook backups carried charge packs, trauma kits, and an assortment of deadly additions to the standard kit. A legionnaire could fight for days on end without resupply.

Each soldier was a fire team condensed into a single man focused on two things. He would kill the enemy first—and attempt to do it better than any other leej around him.

The MCR had kicked the trash and fanned the embers beneath to reignite the dumpster fire that was the galaxy. But like any political movement where freedom was a front for the elite to grab even more power, they only thought about the fire in the dumpster. They didn't care if it spread. The Legion did, and woe to anyone looking to fan the flames.

A HUD window pressed for Chhun's attention. "Chhun, it's Deynolds. SOAR marines just took the orbital station. They're putting it back together now. MCR were monitoring the system for us. Some of their ships just exited hyperspace but are pulling away from orbit. Looks like they didn't expect we were going to bring this many boats to the party."

"How many jumped in?" Chhun asked. Kill Team Victory, along with Wraith, had uncovered a plan for the House of Reason loyalists to support the Kima takeover with stolen Republic warships. Those had briefly materialized at the start of the planet's turmoil, but had left just as quickly. Now it seemed they had stayed free and near enough to answer the call for help should the Legion arise.

"A carrier with a battleship, two destroyers, and four corvettes," the admiral answered. "They're launching fighters, so we're responding in kind. You should be good with the Star Reapers already riding your wing for cover."

"Good copy, Admiral. I'll catch you when I'm on the ground. Good hunting. Chhun out." Chhun flipped the window in the HUD to see Bear's smiling face. "What do you have for me?"

"Sir, we just intercepted traffic to suggest he's alive."

Chhun already knew who Bear was talking about. A flutter of excitement went through his stomach. This was among the best news he could have dreamed of hearing, though he knew that assessment was driven by personal feelings and not the overall mission. "You sure it's him?"

Bear laughed at the question. "Right place, right time-frame. Feed was grainy as hell, but I know the way that kid moves. It's him. Plus, MCR put a bounty on his head. Who else do you know can piss someone off that bad aside from Masters?"

Chhun risked half a laugh in the confines of his bucket. Hope was a powerful motivator, but it could sour and turn to poison if the facts didn't support the theory. "You got a lead on him?"

"Putting it together now, sir."

"Keep me updated. We'll task a crew if you've got a loc, but I need you to stay on mission."

"Always, sir. Speaking of which, I got *Centurion* REPO on the line ready to patch in. Go ahead, REPO."

A second flash window opened in Chhun's HUD with an active video feed of *Centurion*'s intel officer. "Thank you, Captain. General, we have a full AI scrub of the data package sent by Victory-7. Sir, the majority of personnel in Blake are alive. The MCR has them under guard in tents at the running track."

More images flashed at the outskirts of Chhun's HUD. Multiple screen captures depicting people in huddled lines under guard outside of a makeshift tent city. In some holos, they were digging graves for stacked bodies waiting to be attended. But Chhun's attention was drawn to a holo of a woman in a torn RA uniform being pushed from behind, controlled anger on her face. She fell to the ground after another hard push but remained defiant.

Chhun felt the fire rising in his belly. He burned that woman's resolute face into his mind. Battle plans formed around the image in a miasma of rapid-fire calculations that was the hallmark of every good general.

"Changes in the target defense capability?" Chhun asked.

"Kalo Company scouts are pushing reports of teams moving into the forest," the intel officer said. "They noted MK-2 LADS among the teams. Of the Repub Marine longbow air defense systems from back in the day, the MK-2s were the units with the track-and-sack technology. As long as you could paint the target, that missile could knock it out of the sky."

Now there was a wrinkle, Chhun thought. "When did those show up and how was this not on our radar?"

The intel officer sounded determined to not sound like a chastised little girl in front of her dad. "Unknown, sir. They weren't deployed in the planetary takeover, and this is the first appearance of the units on planet as noted by militia scouts or Kill Team Victory."

Chhun pressed his hand against the hull. The rattling he felt was a clear sign that they were breaking atmo inside of the dropship they were riding like a lightning bolt into the ground. This was going to have to be handled quick.

"REPO, stand by for further, break."

Reaper Squadron
Flying Combat Escort for Insertion Team Alpha

Dax Danns adjusted the combat symmetry holo-matrix in his HUD a micron more to the right. Even though this was a Legion op, they still had to run with the same gear they'd been doing the workup with to shake out the bugs. The promised "vast modernization of the military" had thus far only affected the Legion. Danns wasn't one to complain about that sort of thing—the life expectancy for a legionnaire had always been shorter than that of a fighter pilot—but the big problem here was that some of the bugs had laid eggs when the techs went through the last time. One of them just so happened to be a deviation shift to the matrix.

The holographic HUD would, by design, disappear in the line of sight if the pilot looked away from the flight threat display, sometimes called a canopy by some of the older featherheads. This was a safety feature to allow the pilot to look at his various hard displays or the mission data card strapped to his right thigh. The bug was that looking away from the flight threat display and then back again caused a single-micron shift to one side. While it wouldn't matter much when rubbing wings with the incoming bandits, it would throw off targeting and threat acquisition at the crazy distances they often had to deal with as starfighter pilots.

The shift usually only happened in the first few minutes of flight, before some algo or another caught up to the waves of information passing through the semi-autonomous Attack Flight System onboard the new model starcraft they found themselves in. But it could be the difference between life and death.

Danns looked outside of the FTD at the cockpit of the newest Republic Raptor, the Model Kilo. Affectionately named the K-Raptor, the Kilo model had been a significant upgrade to the previous Raptor in terms of both armor and weapons, and even included the addition of a bot acting as a weapons systems operator, or Wizzo. Beyond the wing, Danns saw a horde of dropships carrying an entire Legion battalion. This would be only the first of the many tidal waves of Legion knuckle-crackers that were about to assault the planet.

A series of high-pitched tones in Danns's HUD announced an incoming comm burst. When Danns didn't accept right away, the onboard Wizzo bot, little more than a cube-shaped machine with retracting treads that fit snugly into what was a computer core compartment in the older models, spoke.

"You are not of sufficient rank to ignore the incoming call from the Legion commander," it said.

"Wasn't ignoring him, Lucky," Danns replied. "Just gotta get in the right headspace for royalty is all." He accepted the comm burst. "Go for Reaper One."

"Reaper, this is Harvester. We have news of MK-2 LADS on the deck over Objective Broken Window. We have teams on the ground attempting to neutralize. Have all available ECM on hot when you pass over, how copy?"

"Good copy, Harvester," Danns replied. "Reaper One out."

He killed the connection, taking enough time to signal to Lucky—officially, designator LK-E1—that the message should be transmitted to the rest of Reaper Squadron. It wouldn't do to get them all the way down to the planet only to get dusted by some MCR puke who'd picked up some outdated rockets from a night market hack running his own Army-Navy surplus. Of course, that didn't mean the rockets weren't dangerous. On the contrary, the MK-2 had sights installed that could be linked to the drop lenses in a marine's combat helmet. All it took was to keep line of sight on the target and the missile would do the rest.

Another call was incoming, and this time the ace accepted it immediately.

"Reaper One, this is Red Lead. I have multiple bandits bearing down on track. Please advise."

Danns switched his view to the other wing and took in the sight of the arriving MCR craft disgorging multiple smaller vessels. "Lucky, you got a read on that trash?"

"Preyhunters," answered the bot. "Outgoing sensor sweep indicates they are running a highly advanced broadcast module in each ship, but otherwise they are the same ships as traditionally used by MCR forces."

"Red Lead, stand by. Linking us to REPO, break." Danns entered the command net, dragging all of his flight leaders along for the ride. "*Centurion* REPO, this is Reaper One. Do you have a peep on those incoming bandits? Got some strange signals coming off of them."

Super-Destroyer *Centurion*
Combat Information Center

The intel officer crossed the space to hover over the sensor tech at station two. "I need everything you have on that signal running off those birds."

"Aye, ma'am," the tech responded.

"We have a problem, Lieutenant Apollo?" Deynolds called over the bullpen.

The intel officer turned to face the admiral. "Admiral. We have a few surprises that on their own wouldn't warrant a problem, but together make me think we're about to shake the mummy-bee nest and forgot the special mittens. We have a host of high-bandwidth broadcasts coming off that MCR ship which is currently being beamed to those fighters. Reaper One picked it up when the enemy launched fighters. We're copying our pull over to the EWO to see what he can find."

Deynolds nodded to her, waving a hand to signal that she should continue her part of the mission. The admiral then switched her attention to the other side of the room. "Fire Control Officer, I need a situation on that LZ."

"Aye, ma'am," First Lieutenant Marinkovich called back. "I have two co-opted airstrips ready to launch SLICs and more of those Preyhunter variants. We have victory locks on both targets."

"Well then, let's not keep our friends on the ground waiting. REPO, do we have friendlies in the target zones?"

"Negative, Admiral," Apollo answered. Though he was across the room, the micro-comms in all ears made even a quiet voice rise above the noise of the bridge when necessary. "No friendlies in target locations."

Deynolds nodded. "Fox-Con. Plot a firing solution on target package and execute."

The order was shouted about the bullpen, first as Captain Aguiar relayed her commands, then as the echoes of that order continued across the space until they reached the personnel who would put her call into action—a verbal chain that kept communication flowing even in the event of comms loss.

Marinkovich held up his hand as he called, "I have the lock!" Around him, a hologram projected into the space, showing the planet below with orbital tracks and fig-ured statistics displaying launched munitions to target. "Execute, Target Package Alpha."

The tech at the weapons station double-checked his parameters and confirmed them with a nod from the shipboard AI monitoring the operation. "Aye, sir. Firing on Target Package Alpha."

Holodisplays showing the exterior ventral gun mounts of *Centurion* shuddered as the weapons erupted in a cataclysmic volley of massive particle bolts. Long-range sensors painted the image of the planetside tar-gets slated for the onslaught. Primarily, these were ships that the Republic had once sold to Kima for its planetary defense, but had been subsequently hijacked by the MCR at the start of their planetary takeover.

The zoomed-in AI-constructed views from the orbital cameras washed out temporarily as the first bolts struck. Volcanic explosions of a duracrete flight deck and runway spewed into the air among sedate aircraft waiting in or-ganized rows, turning their dress-right-dress into neatly arranged graves. The next volley of orbital bombardment decimated the Quonset hut-style hangars, causing sec-ondary explosions that caught fueling stations at both target locations. The attack rendered the zones into kilometer-long craters of smoke and ash under the umbrella of a massive mushroom cloud.

A slight smile crossed the face of Marinkovich. "Target Package Alpha eliminated."

Harvester Command Element
Heavy Drop Shuttle *Bulldog Four*

Chhun keyed his L-comm to reconnect with Bear. "Got confirmation from *Centurion* that both airstrips within range of our touchdown are smoked. We still have those reports that those MK-2 LADS are deployed along our drop. Can you work anything on that?"

"Got the scouts on Kalo Company working it now," Bear answered. "Bombassa is going to clear the village on the ODP and then make for Broken Window. He can dust any rocket jockeys he finds."

"That's solid. With him on task, we should be good for landfall on time and on target. We'll punch through Broken Window and make our way to you."

"General, they have this place locked up tight. Lots of fighters. But what has me worried is some of the talk coming out of the old men toking hookahs and watching this go down. They're on about some special hit squads or something. It's got the old guard spooked. They say whatever these units are, they've made deals with the devil to make them more than a match for the Legion."

Chhun considered how likely that was. His teeth had already been itching over the fact that Blake, a major forward operating base for the Republic, had been toppled in a matter of hours. And while it was possible that a Repub officer or high-level civilian working the base might have thrown the keys and codes over the fence so the MCR could make their way in, that still wouldn't account for the Repub forces on the ground being so easily taken. Blake had been staffed up. The camp sported a light infantry battalion, two military police companies, artillery batteries, and tons of support elements including an air wing. These were not slackers or lightweights, but some of the best the Repub military had to offer. It didn't make sense that a whole base full of hyper-motivated war dogs had been beaten and subdued by what the footage showed to be handfuls of MCR squads and a few well-placed IEDs.

Then there was the other aspect to Bear's comment. The MCR had taken the city that fed the base: Kam Dho. Kam Dho was a thriving metropolis with professionally trained Kimbrin police as well as the Kimbrin Defense Force. Of course, much of their training had happened on the House of Reason's watch, which might explain the lion's share of what was going on. There would never be a shortage of people happy to be paid credits for "training" that only ever happened on paper.

Chhun shook his head. "It doesn't matter, Bear. Whatever they've got planned is for the Legion that existed after Psydon up until Nineteen happened. They're not ready for the beating we're about to dish out."

Bear grinned wide enough to fill the HUD window. "Love it when you talk dirty, General. KTF, sir."

16

**Reaper Squadron Insertion Team Alpha
Flying Combat Escort**

"Red Leader, Blue Leader, this is Reaper One," Dax Danns announced through his comms. "I want you to peel off and intercept those bandits. Engagement line is set at one hundred klicks. Kill anything that crosses. Attack and screen pattern one zero four."

"Red Leader copies, one zero four, out."

"Blue Leader, roger out."

Good. No comm chatter. No banter. Get the info, pass it on, and kill anything according to instructions. That was exactly what Danns wanted. So many fighter pilots coming out of the regular navy were hotshots who wanted to run a stick like the stupid holovids showing guys with pearly teeth and pretty hair doing insane combat maneuvers and grandstanding all the while. Those kinds of featherheads were soft, and vain, and had no place in his air wing.

Sure, Danns and his Reapers might have had a reputation for being flashy, and perhaps a bit cocky, but no one would ever accuse them of being *soft*. And it wasn't vanity to know how good you were or what you were capable of, either. They had one mission, and one mission only. Support the Legion. Translation: kill them first and kill them all.

"Black Leader, this is Reaper One. You got the duty on the old man. Split into Offset Trail and Spread Four to max the escort."

"Copy, Reaper One," Black Leader called back into the comms.

Lucky quickly reminded the ace of his own objectives. "You're supposed to be running screen for the force commander."

Danns gave a fractional shake of his head. "I am, but that doesn't mean I have to do it personally." He switched to his wing channel. "Steep, Jig, we're batting cleanup."

"Why are we getting benched?" responded Mariella Cruise, call sign Steeple.

Chris Thompson, call sign Jigsaw, answered. "You really want something to slip through the net and have the B team not be there to catch it?" Typical Jigsaw. He just had to answer a question with a question.

Danns checked the scope again. One hundred ninety klicks and closing. The bandit formations were tight and organized, almost textbook. "There's something off about this," he said. "I don't like it."

"You wanna turn around?" Jigsaw teased.

The first wave of dropships were almost to the upper atmosphere. In another few minutes, the rifle riders in the SOAR would have that orbital weapons platform active and could start pelting the MCR with particle beams that would shred almost anything in the void. If the Legion maintained control of the ODPs on the ground and in the sky, the mids had to know they were karked.

So why were they waiting?

Danns keyed his comms. "*Centurion* REPO, this is Reaper One. I need you to run a high-gain sweep of the battlespace all the way to the ground. Filter atmospherics and other anomalies that may be hiding more ships. Over."

Steeple filled the silence that followed. "What are you thinking?"

"Berycals."

"The birds we saw on Espania?" Jigsaw asked.

Danns's thoughts went back to the training camp they'd run on Espania for the local pilots. They'd had quite a bit of R&R on that trip as a result, which was the whole point in taking the assignment; prior to that the Reapers had been operational for months with barely an hour to themselves, and needed the opportunity to recharge the batteries. They'd gone to beaches, ate amazing food, and sampled the nightlife. All much to their chagrin in the morning when they had to be up before any of the trainees.

Wouldn't be proper for a Reaper to be late.

One day, while soaking up the glorious sunlight and enjoying the feeling of waves washing over their feet, they'd observed a local bird, the berycal, hunting for its breakfast. It wasn't quite a bird, more like a flying reptile, but evidently it was warm-blooded. A monster with strong leathery wings, sleek profile, and a beak that resembled a weapon. A sky-dwelling Reaper made flesh.

But what made the berycals memorable to Danns was how they hunted. The creatures would burrow into the sand and the cliffs, then wait for flocks of sea birds to pass overhead. The moment their prey's flapping and calls echoed over the waves, the berycals would dart from their holes directly into the center of the flocks, eagerly spearing and devouring the smaller birds and causing blood and feathers to rain down below.

Danns had a terrible feeling that—somehow—the big wave of dropships and accompanying fighters was the flock in this metaphor.

So what was playing the role of the berycals?

"*Centurion* REPO, I need that scan, over."

"Reaper One, this is *Centurion*. Bandits on intercept from the planet! Time to target, ninety seconds!"

"Jig, Steep, turn and burn on new track!" Danns called over the radio.

He triggered more power to the inertial drive field that the fighter pilots in the squadron affectionately called "the coaster." Set in the nose of the aircraft was a projector that sent out a stream of energy pulses just ahead of the fighter. These pulses had a charge that was the same polarity as the energy shields protecting the ship from damage. When the shield contacted the pulse, the two would repel each other, allowing the ship to fly as if it was in atmosphere affected by a planet's gravity.

Thrusters silently screamed into the void from the back of the three fighters, shaking the hulls but making no sound in the vacuum of space. They instinctively formed into a wedge aimed at the descending formation of Reaper Blacks and the assault force.

"Black Leader, this is Reaper One. Tighten the package and ride it into the ground. Do not break formation on assault force."

"Copy, Reaper One," the Black Wing leader called back. "Going guns."

"Passing package," Jigsaw roared into the comms, his excitement at the coming fight getting the better of him. "Time to target, six seconds." Danns knew what that adrenaline pump felt like, particularly to younger pilots. Even good ones like Thompson.

The wing soared past the fighter escort surrounding the assault force. Blaster cannon bolts raced from the protective detail, lighting up the dawn horizon as the system's sun crested the planet.

"This is Steeple, Fox-Three!" Danns's wingman announced that she was launching a defensive countermeasure for fighting another air wing capable of fielding more than just blaster cannons. She launched two KX-60 torpedoes, each carrying a complement of two hundred space-capable drones. The weapon fired ahead of the protection detail and detonated in the space between the two fighter groups. The bots deployed with shield technology that allowed them to act in much the same way as the ships' internal coasters, flying at a constant pace ahead of the ships they protected.

Danns raced past the entire affair toward the rising threat as Jig fired his own sixties.

"Reap!" Steeple called over comms, a clear sign that she was neither expecting nor happy with whatever the wing commander was about to do.

"Lucky—reverse shield polarity and set inertial dampeners to max!" Danns screamed to his Wizzo.

He flew so close past the enemy fighters that he was able to make out the surprised looks on their faces. Then he slammed off the coaster for his ship, allowing the oppositely charged shields to pull on each other. The result felt like the ship had just gotten caught up in a mithrik spider's web. Danns shook off the image of the massive arachnoid capable of trapping light-to-medium freighters in its traps as the twin fields slowed his speed to a crawl.

Overcoming the urge to revisit his breakfast, the starfighter ace fired angling thrusters to spin him one hundred and eighty degrees so that the nose of his ship, its weapons, and one hundred percent of his murderous focus was lined up on the back of the enemy fighter wing.

"Danns! You still with us?" Black Leader shouted into the comms.

It was a valid question. The sheer force of the maneuver, in addition to making Danns feel sick, nearly made him black out.

"Going guns," he grunted into the comms, blinking away the swirling black spots that nearly claimed his consciousness. With blood running from his nose, he squeezed the trigger on the stick, firing a fusillade of energetic fury into the engines of the bandit leader. The ship detonated in front of him, causing the twelve interceptors to scatter.

Black Leader and the rest of the assault force raced past in a frenetic charge toward the atmosphere, still escorting the transports. Reaper Squadron's flight leader was nevertheless able to dump a payload of blaster cannon fire into one of the scattering enemy Preyhunters, the bolts turning the ship into debris and momentary flame as the cockpit's artificial atmosphere erupted.

But the enemy intercept wing wasn't ready to break off their attack. They quickly regrouped even as Danns chased them toward Black Wing and the Legion dropships. When two of the Preyhunters peeled off, Danns knew they'd be swinging back around to try and get him.

"Not before I vape a few more of your friends..."

Blaster cannons lashed forth from the Raptor, destroying two more Preyhunters. But the main group continued on, seemingly willing to die to the last man before giving up their attack. They focused their assault on the trailing dropship, punishing its shields with blaster fire.

The deluge might have been enough to cook the legionnaires inside had one of Black Wing not fallen back to put herself between the ships. As advanced as the newest mode of Raptors were, they weren't sufficient to stand up to the concentrated attack. Shields failed and the craft blew apart, a small flare from the cockpit lighting up the black as it spun wildly away from the rest of the ship.

"That was Kemba..." one of the Reapers reported.

"Black Leader to *Centurion*. I have an active beacon along our track. Deploy Valkyrie..."

Danns ignored the rest of that comms traffic. He had bandits to kill and he couldn't be distracted by Black Leader calling in the beacon locks for a future recovery team to track. Even if it was one of his featherheads. While the starfighter had come apart, the protective cockpit had done its job and allowed the pilot to be ejected clear of the wreckage. Now all Kemba had to do was hope the trajectory was right to keep her from floating into the middle of a gunfight or being taken into the atmosphere.

Meanwhile, the Preyhunter variants were flying like nothing he'd ever seen from MCR before. These guys were good. Breaking off into three-man wings, the ships darted and evaded as the members of Reaper Black and his own fighter wing fought to keep them away from the dropships.

Another member of Reaper Black got vaporized when a Preyhunter ran straight for him in a game of high-velocity chicken. The fighter banked, looking to get an angle on the departing Preyhunter, only to be dusted by another bandit coming from beneath.

Jig's and Steep's missiles had dropped nearly a thousand of the defensive drones, and the Preyhunters had gone to work on the screen with a combination of blaster cannons and torpedoes meant to chew the protection to bits. The Legion drop shuttles kept themselves in tight formation inside the screen as the members of Reaper Black flitted and fought against the acrobatic interceptors looking to do them in.

"Reaper One, this is Steep. You see that trio that just dusted one of ours? They used a Clarkson on him."

"I saw it," Danns confirmed. "MCR finally found a way to study our tactics and use them against us."

"Reap, it's Jig. I got triple bandit that just drafted us. I guess they ain't too cozy on us vaping their buddies."

Danns kept his eyes on his flight displays. The Preyhunters destroyed another of the Reapers. "Dammit," he muttered to himself. Then, to his wing, "Let's put these kelhorns down. Not happy!"

"Go asymmetric," Steeple suggested. She waved her wing to avoid a swarm of blaster bolts that sailed by into the void until impacting on the shields of *Centurion.* "Strangers on a skytrain?"

"Are you crazy?" Jig called.

"Lucky: run it!" Danns shouted.

The cubical bot immediately dove into the series of combat flight maneuvers, finding that he had to dig considerably for this particular tactic. Priming the engines, dampeners, and the coaster, the little machine signaled to his pilot that he was good to go... "Unless you wish to change your mind."

"'Fraid not." Danns cut the coaster, using his thrusters to flip around into the direct line of sight of his opponent. At his order, Lucky then popped and vented the ventral angling jets in such a way as to make the Raptor bounce up and down wildly, resulting in a consistent series of misses by the Preyhunter's main cannons.

"Jig," Danns called out, his voice rattling from the maneuver.

"Steep," Jig answered.

That left Steeple to cover Danns. The three Reapers, through the erratic up-and-down motion of the maneuver, had arranged themselves so as to bring their tails into the targeting reticles of one another. Danns didn't hold back on the rapid blaster cannon fire, and quickly vaporized the Preyhunter following Jig. That freed the wingman to shoot through the middle of their formation to nail the one following Steeple. She followed suit from her position just below the entire affair, wrecking the interceptor helplessly trying to get a bead on Reaper One.

"Pretty sure that scorched my wings," Jig said of the tight maneuver. "Thanks, Dax."

"Just glad to still be alive after that," Danns said to his wingmen. "Swoop and loop to pick up the package. Break. Black Leader, this is Reaper One."

"This is Black Lead. We're getting chewed up by these remaining fighters! We got a triple threat and a single doing damage. Lost two more and they crippled one of the drop shuttle engines on the last pass."

"We're front steps and ready to ring the doorbell, Black Leader," Danns assured him. "Hold what you got and get that task force into the atmo."

The Reaper wing kicked the throttle as hard as it would let them, propelling them back toward the assault force. Only the best featherheads the navy had to offer made it to the Star Reapers, and Black Leader—Lieutenant Jaeger Falco—was one of the premier defensive escort fighter pilots in the entire Republic. If anyone was going to get this crew to the ground it would be him.

Yet as Danns glanced out of the cockpit, he saw that Falco's ship was trailing some kind of coolant or gas that would probably ignite in the atmosphere—the price of having used his Raptor to take multiple hits meant for the drop shuttles. In addition, the Preyhunters were lurking beneath the column, using the rising sun bursting over the horizon to hide themselves from line of sight. While it wouldn't keep them off the sensors, it did obscure what the featherheads could see, forcing them to assess what was happening through their HUDs and costing them precious seconds to react. They were in trouble, especially if this wing broke up and came at them from multiple angles. And where was the lone fourth ship?

"Reaper One, this is *Centurion* REPO. We have a line on that frequency coming off the ship. They are network-enabled and passing mass amounts of data between the fighters and the main MCR carrier. Our EWO thinks a full combat controller AI is helping the pilots. The Preyhunters coming off that carrier are giving as good as they're getting. Over."

A hurricane of combat possibilities swirled through Danns's mind. "Lucky, what do we got to jam that noise?"

"Nothing to speak of," the bot answered. "We would have to jam all transmissions in the AO in order to stop hypercast-encrypted burst traffic."

Danns frowned. "*Centurion* REPO, this is Reaper One, can you jam the traffic coming off that boat?"

"EWO is working it, Reaper One. Should be a few mikes to isolate and terminate."

Danns shook his head despite the fact that Apollo couldn't possibly see it from her place on the *Centurion* bridge. "*Centurion* REPO, this is Reaper Lead, I need a blanket on all traffic for thirty seconds starting at 0545

OP-TC." He watched the chrono counting down as the Preyhunters riding the horizon stormed toward the noses of the dropships just starting to redden as they met with the first wisps of the exosphere.

A network-wide communications burst sounded through the battlenet. "All Harvester units, this is *Centurion*. All comms blackout to occur in thirty seconds. Duration, thirty seconds. *Centurion* out."

"Everyone catch that?" Danns shouted to his wing. "Light 'em up!"

All communications coming from the task force ceased. There was no waiting. No further signals to his wingmen. Danns just punched his throttle so hard it threatened to go through the front of his ship.

The engines flared, driving the Reaper Leader back into his seat. Danns and his wingmen darted past the task force, racing toward the incoming interceptors. The Preyhunters, who up to this point had been showing an exceptional amount of skill in evading and returning fire toward Reaper Squadron, were suddenly flying like a bunch of drunken moktaar. Steeple splashed the first one across the atmosphere, sending it to burn up in reentry as Jig raced through the debris to fire a missile at one of the remaining. The rebel managed to dodge the incoming weapon and then clumsily leveled its own shots at the deadly Raptor racing toward it.

Danns swerved out of the direct line to come at it from above. The combat symmetry holo-matrix barked out a relentless stream of battle data for the Reaper Leader to follow straight to target. But he never got the chance. Heavy thumps against his hull spun him off his flight path, putting him out of line with the attack.

"What hit us?" Danns looked around, knowing that neither Lucky nor anyone else would be able to hear him, let alone answer. Then he saw it. "Fourth fighter."

Pushing his external sensors to max, Reaper One brought in a render of the Preyhunter's cockpit as it passed by. It was empty. The entire bay where a pilot should be sitting was filled by a hard shell with a glowing globe at its center.

"Flying by AI, huh?" Danns put his fighter into a tight turn. "That's one way to do it."

"You are not going to be able to outfight an AI by yourself," Lucky announced. "Comms are back up, by the way."

Danns called to his wingmen that he wasn't in shape to take on the remaining fighters. But a solo dogfight? That he could handle.

He put max push into his two functional engines and a struggling third to circle out of his attack vector as he pushed his sensors for a track on the interceptor that had clipped him.

"This course of action will likely result in your death and my end of runtime," Lucky said. "Just so you know."

"And I should have died doing that slingshot maneuver with the shields, but here I am," Danns said. "Now find me that ship!"

The fighter ace's eyes swam in a lake of combat data across his HUD. Steeple was the first to figure out that he wasn't just pulling back.

"Reaper One, this is Steeple. What're you up to?"

Danns checked his damage reports again, pushed to the forefront by an insistent Lucky. One aft outboard engine destroyed, another on life support. A high probability of ruptured power cells. Yeah, this was dumb.

"Steep, I need you to find that last fighter. I'm going to switch places with Black Leader for the rest of the op."

"Black Leader copies. Switching roles," Falco said. The Raptor waved out of formation in the offset trail, making room for Reaper One to take his place.

"Steep, this is Reap. I'm in position. Any sign of that fourth bandit?"

"Nothing and nowhere, Reaper One."

Danns let out a sigh through his nostrils. "All right, take the wing up and back up Red and Blue. I'm riding these boys to the ground. I'll catch up to you on the slingshot."

He watched as the trio pulled out from the atmosphere toward the blaster-laden expanse. *Centurion* and its retinue of destroyers and corvettes were laying into the MCR contingent. Small explosions dotted the azure glow of the sun dusting the atmosphere as it came around the horizon.

"Reaper Black, this is Reaper One, I have the flight. I say again, I have the flight. Signal confirm on COMTAC." When all the ships remaining in the escort wing signaled their confirmation, Danns issued another directive. "Eyes out for that lone bandit. The ship is a drone and should only be taken on in pairs. Change formation to Split Wedge. I'll play Oddball."

Danns burned his way out of orbit and into the atmosphere, with the drop shuttles trailing close behind.

"Incoming out of the sun!" Lucky shouted into the net.

The AI interceptor screamed across the formation with a heavy drop of blaster bolts slapping the heavy shuttle shields and skipping into the waning shields of Danns's fighter.

"Oh, this sucks!" Danns shouted. And there it was again—his mind going to thoughts of the berycal, that lizard-bird creature that was a Reaper of the sky. "Bulldog Four, this is Reaper One. I'm going to saddle up to your belly, near the nose, and take some of your heat."

"Good copy, Reaper One. Bulldog Four out," came the pilot's reply.

The Bulldog pilots ferrying the legionnaires to the ground had seen the entire dogfight go down and knew what the Raptor featherheads were willing to do to protect them. The pilot didn't question Danns. He'd keep the nose of his dropship steady for Reaper One.

Black Six took several bolts as the interceptor passed over again. The fighter's shields held but one of the stabilizers was damaged, leading to a wobbling, clumsy flight path. The Raptor's Wizzo might be able to fix it in flight, but it would take a minute. One they didn't have.

The interceptor dodged several missiles fired at it and disappeared into the dense cloud cover over the terrain below. The dropships shunted power from life support to shields in hopes they would take the damage from the precision fighter still tearing them to pieces. In the confusion of the flyover, Danns's Raptor took position beneath the shuttle, taking the majority of its heat from burning through the atmosphere.

"We're gonna hide in the heat," Danns told Lucky.

The bot didn't have time to complain before the interceptor was again coming at the shuttle from behind one of the cloud banks. It launched a missile straight into the center of the formation. This was a textbook attack on a convoy, repeatedly hitting the formation so they tighten up on the asset—in this case the dropships. After crippling or shrinking the fighter escort, a missile strike on one ship at the center of the formation would often cause the rest to suffer sufficient damage to go down with it.

But Dax Danns was intent on tearing the textbook apart. He punched the throttle, racing as fast as his fighter would carry him from beneath the shuttle. Hidden by the heat signature of the other ship, he catapulted into the flight path of the interceptor while launching every missile he had along a path marked by cannon fire.

The AI ship came apart in flight just as its missile collided with Black Six, who had raced to take the hit for the intended drop shuttle. The ruined AI fighter's shrapnel penetrated the shields of Danns's Raptor and dug into the hull, hastening the machine's death throes as he struggled to control its descent.

"Bulldog Four, this is Reaper One. I have good chute on Black Six. I say again. Good chute on Black Six. Flight recovery marker on his position is good."

"This is Bulldog Four. Good copy, Reaper."

"Bulldog, I have sustained engine damage. Can't hold this girl together for much longer. I am going to ride you to the ground until I can't."

"Roger, Reaper. We have also sustained damage from that last pass. Harvester is going to ditch. Come down close to us and we can ride the dirt for rebound."

Rebound—that was task force pilot lingo for multiple damaged birds trying to reach a target area before ditching the aircraft. With any luck, they could link up with each other on the ground to maximize any escape and evasion necessary to get back to friendly forces.

"I copy rebound, Bulldog Four. I'll see you when I see you," Danns said. "Reaper Black Two, you have the stick."

"Roger, Reaper One. Black Two has the stick. Good luck, Reaper."

Danns flanked the descending shuttle. He saw the landscape coming up to meet him and marveled at how beautiful the rolling hills on this side of Kima were. He checked his scope and his instruments, cursing when his matrix was a micron off again. Just as he was making adjustments, an explosion burst in the air beside both aircraft, buffeting their flight path with a mass of turbulence and flak.

"Bulldog Four, this is Reaper! Get low! I say again, get low! AA guns on the northwest ridge!"

Danns angled the aircraft away from the shuttle, blowing off chaff rounds in the air around him. Dazzling suns trailing smoke in the chill morning air flitted away from the fighter, hiding the signature of the shuttle as it limped away along another path.

"Gun locations are locked on your HUD," Lucky noted.

"Got it. We're out on missiles. Time to improvise. Set the blaster charge cyclers to overload and then give me everything we got into the engines we have left."

And with that, Danns beat the throttle like it owed him credits. He raced along the valley straight into the path of the guns, juking and flashing through the incoming anti-aircraft fire. Flak pelted his canopy, cracking the glass to the point of zero visibility and shorting out the digital display.

Danns recovered from involuntarily covering his face to pop the Raptor's canopy explosive, shattering the rest of the structure like a cracked eggshell that came apart in flight. He could see again and it looked like he was coming down at just the right angle. He traced the first gun emplacement with blaster fire, tearing up the mountain and rupturing the power cells on the gun in a volcano of fire and fury.

"Lucky! We're leaving!"

The little Wizzo slid from his compartment to attach to the ejection seat. With a hard connection made, the seat blasted from its locks in the frame. The thrusters under the seat rocketed them farther into the air as the plane sailed away from them. At the point where the fire from the remaining two AA guns ruined the sky, the Raptor exploded. Its charge cyclers having been sent to critical at Danns's command, the starfighter erupted with the force of a suitcase nuke, blowing the remaining AA guns to cinders.

The chute popped above the ejection seat and the shock of the arrested fall nearly cost Danns his head. "Well, that worked out better than I thought."

Through the comm in his helmet, Lucky said, "Your improvisation resulted in the loss of a multi-billion-credit fighter aircraft which was not meant to be used as an impact weapon. They will probably send you for remedial training."

"Gonna have to live through this first," Danns said wryly.

"You need not fear. I am lucky after all."

"Was that a bot joke?" Danns asked, smiling despite himself. "If that were true, we wouldn't have got shot down."

The fighter ace watched as the sun broke through the clouds, highlighting the valley in a display of beauty he hadn't seen since they were on that beach on Espania.

The little cube of the bot, fixed in its place attached to the ejector seat, said, "At least it's not raining."

17

Harvester Command Element
Heavy Drop Shuttle *Bulldog Four*

"Bulldog Four, this is Reaper! Get low! I say again, get low! AA guns on the northwest ridge!"

Sooty black explosions rocketed across the sky as the five dropships scattered along their flight path. They descended to an altitude obscenely close to the ground, forcing them to arc around mountains and jungle canopies and dash across bodies of water.

"Who was the kelhorned maggot that ordered the nap-o'-the-earth-style landing we got goin' on here? 'Cause I'd like to punch him," MakRaven said through his personal channel with Chhun.

Chhun pinged the pilot over the shuttle's internal comms. "Hey, Lieutenant. Things don't sound like we're doing too hot out there."

"Not going to lie, sir, I've had better flights. We have multiple system failures after we took a bunch of hits that got through the shield and scrapped one of the engine thruster ports. This bird can take a beating to the armor, but the weak point is all the thrust coming out of the back."

"Do we have repulsors?" Chhun asked.

"It's a maybe, sir. Co-pilot is re-routing power now. But first we have to get away from those AA guns or they're going to rip us to shreds."

The HUD inside of Chhun's bucket flashed over to the command net. "Riggs, get your boys up and tell 'em to jock for a quick exit. We're testing out the jump jets on the new gear."

"On it, General," Major Riggs growled.

"We gonna ditch, sir?" asked MakRaven.

"Looks that way." Chhun broadcast up to the pilot. "LT, it's Chhun. This flight's been terrible so we're going to jump."

Despite talking to the task force commander, the pilot couldn't help but laugh through the comm. "Roger that, sir. I won't expect a glowing review, then. I'll keep it steady and get you boys to a spot that won't be that harsh for an early exit."

"Negative. You're jumping with us. I'm forwarding you coordinates for a small water source twelve klicks from here. Set for an AI assist remote and pilot it to the edge of the water if the repulsors hold. If they're karked out, let it hit the water and we'll recover it once we're down."

"Roger, sir. Notifying Reaper One."

"He's still on our wing?"

"Technically, sir. Traded places with Reaper Black Leader. He just took out the AA guns before taking the sky chair."

"Good. Get up here now." Chhun unstrapped from his seat and reached for the drag cable on his side of the aircraft to stabilize himself. "Domino! We're going to ditch, and you're coming!"

The crew chief slapped a panel on the skin of the aircraft ramp to yank a ruck from the enclosure. Two other navy personnel followed suit before reaching for parachutes strapped to the bulkhead.

"Leave it!" MakRaven shouted. "You spacers are riding down with us. Kick open that ramp!"

As if the shouting of a Legion sergeant major con-trolled the universe, the ramp popped its seals, and thun-derous airflow rushed through the cabin. Domino sig-naled with a thumbs-up followed by motioning the four lines of legionnaires toward the end of the ramp.

"Sergeant Major! We're still too low for repulsors!" the crew chief called into the shared battlenet.

"And I told you to *leave* the repulsors! Find yourself a heartbreaker and hold on for your life."

Above them, the cataclysmic echo of AA guns died in the distance. Their fury had been silenced by a Kilo-model Raptor detonating into the side of the hill. Distance to tar-get indicators in the general's HUD gave him an idea of where to drop. It was all about the timing until it became all about luck.

"General. I have the pilots," Riggs reported over L-comm.

"Roger, we'll get the crew." Chhun sprinted forward to-ward one of the air crew standing near the ramp. "Comin' at you, spacer!"

The former Legion commander tackled the navy crewman on the way out of the drop shuttle. The pair tum-bled in the air in freefall before a powerful jet thrust blast-ed from the general's calf and waist. With the fall nearly arrested, the two men were brought into a controlled arc toward the tropical canopy below. Chhun protected his passenger by letting his armor take the brunt of the im-pact as they broke through branches and vines. Another jet blast sent them away from the trunk and brought them closer to the jungle floor. After a third controlled burst, they landed with no more difficulty than stepping down off the last step in a flight of stairs.

"Damn, sir! That was wild," the spacer said through the facemask clipped to his helmet.

Nearby, the crew chief scowled as she disentangled herself from MakRaven. "You will show the general proper respect, spacer, or next time I'll kick you from the bird without the benefit of the boost." Domino looked between MakRaven and Chhun. "Sorry about that, Sergeant Major, General. They don't get out much. Still, thanks for the ride."

MakRaven nodded. "You're on our six until we can link back up to your workspace, Petty Officer."

"Aye, Sergeant Major." Domino removed the shorty carbine from her ruck, slapping the folding stock into place to set it for patrol ops. She looked into the trees and took a half-step back as the color drained from her face. Her voice went to a hushed whisper. "Um, Sergeant Major? That going to be a problem?"

Legion buckets turned to follow the crew chief's gaze. They tracked to a line of trees ahead of them with a massive beast resting under some of the fronds. MakRaven figured it to be three point five, maybe four meters in length. It had orange fur with black stripes, and as it brought its head up to sniff the air, teeth the size of a Drusic's fingers appeared in a snarl that suggested this beast was all too used to sinking its fangs into things.

"Just a wobanki without pants," MakRaven said. "Don't mess with the wildlife and it won't mess with you."

The big predatory cat took a step from the tree cover providing it shade, and Domino pointed her weapon as an argument against the sergeant major's wisdom.

"Do not shoot that animal," Chhun said. "We have our own set of teeth for these occasions."

A wave of the general's hand brought forth a legionnaire from the surrounding foliage. The man was nearly as large as the creature, and trailing by his side was a mottled brown dog whose pointed ears stuck up on either side of the muzzle it was wearing. Form-fitting body armor around its torso acted just like the Legion version, mimetically capturing the surrounding colors and patterns to hide its wearer in the bush.

"Hold on to your skull, lady," MakRaven said. "This is where it gets weird."

The predatory feline growled as it took stock of the new animal. Its focus suggested it saw the dog as a greater threat than the armored humans. It took several steps forward as its growl intensified. MakRaven's assessment wasn't far off, even if he was joking: the animal *did* look like a wobanki that had forgotten to stand, and much like a wobanki, it was intent on murdering anything that happened to enter its territory.

The beast was priming itself to rush forward when the legionnaire handling the dog unclipped something from the back of the animal's muzzle. The motion served as a starter gun to the race, and the dog launched toward the feline like it had been fired out of a blaster. Startled by its fury, intensity, and barking, the several-hundred-kilo cat jumped backward, apparently uncertain about something so small rushing so fearlessly at something as big as itself.

As the dog approached, the cat raised paws that were made for digging graves. It looked like it intended to club the dog in the side of the head, but then suddenly it lowered its paws once more and sat down. A guttural growl issued from its throat, like some alley cat cornered among trash cans with no avenue of escape. It looked from shoulder to shoulder before backing slowly away from the canine, dropping its considerable bulk to the ground and practically slithering back into the leaves to whatever den it had crawled from.

The dog loped back to its hulking Legion handler, who patted him on the flank in a powerful display of affection that would have fractured the ribs of most spacers.

"What in Oba's underpants just happened?" Domino asked.

MakRaven clapped her on the shoulder. "That, my friend, is a dog called a Malinois. But the version that the Legion uses is kind of a trade secret. That little clip that got yanked before the dog went into action? It keeps his considerable superpowers in check. If he didn't have it on during the ride into atmo, that dog would have voo-doo mind-tricked the lot of us to jump from orbit and land on the enemy like some pain-seeking missile of saintly vengeance."

"The dog has mind powers?

MakRaven smiled. "Best to keep that to yourself. Lest we let Bubbles have his way with you."

"Mount up," Chhun ordered, and a Legion squad materialized from the direction that had spat out the dog handler.

"General," said the squad leader, "we have the air crew. Pilot says the repulsors held but are fried after land-ing. Ship is a klick on this bearing, sir."

"Lead the way, Legionnaire."

The group fell into position as they moved through the underbrush. The legionnaires moved silently in their environmentally sealed armor, stalking through the vine-strewn vegetation as though it were their natural envi-ronment, but the air crew repeatedly got hung up. During these moments the leejes vanished into the terrain to stand guard, then reappeared when the whole affair was ready to continue forward.

The group crested a hill, showing the forest thinning into an open expanse where a low portion of the terrain had formed a pond. Just at its opposite edge was the ship, *Bulldog Four.*

MakRaven knife-handed in two directions, and the assembled leejes scattered as though they were haunting spirits fleeing the sunrise.

"I've been in this Republic's navy for a bit now, and not since stitching in my stripes have I felt like such a rank amateur," Domino said.

"Don't give it a thought," the sergeant major replied through his external speakers. "You've trained for this situation. The leejes live for it."

Another set of legionnaires appeared out of the wood line close to the water on an intercept course with the task force commander.

"Talk to me, Riggs," Chhun said, shaking the Victory Company commander's hand.

"Bird's engine took a whole lot of flak but the rest of the armor held," Major Riggs reported. "All of our gear is five by five. We're cutting and kicking now. If your plan is still to use one of the APCs as a TOC, we can bring down one of the other birds that ain't so crooked, sir."

"Negative. Crooked works for me." Chhun nodded toward the air crew. "Collect your gear and move out, Major. We have a timetable to keep."

"On it, sir." Riggs waved, and the assortment of leejes around the air crew disappeared into the bush with their commander.

"Now comes the hard part," MakRaven said.

Domino motioned for her crew to skirt the waterline and head for the APC. "What's that, Sar'nt Major?"

"Trying to keep a general from jumping into the action and getting in everyone's way."

Chhun saluted the man with a solitary finger and followed the flight crew. "How about getting me an ACE report."

Dipping into the L-comm, the general watched as the hammer that was the Legion descended toward the anvil.

Orbital Defense Station
Outskirts of Kam Dho City

"They're squirting back over that ridge!" Toots fired three shots on the retreating Kimbrin squad. They struck the hill with puffs of smoke as bolts met mud.

Pina called to him over L-comm. "Rolling out left!"

"Take it!"

Pina sprinted to a pair of trees growing out of the forest nearly on top of each other. While the trunks offered more concealment than cover, they became a point of confusion for the enemy as his armor took on the natural colors and textures of his surroundings. "Set!"

Toots switched the grip for his firing hand to just ahead of his mag well. "CS out!"

Two twenty-millimeter rounds coughed from the end of the rifle with a resounding *poot*. There was a pregnant pause in which all the fighting seemed to hold its action in order to learn the result of the uncharacteristic noise coming out of the end of a Legion rifle. Then twin pops echoed from over the hill, followed by coughing and hacking.

Pina keyed into the L-comm. "Harry, I need eyes on the other side of the hill marked as one-six-bravo."

The response crawled along the bottom of his HUD. *Approaching at 121 degrees magnetic and cresting the hill. Shift fire to 91 degrees.*

Combat overlays in the augmented reality of their buckets pointed to the spot where the incoming R-CSM mech—designated Harry—could maneuver around the terrain without getting shot by its buddies. As the twin leejes sent rounds toward the hill to suppress the MCR squad, the mechanized headless bullitar stomped through the vegetation. A brush bar on its front knocked down any limb or vine that blocked its path as it picked its way over the terrain.

When it reached the back side of the landscape obscuring the enemy, Harry deployed a prehensile, serpentine neck with a sensor node painted on to make it look like it possessed a snarling mouth.

"Do not move!" the massive armored bot shouted in the local Kimbrin dialect. "You are hereby ordered to drop your weapons and move down the slope where you will be taken into custody."

A single blaster bolt winged off the mech's right shoulder. The serpentine head dropped back into its housing and the dual gun mount on its back turned in the direction of the attack. A rotary blaster spun up, pelting something on the opposite side of the chemically choked hill. The destructive burp lasted only a second, and the spraying of dirt and plant matter in all directions was the only indication to the leejes on the safe side of the hill that something had been truly and resoundingly pounded.

Harry once more raised its head. "You are hereby ordered to drop your weapons and move down the slope where you will be taken into custody by Republic legionnaires."

Nine members of the choking MCR squad limped over the hill with their weapons raised above their heads. Toots stripped them of their gear and sent them to Wello at the edge of the village. There, each man was dragged into a kneeling posture and fitted with ener-chains. The prisoners were strung together using synth-cord, with a slip-knot loop wrapped around each man's neck and descending through his ener-chains before connecting him to the next prisoner. Should one of them try to move away from another, the noose would tighten on the other man.

Old-school pain, compliance, and guilt. No one wanted to be the guy that strangled his buddy so he could escape.

Sounds of gunfire on the opposite ridge echoed through the village. The L-comm lit up like the starting line at the Levenir Gran Prix.

"Heads up!" Nix shouted over the comm. "Got the other squad of Spikers laying some hate our way. One of them has an RPG."

On cue, a rocket fired from that side of the operations area. The wispy trail of smoke from its tail motor carried the weapon into the sky in a lazy arc. Lancing rotary cannon fire sent a whirlwind of blaster bolts after the errant projectile, a red streaking energy buzzsaw that blazed a path across the sky before cutting the rocket in half.

"Rocket destroyed," reported Henry, the other heavy munitions bot, over the L-comm. "Moving to capture point."

"All Victory elements, this is Nobes. Drone feed shows one hundred percent roundup on Spiker elements. Collapse on the dock to await incoming 2-FR support."

The kill team rounded up their prisoners and escorted them to the dock. Two leejes stood over them like silent sentinels, waiting for their relief to show up somewhere downriver. As the troopers assembled on the rally point, Bombassa pulled Pina aside.

"I need your eyes on something."

"On you, Top," Pina responded.

The two walked over to one of the tables used for cleaning fish. Neck hovered above the surface, spreading out an assortment of ruined tech for them to inspect. "Now see here, this junk came out of that rocket old Henry dusted a minute ago. You ever see anything like this?"

Pina nodded as he took hold of one of the more complete machines. "This is combat drone tech. If I had to guess, it's from a Valhawk missile. Do you have the launcher?"

"Nope. Henry put a grenade round on the gunner before wiping the sky with the blaster blender. We found less of him than we did of the weapon."

Pina turned to Bombassa. "Top, this coulda been bad news. Two-stage weapon. Stage one sends up small bots to hover over the area to provide battle info to units on the ground. Talkin' reep-flies as a size comparison. Stage two is gonna look like, well... bigger bugs—and these carry a concentrated payload. Small ones find the targets and the big ones blow 'em up."

"Will the payload in question be capable of piercing the new armor?" Bombassa asked.

"One drone? No. Two or three, I wouldn't be the guy inside the armor."

Bombassa sifted through some of the drones, then peeled back one of the casings to see the explosive charge underneath. "Who fields these?"

"This is old Psydon-era tech. Back in the day, a bunch of colonels in the Regs got busted for funneling these through the Nether Ops guys for 'friendlies' on Psydon. It turns out the majority of them went missing and ended up in some of the skirmish wars out on galaxy's edge. Good news is that they aren't that effective if we have jammers up. The AI is in the launcher and broadcasts to the drones. The range is actually pretty limited."

Bombassa looked over his shoulder at an approaching gunboat loaded with Yawds. They waved to Wello on the dock, who nodded and waved them in. "Scan and shoot all of this to Harvester Ops now that they're on the ground. Everyone jock up and be ready to move in ten. We're moving to phase three."

Harvester Command Element
Temporary Ops Center
Bulldog Four

Chhun used his entrenching tool to fill the bag with the last bit of sand, then gave the bundle a spin until the top cinched closed enough for him to tie it shut.

"Sir, shouldn't you let one of us do that so you can concentrate on something more important?" Domino asked.

"Negative. Multi-tasking. Speaking of which, how go the repairs?"

"Number four engine is shot, sir, but we got power routed back to the repulsors. We can flatten this thing out so you won't have to use that sandbag."

Chhun lifted the leg of the table in his makeshift ops center and slid the sandbag beneath it. "I'm good. I like the angle this dropship is sitting at. A quick sandbag will hold my table level, while the angle gives us a little extra cover from a surprise attack. A ground-level sniper doesn't have a straight shot into here. But... if you're looking for something to do, work with the leejes outside running security and provide a linkup to the mech crew landing in twenty to get this bird operational."

"Aye, sir." Domino turned and headed out of the craft.

MakRaven leaned on the table, nearly toppling the leg off the sandbag. Chhun caught his helmet before it could tumble off.

"Good kid," MakRaven said.

Chhun nodded.

Both men looked up to see an armored bot coming up the ramp to join them in *Bulldog Four*. It was nothing short of a bulky, mechanical legionnaire.

"General Chhun," the bot intoned with a clipped, military style of speaking. "I have an update for you, sir."

"You got a bot to bring you your kaff, sir?" Mak said, shaking his head. "That ain't progress. I miss the old days when some leej officer who'd caught hell was tasked with makin' the kaff. Them boys always went the extra hyperjump just to get the hell out of kaff duty and back to the line. Plus it was the best kaff I ever tasted."

The bot seemed eager to answer, probably the work of a boastful programmer somewhere way back on the core world that had developed the machine. "Negative, Sergeant Major MakRaven. Legion operating directive

90411-stroke-5 requires that all regimental staff officers employ a robotic CCASS unit for directed Legion operations so that real leejes can lead on the ground."

MakRaven dropped a kaff tablet into his mug of water and watched it brown and sizzle as it heated. He took a sip, once more ignoring the bot to address the general. "That one o' your orders?"

"I wanted my officers leading, and my spacers spacing." Chhun took the cup from MakRaven, pirating a sip before handing it back. He grinned. "Besides, who needs an officer to make kaff when you're around?"

The sergeant major looked at his cup as though its sanctity had been violated. He wiped the lip with a gloved finger. "Point taken."

Chhun nodded to the bot. "I'll take that update."

"Of course, sir. Victory Company has departed with all associated assets toward Objective Broken Window. Major Riggs reports being on target to link with elements of the Second Free Rifles in support of Kill Team Victory to retake the base. First Battalion Commander, Colonel Blaine, has positioned *Bulldog Two* as his battalion Ops CP on the far side of Kham Do City with Venom Company deploying to take the remaining Mechasaga-381 mobile gun platforms. Colonel Shaman is prepping Second Battalion for phase four aboard *Centurion*."

Chhun nodded. "Keep an eye on things while I coordinate from here. Advise me on anything out of the ordinary."

The robot spoke again. "I have one incident from Kill Team Victory that matches that description, sir. Kill Team Victory, while defending the orbital ion gun platform, encountered a missile team in the hills."

"We got that in the briefing on the way down.," cut in MakRaven.

"Negative, Sergeant Major. This was not the MK-2 LADS system as put in the FRAGO. They have encountered a unit with a Valhawk missile launcher."

The crusty sergeant major set down his cup to free both hands to lean on the table. "Saw those on the back end of Psydon when I was just a young pup with too much testosterone for my own good. Nasty pieces of work. Launch a bunch of drones that chase you like a swarm of mummy-bees and then blow up in your face."

"I've never encountered them," Chhun said.

"They went off the radar after Psydon. One RTO running an ion pulser and they were useless."

Chhun kicked the sandbag to straighten the table. "And we don't have a workaround."

MakRaven frowned. "No, sir. We do not. When was the last time you had an RTO with an ion pulser as part of his kit?"

18

Kill Team Victory
En Route to Fort Blake

Nobes crested the hill, then motioned to the rest of the team that they were clear to advance. The heavily camouflaged unit slithered quietly through the underbrush to a break in the jungle. A series of pools divided by berms acting as walkways lay ahead of them. Grain paddies. But today must have been a quiet day for the farm, as there wasn't a soul in sight.

"Remember back in the day on Kublar when we were about to get hit?" Neck asked into the comm.

"I wasn't on Kublar," answered Bombassa, shutting down the discussion. "Toots, break right and we'll skirt the paddy just beneath the berm on this side of the trees."

"On it, Top," said Toots, backing into the concealing embrace of the wood line.

"Top, just got traffic from *Centurion* REPO," Nobes said. "She's tracking a buildup of forces in the cities and around Blake. They're also tracking some radio chatter primed on our grid. Something about deploying a thresher."

"Thresher?" Nix asked.

"That was the closest they could get on the translation from the Kimbrin."

"Low and slow," Bombassa warned.

Victory Company,
Second Platoon, Zombie Squad
Approaching Phase Line Rappex

Sergeant Lynx called his men to a halt. Legionnaires scattered into the bush with barely a sound, allowing the NCO to direct his attention to the chatter coming over the platoon channel in the L-comm.

"Somethin' bugging those ears o' yers, Sar'nt?" Diggs asked.

"Negative. LT called us to hold up while we effect link-up with local militia scouts."

"You can't clint me, Sar'nt. You can't dress up a bullitar and run it through the jungle on its own to call it a scout."

"Be that as it may, it's what we got so it's what we got."

"Roger that."

"Hey Diggs, what's that PFC doing?" Lynx asked.

Diggs slipped into the foliage. If Lynx didn't know any better, he'd swear the man had just gone native reptile on him. The legionnaire seemed to be swimming in the grass, wriggling his rear end as though a colony of lava-ants had eaten their way past his armor and synth-prene. After a moment of discussion between him and the PFC, Diggs crept back.

"He launched a micro-peeper. Sent it to the trees to do a quick sweep of the ridge and the open grain paddy off to the left."

"That's good thinking on his part. Just remind him to call that out next time."

"Will do," Diggs said. "Still, not bad for a PFC right out of L-SAT."

Lynx laughed. "Is that what they're calling selection now?"

"Yeah. I think War Boss Chhun, or Cha-hoon or whatever, probably changed the name because LASP sounded a little limp."

Lynx's bucket bobbed in agreement with the man's guess. "Hey, your boy is looking for another date."

"Ugh. Karking privates." Diggs once more slunk down to his trooper, dropping into the shallow berm next to him. Lynx set his L-comm to monitor so he could listen in.

"You can just hit me with a ping, Drag," said Diggs. "You don't have to call me over. Don't they show you how to use the L-comm in L-SAT?"

"Yes, Corporal," PFC Wells answered. "But the drone feed is picking up a mass heat signature and I wanted you to come over and make sure I wasn't slagging it."

Diggs looked over the settings on the battle board strapped to the kid's wrist. The display was set so that only someone with a Legion bucket could see the active screen. He ran his hand over the device, noting that everything seemed to be in order. The kid was right. One of the huts on the other side of the grain paddy did have a heat signature that was wavering. It could be a stove attempting to boil water... or it could be something much worse.

"Sar'nt Lynx. Sending you a feed from the Drag's peeper."

"When do I lose the nickname and get a real call sign?" Wells asked.

Diggs pushed the kid's bucket. "When you're not an anchor around my neck pulling me down. Actually, Anchor's not bad. I'll think about it."

Lynx stared at the display inside his HUD, then switched to the platoon net. "LS-339 to LS-059A."

"Go ahead, Lynx," came the reply from Lieutenant Chopisan, call sign Chopper.

"Got a strange heat sig on the following grid. It's a ways away, but if we're not careful, and we just happen to hop the wrong fence..." Lynx let the end of his statement run cold.

"Stand by," Chopper responded.

In the half second it took for the L-comm to go on standby, the shed in the distance exploded. A half second after that, the top of the hill they were all hiding behind blew apart, sending mud, stone, and bone tumbling.

"Zombie Squad! Call it!" Lynx shouted into the L-comm.

The sergeant's two team leaders rattled off that they were all okay, and that the leejes they were responsible for were chomping at the bit to get after it, whatever it was.

Lynx broke into the platoon net. "I have enemy armor at seventy-one degrees magnetic at two hundred meters. Pushing feed to you now. Tank is an LM-3 Red Foot light armored vehicle."

Wells shouted over his external speakers. "Got another one poking up."

"Chopper, this is Lynx. Got a second LM-3 on the hillside tucked into some lumber at eighty-four degrees magnetic at three hundred and seventy-two meters. That victor is aimed toward the farm road. I don't think we were the target."

"Roger that," Chopper sounded back. "I have the militia team at our flank. Looks like they skirted too close to the road and woke the dogs. Your find, your kill, Zombie. Call it!"

"We'll take the one on the hill. That will let us recon by fire and see if there's only the two dogs barking."

"Take it, Leej."

Lynx switched the settings in his bucket from patrol ops to objective assault. "Digger! Split off and run wide below the ridge line. Keep it on the compass. Everyone else with me!"

The leejes split into the wood line. Diggs took his team well below the lip of the hill while Lynx took the rest of the squad on a more direct route hugging the top. Both were well below where enemy sensors could detect unless they were running drones or had planned for someone to come through the triple canopy like Victory Company was doing. The rest of Second Platoon opened up on the main tank, dousing it with copious amounts of blaster fire to suppress any ground troops while rigging heavier weapons to deal some more serious damage.

The company commander, Major Riggs, sounded over the L-comm. "Harvester, this is Victory Actual. I have hardened emplacement of forces on Phase Line Rappex. One RV in the open and another under cover on the following grids. Request air support on phase line, rear of my position, how copy over."

Lynx shunted that net to the background, bringing the squad net to the front. Gliding through the forest, the NCO pushed a squad halt through the L-comm. "Trent! What is that under that moss? HUD is showing it as reflective."

The legionnaire moved up to the tree trunk, not bothering to be quiet as the sounds of battle over the ridge intensified. He pulled the moss from the tree, exposing what looked like a tiny drone that had settled into the crook of a branch. He smashed it with the enhanced knuckles on his gloves.

"Crap. Hoof it, Zombie!" Lynx shouted.

Both sections of the squad took off at a sprint, crashing through the thick foliage like bullitars to breakfast. They climbed and ducked, scampering as fast as the terrain would allow.

"Put those buckets on signal catch. I want to know if we have any more eyes on us!" Diggs yelled into the L-comm.

The first mortar rounds impacted the area roughly fifty meters behind them. The next volley walked the rounds deeper into the forest, shattering the landscape in the hopes of catching the wily legionnaires.

"Lynx, it's Chop. We plotted the track for that mortar team. We know where they are but can't hit 'em."

"No worries, LT. We're on the run. We'll set up on the mortar team and RV in a few blinks."

"You already on that hill?" Chopper asked.

"On it and own it!" Lynx called back.

The ground swung to the back side of the rise, crawling along the green as their mimetic armor captured the look of the landscape and pasted it on their armor.

"Lynx, it's Diggs. I have the mortar team."

"I want that gun!"

The smile on Diggs's face could almost be heard through the L-comm. "You know I always get you the best stuff."

Lynx and his crew belly-crawled up to the lip of the slope. The initial rush had been to get them here. Now a quick peek before the reap would allow them to gauge what they were walking into just on the off chance this was more than it seemed. As two tanks and a mortar team seemed like the wrong play for guarding a road against legionnaires, Lynx couldn't shake the feeling that there was something he hadn't sniffed out yet.

"Freeze in place," came the emergency action message flashing in Zombie Squad's HUD. When the squad froze, Diggs spoke. "Mortar belongs to us. You got motion sensors on the back side of that ridge. IR interrupt trips." Sergeant Lynx mumbled a silent curse. "Trent, kill those trips."

Trent took a bot from a belt pouch and spread the legs into a crab the size of a Drusic stone spider. The little thing scampered over the hill, working its magic on the infrared projectors and their receivers that acted as invisible tripwires. Real trips with actual wires as thin as a human hair were harder to spot and could be rigged to be harder to defeat.

"Laser out," Trent reported.

The leejes crept up to the top of the hill and spotted the tank just below on the other side, in what looked like a small kids' fort in the side of the slope. The MCR troopers had dug out a flat terrace with plenty of tree cover remaining from which to hang tarps and camo netting. A wall of interlocking logs were set up behind sand barriers, and everything was hidden by what looked like rotting lumber made to seem as though it had fallen over.

The LM-3 Red Foot tank sat on top of heavy struts. It was only a little longer than a Republic combat sled, but sported triple-layer armor with reactive plating and a low-yield shield generator. The Republic had never bought them because the generator not only powered the shield, it also ran the repulsor array the tank floated on—which meant that for maximum protection of the deflector screen, the tank had to be stationary. The name "Red Foot" had come from the crimson glow coming off the repulsors when it was moving at max speed.

Two Kimbrin on foot leaned against the lumber, smoking stim sticks and watching the battle on the lower ground play out with field mags. They obviously had no idea they were now being monitored at short distance by the enemy.

Lynx waved his hand toward the two Kimbrin, then duck-walked down the slope toward the back of the tank. As he put his palm on the vehicle, Trent and a second legionnaire used their suppressed sidearms to dump rounds into the backs of the MCR skulls.

"Forward down. Clear to hatch," Trent called to his squad leader.

Lynx, waiting at the back of the cupola, rapped his knuckles on the top of the tank. He waited two heartbeats, then knocked again.

"Hey, stop messing around," a voice called in Kimbrin from the inside of the tank, its top hatch open. "Did you get ahold of Vixx yet?"

The tank commander popped his head up, then raised himself slightly higher to get a better look at the ruined skulls of the two men who were supposed to be his target observers. Lynx quickly wrapped a hand around the man's mouth and yanked him free of the vehicle.

"Hey! I can't do this by myself, you know," said another Kimbrin voice from inside the vehicle. A second head shot up to see where his commander had gone, only to find himself staring into the waiting barrel of a suppressed pistol. The round sprayed the contents of his skull across the front of the cupola and the gun barrel, giving the Red Foot a matching red top.

Diggs, observing on overwatch, pushed his message into the L-comm. "All threats buried, Sar'nt. You got all the goodies."

Lynx motioned to Trent. "The tank is elevated to send the gun out to long-range targets and the opposing hills on this valley. If you feather the repulsor and tip the nose at a down angle, you might be able to give our friends down there a hand."

"Always wanted to drive somethin' like this, Sar'nt." Trent dove into the cupola, while Sergeant Lynx watched the legionnaire's bucket feed in a corner of his HUD.

A red shimmer appeared beneath the tank as the repulsors hummed to life. Clumsily at first, the legionnaire coaxed the repulsors to hoist the back of the vehicle in such a way as to give them an angle on the armored vehicle harassing the company below.

"Easy enough. Rolling the next round to chamber."

"Come down five more clicks," Lynx said, passing off his prisoner to a legionnaire who stood at the base of the tank. "There it is. You good?"

"Locked, Sar'nt," Trent responded.

"Send it."

The camo netting and palm fronds fluttered from the concussion of the blast, showering the terrace in dust and thunder. The round sailed into target at nine klicks per second, detonating on the sunken MCR tank in the field with a shower of sparks. A luminescent shimmer poured off the tank like water off a freshly washed grav sled as its shield died away.

"Reload and repeat," Lynx said over L-comm.

"Reloading. Repeating shot."

The gun barked again, whipping up a cyclone of dust to obscure their vision for a half second. The round impacted the upper armor with a secondary explosion as the reactive plates detonated the force of the blast outward, away from the tank crew. Repulsors flared from the mud-encrusted vehicle, throwing off bits of muck in all directions as the vehicle jumped from its entrenched position.

Lynx got on the comm. "Chopper, this is Lynx."

The second platoon commander's voice came on clear and crisp, no sign of the flurry of shouts and battlefield sounds penetrating the bucket. "Got you, Lynx. Good hit. Let 'em run. We got 'em right where we want 'em!"

Lynx watched as the trees on the other side of the grain paddies bowed outward, vomiting out a Legion main battle tank. The armored juggernaut splashed into the flooded fields, its repulsors creating a cyclone of water around its base. Massive geysers of mud and water trailed it as it raced to flank the enemy vehicle.

"Say good night and suck it," Trent called from inside his own tank.

A shock wave pulsed out from the skin of the MBT, flashing across the paddies into the smoking enemy Red Foot. Its repulsors died in the wake of the energy pulse, and the bulky armored vehicle splashed into the water of the paddy, leaving its back end up in the air, a perfect stationary target for the advanced AI-assisted systems on the MBT.

The MBT's main gun barked with a thunder crack that sent water venting away from the vehicle in a wave that nearly left the paddy dry. The round struck the enemy tank near the cupola, detonating the entire vehicle in a shower of sparks and fire.

"Lynx, it's Chop. Sitrep."

Harvester Command Element
Temporary Ops Center
Bulldog Four

Chhun watched the holoboard that flared from his helmet. The bucket's projection emitter would do until he could get the combat control bot to set up a real battle board projector. While he could work everything from his bucket, other command staff might need to study the map to get an idea of things he needed or what they could do to maximize operations.

"General Chhun," said the control bot.

"Yeah, Chaz."

"Update from Major Riggs. They've encountered an armor element using LM-3 Red Foots to guard a hidden mobile gun platform. "

Chhun shook his head. "How many of those things did the MCR steal?"

"Unknown at this time, sir. Six are now accounted for, four of which are under our control. Venom Company is dispatching a unit to take control of the site and the remaining Red Foot."

"Casualties?" Chhun asked.

"Sixteen E-KIA and no friendly forces."

That was good. Legionnaires weren't immortal by any stretch, so it was nice to hear that the men were rolling on without taking casualties thus far, even while attached to indigenous fighters.

"Thank you." Chhun waved to the bot, dismissing it to go back to whatever it had been doing before it rolled up. Then he opened a channel to *Centurion*.

"I was wondering when you'd call," Admiral Deynolds said over their private comm.

"How are you looking up there?"

"We just cracked the spine on that carrier. The destroyers are moving to protect the battleship. Their tactics aren't awful and they've handed us a few surprises—namely, knocking our task force commander into the mud."

"I'm good," Chhun remarked.

"Second Batt is rigging the last of the gear now. They'll be ready to jump when you need them."

"Good deal. We're advancing to Broken Window now. Once we have that, we'll go to phase four."

"Lots of moving parts here, Legion Commander," Deynolds noted.

"*Former* Legion commander. As long as we shoot, move, and communicate, we'll roll this up and return this planet to the people."

19

Kill Team Victory
Staging Outside Fort Blake

"*Centurion* REPO, this is Victory Seven. I have eyes on Objective Broken Window. I confirm hostiles in prep for indirect fire on friendly forces." Bombassa flipped through the targeting algorithm in his bucket, marking enemy troop movements priming the main artillery batteries for use against the Legion approach. "MCR regulars are moving into support positions throughout objective area. Tagging all available locations through active targeting and monitored enemy net."

"Good copy, Victory Seven. Stand by for Harvester Actual."

Bombassa kept his vigil on the base some distance away, using a combination of pirated video feeds and the team's NS-151 spotting scope. The crew had spent the last hour running confirmation reports back and forth to *Centurion* in order to coordinate the attack with the Legion elements on the ground. What came next required precision, and Chhun had OP-conned them to Lieutenant Apollo to give them the best chance of success.

"Bassa, it's Chhun. Heard you ran into some trouble earlier."

"Not us, sir. Although we were close by and warned V-Co that there could be enemy units along the route to Broken Window."

"Good deal. They got it handled. Ready for the handoff?"

"I am. The feeds are yours, sir. Good luck."

"See you on the other side, First Sergeant."

Bombassa turned away from his observation point to survey the rest of his kill team. They'd pulled tarps, un-strapped equipment tie-downs, and rigged their gear to the two all-terrain vehicles hidden at the base of the cliff that marked the entrance to the Kam Dho Valley. He climbed into the TC seat beside Nobes, who'd taken the wheel on the first GMV. Nix stepped on the side rail and climbed into the gunner's roost where the N-50 waited for him to paint the landscape with its deadly blaster fire.

Neck and Toots checked the bundles strapped to the twin repulsor bikes they'd had Bear "requisition" for them. The two hovering riders were ahead of the GMVs and primed to go.

"Ya know, I usually don't agree to ride a rocket straight into the teeth," Neck huffed.

While the helmet hid his look of disappointment, Nobes's voice made the sentiment clear. "You were prac-tically a hullbuster when we recruited you!"

"Ready up," Bombassa cut in. "Time to hit this and take our toys back."

Harvester Command Element
Temporary Ops Center
Bulldog Four

"Tell me when you've got me on the nets, Chaz."

The robotic assistant continued to manipulate the planetary broadcast and network systems while it turned to address its superior. "Yes, General Chhun. We are keyed into all the required broadcasts. You may proceed when ready and I will switch to live."

A floating holocam swished slightly from side to side, its recording light not yet red.

MakRaven, who was being careful to stay out of the floating holocam's line of sight so as not to be caught in the eventual broadcast, winked at Chhun. "You know, the last time a Legion commander decided to put his mug across the holochannels from the battlefield, we got a galaxy-wide civil war and a brand-new government out of it."

"I'm going for something a bit more low-key than a summary execution on an intergalactic net," Chhun said. "This message is only for Kima."

He pointed to Chaz, letting the bot know he was ready. A heartbeat later, the outer ring of the holocam's main lenses glowed a faint red, a signal that Chhun was now addressing all of Kima.

"My fellow Republic citizens. My name is Cohen Chhun, former commander of the Legion. I am broadcasting to you today from an undisclosed location on Kima. I am here because the leaders you elected to represent you within the Republic petitioned the Senate and the House of Liberty for aid after the brutal takeover of your government by factions within the Mid-Core Rebellion. It is our sincere hope that we can address this matter with the utmost speed and professionalism, and return control of the planet to its lawfully elected legislature. Members of the Republic military, working in concert with the 131st Legion, will do everything in our power to safeguard the citizens of Kima as we work to set things right.

"I have a message as well for the members of the Mid-Core Rebellion, those who would slink out of the shadows and murder innocent people in order to take something that is not yours. I offer you this one chance to abandon the places you've taken and release the hostages you hold. Doing so will gain you some measure of goodwill from this point forward. Those who refuse this offer, or who attempt to hinder our efforts to restore law and order, will be met with the assembled might of the 131st Legion and our allies. May whatever higher power you pray to grant you mercy, because we will not.

"Finally, to those fighting for democracy, my message is simple: Stay strong. We're coming."

Chhun snapped his fingers to signal the bot to end the broadcast. Chaz unplugged from the ship-based transmitter inside the APC, retracting the wire so it could move freely around the cargo bay again.

"Oba, sir," said MakRaven admiringly. "You were the very epitome of the Republic mouthpiece until you went all serial killer, and then all warrior poet with that 'We're coming' business. No signoff, no 'Oba bless the Republic', just 'We're coming.' That was some attack-dog-level bark. You sure you weren't cut out to do the job back at Rep-One?"

"When this is over, we want the Republic to see that we stand guard on the walls, Sergeant Major," Chhun said. "We don't want the people we're trying to defend thinking that we'll go back to that shiny armor tax collector nonsense from the House of Reason. That means be person-able, be polite, but have a plan to kill everyone."

MakRaven rolled his hand as though reporting to some posh head of state. "You got my vote."

Super-Destroyer *Centurion*
Combat Information Center

Admiral Deynolds watched the combat clock count down to the next phase of Operation Atlas Wake. The maneuvers and feints to this point had been only the opening salvos, and the suffered so far—the loss of pilots and ships and the injuries to a few legionnaires—were merely the initial scrapes in the very brutal fight that was to come. The fight that happened when that clock reached zero.

"We are go for second strike in two minutes," Apollo said. The naval intelligence officer aboard the ship was one of the best intel sources Deynolds had ever worked with, and Apollo had leveraged all her resources to give them the sight picture they had thus far. There had been some intel misses, like the enemy's light tanks, which they should have anticipated seeing as those were a relic of the Kimbrin civil war. The Valhawk drone missiles were a much bigger surprise.

But Deynolds was less worried about the misses they now knew about, and more worried about the ones they didn't. What other dangers did the leejes on the ground and her fleet in orbit face?

As orbit was her territory, she reviewed the last few hours as she watched the numbers on the clock. They'd cracked the MCR carrier ship with a combination of concentrated fire from *Centurion* and the cruisers flying escort, and the other Rebellion craft pulled away from the planet when the MCR carrier split in half. They knew not to jump out of the system for fear that the heavy Republic ships at the Lagrange point would use a combination of tractor tech and the planet's gravitational fields to shatter their hyperdrives, but they were effectively out of the fight for now.

It could have been worse. Legion intel suggested that there was a call for House of Reason loyalists to come to the defense of Kima. So far, that hadn't happened. And maybe it wouldn't. Maybe those rogue captains and crews were content to play pirate, assuaged by their sense of moral superiority. And maybe they recognized that a showdown with the Republic could end all of that in a hurry.

Still, there was a feeling settling into the pit of Deynolds's stomach that she just couldn't shake. The same feeling she'd had when they faced the Black Fleet. There was something they were all missing. The Mid-Core Rebellion had some groups of Kimbrin running around with tech that could barely scratch the paint, and yet other groups were dropping advanced drone and battle gear. The MCR was a disjointed organization, certainly. It always had been. But this was a giant step beyond. And where did they get all these ships without setting off alarms with every intelligence community in the Republic?

The House of Reason had legitimized the MCR in a final fit of desperation during Article Nineteen. Had that alliance of convenience carried over to the present? Were those loyal to the House of Reason now one and the same with the Mid-Core Rebellion? The two groups had always seemed mutually exclusive, but the galaxy had been rife with strange bedfellows and stranger things. There was no telling what some might do to retain—or take back—power.

As the clock ticked down to zero, Deynolds pocketed those thoughts for another time. "Fire when ready."

Captain Aguiar adjusted the holo-lenses feeding him real-time data in augmented reality about the nature of his ship. He reached for the ghostly image only he could see, the glasses reading his motions to translate them to commands inside the computer network under his control. The pink-skinned Endurian primed the holo for the fire control center so he could watch as his subordinates enacted his orders. "Fox-Con," he said. "Plot a firing solution on target package Bravo. Insert a five-second delay and execute Charlie."

Knowing the procedure, First Lieutenant Marinkovich read his lines to the letter, knowing that the audience for this next performance would be the enemy at Fort Blake and possibly the entirety of Kima. "I have the lock. Execute target package Bravo. Insert five-second delay and launch Charlie."

"Aye, sir. Target package Bravo is locked. Firing," repeated the fire control technician.

Somewhere off *Centurion*'s flank, a Republic guided missile cruiser launched an orbital-to-surface missile. Sensor data flew back and forth between the launch point and the projectile headed for the ground around Fort Blake.

As the weapon entered the upper atmosphere, *Centurion* drifted closer to the pole to get a better angle on a target in another hemisphere. At five seconds past the missile's launch, the super-destroyer leveled a barrage of super-blaster cannon fire into an unsuspecting target on Kima.

Nadurn Industrial Hangar
Kantro Star Port, Kima

Nadurn Interplanetary Shipping had suffered more than once at the hands of Republic customs inspectors cracking down on cargo moving to known MCR hot spots. The government had even imposed sanctions and embargoes on those planets so as to discourage anyone from shipping there. As a result, most of the shipping to those locations had been contracted out to edge world companies or private contractors who didn't give one iota what the Republic imposed or discouraged.

But Nadurn had settled on Kima, hoping that by locating itself in the Kantro Star Port, a continent away from Kham Dho City and the nearby Republic military base, it would keep critical eyes off of it. Kima made for a great jumping-off point for all their legitimate shipping enterprises—which delivered primarily to core worlds—while still allowing them to cash in on the big-money MCR contracts. It was risky, as getting caught would result in the Republic shutting down the company and selling its assets, but the MCR made the risk worthwhile.

Unfortunately for Nadurn, they'd shown up on a few too many intel reports as a suspected MCR supplier, and as a result, they had caught the notice of Cohen Chhun. The former Legion commander had reached out to his contacts in the House of Liberty and identified the prolific shipping company as one of his prime targets during the initial phases of the campaign.

The first rounds from *Centurion*'s ventral heavy cannons blasted into Nadurn's dedicated landing pads, turning the duracrete into a volcano of magma and shattered stone. Fragmentation and debris flew for kilometers. The next few hits were direct attacks against the Nadurn shipping facility. The company had just received a shipment of micro-reactors that were to be used to put mothballed starships back into operation for the liberation of the planet from the Republic. Legion Dark Ops had followed targeted executives and shipping managers for weeks in order to confirm the shipment was on scene when *Centurion* made its strike.

The presence of the micro-reactors on site made the strike exponentially more effective. When *Centurion* hammered the building where the reactors were housed, the reactors went critical, and the resulting electromagnetic pulse decimated electronics everywhere on the continent—and wiped Nadurn Interplanetary Shipping from the face of the galaxy in a fireball that could be seen from orbit.

Kill Team Victory
Assault on Fort Blake

The repulsor whine of the rocket bikes over the wet terrain on the approach to Fort Blake served as a backdrop for the ground mobility vehicles favored by Legion reconnaissance. With their fording kits keeping the water free from the engines, the machines crashed and juked through the paddies until reaching a dirt road that gave them a straight shot into the back of the camp.

Blake was immense by military standards for deployed off-planet bases. Covering roughly three point five kilometers, Blake housed a multitude of military units as well as the RIAS, the Republic Interplanetary Air Station, which was dedicated to atmospheric monitoring for the entire planet of Kima. The base terminated in a peninsula jutting into the Kam River, where several estate houses had been converted into military headquarters.

The rocket bikes picked up speed as the two GMVs pounded the road behind them on their rugged all-terrain tires. Neck set the controls on the machine he was riding and then waved his knife hand like a shark fin against the front of his bucket. Nobes raced up to the rocket bike, bringing the GMV alongside so Neck could make the climb over to the vehicle. He climbed into the passenger seat behind Bombassa, locking his N-4X into the pintle mounted to the door.

Bombassa swiveled the heavy squad automatic blaster on its gyroscopic mount on the frame of the vehicle. He aimed the weapon and then pointed along the barrel. Neck followed the man's direction, noting a gaggle of repulsor-driven technicals exiting the front gate nearly a klick away and uselessly firing small arms from the beds.

One of the converted utility trucks had an old-time MK-1 SAB on a fabricated pintle.

Warnings blared in Neck's HUD. Something had set off the indirect fire warning indicator.

"Incoming!" he shouted. A force of habit. The others would have received the same warning from their own buckets.

The trucks veered from the road to splash down into the grain paddy. They cut across several plantings before they found another road. Toots had jumped to the other gun truck just moments prior, taking the heavy frag launcher at the back of the vehicle. He cycle-charged the weapon, bringing the battery core to full capacity.

The road they'd just left exploded in clumps of packed earth and water. The MCR running the mortar pit inside of Blake had fired on the most likely approach—the main back road toward that side of the camp. By switching to a less improved road along another track, the kill team had evaded the targeting line the MCR had on them, leaving them free from fire.

"Got a heavy coming out of the gate. Give me some smoke to obscure that thing's main gun!" Nobes cried out from behind the wheel.

The base's main gate had spit out a six-wheeled monstrosity in the form of an L-TAV. Massive, mud-chewing tires supported an armored body with a long-barreled twenty-five-millimeter blaster cannon on top. The light tactical armored vehicle gun ports were slit down the length of the armor so that those inside could fire their small arms outside. Smoke dispersion launchers on the back hatch, along with external container racks, rounded out the beast's gear. It was a perfect support vehicle, except that its high center of gravity made it unsuited to negotiating the dips between the paddies and the roads.

The L-TAV rumbled behind the technical trucks, which slid across the terrain on repulsors, seeking to find an angle to engage the legionnaires.

"I see it," Toots said. "Let's worry about those technicals first, huh?"

He depressed the butterfly trigger on the automatic grenade launcher. The weapon chewed through its twenty-millimeter linked ammunition, sending out a nine-round burst toward the approaching trucks. High-explosive dual-purpose rounds slammed into the advancing technicals, detonating the engine cores of the front two trucks and turning them into a conflagration of caustic, inky smoke and slag. The battery cores soon detonated as well, engulfing both trucks in green flame. With the burning wreckage stopping up the road and the awkward decline into the grain paddy to either side, the L-TAV had no choice but to reverse direction.

Nobes swerved around to yet another road, giving further headache to the forward observers trying to sight them in. Several drones were launched to gain a target lock on them, but with Bombassa and *Centurion* REPO pirating the feeds, Nix was quick to be notified and let off his leash with the N-50 mounted to the back of the GMV. It was always tough to keep aerial bots in the sky when it was full of heavy blaster fire.

A series of pops in the air announced the unleashing of a torrent of drones. For a moment they were a swirl of chaos, but they quickly formed an organized whirlwind of coordinated flight patterns. Nix turned his N-50 on the swarm, attempting to shoot them from the sky as they darted and zipped in unison like a flock of birds evading a predator.

"How's my clock?" Nobes asked.

"Fifteen seconds," Bombassa shouted.

Behind the cloud of murderous machines forming into a swarm, three Psydon-era SLICs rose from the security walls near the air station. Updated with fresh paint, some new armor, and that same wobbly vertical boost before the repulsors gave way to the thrusters, the SLICs were fully kitted out with side-mounted machine blasters and full of battle-hungry Kimbrin looking to do some damage to the tiny Legion team they planned on pummeling.

"How's my distance?" Wello shouted from the driver's seat of the other vehicle.

"Stay along this track and we should be good!" Nobes said.

Bombassa shut down all side conversations in the two trucks as he started counting down. "Five... four..."

Doc Chance took the countdown as his cue for the autopilot-driven repulsor bikes to increase speed and head straight for the camp's outer wall. The first bike struck the barrier head-on, and the five kilograms of synthetic high explosive on its back erupted, sending out concussive waves of force and heat that blew through the duracrete wall in a maelstrom of stone and powder. The second bike raced right through the gaping hole and into the camp, heading straight for the largest broadcast tower on this side of the base. Its explosives had a similar effect, shattering the struts on the tower and nearly taking out one of the SLICs in the process.

"Two... one..." Bombassa finished.

A missile raced in from the atmosphere and detonated above the base in a brilliant flare of white light. The

SLICs, full of armed Kimbrin ready to take the fight to the annoying little leej team, suddenly powered down and fell back into the base. Though they dropped out of sight behind the wall, the sounds of the horrific crash told the kill team all they need to know.

Fort Blake—aka Objective Broken Glass—just had its lights put out.

"Take us in!" Bombassa shouted. Diving into the L-comm, he made contact with the Victory Company command element. "Riggs, this is Bombassa. I confirm positive EMP strike over Objective Broken Glass. We are going in for the guns. I say again. We are going for guns before they reboot."

"Copy, First Sergeant. We'll meet you in the middle," Riggs responded.

"KTF, sir! Bombassa out."

Victory Company, Zombie Squad
Assault on Fort Blake

"Sergeant Lynx, this is Chopper!"

"Go for Lynx," the legion NCO said into his bucket.

General Chhun's unorthodox EMP strike over Fort Blake had put out the lights. Sergeant Lynx, watching from his staged position, saw that intelligence had been correct; the MCR had been relying on the Republic goodies they'd taken for defense of Blake. The base was in various stages of chaos as soldiers and technicians rushed about madly, trying to get systems back online.

Lynx knew what would be coming next. A variation of orders that ultimately led to the same goal—get inside Fort Blake and pave the way for the rest of the 131st to do the same.

"Got a change of mission for you, Sergeant. Take Zombie Squad and roll behind that MBT straight into the entry control point. The auto-turrets and sentry guns are down for the next few minutes until they can reset. I need you to take the ECP tower and eliminate anyone trying to get a reboot on those guns so we don't get torn to shreds."

"Moving, sir. Lynx out." Switching to his squad net, he broadcast to Diggs. "You catch that?"

"Orders issued and we're already shambling!"

When Lynx was first assigned to the Zombie Squad, the men had already come equipped with the nickname. The previous squad boss had been given some of the most intense intrusion missions on behalf of Second Platoon, and the squad had proven themselves impossible to kill unless you got a headshot. Which was exactly what happened to the previous squad leader. The Legion had access to some of the best medical tech in the galaxy, but there was no coming back from a high-gain kinetic round to the head.

The team broke into a trot, catching up to the MBT about to crest the hill into the no-man's-land clearing that led to the base. The jungle had been deforested at half a klick as a matter of security so that anyone trying to rush the main gate had no cover or concealment from the entry control point. Leading up to the gate, the serpentine road had been partitioned off with cement barriers and razor-mag wire in order to force anyone driving up to the entrance to take a slow and meandering path.

With all the powered security measures down, the MBT increased its repulsors for max height in its hover over the terrain. It easily cleared the barriers, and the heavy thrust keeping the sixty-ton battle tank floating above the terrain crushed the razor-mag wire into the mud. The Zombies continued their jog behind the armored behemoth until it got to the entrance.

Tire depressions ahead of the tank served as a visual confirmation of what the Dark Ops team had reported—an L-TAV had run from this side of the camp to try and take out Kill Team Victory on its rush into the back of the base to take out the artillery batteries. With the L-TAV gone to pursue the Dark Ops kill team, the opportunity for the Zombies to get their own tank inside the vehicle gate became too easy to resist. The MBT would wreak far more havoc from here than it would trying to squeeze its ways through the opening the kill team had taken. On top of which, a tank entering through the main vehicle gate would be able to cover any legionnaires who poured in through the smaller personnel gate, once they bypassed the security shack and tower.

Lynx and Diggs ran by the Legion tank, careful to stay an arm's length away to avoid its repulsor field. The projector's hum was still powerful enough to vibrate the plates of their armor on the way by.

Diggs pulled a control plate from the door housing. "Power's still down. Patch me."

Lynx punched in an access code they'd been given to interface with the tank in the event they needed the machine's entry kit for situations just like this. He dragged a cable from the opened plate into the waiting hands of his team leader.

"Ten seconds," Diggs said.

Lynx looked back to make sure the dispersion on Zombie Squad was as tight as they'd trained it. They'd positioned themselves around the various barriers and holes formed by the serpentine road, each man taking a sector to make his own. Anything that popped its head out would get vaporized thanks to the copious range and VR house drills courtesy of Republic tax credits at work. Lynx looked to the top of the tank and was satisfied to see that from somewhere in the depths of the armored vehicle someone was working the coaxial repeating blaster.

"System is powered. Punching the door," Diggs called into the L-comm.

Lynx pulled to a barrier, wishing he had a CROWS system like the one on the tank. At times like these Lynx would have preferred that the Legion didn't put so much stock in their buckets keeping their skulls set onto their necks. A little extra armor goes a long way.

The massive impervisteel door separated at its center and recessed into the meter-thick duracrete walls on either side. The base seemed eerily quiet once the door opened, with no sign of the MCR forces reported to be in control of the camp.

Diggs pulled the power feed from the wall, which turned out to be the catalyst for a wave of blaster bolts that sailed through the now-open vehicular entry gate. The bolts impotently pinged off the front armor of the tank and ricocheted to other courses, forcing the hunkered legionnaires to keep their heads down.

Farther down on the serpentine road, Trent threw a drone into the air. The flying bot flashed from his position behind a duracrete barrier to sail over the wall. "Boss!" he called over the comm. "We need to breach. Got a triple at fifty meters looking to ruin our day with a double Rippy!"

Double Rippy was squad lingo for a recoilless rifle that fired seventy-five-millimeter, chemically projected shells to harass or disable light armored vehicles. While the Legion-model MBT was anything but light, with the right warhead the enemy rocket could damage crucial armor or weapons, taking the armored vehicle out of the fight while it underwent repairs.

"Rocket inbound, Rhino Zero Two!" Lynx called to the tank.

Without warning to the leejes around it, the sixty tons of weaponized aggression moved laterally, crashing through more razor-mag wire and duracrete barriers designed to keep anything that wasn't a Legion tank on the road. An instant later, the projectile rocketed through the open armored doors, flew through the expanse, and turned the trees in the distance into a smoking ruin.

"Lynx, it's Gekko. I have a LOS to the Rippy."

Having the squad long-range precision marksman telling you he has line of sight to the guys making your job a lot harder is like having someone tell you that they paid for your kaff in the morning. It's all just sunshine and giggles after that.

"Take it!" Lynx ordered into the L-comm.

"Firing."

The first bolt out of the N-65 variable output rifle sailed through the doors in answer to the recoilless rifle round. The gun team was in the process of loading the next shell into the back of the Rippy when the loader had his head splattered across the rest of the team.

"Hit," Gekko sounded to his crew. "Firing."

Another round sailed through the doors, and this one punching a hole through the shoddy plate carrier of the Kimbrin running the gun. The remainder of the team scattered behind buildings, vehicles, and anything they could find to get away from the scope being run over them by the Legion's Grim Reaper.

"Hit. Gun team is running but that security squad is being stubborn. They're dropping rounds on my position to keep my head down," Gekko announced to the squad.

"Digg, take the Drag on my go," Lynx said.

"Set!"

Lynx fired off two grenades from the underslung launcher on his blaster carbine. The rounds detonated just ahead of the recoilless rifle position, blowing apart several Kimbrin who were laying fire at the entry. Diggs and Wells rushed through the nearby personnel gate, blown up earlier courtesy of Kill Team Victory. Using the duracrete pylons for cover against the outpouring of blaster fire from the remaining MCR team, the two leejes slipped into the security shack on their side just beyond the entrance.

Lynx waited for his crew inside to lay suppressing fire before he ran diagonally across the opening. He slid behind the protection of the barriers and signaled that he was set. Outside, the remainder of his team sent a wave of blaster fire inside, dropping heads and giving the entry leejes room to move.

Ducking through the sandbags and duracrete pylons that led to the security shack on his side of the entrance, Lynx moved with the soft-footed grace of a mountain cat looking to get his murder on for lunch. A Kimbrin just ahead, with several scars and missing facial spikes, wrestled with a weapons malfunction in the PK-9 he was carrying. The sergeant, not slowing his pace, punched the back of the Kimbrin's skull with his kerambit knife, hooked the curved blade as it pierced the flesh, and severed the alien's spine.

As the enemy fell over dead, Lynx let his own N-4X magnetically lock to his armor to make room for him to draw his suppressed pistol. He snapped out the shoulder stock to give himself better control over the weapon on his advance through the space. As he exited the passage leading to the security tower, he stepped right into the surprised stare of another Kimbrin reloading his weapon. A freshly lit stim stick dangled from the Kimbrin's open mouth as Lynx put a round through his eye.

Just as the main security gate required passage through a serpentine maze of obstacles meant to slow down any vehicles who might wish to ram it, the personnel gate featured a six-lane checkpoint sized for personal vehicles. Five lanes went into the camp with one going out. A security shack—really a reinforced square bunker with blaster-proof glass and an inexplicably unmanned repeating-blaster nest on top—typically housed the soldiers who made sure there was no trouble at any of those five lanes. The rest of the MCR appeared to have holed themselves up inside the shack, looking to defend themselves from there.

With the rest of the fort still in chaos from the EMP attack, Zombie Squad pushed on the shack. Sergeant Lynx stacked against one of the shack's corners, not needing to stare off into the combat tracker in his HUD to know that Diggs and the new guy had done the same on their side of the entry. Farther on was a flight of spartan metal stairs that zigzagged their way up to an elevated security tower. The tower's previous occupants, providing overwatch of the Legion advance, had been eliminated by Victory Company snipers.

As Lynx and his squad held down the corners of the security shack, two legionnaires hurried their way up the tower. "Haul ass, leejes," Lynx growled into the L-comm. "I want blasters on this shack's roof before some mid gets the idea to get that gun up top firing."

The Legion tank boomed its main gun, and though it was not yet inside the gate for fear of being hit by someone in the tower or security shack, its blast was a violent addition to the chaos of those MCR troops who were still trying to figure out what to do while their systems desperately rebooted.

The legionnaires tasked with ascending the tower reached the top and sat down against the wall to cover the space to the security door. "Set on top. Bring it."

"And no kelhorn is trying to get up to the roof on that nest?" Lynx asked.

"Negative, Sar'nt. Scared sketless."

Lynx laughed and then gave the order for his team to stack up on the security shack door.

Diggs was first man up. He pulled something from his pack that looked like a bluish-gray donut, and slapped the thing against the combat glass of the shack. Then he cranked up the gain on his external speakers and broadcast to the MCR within. "I've just attached over two hundred grams of high explosive to this dinnik nest you're holed up in. Either you come out now, or I blow the thing and pour what's left of you into the street."

Moments later, Kimbrin fighters with their hands interlocked above their heads filtered from the shack into the waiting hands of the rest of Zombie Squad.

The tank was now free to move inside. It would only be a matter of time before more elements pushed through and really let the MCR have it.

Lynx broadcast to the Legion armor. "Rhino Zero Two, this is LS-339. You are clear to enter. We have tower and both gates secure. Hurry up so you don't miss the fun."

20

Kill Team Victory
Inside Fort Blake
Target: Artillery Battery

While Zombie Squad secured the vehicle and personnel gates, the members of Kill Team Victory barreled through the wet duracrete streets of Fort Blake until the tires of their GMVs caught enough traction to launch them forward again. They were well ahead of any friendly Legion elements, and were being hotly pursued by MCR technicals and at least one L-TAV. It was clear that the MCR, the newest inhabitants of Fort Blake, didn't care too much about getting their deposit back; buildings and sections of road alike exploded as the mids fired furiously at the nimble operators driving through occupied streets.

"Victory Seven, this is *Centurion* REPO. We have ISR drones on station. You have priority tasking."

"Roger out," Bombassa confirmed. Then, to his team, split up in two GMVs, he said, "Time to take different routes. Go!"

The side of the building next to them detonated in a shower of debris that pelted the second vehicle in their truck team. Both GMVs sprinted through the dust cloud, racing away from each other to make them a more difficult target.

"It's a good thing we have priority!" Neck shouted.

"If you're not too busy complaining, how's about you pull a dancer out of my bag and give them something else to shoot at?" Nobes snapped back.

"Hey, I can multitask." Neck swiveled in the vehicle's seat and groped at the rucks settled between Nix's feet.

The legionnaire manning the truck-mounted N-50 flashed dozens of blaster bolts in twin bursts toward the rallying enemy, who despite having lost most of their defensive capabilities in the unexpected EMP attack, knew enough to take up arms against a hostile vehicle drag-racing through the base. The legionnaire's intense N-50 bolts struck the sides of Q-hut-fabbed buildings and duracrete bunkers, catching a platoon's worth of Kimbrin that had come from the shadows to strike at them. Any living thing hit by the immense energy spears came apart like overcooked meat.

Rolling into the street on a parallel track to theirs was another of the regular army L-TAVs, using its heavy gun to try to slow if not outright stop the kill team. Often used by Republic army and marine armored cavalry forces, the L-TAV was well suited to its task. The light tactical armored vehicle rode on hyper-maneuverable run-flat tires that gripped the road while auto-targeting systems for the main gun kept the barrel steady enough to make shots on the run.

To a Republic military unit facing off against their own stolen gear, this would be a nightmare, especially since the systems inside were hardened against extreme ion attacks and could reboot in under a minute. But to a Legion kill team, this was just Tuesday.

Neck flipped the switch on what looked like a me-ter-long remote-control car with tires that matched that of the GMV. The little device flashed a ready signal in Neck's HUD, signaling that it was ready for diversion operations.

"Okay, Dancer," said Neck. "Get out there and show them what's up. But no kissing the clientele."

The little truck bounced and tumbled as Neck dropped it into the street, but small, stabilizing repulsors made sure the little unit ended up right side up.

Another heavy blaster cannon bolt shattered the street ahead of the GMV, putting a hole in the duracrete. The front tire on the truck went right into the hole and effectively turned into an anchor that smashed the brush guard into the ground and spun the vehicle to a stop facing the wrong way.

"Nobes!" Bombassa called out.

"Struts and train held. We're good!"

"Someone tell me why we couldn't get a repulsor truck!" Neck shouted.

The engine revved as Nobes bounced the wheel from the crater in a backwards rush out of the debris and smoke from the shot. The intel-sergeant-turned-death-race-driver then built up enough speed that applying the emergency brake and giving the tires a little turn sent the truck into a spin that put it facing in the right direction once more.

"Nice one," Bombassa noted as he sent scores of blaster bolts into a Q-hut that was forming up as an attack position for a squad of Kimbrin.

"I try," Nobes answered. He swerved the truck into an alley between a row of regular duracrete buildings until he found enough room to bring it into a tight skid that brought them back onto their original track.

Neck had taken advantage of the smoke cloud to instruct the dancer to project a hologram that looked exactly like another ground mobility vehicle, and had sent it racing from the cloud, down the side street toward the enemy L-TAV. Now he shared his display from the dancer to Bombassa. "Top, I'm watching the feed from the toy. The L-TAV is buying the hologram. It's trying to engage it. Should buy us a minute."

"Good," Bombassa grunted. He toggled into an incoming call from *Centurion* REPO as he decimated a fire team with his heavy blaster. "Go for Victory Seven."

"ISR shows another L-TAV spinning up at the motor pool to join the fight, and we have two combat sleds moving in from the palisade to your two o'clock."

"Roger, REPO. Break. Victory Seven for Harvester."

Chhun's voice was there in an instant, as though he was a guardian angel just waiting to be called upon. "How're we looking at taking control of those guns, Top? I can't fly air anywhere near that base until we get those guns and the ADA handled."

"We're on the wrong side of a rapidly closing net, sir. The base cannons are the LR-61s. They're hardened against EMP, so as soon as the blast washes out, the guns will attempt to reset. This Kimbrin force is surprisingly well trained, and they know exactly what we're gunning for. They're using other mounted assets to hem us in."

The team continued to race through the streets, aided by the fact that the L-TAV had been fooled, for the moment at least, by the holographic truck projected by Neck's dancer.

Bombassa ordered a hard stop as his vehicle sped alongside an empty barracks that had almost toppled when the L-TAV hit it earlier with its rear-mounted mortar system. "Nobes! I need markers on those two vics!" he shouted. "Get in there, find a place to hide, and launch the bot."

"On it!" The intel sergeant hopped out of the GMV, which quickly sped on its way, leaving Nobes to pick his way into the building alone. It was in rough shape, but luckily the duracrete had taken most of the blast, leaving the impervisteel frame relatively unharmed. Not so fortunately, the stairs hadn't made out nearly so well, and it took some creative climbing by Nobes to make his way to the second floor. He figured from up there he'd have a good enough hide to launch and monitor the drone undisturbed.

The instant he arrived, he threw a small bot, which rose on micro-repulsors so quiet they'd be hard to hear even without a war going on just outside. The little bot whizzed from the window and took a wide arc over the buildings and avenues. When it spotted the L-TAV supporting the two combat sleds, it dipped toward the ground, flitting between ruined structures and diving directly beneath the armored beast. From there it magnetized itself to the undercarriage of the machine, and as its drive motor died down, it began broadcasting a steady signal back to the legionnaire.

"Okay," Nobes reported over L-comm. "Tracker in place. You guys gonna swing back around to pick me up, or am I walkin'?"

21

Chhun scanned his battle board and the myriad assets at his disposal. Vindicator drones were almost set to fly but wouldn't get there in the time needed to save the first sergeant and his team. Meanwhile, the temporary ops center was starting to look a lot more permanent as more and more elements coming down from *Centurion* began staging near Chhun. Combat sleds, additional legionnaires, and a score of other munitions and supplies were piling up. But none of that would do any good when it came to helping Kill Team Victory unless Chhun could come up with a plan. And thinking of that wasn't getting any easier given the commotion that was taking place outside the dropship.

The general could sense his armored admin bot nearby. "Chaz, what's going on out there?"

"Sir, recovery teams have just returned with the downed pilots that got us to the planet. All were wounded and won't be flying again today. One was severely concussed after ejecting. That's the man screaming outside. He's adamant he gets back into the fight."

Chhun stepped out of the dropship into the middle of the argument, and everyone took a step back at the sight of their task force commander.

"Name, pilot," Chhun barked. Then he saw the man's face and declared, "Commander Danns."

Dax Danns had flown a mission in support of Chhun when he was still on Kill Team Victory. He had fought it out as long as he could when the Cybar appeared and very nearly wiped out Dark Ops altogether. He was a good man.

"Aye, sir!" Danns barked back.

Chhun turned on one of his legionnaires. "Tag and track, Leej."

"LS-731-Victor, sir. Call sign Knox."

"You're the Valkyrie team leader. Is Commander Danns good to go?"

"General, I wouldn't let any of these men fly today after what they've been through. It could be a risk to them as well as the mission, sir."

Chhun turned to Danns with a no-nonsense look. "Commander?"

The pilot brought his A-game. "I took a hard hit, sir. The ref is gonna start countin', that's his job. But this was a slip, not a fall. You let me climb into that bird and I'll choke-slam the sky, sir."

Chhun couldn't help but smile. Back before he'd become Legion commander, he'd blown off steam as one of the premier combatants in his weight class in the LCT. Legion combatives training was standard for all legionnaires, but there were those like Chhun who took it a step further and fought for pride in what passed for an amateur fighting federation onboard the various destroyers he jumped across the galaxy in while in Victory Company as a sergeant. Legion Combat Tournaments were a way for members of the Legion to test their mettle against the only opponent in the Republic capable of giving them a challenge: themselves. Back in the day, Chhun was legend in the Legion for his ferocity and tactical ability, and some of those old holovids still circulated.

Whether Danns somehow knew all of this—Chhun was as close to being a celebrity as the Legion had—or whether it was a lucky turn of speech, it was working. Chhun knew that urge to get back after it. He'd seen it in Twenties on Kublar and had done it himself countless times. And while sometimes you had to force a man to sit down for his own good, now didn't seem like one of those times. Not for Danns, anyway.

Chhun looked to the legionnaire. "I'll take the hit if you're right, LS-731. Let's get the commander back in the air."

The legionnaire simply nodded before he and his men escorted the other two pilots to the med unit operating out of a dropship.

"I expect you to deliver on that choke-slam," Chhun said, shooing Danns away. "*Centurion* is staging fighters on the ground so we can get up and in the action as soon as Blake's guns are asleep. I'll send the orders to make sure you get to the staging area."

Danns grinned and sprinted away from the general toward the nearest transport, his cube-shaped Wizzo bot following dutifully.

"Commander Danns," Chhun called after the pilot. "I may need someone in the air *before* those guns are asleep."

The smile on Danns's face only brightened. "I'm your ace, Legion Commander."

As the pilot climbed aboard a four-man repulsor sled that took him racing toward the flight staging area, Chhun turned and saw in the distance a huge boom of water erupting from the center of the pond where the downed shuttle, *Bulldog Four*, had once been stationed nearly a kilometer away. A boom sounded a split second after. Mud, muck, and rain surrendered to gravity after the explosion pelted the now-empty location. Three more shells sailed into the space in landscape-shattering explosions that echoed all throughout the valley.

The task force had received a warning via leejes on the ground, as well as through pirated drone assets coming back online after the EMP, that Fort Blake's cannons were back in the fight. And here was the proof. *Bulldog Four* and the three other dropships that had come to cohabit the space around the pond had moved to the new location just in time to avoid the MCR's latest pounding. Still, they hadn't gone far. Though they'd gotten the repulsors fixed and could make short jumps with the ship, long-range flight was still out of the question.

Which meant if the MCR was able to get eyes on Legion staging grounds—no easy feat while the Republic owned the skies, but possible with time and foot patrols—the result wasn't going to be pretty.

Chhun stepped back onto *Bulldog Four* and returned to his workspace. This was maddening. He knew the time would come where he would have the opportunity to go full General Rex and participate in direct combat, but for now, rank had its requirements.

"Chaz, give me an ACE report."

The Legion staff assistance bot stepped to the table in order to project holodisplays for its commander. "Bulldogs One through Four are intact with zero casualties reported. Basher Company, First Battalion, 131st Legion is reporting twelve legionnaires injured with four ambulatory."

"Did they not get the warning in time?"

MakRaven answered as he stomped his way up the ramp to Chhun's makeshift desk. "Negative. Kelhorns wanted to see if they could catch the incoming rounds and toss 'em back."

The bot added its own assessment. "My input does indicate that Basher Company would be amenable to attempt that tactic based on their previous missions. However it was most likely a case of bracketed fire on behalf of the artillery batteries attempting to spread the damage across our assembly area."

"I like my version better," MakRaven said. "And we did have to tranq some leejes attempting to crawl away from the medics so they could stay and fight. They're on their way up to *Centurion* for an oil change and should be back at it in a matter of hours."

"My concern is that it wasn't a lucky hit," Chhun said. "They may have units on the ground calling back positions over radio."

"We have not intercepted any such radio transmissions," Chaz said. "Their encryption is almost non-existent."

"Other ways to deliver a message beyond L-comm and radio," MakRaven observed.

Chhun stroked his chin. "Do we still have access to that dog handler?"

MakRaven nodded. "LS-1310, call sign Bouncer. Yes, sir. He's still out there."

Chaz followed up with more details. "His crew is a part of the Legion reconnaissance company for the Special Troops Battalion, sir."

MakRaven smiled devilishly. "I think it's the dog that's in charge."

Chhun had heard all that he needed. "Chaz, contact his CO and have them task Bouncer for an interdiction sweep of the AO using the dog."

"The dog is LWD-2060, call sign Bubbles, sir. I am tasking now."

"Bubbles? I ain't callin' it that," MakRaven said with a grunt. "What the hell kinda name for a dog is Bubbles?"

Chhun swiped away the holos projected by the bot, leaving the table empty so he could fill it with his own. "With telepathy powers, that dog can make you call him whatever he wants. But I'd rather we use him to locate any MCR spotters and knock them out of play. Then, as soon as Bombassa clears those guns, we can spin up Task Force Twelve and get them ready for the airfield. Once that happens we move this whole show to Blake."

"You mean if Bombassa knocks out those guns *and* we don't suffer another volley," MakRaven said in a tone even more dour than usual.

Chhun grimaced. The sergeant major was right. Kill Team Victory was going to need some help, and quick.

"Chaz, get me on comm with Commander Danns. He's with the Star Reapers."

"Yes, sir. You are connected."

"General Chhun to Commander Danns. Have you reached the airfield?"

"Yes, sir. Thanks again for the ride."

"Any chance you can get one of those birds in the air for me? I've got a rapidly accelerating timetable and I need someone up there to help me."

The smile on Dann's face was unmistakably represented in his voice. "Yes, General. I see a pretty little Raptor right now, and someone left the keys inside."

22

It was perhaps the most specialized mission Dax Danns had ever been given, which was saying something given his time in the Star Reapers. A single attack craft, with a fighter who, let's face it, was concussed, flying over heavily defended air space in support of a single kill team. There was a first time for everything.

"What's that sensor track?" Danns called to his Wizzo.

"They have the ATC back online after the drone strike. They are tracking us," Lucky replied.

"That's why they call you Lucky. I have the ball from Victory Seven. Mark and lock that sig."

The terrain below the belly of the fighter whipped past as the ship poured more power into the engines. To any creatures in the jungle below, the screams of the ship's thrusters would be quickly followed by the drag of air in the Raptor's wake. Focusing on the belly display in his HUD, Danns watched the canopy disgorging leaves as the monstrous warbird swooped overhead at blazing speed.

"Lucky, rig me for max burn in atmo and quick-trip me to combat config."

Countless hours spent together during the train-up for this mission meant the weapons system operator bot was already anticipating the request before Danns even spoke it. In the span of a few op-cycles, the bot rigged the starfighter for maximum maneuverability in atmosphere. Since humans had a tendency to squish under high gravitational forces, Lucky also turned up the inertial dampeners to compensate for the insane level of risk-taking his pilot was known for. Lastly, he sent all remaining power into the shields because—well, because of the insane level of risk-taking his pilot was known for.

Danns let the kill team know he was coming. "Victory Seven, this is Reaper One. I have your target. Engaging."

Friend and foe identifiers appeared in his HUD as blue and red dots moving throughout the base. There were also green dots scattered throughout the jungle surrounding Fort Blake, marking the movements of the Second Free Rifles Regiment in position to assist Victory Company and its forward-deployed kill team when called upon.

Danns took note of the current movements of the red dots. One mass of crimson rushed the front gate in an effort to bottleneck the Legion's advance. *Yeah*, thought Danns, *good luck with that.* A second mass of dots was rapidly pouring out of the three firing points for the long-range artillery batteries set throughout the base. With gunfire that could reach for miles, Fort Blake's long guns could drop both traditional and magnetically accelerated large-bore rounds nearly anywhere in this part of the world. General Chhun had asked that these guns be taken intact so they could be put to use in the defense of the camp once Objective Broken Window was once again under Republic control.

It would have been a hell of a lot easier to just blow them up, though. That was for sure.

The air-defense artillery scattered throughout the base picked up on Reaper One's approach, and multiple explosions sounded almost as if they occurred right in-side the cockpit.

"That was close," Danns grunted.

Lucky gave his analysis. "That is their objective. To come close, not to hit us. They're firing DSMs."

Drone swarm munitions were a particularly nasty bit of work that the Republic had had no compunction in stealing from their enemies during the Savage Wars. A drown-swarm missile would paint a target and follow its digital signature like a tether, but its goal was to detonate close by, where it would release a swarm of hundreds of drones. The tiny machines would then pursue the aircraft with a variety of bots—some rigged with slicer tech, others loaded with high explosives to dust anything in their sensor fields.

"First defensive battery launched six missiles, yield-ing a swarm of seven hundred and twenty-one drones," Lucky reported. "The drones have a lock on our flight pro-file and are chasing. We have already faced two hundred thirty-three slice attempts. I have intrusion countermea-sures active, but it is only a matter of time before we suc-cumb to the attack."

"Worry about that in a minute." Danns gritted his teeth as he focused on the target. He keyed the weapons sys-tem to let the ship's most dangerous direct-fire weapon—the Hell Bat missile—off the leash.

The Hell Bat missile occupied a special place in the hearts and minds of Reaper Squadron. A semi-autono-mous AI guided the missile to target, ignoring ship-to-ship countermeasures and attempts at jamming active guidance systems. The pilot had the option of program-ming the missile for a standard impact detonation or for proximity. Either way, upon detonation its warhead would generate a displacement field that caused an implosion in or near the target. Though brief in duration, this massive energy wave would drag matter from all around the object into a crushing field that would collapse in on itself.

And that was just the first stage. The weapon would then explode with enough force to crack a small frigate in half.

"Good tone on target. Reaper One, Fox One."

The missile flew away from the ship and roared over the landscape. The echo of the fighter's engines served to hide the growl of the Hell Bat's flight motor as it descended on its prey.

Kill Team Victory
Assault on Fort Blake
Target: Artillery Battery

The GMV came back for Nobes, but they brought trouble behind them. The MCR-operated L-TAV had figured out that it was chasing a holographic target and had since found the real deal. Now it was in hot pursuit.

"Add two CS's to the pursuit," Neck called into the L-comm, noting that a pair of Republic combat sleds had joined the L-TAV in chasing their GMV. "You better be ready to go, Nobes! No time to put on your makeup."

Nobes was already sliding down the debris of the tumbled-down barracks he'd launched his trackers from and was moving to street level for pickup. "So hurry up already!"

The GMV slid to a screeching halt, fishtailing as the legionnaires inside called for their teammate to get on board. Blaster cannon bolts from the pursuing vehicles zipped past the Dark Ops vehicle and shook the barracks, blowing doorway-sized holes in the duracrete. With each shot, more of the structure fell around Nobes as he sprinted toward the truck, occasionally forcing him to halt or jump back to avoid being crushed.

"We're not getting clear soon enough," Bombassa growled. With the tracker in place, Bombassa had requested a fire mission that would destroy the L-TAV via targeted orbital bombardment—or via the much riskier option of a flyover if Command had someone crazy enough to give it a try, which, as it turned out, they did. But now any hopes of racing away from the target area before the strike was effectively finished. Not unless they left Nobes to fend for himself. Something the kill team was not about to do.

"What's the plan, Top?" Neck asked. "The featherhead is gonna be here to blow the L-TAV any second now."

Proving those words prophetic, Dax Danns reported his approach over the comm. "Victory Seven, this is Reaper One. I have your target. Engaging."

"I'll call him off," Neck announced.

"Do *not*," shouted Bombassa. More blaster bolts punished the street around the GMV and the building itself. "Get us to cover. Inside the building. Nobes—watch out!"

The GMV powered into a swiveling reverse as it raced into the mostly collapsed structure. They would be easy pickings for the pursuing MCR vehicles, but the hope was that those vehicles wouldn't be in action for much longer.

"Cover up!" Bombassa ordered.

Neck went to work ripping open the reinforced doors on the vehicles and placing the interior protective curtain—meant as a final line of defense for any RPGs that might penetrate the outer armor—over the reinforced glass of the front windshield and all the rest. Nobes arrived to help, turning the GMV into a multi-layered shell to shield them against what would come next.

The wail of a Republic Raptor tearing up the sky intensified above the sound of relentless twin blaster cannons hammering the kill team and the occasional heavy cannon bolt trying to topple what was left of the building down on top of them. The fighter raced by a mere hundred or so meters off the deck, shattering windows and likely deafening anyone without a solid Legion bucket on.

"Good tone on target. Reaper One, Fox One."

A high-pitched drive motor zinged overhead as the Hell Bat missile shot to target. The initial sound of the implosion field detonating was like an entire Legion training class firing blaster rifles on steel targets. The energy field tore steel girders and duracrete from the surrounding structures and swept it all up as soon-to-be shrapnel. The L-TAV and two combat sleds were crushed like used star-hoppers that jumped into a gravity well. Half a heartbeat later, the explosion followed, turning the street into an inferno. Kimbrin who'd run into the fight to shoot their blaster rifles in the direction of the legionnaires in hopes they could later brag about the lucky shot that took out one of the Republic demons, were crushed before being flash-burned to ash. The wreckage of the L-TAV flipped three times in the street before the shattered rubble of a building arrested its death roll. The explosive wave battered the remains of the barracks as well, and it sent the armored truck inside hopping and skidding wildly, though thankfully it didn't tip. The legionnaires inside were tossed against the frame and one another, but their armor kept them from harm.

A quiet followed the attack. Bombassa was the first to shake himself from the battered haze, and he pushed away the additional armor from the front windshield, which had been blown apart by the blast. The GMV was facing the street, and the legionnaire looked out at the scene with the grim fascination that comes from your enemies getting slogged.

"Victory Seven, this is Reaper One," called Danns, now several kilometers away, over the comm.

"Go for Seven," said Bombassa.

"That buzzing sound you hear above you is the active drones from a DSM trying to lock on to me when I come back. I'm running a tight track and will make another pass before I go orbital."

Bombassa's brows furrowed. "Why give them another shot, Reaper One?"

"Most kill teams like yours carry track-and-crack technology, do they not?"

Bombassa started to see what the suicidal but clever pilot was thinking. He didn't wait for the full plan to form in his head before barking orders to his crew. "Nobes, fire up the signal trap!"

"The what? Oh! I'm on it!" The leej dove into his ruck and snapped aiming sight and tripod together while Nix dug in his own ruck to grab the power supply. "If that rocket jockey wants us to do what I think he wants us to do, then we probably only get one shot at this."

The attack fighter screamed directly over their position at speeds that weren't safe for anyone in atmosphere. Thunder and fury washed over them, along with a cloud of dust and cracked stone that was dragged in the wake of the pulse emission engines. The dying sound of the war bird's growling echo was soon dwarfed by the incessant buzzing of hundreds of drones speeding to catch it.

"On it. Out-loads set," Nobes said. "Signal locked and slicing."

The Raptor had barely flown past them when its nose shot into the air, leading the rest of the starfighter in a mad dash for orbit. High-gain pulse engines flared almost white as their scream became the roar of power plants pushing escape velocity from a planet's gravity. The drones followed the plane on its race to the black, winding around the contrail like a reverse tornado in an attempt to max out their signal reach before the fighter escaped. All it would take was a single hack and they could kill an engine, leaving their prey to fall into the swarm and be destroyed like so much scrap.

Suddenly the drone tornado fluttered, slowed, and then fell back along that same contrail. Nobes struck his combat gloves against the roll bar of the GMV. "We got 'em!"

The drones folded in on themselves, powered down to ride out their frenetic flight back to the deck.

That threat was finished, but a new one had already revealed itself. Kill Team Victory, still parked inside the smoldering barracks, were being angled on by Kimbrin forces.

"Get us going," Bombassa ordered.

"On it," said Neck. "Oh, sket! Never mind!"

A new combat sled had just raced up and was unloading a complement of MCR soldiers who used the smoking armored L-TAV as cover to lay down suppressing fire in an attempt to keep the Dark Ops GMV penned inside the barracks. Meanwhile a second sled arced around multiple ruined buildings and between the wreckage of the two previous sleds, seeking a shot at the back side of the single kill team truck; there wasn't enough wall left of the barracks to protect the GMV from any angle. Should the combat sled use its twins to dump enough blaster fire, it would surely finish the legionnaires off.

The MCR's plan was solid. An L-shaped ambush with two combat sleds might have worked if the MCR had just laid quiet and waited for the kill team to drive out of the building. Instead they fired early and announced their presence.

"Gun it or are we staying?" Neck asked.

"Dig in," ordered Bombassa. The legionnaires had plenty of gear within reach. And better yet, they could reactivate the drones that were still falling from the sky. "Let's turn those drones on the kelhorns."

Nobes gave a huge smile. "Keep talkin' dirty, Top."

The legionnaire reactivated the drones they'd hijacked only moments before and sent the newly re-formed swarm flashing by the barracks where they stood in a chaotic buzz. The sound of the swarm didn't make it through the sound cancellation in the kill team's buckets, but they could feel the hum vibrating the debris-strewn ground through their boots.

Hundreds of drones flashed across the battlespace, catching the first combat sled in a series of explosions that killed the gunner behind the twins. The gunner's body fell down into the vehicle, which turned the vacant gunner's hatch into a giant welcome sign. The entire vehicle shattered from the inside out as multiple explosive-carrying drones fulfilled their mission with a teeth-rattling boom.

The next combat sled took several dozen hits from the weaponized swarm, knocking out its repulsors and destroying its power core. The slicer drones in the mix hacked into the sled's CROWS system, overcharging the twin blasters for an armor-piercing shot, but never cycled the trigger. Godlike fingers of fire arced along the vehicle as it detonated in place.

Still in their GMV inside the ruined barracks, Bombassa's half of Kill Team Victory watched as two of the artillery pieces roared to life. A multiple-shell barrage left the first battery in a trajectory that spoke of mountains. The second battery aimed along the path taken by Victory Company.

There were three big guns in all, spread out across the base and well protected by ground forces and smaller anti-air batteries. The two that fired were the ones that Bombassa's truck had been responsible for neutralizing. The other gun was meant for Pina and the leejes in the second GMV that had split off to better escape the pursuing L-TAV, technical trucks, and eventual combat sleds. The fact that the third gun didn't fire spoke well of Pina's efforts, which the legionnaire soon confirmed over L-comm.

"Bombassa, this is Pina. We have control of our target arty battery. What's going on?"

"We got waylaid by enemy armor. We're making a run at the far side battery now."

"Copy. You need help with the central battery?"

"I'm requesting assistance from Victory Company. If the opportunity to assist them comes—or an opportunity to take it sooner—do it. But not at the expense of losing what you've already captured."

"Understood, Top."

Bombassa gave a fractional nod. "Will make contact again as soon as we have the next gun." He flipped his

L-comm to establish contact with Victory Company's CO. "Riggs, this is Bombassa. I need boots and blasters on that last arty site closest to your insertion point."

"Tasking a crew now. Riggs out."

"We got a plan, boss?" Nobes asked.

"Yeah. Take the drones and see if you can't buy our friends from Victory Company a few minutes to get in place."

23

Harvester Command Element
Temporary Ops Center
Bulldog Four

"Crank those shields to maximum! Domino! Get your people back in here!" MakRaven shouted. "Time to find a new neighborhood!"

Outside, the second of four drop shuttles, the one carrying the medical team, lifted through the canopy and sent its engines to max burn.

Sergeant Major MakRaven and General Chhun dragged their security teams and a squad of close-by legionnaires into the shuttle's cargo bay with just time enough for them to close the ramp. The first two dropships had already been spun up when Bombassa announced another volley of artillery fire incoming. But *Bulldog Four*—along with *Bulldog Three*, the shuttle containing the MBTs and assorted other toys—had gone to standby. It was a risk, but one they had to take if they were going to get both ships ready for phase four.

Chaz watched as the legionnaires moved by. The bot voiced a concern its programming identified with how things were going down. "Sergeant Major MakRaven. As it is your job to safeguard the well-being of the legionnaires in the task force, I should advise you that a team from the commo section is running toward the ships. Based on

Victory Seven's warning call, they will not make it before the rounds hit."

MakRaven slammed his hand on the release for the side hatch and ran out from the drop shuttle while throwing his bucket on his head. "Hiccup the shields, LT!" he shouted into the net. The pilot—fearing a world where a flight lieutenant told a Legion sergeant major *no*—did as he was told, causing the shields to pulse long enough to let the crusty leej through.

MakRaven sprinted through the jungle, his armor hiding that his aching knees sounded every bit like that crispy rice cereal all the Republic kids ate. Anyone watching would see a leej vaulting over downed tree limbs like a pro athlete sailing to victory in the Pan-Galactic Games, but to the man beneath the armor, there would never be enough pain relievers or whiskey to stave off the aches when this was through.

Altered reality geo-mapping in his HUD brought him on a collision course with the commo team hoofing it back to the protection of the shuttle. Sound amplification in his bucket registered the first hints of a whistle as the incoming rounds descended to target.

Several meters ahead, the sergeant major saw a lone Legion communications trooper diving into the underbrush.

MakRaven skidded to a halt as he came hip to nose with a Legion working dog. Out of nowhere, a spoken command appeared in the sergeant major's mind. "Jump." The command came with a sudden urge.

Had the dog just told him to...?

The dog launched itself into a hole in the underbrush that led into a cave mouth. MakRaven followed.

He had barely dragged his boots into the cave when the world outside exploded. Gargantuan mounds of earth flew toward the sky as artillery rounds turned the landscape into a hellscape. Rolling fire-breathing turbulence buffeted MakRaven and the others in the hole, and globs of mud slapped against his back armor as gravity reclaimed what was thrown into the sky by the detonation.

Almost as quickly as it had struck, the thunder of Republic artillery being used against the Republic legionnaires subsided, leaving only the distant rumble to vibrate the stone around them.

MakRaven addressed his fellow leejes, most of whom were pressed up against him in the tight space. "Everyone good?"

He received a chorus of affirmatives, and the working dog licked the front of the NCO's faceplate before barking twice.

They had to kick their way out, dislodging mud and loose rock before they could push themselves free of the burrow. When the last of the commo team had cleared himself from the destruction, MakRaven saw that the dog was frantically barking at a pile of trees at the bottom of a recess some meters away. He moved over to the animal to see what he was keying on.

Most working dogs that had been trained for detection would, upon finding the object they were searching for, merely sit quietly in front of it. Some, including the Malinois assigned to the Repub military, would also bark like a maniac. But this dog—MakRaven still refused to think of it or call it by its name—added another wrinkle. The Malinois employed by the Legion had empathic abilities bordering on the mystical—a connection with humans that bordered on true telepathy, much like the

Gomarii species's ability to wordlessly feel and communicate through emotion.

"You wire cutters get over here and help me dig!" MakRaven shouted.

The makeshift work crew pounded at the broken terrain to uncover whatever lay underneath.

"Holy sket!" called one of the leejes, prompting the rest of the crew to shift to his side. "Leej down!"

First an arm, then a shoulder, and finally the entire body of a massive legionnaire in tiger-stripe armor came free from the timber and soil.

Bouncer, the dog's handler. No wonder the dog had been so anxious.

As the man got himself to his knees and removed his bucket to wipe his brow, he was tackled by nearly thirty kilos of hyperactive combat hound. The licking reunion went on for as long as the handler would allow, which wasn't long given the danger they found themselves in. Waves of elation emanated from the animal. MakRaven could feel it.

MakRaven ordered the survivors to double-time it back to the ship. Then he keyed into the L-comm. "Harvester, this is Harvester Zero Seven. Coming back with commo team, and a story you're not going to believe. Bubbles just saved my life."

24

Kill Team Victory
Assault on Fort Blake
Target: Artillery Battery

Bombassa had expected to have to drive the GMV to the right-most artillery piece and take it directly. But Nobes, in possession of the MCR drone swarm, convinced the kill team leader that they could do it faster and from a distance if he could just have a few minutes alone with the controls.

"All right," Bombassa agreed. "But not here. We've worn out our welcome."

Bombassa's half of Kill Team Victory, along with their GMV, left the ruined barracks and fought their way to a Quonset hut structure that had originally served as a classroom for the Fire Direction Center.

"Looks like we wore out our next welcome before we even arrived!" Neck shouted as he worked the N-50 atop the GMV.

"Turn here!" Bombassa ordered.

The team entered the Q-hut and quickly dismounted. They flipped desks, chairs, and anything else they could pile into a barrier so that bolts coming off the MCR security team harassing them didn't pass through the thin skin of the building and into themselves. Still, the occasional bolt got through.

Nobes, who had been doing nothing this whole time but working the bots, let out a triumphant whoop. "I just jailbroke the target gun on that far artillery platform using our stolen drone swarm," he told the team. "That's two down, and it should buy the CP enough time to get up and moved to a new loc before the last gun can catch up."

"Good work, Leej," said Bombassa.

"Aw, Top, you're gonna make me blush."

Just as Nobes finished speaking, a blaster bolt zipped off the flipped presentation desk and terminated its flight as a scorch mark on the ceiling fan.

Nix dropped into the GMV's seat, preferring the impervisteel struts and plates on the armored truck to taking any stray bolts. "They must really not want us to take the last gun, eh?"

"Someone should tell them that's Victory Company's job now," chimed in Neck. "They can leave us the hell alone."

"Sket!" Nobes shouted. "Technicals rolling up!"

Two advancing units in the trucks showed up to make sure the legionnaires didn't have too easy a time of it. The enemy vehicles were just ordinary trucks, the kind made for the everyday utility of hauling equipment on base, but each one was packed nearly ten Kimbrin deep in the vehicle beds, with every hand either holding a gun or running a borrowed Republic medium squad automatic blaster. Kill Team Victory had decimated the first squad to arrive but were unable to lay enough firepower on the maneuvering second squad to keep them from reaching the building.

The ground shook hard enough to throw dirt and debris from the floor almost a meter high. The sound of another volley of targeted cannon fire out toward their friends made every leej in the room shudder at the thought of who'd be on the receiving end.

Nix keyed the start sequence for the CROWS system and linked it to his battle board. "You know what I hate? Cocky bad guys. Like this doofus across the street, trying to hack my N-50 remote. Like, who does that?"

"I just locked said idiots out of the FDC," Nobes said. "These guns are locked until the power cells on those drones go tango uniform."

"Good," said Bombassa. He lined up a shot with his N-4X, putting a blaster bolt through a Kimbrin rebel—not one of the regulars, but a street thug dedicated to the cause—trying to get an angle on them. The bolt sailed through the man's hoverbike helmet, splattering brains on his inadequate armor.

Neck gave a chuckle at the spectacle. "Some of these MCR are just tourists who ransacked a pawn shop." An odd-sounding report, just a single shot, sounded over the battlefield. "See? There's another one. Like who brings a hunting rifle to a major gunfight?"

"Wannabe mids looking to take trophies?" Nobes suggested.

"Right? Who does that?"

Bombassa hit the bantering operators with a dose of reality. "If enough of them do that, we're karked. Nobes, can we use what's left of the drones to clean these guys out?"

"On it, Top."

The drones remaining from the DSMs raced through the street into the MCR security element. Slicer drones slapped into the Kimbrin fighters, throwing off their aim and knocking them against the Fire Direction Center. Rising over the security wall to take aim at their Legion targets, the Kima natives exposed themselves to the last of the explosive-laden machines whizzing into the side of the barrier. Duracrete from the wall transformed into a fragmentation-tinged cyclone as the security team were blown from their position.

The MCR assaulting the kill team had been neutralized, but there were sure to be more.

"How's the GMV?" Bombassa asked. The vehicle had taken another pounding of small arms fire during the conflict.

"We paid for the extra insurance package, right?" asked Neck. "Because she's not looking so hot."

Annoyed, Bombassa pressed. "Does it run?"

"It runs, Top."

"Let's go. Nobes, Nix, in the truck. Neck, with me on foot." Bombassa gave the hand signal for the team to move.

Nobes and Nix kicked the accelerator and raced around to the other side of the FDC. There, a three-story tower stood conspicuously with blacked-out glass in the control center—which the regular soldiers called "the roost." The dark glass kept most troops from looking inside, but optics set into Nix's bucket had no such problem, allowing the N-50-wielding gunner a view of the Kimbrin inside going frantic from their security detail getting dusted.

"Top. Got three in the roost. Not sure how many on the other floors."

"Roger. We'll go low."

Bombassa and Neck slithered past what used to be the duracrete security walls on the perimeter of the FDC. He stepped over the bodies of the Kimbrin defense squad they'd shattered with a combination of the DSM remnants and Nix's N-50 machine blaster. Flashing through optics modes in his bucket, Bombassa peered through the smoke and ruin that was the firefight from the last few minutes to scan for MCR stragglers hiding in the chaos. Seeing no heat signatures or anything moving, he resigned himself to the next step in taking this element of Objective Stovepipe.

He tested the door to gauge if it was locked, and was rewarded with a click. He stepped to the back side of the portal and Neck took the spot opposite him, bringing his N-4X to the patrol ready for the second Bombassa opened the door.

Neck tossed a smoke grenade to the opposite side of the tower, clouding the structure in bright orange smoke. This gave cover to swing the door open so that Nobes could peer in from the truck, using his optical sensors to see what lay inside.

"Flat scan shows no wires or passive sensors. The hall is clear, Top."

Neck poured into the hallway, his bucket tracking the resting points in his field of view to mark doorways that needed to be cleared. First door, supply closet. Next two, offices.

"Advancing to second level," he announced over L-comm. He boosted the sound amplification to max for the combat controller in his bucket. Normally the helmet was set for passive scanning, only pointing out something that the average soldier would see as a legitimate threat. The detection algorithms could be tweaked as needed, serve their purpose, and be reset to normal so the leej wasn't jumping at every shadow and mouse fart in the battlespace. Weapons could fail, charge packs could run dry, and everything this side of the spiral could blow everyone off course, but as long as the leej kept his head in his bucket, he was a force to be reckoned with.

The hum of the data center was clear as day to Neck as he crested the stairs of the building. That was the room to their right. On the left was the battle control station, where most of the large-scale tracking went down. Technicians in that room could follow key control points of a battle outside of Fort Blake and relay priority targets to the fire control station upstairs.

Neck and Bombassa entered and cleared the data center first. Monumental server racks and supercomputer stations lined the room. Neck slid an interface card into the data port on a terminal, watching just long enough for the card to be swallowed by the slot. When they were satisfied that the room was clear, the leejes exited back into the hall.

Bombassa held Neck from going forward. He flashed into a different vision mode and shared the results with Neck. A single Kimbrin ran back and forth between what appeared to be multiple workstations in the battle control station. The person appeared erratic, as though he wasn't sure where things were. Then he came rushing out of the room, and Bombassa was on him in an instant. The legionnaire kicked out the back of the man's knee, causing him to bend backward before pitching forward. The Kimbrin reached out to arrest his fall, but his hand never made the connection. Bombassa took hold of the man's wrist and the back of his head and smashed his skull into the duracrete wall with a wet crack.

They entered the battle control station, and while Neck went to work checking the computers, Bombassa keyed up the L-comm. "Nix, this is Bombassa. Take it."

When Bombassa had told Nix and Nobes that he would go low, the legionnaires knew that their job was to get to the top of the tower. Not wanting to lose the N-50, they had decided to send Nix up while Nobes manned the GMV's big gun. Nix had now reached the roof, and Bombassa could see the legionnaire's view in a HUD portal in his display.

Nobes uncoiled something that looked like a length of cord with a bulb at the end of it. He swung it like a sling, and the bulb disappeared under the lip of the roof. The leej ran to follow, then jumped from the structure into a hard jerk that rattled the feed. The trooper had reached the end of the line that attached him to the tower and swung into an explosion of frosted glass as he sailed into the FDC.

The team had already spotted the four armed Kimbrin in the room. The first one barely got his rifle to his shoulder before the front of his head was blown through the back by the Legion NK-21 Scorpion variable capability pistol. To the side of Nix's first victim, a fighter lost his eye as another round fired from the suppressed pistol, passing through zygomatic bone and into the face of the Kimbrin directly behind him.

The wound wasn't fatal, and the Kimbrin clutched his face and howled as he turned his back to Nix. Nix kicked the rebel in the center of his back, sending him stumbling forward and putting him in a direct line of fire between Nix and the remaining fighter. That last shooter never even got the chance to dodge as Nix rode the tripping Kimbrin into his partner and skip-kicked his knee backwards. Growling against the impact, the final MCR soldier didn't have to wait long for a pain reliever as Nix slapped him into the ground with the pistol.

He had just finished putting shots into the downed MCR troopers to make sure he wouldn't have to check for a pulse later, when a panicked, fear-soaked sob sounded from underneath a desk.

"And who are you supposed to be?" Nix said, peering at the man cowering beneath the furniture.

The meek-looking soldier wore trademark MCR gray pants along with a stylish black coat with gold stripes set onto the epaulets. He held a service pistol against his chest, finger on the trigger, but was clearly not in any mood to fight. Still, despite his fear, the hate on his face was all too familiar to leejes who had spent any time deployed on a foreign world.

"You trigger-flick that weapon and you're gonna end up like your buddies here," Nix warned.

The enemy soldier gently removed his finger from the trigger housing and set down the pistol with the grip facing the leej.

Bombassa clipped the feed, reverting to the message hub with the other half of his kill team. Pina had taken advantage of everyone trying to take a swing at Bombassa and moved to assist Victory Company in taking control of the final Fire Direction Center, thereby neutralizing the artillery battery. Now that all stations, as well as the entrance to the base, were under Legion control, they could move to the next part of the operation.

"Harvester, this is Victory Seven. We have Stovepipe. I say again, we have Stovepipe. You are clear."

25

Harvester Command Element
Temporary Ops Center
Bulldog Four

"Riggs, it's Chhun. Give it to me."

"We have the entrance and are going house to house. Down one squad to assist the kill team in taking down one of those guns. Got some big issues in the motor pool but we're handling it."

"Define issues, Major."

"We have a significant MCR presence holed up. Plus in our initial push, we had to fall back in support of the Third Bat, 2-SFR. They got hit by some of that artillery and MCR support forces outside the wire. We got it turned around, but that left a gap for the little rats to run through as we pushed deep into Broken Window."

"So you have a majority of the MCR on Blake making a run for the armor in hopes they can smash their way out."

"Roger that, General. Are you ready to hit Star Deck? I have my Second Platoon lined up on Deep Space and we have a company from 2-SFR ready to do the job."

"Line up to make the play. Drop time in seven mikes."

"Good copy, General. Riggs out."

Chhun pointed at Chaz, and the bot turned to face the general. As a bot with a 360-degree sensory, it really didn't need to turn anywhere, but it had been corrected several times in its person-to-simucron training that eye contact was important, even if it was just a person looking into his central lens.

"I have First of the Forty-Fifth on line, General. They are half a klick out and making their pass now."

"Thanks, Chaz." The bot was certainly helping things go smoothly. As an added bonus, it only spoke when spoken to, and Chhun didn't have to feed it. "Signal to the other Bulldog elements that we're change of location in the next thirty minutes. Is *Bulldog Three* jocked up?"

"Yes, General. Warlock Company are primed and ready for deployment. That will clear all current legionnaires from the ground with the exception of our security element and two sections from the STB."

Chhun acknowledged the bot's contribution before moving to his next directive. "Knight Hunter Actual, this is Harvester."

"Go for Actual," came the muffled response over the net. The featherhead's bucket was probably suction-cupped to his face to prevent the avionics from messing with the transmission.

"Knight Hunter, deploy all Sidewinders and stay on station for follow-on tasking. Have your flight leader make room for *Bulldog Three* carrying Warlock on Objective Star Deck. I also have a tasking on Objective Deep Space."

"I copy, make room for Bulldog and prep drop sight for Star Deck. Follow-on tasking received for Deep Space. We're in the wind, sir."

Chhun smiled. If there was an air cavalry regiment better than the Knight Hunters, he didn't know of one. He signed off with the squadron commander to watch them roll past the horizon. Seven shuttles flying an offset wedge formation put them at a diagonal approach with Fort Blake. The tactic kept the heavy hauler ships out of the direct line of fire of any remaining air defense artillery while the much larger signature masked the drop of the other aircraft it was carrying.

Unit identifiers and info lit up his bucket display as he zoomed in on the formation. Seven Condor air deployment shuttles streaked across the sky carrying an assortment of aircraft. The outside arm on the short side of the flight formation dropped its complement of short multi-purpose strike aircraft, the NH-3 Sidewinder. Sometimes called the Baby Snake due to its small profile, the Sidewinder had an arrowhead-shaped cockpit with a narrow tail ending in a vertical stabilizer and fin. Twin turbine engines in the back took over for ventral-mounted repulsors to make the Sidewinder one of the most agile new ships in the Legion arsenal.

As the Condor dropped its load of aircraft, it also dumped tremendous amounts of counterfire measures over the jungle. White star clusters, signal-lock-defeating drones, and ram-jam tech flew away from the aircraft.

"Knight Hunter Actual, this is Harvester. Sitrep, over."

The harried voice of the squadron leader crackled over the net. "We have ADA from the ground. SIG-ID pegs it as a Mark Two LADS missile. Lock breakers took it but that was close. WALOS has a platoon-sized element supported by some sort of old combat drones. SIG-ID is having a tough time sourcing it. Looks like they were headed for you when they tried to take a potshot."

Image magnification in his HUD brought a snarl to Chhun's face as he watched tracing and trapping fire erupt from the ground. Tracer ammunition in the form of actual bullets lanced the sky and smacked into the trailing end of the Condor formation. Chhun watched in ultra-high definition as the two rearmost ships, Ram Wings by the looks of them, were pelted by rising fire.

"Harvester, this is Knight Hunter Actual. We got a Ram Wing's Papa WIA from that drone. We're going to run a pass, but that gives us less ships for Objective Star Deck."

"Negative, Knight Hunter," Chhun countered. "We have the fix. Keep those Sidewinders under your flight to hide their sig and we'll take the ground."

He scrolled through his battle board. "There we are. Chaz, task a Vindicator to get eyes on that enemy platoon. They're not going to stay in place after Knight Hunter spotted them. Get me a location. "

"Yes, sir," the robot answered.

Chhun deftly pinged his kill team over L-comm. "Bombassa, it's Chhun. Do you have those batteries up and running?"

"Negative, sir. The artillery fire control system is down pending a scrub. Seems like the MCR on station dropped some poison code into the system. We do not want to link it into the various networks until we are sure it is clean."

"Roger out," Chhun growled. He sifted through elements on his battle board before handing it to Chaz. "Get Venom Company up. Tell them I want that yesterday."

The bot took the offered slate and silently dove into the L-comm to hot drop the general's orders to the company commander, call sign Butcher.

Chhun leaned out of the side hatch on the shuttle, checking out the devastation to the jungle that had been leveled by Blake's artillery before his legionnaires silenced the weapons. The trees all around them were smoking and more than a few were still on fire. Shattered timber and the carcasses of several animals were little more than ash that had forgotten to fall apart after the shelling. The two shuttles that couldn't lift off to get clear of the assault—Chhun's included—still had active power cores online, which they'd used to crank their shields to maximum. They'd weathered the storm despite Chaz's insistence that the senior-most leej on the ground be evacuated.

There was no chance Chhun would leave his legionnaires in harm's way. He had offered to let the flight crew of *Bulldog Four* take his spot on a ride out. But neither the pilots nor Domino's section would leave their ride—or the general who had chosen to stay. The pounding they took was intense, but the shields held against the onslaught of the long-range guns.

Chhun heard MakRaven moving through *Bulldog Four*. "Sar'nt Major. You pick up that traffic from Knight Hunter on the command channel?"

"Yes, sir. You were gettin' ready to send that dog out to find any spotters, and I'm thinkin' me and Bouncer— that's the handler, sir—are gonna set up an ambush on those mids. I take it you're having Ven-Co hem them toward us?"

Chhun laughed. He couldn't surprise the old man if he tried. "I was. But shouldn't you be making sure the hit team has all the right glint tape on their armor before they go out, and not traipsing the woods with them, Sergeant Major?"

"Sir, that's a Sar'nt Major's job. I demoted myself so I could go out on the mission. Heard you talk about them General Rex rules so much, figured I'd try it out m'self." MakRaven used the mimetic function of his armor to change the subdued rank on his shoulder pauldron to reflect a staff sergeant in the Legion.

"I'm only a general, but as I recall, you need a field grade officer to do that to you." Chhun couldn't hope to hide the smile on his face.

"Well I guess you're going to have to bust me, then." MakRaven whistled in a summons that brought out *Bulldog Four*'s air crew like Denadian meerkats. "You kids want some time on a trigger? I could use the help."

Domino looked to the general, who stepped aside to let them walk by if they chose to.

"I can't speak for the two of you," Domino said to the rest of her crew, "but I'm going wherever that leej is headed. Call it proactive defense of the ship. Technically that falls under my job description. If you want to stay and keep the general safe, no one is going to fault you for it since technically that's your job, too."

Without a word, the two members of the flight crew stepped from the ship and fell in behind the sergeant major.

MakRaven nodded in approval. "You move when I say move and you shoot when I say shoot. You feel me, Navy?"

Domino nodded. "Let's get after it, Sar'nt Major."

The enhanced audio sensors in a Legion bucket can filter out the most terrifying explosions or elevate sound so a leej can hear a slag mouse sneeze at ten meters. MakRaven had to dial his back so he wouldn't have to hear the navy kid's heart beating straight out of his armor. "You're going to sprain that delicate little trigger finger if you keep trying to put the Zerachi death grip on that weapon, kid."

Domino frowned from her position behind the blaster roost she'd claimed as her own. She went to correct her crewman, but MakRaven waved her away. The legionnaire had more wisdom to impart.

"Listen, that feeling, like someone tried to turn you inside out with a kick between the knees? That's fear. Now in spacer basic, I'm sure they tried to burn that out of you with a lot of motivational holos and ice cream every Sunday. Reality is, you find yourself, like we do now, sitting inside a Legion combat sled ready to face down a company-sized element with only six leejes, one burnt sergeant major—newly demoted—and a dog with about the silliest name I ever heard, and you gotta be asking yourself the same kelhorned question I'm wondering about you, kid: Can you really be the warrior they told you that you were?"

Domino coughed to get his attention. "Um, Sergeant Major, is that really what Spacer Hail needs to hear?"

MakRaven stared at the crew chief like she'd just asked the dumbest question he'd ever heard. "He's got to hear it before we kick the fires on this gun puppy, Petty Officer Damiano. Because he's gotta remind himself that at some point our military put their seal of approval on him. He passed the tests and finished the courses that put him here at this moment. Standing with a bunch of leejes about to pour a bucket of stupid all over the enemy just to see if they flinch."

The combat sled driver walked from the cockpit at the front of the vehicle. While he definitely wasn't Legion, he had a swagger that marked him as Legion adjacent.

Kildane, the spacer Chhun had requisitioned from the StarEx aboard the *Centurion*, didn't have to think before answering. "Sergeant Major, the sled's rigged and ready hit the mud."

"How 'bout you? You ready, son?"

"Born to ignore the brake pedal, Sergeant Major."

"Yeah, yeah. Save it for the Spikers, kid."

MakRaven left the confines of the sled and waited just outside the ramp with hands on hips. The first of a Legion team arrived and slapped his own forearm against the sergeant major's. The same greeting occurred for each of the additional five leejes who boarded the sled. Two more then arrived on what looked like repulsor bikes that had crashed through the terrain more than glide over it. Riding on the engine cover of the lead slip was the Legion working dog. Bubbles was still proudly wearing his Legion-issued armor and in addition sported an armored wrap around his ears with a set of combat goggles placed over his eyes.

"Does that dog have a doggy Legion bucket on?" Kildane asked with his mouth near to his chest.

"Special issue," MakRaven mumbled back. "You want one?"

MakRaven put his helmet on his head before giving the Legion pup a head pat. He then whirled on the ramp and strode inside the vehicle, and the ramp shut behind him. A holomap dispelled the darkness and cast shadows, making the legionnaires in the back of the sled look like gargoyles.

MakRaven addressed the spacers that had come in with Domino. "Hail and Lahgari. I got somethin' to make you feel proud. Our driver is also navy. How about that? Four spacers ready to go to war with the big dogs. See if they got the teeth to bite."

There was a congenial amusement in the sergeant major's voice that vanished with his next statement, wiping the smiles off the faces of Hail and Lahgari. "If you have any doubts about running this mission, you should step out right now."

When no one moved, he pointed to the map and continued. "This right here is where we have to run so we can slap this incoming MCR force across the mouth. We need speed, surprise, and violence of action to take them out. Venom Company firing stolen artillery is here and will use bracketed fire to move them into our kill zone. Domino, you understand basic fire and maneuver?"

"Yes, Sar'nt Major."

"Then you're in charge when I'm not in the vic. Think of this sled like an armored shuttle that is so trimmed up with guns, gadgets, and dear gods-a-mighty that she won't fly but a meter off the ground. Can you run a crew like that?"

"Aye, Sergeant Major!"

"Damn right you can. And you. Heartbeat Hail or whatever. This is the part where you pack up that fear and use it like radar to keep you and yours safe during the fight. Fire when Domino tells you to fire. Stay sharp, tight, and keep it right. Those MCR out there are nothing but prey for us, and the general just rang the dinner bell. You hungry?"

"Hell yeah, Sergeant Major," Hail almost shouted.

"Ain't basic training, Heartbeat. Save it for the mids. And you, Snack Shack."

"Me, Sergeant Major?" Kildane asked.

"'Cause there's so many fruit stand operators in my sled. Yeah, you! Get up there and drive this sled like it's on fire." MakRaven moved out of the way for the driver to hurry toward the cockpit. "Bounce, it's Mak. Hit it."

The whine of high-cycle repulsor-bike engines squealed outside of the sled. MakRaven toggled a control in his bucket, launching a hologram into the space to replace the map. The walls of the vehicle seemed to turn translucent, giving the flight crew a full view of what was going on outside. Twin turbo-powered repulsor bikes revved their engines to full power. Bubbles hopped over his handler's shoulder to rest on the armor at the end of the seat. Bouncer spun to rig suspension lines on the canine so he wouldn't fall from the ride.

With a kick of the throttle, the leejes riding rocket-propelled razor blades catapulted into the forest. The engine whine sounded off in the distance like a haunted wail as the combat sled gave chase. In the back of the troop bay, MakRaven launched two holodisplays showing the points of view of the two riders on the bikes. They dipped and jumped, slid, and juked in every conceivable direction on a mad throttle across a heavily forested landscape. They seemed to pour through the terrain like water through a river in any number of hair-raising stunts that should have smashed them into fiery bits of twisted metal and angry leej.

26

MakRaven moved through the jungle, taking in observation bot data that estimated the MCR they were hunting to be at company strength with drone support. The feed zoomed in on a tight shot of twelve Kimbrin fighters making their way through the forest along with a Hool holding a machine blaster big enough to have been stolen off a combat sled.

"What the hell is a Hool doin' with a bunch of mids?" MakRaven grumbled to himself. The dangerous alien species were often criminal, occasionally mercenary, but never caught up in causes. Their presence suggested that the MCR must have hired them, but given the MCR's already overwhelming numbers on Kima... why?

Of larger concern was the machine moving with them. A heavy turret sporting a dual weapon mount and exterior rocket pods sat atop a tread-based tank body.

Targeting data and machine specs flashed across the screen, identifying it as a Korodon-19 Infantry Support Mech. The K-19 was a relic of the Kiomar Conflict where a Savage incursion landed on a city in the middle of a desert. Dotted oases allowed some relief for the Legion fighters, but the one thing that the desert on Kiomar didn't have was cover. So the Repub responded by constructing a heavy war bot packed with armor. Basically a driverless armored vehicle, the K-19 was the first to use hybrid armor systems to provide rolling cover for the troops.

Impervisteel, high-grade ceramics, and carbide glass packs made for massive protection for the war bot.

Moving along one of the larger tributaries, the MCR company split into platoons to maximize their coverage of the battlespace while minimizing the likelihood they could be taken out by a single drone or flyover. They moved quickly, with the polish of military-trained troops rather than the hodgepodge of separate militias and terrorist cells that typically made up the MCR.

Farther out, Bouncer maxed out the magnification in his bucket, marking the next in a series of movements of the errant MCR squad that had changed course to intercept them. That meant there was a drone nearby they had to deal with. He let his mind drift into the bond he shared with Bubbles until he could feel the canine's response.

"Hey Finn, get ready to move," Bouncer said to his co-rider.

"Do you think we got a creeper tracking us?" Finn asked.

"Yeah. Won't matter in a sec, though." Bouncer spread his arms, waiting for the tackle that was to come as his dog sprinted over the berm in a four-meter leap that rocketed the animal straight into the waiting leej. Bouncer swung in his seat, using the momentum to whip the dog into the saddle behind him. "Good recon, Bubs!" He locked the dog into the seat of the bike.

"Here it comes," Finn said. "Let's go!"

The two bikes rocketed from their concealment, shooting into the terrain away from the maneuvering squad. Legion observation bot data played in the Legion buckets, showing the squad picking up the pace in order to try for an intercept.

"Three seconds," Finn called.

The bikes briefly shot into the expanse as they came to the end of a saddle in the landscape. Gravity took hold of them, slamming against the invisible force of the re- pulsors keeping the bikes at a hover above the ground. Grating howls sounded from the engines as they sped through the vegetation.

Resounding whistles streaked in behind them for a fraction of a second before the first explosions made landfall. Even on a cushion of energy coming from the bottom of the bikes, the riders could feel the destructive rattle of the heavy shells behind them.

Venom Company had taken control of the mobile ar- tillery platforms early on in the campaign and were now using them to great effect against the incoming waves of MCR fighters looking to finish off the command group that had parked in their back yard. Like a volcano chain, high-velocity cannon rounds packed to the gills with plas- ma-burst warheads littered the target area, turning the once lush jungle into another hellscape of fire and ruin. The warheads weren't the state-of-the-art munitions that the guns on Fort Blake could send, but the shells did the job they were designed for, state-of-the-art or not.

The staccato explosions went on for several minutes before abating, leaving a lingering echo as a requiem for the dead. Bouncer linked into the observation bot, tasked it for a low orbital pass, and swept all the sensory data the machine could feed him to MakRaven in the combat sled.

"I'm not getting a read on that detachment coming after us," Finn said. He flanked the bike out hard, narrowly missing a tree on their wide track back to the sled.

"That's not good. Hey, Finn, power down your bike for a sec, just in case."

The duo came to a stop. A quick series of hand signals conveyed more than enough to each other so that each was clued into the plan. Pulling bot-poppers from their assault packs, the legionnaires tossed them in opposite directions.

Bubbles whimpered.

"Yeah, I know they make your teeth itch. Grow a pair," Bouncer said to the dog.

The animal's expression was nearly unreadable in a bucket specifically designed for him. Hard goggles and head cover were attached to a locked-in strike muzzle that could be ratcheted off by the animal with a gesture of its jaw. Written on the back of the helmet were the words *Combat Snuggle Inducer. Stand Clear.*

The ionic grenades sailed away into their near-silent detonation. Some meters to their flank, an aerial drone sputtered and died in the vines. Bubbles huffed as Bouncer got clear of the bike.

"I'll get it. Don't strain yourself."

The legionnaire used his vibro-knife to pry out the three sensor mods before running back to the bike. A quick check with his optics confirmed it wasn't carrying a payload of explosives, which meant it could take a ride in his assault pack clipped to the back of the vehicle. Jumping back on the bike, he fired up the engines, giving a hand signal for them to move out.

Twin blaster bolts sailed into Bouncer's back, knocking him forward onto the controls. Bubbles jumped free of the bike in a crouch, and Finn circled his machine in a sweeping arc, putting it between the attack and his Legion brother.

"Going hot!" Finn cried out. The auto-blaster mounted to the underside of the forward power forks sent high-cycle shots into the terrain on fanned burst. "Need a target, Bub!"

Combat data from the dog's bucket raced into the L-comm, identifying half a squad.

"If that's the same crew, they got buddies out there. Get back on the bike," Bouncer shouted. The pain in his voice was evident, but the armor had kept the bolts from doing any permanent damage.

Waves of hostility emanated from the dog and washed over its handler. The little combat monster was primed to run straight into the squad and tear out throats. Only its handler could keep it back.

"Negative! Get on the bike! I'm hit but the armor took it," Bouncer growled. "Finn, get us out of here."

With an excited bark, Bubbles pounced onto the thruster plate and the two leejes bolted off into the jungle.

"Mak, it's Finn. Bouncer's hit, but angry. We're coming back to you. Next barrage is in thirty seconds to change the track on those mids."

"Bring it in, son. We'll trade him out."

MakRaven ran from the combat sled to the approaching bike. "Hand him to me. Hammer's gonna take his spot. Get back out there."

"On it, Mak!" Finn said.

Another leej emerged to help shoulder the injured Bouncer up the ramp.

"Put him on the floor face down!" MakRaven said.

Hail stood with the vehicle med kit in his hands. "What do I do?"

MakRaven pointed with knife hands. "Take that and plug it into the vehicle. You're going to see a menu that has three selections. Choose *Scrub* and then wait for it to sequence. Then hit transmit, and the system will do the rest."

The dog trotted into the sled, holding the busted aerial drone. He dropped it at the spacer's feet, then went into a sit position to wait for the kid to do something with his discarded chew toy.

"Sergeant Major—the, uh, dog has something," Hail said.

"You got that sequence runnin'?" MakRaven barked.

"Yes, Sergeant Major."

"Take the intel from the mutt," said MakRaven. "I got the leej."

Hail flinched at the sound of another artillery barrage pounding the MCR out in the jungle.

"Hey Heartbeat. Remember what I said to you about fear? Time to fuel up and load that scrap into the system so we can pull it apart. Do it now." MakRaven popped the latches on Bouncer's back plate and discarded the mess of smoking, ruined armor. He risked a pat on the head to the diminutive death dealer watching every move made to his handler. "Don't worry, bud. Looks like a second-degree burn but the plate held. Damn, they must have overcharged the blasters to pull off this kind of smoke."

"Feels like Legion selection when they did those wet sand drills," said Bouncer. "My armor is saying I have a broken rib on my firing side."

"Lucky you weren't wearing any of that old shiny garbage or you would have been cooked."

A massive concussion slapped against the combat sled, rocking it on its repulsor field. Finn shouted into the L-comm. "Mak, you have a K-19 behind you. We have their squad approaching off-center from you. Have Domino fire along the following grid!"

"And here I thought you two slagged the drone to keep from gettin' followed."

"Dunno, Mak. Must have gone wide and used the sensor suite to track the engine. We can ask it once we blow it off Kima."

MakRaven smiled in his bucket. He loved working with killers not deterred by having to go off-book. Above him, Domino fired the twin heavy blaster turret. Its throaty bark in nine-to-twelve-round bursts spoke to the petty officer's training as a gunner on the shuttles. The lady sure did know how to run a gun.

Time to do the lord's work and dust some of these kelhorns.

27

"How bad was the hit on Bouncer?" Chhun asked his armored robotic assistant.

"The bio-sig on his armor indicates he has second-degree burns across his back and shoulders and a fractured T-11 floating rib on the left side." The bot seemed almost sympathetic to the man as he called out his injuries. "He has taken a stim pack as well as having his torso armor replaced with spare recon sets loaded into the sled. Skinpacks have been applied. The combat sled is engaging the MCR squad coming at them while Venom Company continues to drop artillery rounds."

Chhun frowned. "Seven leejes and four navy basics against a company. What the hell was I thinking."

"General, you trusted your sergeant major's judgment in his leejes and your own in the character of the navy spacers to work at their various tasks."

Chhun had been speaking to himself, and the bot didn't care one way or the other what its commanding officer said. That was a trick of its programming. Still, Chhun felt compelled to be human to the machine. "Thanks for the recap, Chaz."

He negotiated his way along a new path in the L-comm. "Go for Chhun."

"This is Knight Hunter Actual. We have deployed our complement of ships and are standing by for additional tasking."

"Good copy, Hawk. RTB *Centurion* for second loadout. Report when at fifty percent full, over."

"Roger, Knight Hunter out."

Chhun sent a signal to *Bulldog Three* waiting outside. The working engines pushed power through the repulsors, bringing the bulk of the heavy troop transport from its landing struts. It swung over the trees, and with a blast of its main engines, roared out toward Fort Blake.

"*Centurion* REPO to Harvester."

The general's shoulders sagged a bit. He'd hoped that Chaz would field more of the net traffic, so if this call had reached him, it had to be important. "Go for Harvester."

"This is *Centurion* REPO. Intel packets from Victory One indicate three company elements and support equipment moving to Objective Broken Window. That number is dwindling to two company elements with the long-range strike against Objective Shepherd. Victory One also reports they have munitions casing for biochem short-range missiles."

Chhun nodded. "Harvester to *Centurion* REPO, do we have a chem marker on that launcher, over?"

"Negative, Harvester. No joy at this time. *Centurion* REPO out."

"General, we have the Sidewinder heavies approaching Objective Star Deck," Chaz offered. "*Bulldog Three* is ready for a drop on objective."

"Where are we with Victory Company?"

"Major Riggs reports they have control of the main gate as well as five structures surrounding it. The main battle tanks are employed and ready for work."

"Thank you, Chaz. Keep half an ear on the sergeant major's strike team. I want to know the second they're clear."

"I will, sir. Also, General, it's been twenty-seven hours, fourteen minutes, and thirty-one seconds since the system has last recorded you sleeping. Would you like to take a break? I can monitor the battle for you and wake you if anything significant comes along."

"Thank you for that. But not yet. Too many pieces up in the air for me to stop juggling now."

Combat Sled CS-0018
Pursued by MCR Forces

Kildane had been the kid no one expected. He was thin where the other thugs on his block had been like whiskey barrels. He was smart where many others preferred a hard head. Last up in his listing of what no one expected was that behind the wheel, any wheel, he was Oba's number one guy.

He killed the inertial drive field and, in what seemed like an uncontrolled slide, drifted the combat sled between a tree and a hill, letting MCR blaster cannon bolts skim the sled's shield. They caused next to no damage at all as he quickly maneuvered the sled out of the enemy's field of fire.

"Damn, son! You said you could drive. You didn't say you could drive like the devil! What else ya got?"

"Can I go off leash, Sar'nt Major?"

"The leash is gone and the collar already broke, kid! Give it all to me."

"About damn time," Kildane said under his breath. "Domino, light 'em up!"

The spacer took to the twins like a musician takes to a packed concert hall. She traced the heavy blaster cannons, lancing thuds into the body of the K-19 chasing them, scoring destructive hits marked by plumes of smoke and showers of sparks.

"Heartbeat, Lags!" MakRaven shouted. "Hop on the secondary weapons. They're just like the CROWS!"

"On it, Sar'nt Major!" Hail shouted, not bothering to decry the nickname he'd been given. As far as anyone here was concerned, if a man like MakRaven gave you a nickname, you might as well tattoo it on your soul. There was no changing it.

Above them, Domino continued her destruction of their pursuer by running trapping fire into the K-19 minitank. Bolts zinged off the armor, temporarily robbing the light from the canopy as the sparks flared in each strike.

For its part, the tank used its twin, short-barreled cannons to level another bolt into the sled. Kildane called out the warning to hold on a second before he pulled another feat of stunt-driving wizardry out of his helmet. The vehicle swerved to the side, putting a tree in between the sled and the drone. The bolt sailed by, followed closely by the gun that had fired it. Its sensor suite realized a second too late that the combat sled had slipped in front of the tree and come to a dead stop.

The four independent tread systems on the tank locked up in an attempt to bring the rushing armor to a stop. Kildane snapped the throttle forward, bringing the Legion combat sled to full power in just a few short meters. The plow ram on the front of the sled slammed into the back of the tank before it could get a chance to turn. Its cupola spun for a chance to get away from the advancing combat sled, but its gun barrels struck the side of the brush guard making it impossible to turn. Another slam on the accelerator brought the sled's engines to full power for a push against the armored vehicle.

Gears strained and treads spun impotently under the tank as the heavier, more powerful vehicle sank low and pushed the MCR drone toward its handlers. The cupola panned back and forth, slamming into the brush guard looking for any attempt to gain a sight picture on the sled. Kildane angled the combat craft back and forth as well, using the corners of the brush guard to redirect the tank every time it tried to turn or escape.

"Hail! Launch it!"

A cover housing on the back of the combat sled exploded from the vehicle like a pilot ejecting the cockpit canopy. Unfurling from the smoke, a spider-legged, gun-toting drone sprang from the vehicle into the mud. With its legs tapping out a chaotic rhythm that rushed the mech forward, it lunged toward the tank at a speed that surprised everyone in the sled watching through holo or bucket.

Domino continued her onslaught as the twins pounded against the armor with relentless fury. The petty officer pressed her thumbs into the butterfly trigger until they were numb from the effort, as if the extra strain would strike the bolts that much deeper into the drone's armor. The Legion ground security combat drone leveled its heavy blasters into the side of the trapped machine, shattering its treads and destroying the flank rocket pods on the outside of the twin guns.

"Rockets on first side are down," Hail called out through the VR rig clipped to his helmet.

"Take it, Heartbeat! Make it rain!" MakRaven shouted to the basic, accented by a slap on the shoulder. "These new CSes are a hell of a lot better than the tin-can death traps I used to ride around in." The upgrades Chhun had ordered made to these combat sleds really were something.

The combat sled continued to push the tank toward the enemy squad amid a growing tangle of vines, tree branches, and mud. In doing so, Kildane used its armor against their incoming gunfire. The Legion security drone raced behind the sled, ready to deal out more destruction to the tank's remaining gun.

"Launching APROS!" Lahgari said.

An arrow-shaped device tumbled away from the ramp, coming just short of the ground as repulsors fired beneath it. A jet of fire pushed from the back to launch the new drone into the trees. It sailed above, using its sensor suite to highlight enemy targets for the team inside the sled.

"Squad is closing in, and we have another one of those drones racing out," MakRaven said. "If they have MK-2s in the band, we're cooked."

Off in the distance, another artillery strike sounded through the hull. The MCR combat company running to support the assault squad took the brunt. Swaths of terrain and broken bodies were launched into the air amid the explosive fire coming from the barrage.

"Lags, what's the track on those mids?" MakRaven shouted.

"Got the squad digging into our front. They're sending blaster fire our way but it's mostly hitting the tank. There's a fire team creeping to our side but Finn and Hammer say they have that under control."

Hammer had replaced Bouncer on the bike.

"Our best defense is to be anywhere other than where they're hitting!" Kildane shouted from the pilot's seat. "Domino, get ready to punch that thing's ticket!"

"Bring it to me, baby!"

Kildane spun the sled, slamming the tank into a tree to dislodge it. The twins roared against the armor, slicing a hole in the exterior before warning indicators of an overheated barrel flared in Domino's drop lens. Lahgari's drone sprinted from behind the sled, punching bolts into the shredded armor. The mech fired a salvo of three rockets from its outboard launcher, all punching into the hole. Combat sled and mech raced away as the tank's internals went critical and exploded.

"Shield is down!" Kildane shouted. "Reading sixty seconds to reset."

Shrapnel rebounded across the troop bay inside the sled. Legionnaires jumped at the spacers to cover them from the fragmentary tornado until the pinging stopped.

When Bubbles barked toward the gunner's nest, one of the faceless leejes pulled Domino from the roost to pass her back to the waiting arms of the other legionnaires. A triangular piece of flak had pierced her eye and she had burns across her upper torso and neck, with more pieces of ruined metal sticking from her armor and flesh.

"No! I ain't done. Got to see this through," Domino said through searing waves of pain.

A monumentally stocked med kit appeared from behind one of the legionnaires as he dropped to the deck to work on the spacer NCO. "Skinpacks will hold her, but she's going to need the goods sooner than later, Sergeant Major."

"Work it, Doc," MakRaven said.

Bouncer staggered up from his spot on the floor, grunting in pain. He snapped his fingers to get Bubbles's attention. "We're going out."

"Hold up," MakRaven said from his position by the medic. "Gettin' a status update."

Four legionnaires stood from the bouncing troop seats to shoulder their goodie bags of assorted death and mayhem. Along with Bouncer, they waited for the word.

MakRaven relayed a report from the observation bot overhead. "We have another K-19 creeping on us. Thirty-one strong chasing right at us as a result of artillery. And we have a wounded spacer we need to evac."

Bouncer was the first to articulate a plan. "Me, Bubs, and the bikes will buy you the time you need for all that. Let's show 'em."

"Ooah!" the three other legionnaires shouted in reply, eager to get out of the combat sled and directly into the fight.

The ramp lowered partway, allowing the force to jump from the vehicle without getting caught on anything. They leapt from the sled going full speed, using a combination of proper falling technique and Legion body armor to arrest their fall. Three of the men ran in one direction while a leej and his dog went another.

Bouncer and his dog had crept in close enough to the MCR elements that he could pick up their every word through his bucket's enhanced audio systems.

"I'm telling you," said a Kimbrin soldier, "the riders flew off that way and the sled went that way. They're splitting up to corral us and finish off what the artillery doesn't."

Sporting a PK-9 and an over-under grenade launcher, another Kimbrin redirected the first man's aim. "Focus on your line of fire, Kosh. Stay alert and you can worry all you want at home. Worry out here and you lose focus and your life."

"Yes, Sergeant Vaine."

The group of nine MCR fighters with modern weapons and plate carrier armor rushed through the forest as fast as the dense terrain would allow them. Several times Kosh, who seemed not as accustomed to the bush as the rest, stumbled and bulled his way through the natural tangle.

"Sergeant Vaine. I think Helna is missing."

The scarred Kimbrin let his sluggish junior catch up to him in their patrol wedge. "And I thought I told you to watch your own firing lane."

"Sorry, Sergeant." Kosh jogged ahead to catch up to his squad mates, several times removing his hand from his Psydon-era SAB to adjust the helmet that kept tilting when he moved faster than a stumble.

Vaine watched the line of men for the missing trooper. Sure enough, he had a hole where Helna should have been. He whistled to get their attention and then put them in a patrol halt. At least they paid attention to the training and did that properly.

He moved to the trooper that should have been in front of the missing man. The soldier was leaning against a tree, watching his sector. "Sill. When was the last time you saw Helna?"

When Sill didn't answer, Vaine grabbed the man's shoulder. The motion caused the man's corpse to fall to the ground.

Vaine jumped up from his position, sent out two short whistles, and brought his men into a tighter formation.

"Sill is dead. Helna is missing. We're being stalked. Get up and move to that ridge and we'll set up an ambush. Single file. Move out."

The squad ran into formation and made tracks farther into the wood line. They fell into a rhythmic jog toward a drop-off just ahead when the artillery strikes started again behind them. Vaine cursed the universe for putting him with the unit tasked with hunting down the Legion commander. This was a stupid idea, as even if they got close they weren't likely to kill him outright. The rest of the squad leaders guessed this was all a stalling action to keep the Legion busy so the command elements of the liberation could make the next moves.

An explosion of brush and vines up ahead took Vaine's point man to the ground. The men toward the front of the column raced forward to the savaged Kimbrin screaming for help. Agony flared in the man's ruined body as pain forced wracking sobs across the many wounds inflicted in a matter of seconds. His weapon arm had been dislocated and savaged by what looked like a bite wound. But it was his leg that caused more than one of Vaine's men to empty the contents of their stomachs. The shin bone was sticking up from the leg near the ankle, surrounded by gobs of torn flesh. It was as if a massive predator had tried to bite the bone right out of his leg and then had just as quickly run away.

Then it was in front of them. Fear personified. Brown, mottled with white flecks, probably thirty kilos, and wearing body armor. Its muzzle was covered in blood.

A primal roar escaped from somewhere inside the Legion attack dog. At the same instant, a legionnaire emerged from the brush, and his tomahawk split the nearest Kimbrin's skull before the man could raise his weapon. A second blade, this one a combat butcher's knife, pierced the man's jaw from under his mouth, spinning him around to face his friends. The red eye slit on the legionnaire's helmet seemed to glow the color of blood as promises of pain and death oozed forth.

But this was madness. A foolish frontal attack. The legionnaire would be cut down as soon as—

The legionnaire and the dog both leapt back as a fragger rolled to a stop among the Kimbrin fighters. The double-burst of fragmentation killed four of the seven remaining MCR squad members in an instant. Two more legionnaires emerged from the flanks and put down the rest of the squad, leaving only the MCR sergeant.

"Surrender and you live," came the demonic voice through the external modulator in the first legionnaire's bucket. At the man's side, his dog barked once.

Vaine looked from side to side. A legionnaire to his left. Another to his right. And a devil right in front of him.

"I live for Kima!" he shouted, yanking his knife free from its sheath.

He was shot by all three legionnaires before the blade could be raised above his knees.

"We gotta go," Finn said to Bouncer. Hammer was already making his way back to the hoverbikes. Finn nodded to the lone Kimbrin left from the patrol. "Are we takin' this guy or dusting him?"

The rebel sat in the crook of a tree with his eyes wide and white, a stark contrast to a face that was awash in the blood of his squad.

"Leave him here," Bouncer decided. "Bubbles can watch him until we can swing back to grab him."

It was the dog, rather than the other legionnaire, who protested.

Bouncer patted Bubbles on the head. "I know you want to go with me, but you have to stay to guard this man. We need the intel."

The dog leaned his head into Bouncer's.

Bouncer turned to the Kimbrin. "If you move from this spot, my dog will bite out your spine through your face. Do you understand me?"

The rebel nodded vigorously and pushed himself further back into the tree.

Bouncer followed Finn toward Hammer and the two bikes. Hammer took one, and Finn drove the other with Bouncer in the rear. Together they raced to meet up with the other three legionnaires who had left the combat sled and were running on foot.

Or *mostly* on foot. As they caught up to their fellow leejes, one of the men, a leej known as Prowl, jumped from a log into a jet-assisted leap. Rockets developed by Legion R&D on his rear-facing shin armor and utility belt propelled him into the trees, sending animals scattering and birds taking flight. New predators now commanded this jungle.

The six legionnaires continued on until reaching the rear guard of the remaining Kimbrin company set to assault the temporary CP.

"Mak, this is Bounce. We're about to knock on the back door of those mids."

"We're in position. Give 'em hell, leej."

Blaster flashes lit up the jungle, passing between the combat sled in front and the hyper-mobile leejes behind, with the Rebellion force caught in the middle. A jet-assisted leej fired an aero-precision missile at an old War Scythe aerial combat drone attempting to lay fire down on the embattled combat sled. Crisscrossed attacks from the twin leejes on repulsor bikes shredded the forward lines. Bouncer dismounted and assaulted on foot, shooting until the charge packs on his weapons ran dry and he had to take from the dead to continue the fight. It was over in a matter of minutes, with a handful of the fighters surrendering to the Legion soldiers after the rest were eliminated.

Bouncer moved up beside his brothers. "I'm going back for Bubbles."

"Good deal," Prowl said. "Take Hammer with you."

Taking two bikes, Bouncer and Hammer raced back toward the dog and prisoner. They were closing on the site when Bubbles shared his feelings through their bond. Fear and regret. Something was wrong.

Bouncer had only moments to react, and what he was reacting to wasn't in any way clear to him. He brought his bike alongside Hammer's, ready to tell the man to slow or veer, when he saw it: a lone MCR soldier running toward them, wearing an explosive vest.

With no time for words, explanations, or regrets, Bouncer pushed Hammer off his bike.

"Bounce, what the hell!" Hammer shouted before crashing down amid the ferns and foliage, his bike racing toward the suicide bomber—along with Bouncer's.

Bouncer tried in that last moment to veer, but there was no time. The Kimbrin fighter exploded into a greenish mist right before him, and the blast knocked Bouncer from his bike. There was nothing left of the Kimbrin.

For a moment, Bouncer thought he had gotten lucky. He was alive. Banged up, certainly. But nothing broken. Then he saw the tendrils of gas emanating from the explosion, turning vegetation brown as they snaked out into the trees. Animals and birds not only fell dead but turned black as the mist touched them.

"Sket!" Bouncer shouted. "Hammer! Stay back! And make sure Bubbles doesn't come over here!"

The dog was barking wildly in the distance.

"I'm watching it!" Hammer shouted. "Bouncer, that stuff is corrosive! You have to run!"

But even as he shouted the words, he saw that Bouncer could do no such thing. The mist was already on top of him. Convulsions racked his body, and his bare arms... Hammer could see the flesh being eaten away.

Bouncer had always done the bare-arms thing. Some thought it was a deliberate throwback to the old Psydon leej style, but Hammer knew it was more than that. It was a way to give him flesh-to-fur contact with Bubbles. Part of a handler's bonding procedures, critical to the job.

MakRaven called from the combat sled. "What the hell is goin' on?"

"Bounce got hit with some kind of gas attack!" Hammer reported. "We need Doc!"

"Sendin' him now," MakRaven said.

The Legion medic's voice came over Hammer's comm. "I'm on my way with Prowler. Tell me exactly what you're seeing."

"Looks bad, Doc. Really bad. This stuff is eating the exposed flesh on his arms. It looks like it's also attacking his nervous system."

"His armor's auto-injectors are working," Doc said, his voice calm and comforting. "He's not in any pain."

"Yeah, well he needs to get out of here."

"Mak already has a call in for a Valkyrie team. Time on target is three minutes."

Hammer shook his head. "He's not going to last that long."

Bouncer's flesh was necrotizing right in front of Hammer's eyes, sloughing off his arms in clumps. It was clear the leej was going to die, and Hammer didn't want him to die alone. He decided to take the risk of moving in. Unlike Bouncer, his armor was fully sealed, and readouts in his HUD said the toxic cloud was dissipating. He hoped so.

He rushed to Bouncer's side.

So did Bubbles, appearing from among the trees. Except it was moving slowly, starting and stopping, then barking and growling at something behind it. A moment later, Hammer saw why. The dog was threatening its prisoner to come along, not willing to disobey its final order: to watch over the MCR rebel.

The rebel held his arms close and obeyed, moving quickly but not nearly as quickly as Bubbles would have liked. The dog's barks grew louder, and somehow, even through the cocktail of pain and drugs, Bouncer must have heard them. He sat up, struggled to his knees.

Hammer didn't try to stop him. He would allow his fellow leej the one last dignity of not dying on his back.

Massive convulsions wracked Bouncer's body. Hammer could now see bone in places through the flesh falling from the man's arms, but the dog handler made it to his feet and allowed his bucket to tumble from his head.

Bubbles barked and whined.

"Stay," Bouncer rasped.

The dog held at the edge of the green, commanded not to enter the brown patch of dead vegetation that marked the chemical weapon's fallout zone. It sat, nervously stood, then sat again, whining and barking.

Hammer quickly took possession of the prisoner, freeing the dog of its charge, and Bubbles tried to take another step toward Bouncer. But it was clear the dog's handler was worried about Bubbles's exposure to any remaining toxin.

"Stay," Bouncer managed again. The words seemed a monumental effort.

Bouncer sat.

"Good boy."

Bouncer smiled.

And then he fell back into the soft mud. Foam drizzled from his mouth as convulsions robbed him of his final breaths. A tortured rage crossed his face, then gave way to peace as his azure-colored eyes became pinpricks staring into Kima's clear blue sky.

Bubbles let out a howl that could be heard all the way back at the combat sled.

28

The line of Sidewinder attack had disengaged from their shuttles and now raced toward Objective Star Deck: The recapture of Fort Blake's airfield. This was as far as they could hitch a ride with the larger transport ships until finally having to reveal themselves to any MCR still watching the skies with anti-air.

"*Centurion* REPO, this is Stinger Lead." Captain Quinn adjusted the sensor wave on his system to factor in the assault shuttle full of legionnaires trailing them by five minutes. "I have good stream from ISR on Objective Star Deck. We are approaching low and lean from three one four. Ready on your bang bang. How copy, over?"

"Stinger Lead, this is *Centurion* REPO. I have two air defense towers central to the main runway. Taxi Two has a mobile in place. Task Unit Zombie is on station and ready for your approach."

"Good copy, REPO."

This next bit had to be done right and tight or those leejes would get race tracked until he could get them over the target without something blowing them up. And since he was focused on not getting blown up today, Quinn keyed in on some intel coming in from his wingmen and then got back on comms with the mothership. "*Centurion*

REPO this is Stinger Lead. I have new sensor lock on mobile ADA behind Objective Star Deck. Forwarding target grid to *Centurion* FOX-CON, Over."

"This is *Centurion* REPO. Roger out."

The jungle leading to the mountainous rise behind the airfield loomed closer as the seconds ticked by in Quinn's internal clock. As the anxiousness built in the pit of his stomach, almost prompting another call, a lance of light struck the top of the hill just before the airfield—it was awe-inspiring to witness an orbital bombardment from the sky. The mobile air defense system hidden at the summit detonated, along with most of the hilltop. Another lance struck a half kilometer on the far side of the mountain, mirroring the first explosion and sending an avalanche of rock tumbling toward the airfield's outer wall.

"Stinger Lead this is *Centurion* FOX-CON. Targets destroyed you may start your run."

"Thank you, FOX-CON. Break. All Stinger Elements, this is Stinger Lead. We are go for Objective Star Deck. Start your run."

The trail formation for the arrow-shaped attack ships fanned out into a wedge. They buzzed through the smoke and haze of the airstrike to trace the slope of the mountain down to the airstrip.

"Stinger Lead, strike out," Quinn called into the flight channel.

Fifty meters off the deck, he sailed over the airfield wall sideways as the repulsors kicked into full push. A flight of three SLICs—rebooted and recovered from the EMP attack and loaded with MCR troops—hovered at uniform height above the tarmac waiting for instructions from the Air Traffic Control station. A violent burp of the rotary cannon on Quinn's primary weapon-wing sent a hail of destructive bolts into the enemy ship.

The SLIC came apart like a thrift-store admin bot on the ride home. The other two SLICs ran to flanks to distance themselves from the plummeting hulk onto to suffer similar fates as the next ships in the Sidewinder wedge dropped the hammer on them in the form of Widow Maker Rockets fired from the outboard weapon's pod.

Quinn cycled to the squadron net. "Stinger Lead to Stinger Red Leader. Start your run."

Another wave of Sidewinders came over the mountain with the noses of their aircraft down and their tails up, like some hydro-scorpion hunting for fish. They swept to the far end of the field where MCR troops manned heavy weapons and combat sleds. Bringing their engines to max burn, Stinger Red rushed the field as blaster bolts raced up to meet them.

Outboard high-cycle rotary blaster cannons burped out frenetic waves of violence on their pass over the large hangars. Stolen Repub combat sleds and T-LAV's, more than the MCR had personnel to use, detonated under the onslaught of the rockets and blaster fire from the agile NH-3's. The Baby Snakes made a combat pass over the Q-Hut's, slagging several structures and obliterating MCR troops moving from building to building in an effort to reach the gates, guns, or airfield—the newest prong of the 131st Legion's attack.

"Stinger Gold Lead this is Stinger Lead," Quinn called into the radio. "Got traffic of NBC, I say Nuclear, Biological, or Chemical, from the MCR on ground. Run a sensor pack on that taxiway leading right up to the Q-Hut."

"Roger, Stinger lead," Came the reply.

A third wing appeared flying at a much higher altitude than the other stinger elements scrapping the landscape. Rocket pods flashed from the outboard struts into a devastation-inducing serenade by the agile little warcraft dumping the totality of their weapon system in under three seconds. An entire line of SLICs gifted to the Planetary Defense Army by the Republic and stolen by the MCR during the takeover, had pilots priming them to get into the air and away from the Legion assault. The line of ships ruptured from the projectiles, each one sparking from a ruptured power cell until it ignited into its own arcing explosion. Amid the thunder and chaos, Stinger Gold Leader swept across the field to fire a missile mounted in between the rocket pods on its weapon wing. The missile sailed into the inferno before dropping a load of hundreds of sensor modules.

"Stinger Lead this is Gold Lead. Sensors are up and flashing. No chemical sig on objective at this time. Flash detection on the five. Gold out."

"Hit, hit, hit!" came a call over the comm.

A convoy of combat sleds surrounding an L-TAV swept from the smoke onto the airfield. Quinn switched to the SIG-ID display to see Gold Two had been hit by one of the trucks when they made the break away. "Gold Two this is Stinger Lead. Can you hold it?"

The comm went dead as the primary repulsor flared beneath the ship and arced. The crack of electricity slapped against the drive engine and the entire ship turned into a firestorm raining debris onto the airfield.

A MK-2 LADS missile shot from an operation's building beyond the hangars where an MCR infantry unit of some type was taking the ships down, one at a time. It struck Red Five, sending him into the tarmac as a shower of fire and scrap.

Quinn flared the repulsors on his Sidewinder as he killed the drive engine, putting the ship into a hovering glide. A combination of directional thrusters and ailerons swung the ship into a backwards track. With his nose now aimed directly at the threat, Stinger Lead engaged the drive engines to put his aircraft into a strike position on the enemy lock.

"This is Stinger Lead. Firing on improved structure past the Q-Huts providing cover to entrenched infantry."

"Stinger Lead, this is Stinger Red Seven. Passing your line of fire at thirty high."

Quinn cursed with the practiced efficiency of a navy man that left the fleet to fly Repub army birds. He slammed the repulsor controls, dropping his ship fifteen meters from the tarmac. Next he fired off his rocket pods, sending a salvo of destruction beneath the passing ship and straight into the face of the MCR contingent. The featherhead finished off the volley with a burst from his spinning death dealer. Blaster bolts tore at the front of the building at a rate of one thousand shots per minute.

Just as he was about to climb into the air, a titanic quake shattered the back end of Quinn's vehicle, blowing fire and debris into the cabin. Spikes of impervisteel pierced his right lung through the light combat armor the pilots wore over their flight suits.

"Stinger Lead," Quinn coughed into the net. He pulled the mask from one side of the helmet so he could talk without coughing out spurts of blood. "This is Stinger Lead. I'm hit!"

The main engine on the right-hand side rattled hard as it fought to keep its place in the engine array. The

Sidewinder spun out of control and slammed into the duracrete. By design, the cockpit stayed mostly intact as the ship ground to a halt meters from the building the captain had just assaulted.

Kimbrin fighters rushed from the cover of the still mostly intact building. They swarmed over the pummeled cockpit to pop the latches on the canopy and pull Captain Quinn from his straps in the seat. Yes, the Republic was still actively engaging in attacking the airfield—but having a prisoner, especially an officer, might be the difference between getting killed or having a bargaining piece to leave with your life should things continue to go badly.

Or at least that's how it worked in the old days.

Quinn's body was hoisted above them like a crowd surfer at a heavy metal concert. MCR officers yelled for him to be brought to their position. The shouts continued until the MCR regulars realized the man was dead.

His body was dumped unceremoniously onto the deck.

29

**Victory Company, Zombie Squad
In Support of Fort Blake Airfield Seizure,
Objective Star Deck**

Sergeant Lynx used the kerambit knife stabbed into the man's ear to steer his opponent to the wall. In the second the Kimbrin had come from the door, the squad leader's off hand darted to the weapon's sheath hidden just behind the mag pouches on his body armor. The wickedly hooked knife with the finger loop handle swung onto the rebel's neck, cutting off his airway before flipping over on his finger into a reverse grip. That's when the slam into the ear happened.

Gasping for breath that escaped his ruined pipes, the MCR rebel spasmed against the wall. Diggs slithered from behind to paint the surface with the contents of the man's skull using his suppressed pistol. The weapon's rush of air followed by the metallic tap ended the rebel's struggle.

"Who made a pass at the colonel's wife to get us put on cleanup?" Diggs asked into the squad L-comm.

Lynx ignored the man's comment. Thankfully, he was complaining on the team leader's freq and not on the command net. "Lynx to Chopper. I need a net pass to advancing forces."

Diggs's immense frame passed them both and took the lead in the stack with his SAB configured for CQB, while the lieutenant made contact.

"Chopper, this is Lynx. Entry on tower one. Need link-up with Stinger Lead."

"Stand by Lynx," the platoon leader called back immediately.

The L-comm switched to the secure battlenet used by the rest of the Republic forces—an impressive piece of encrypted communication in its own right. "Stinger Lead, this is LS-339. We have entry on tower one. Rig for control in two mikes. How copy, over?"

"LS-339, this is Stinger Lead. I copy two mikes to clean sweep. We are go to clean the gutters and then moving on to the yard. Remain in the tower until we pass. Stinger Lead out."

Lynx frowned. That wasn't the same voice as last time. Poor featherhead must've gotten dusted.

"Ah, crap!" Diggs shouted. He ripped a cylinder off his belt and chucked it into the stairs. The second it left his hand, the device exploded into a translucent blue shimmering barrier that spanned from wall to wall. A grenade dropped by the MCR at the top of the tower exploded, ruining the entry and decimating the walls. The shimmer lasted for thirty seconds before winking out of existence.

"Sket. Did you have those the whole time, Diggsy?" asked Drag, the junior member of the squad.

Diggs pushed his helmet. "If I want commentary from you, Drag, I'll give it to you." When he saw the tilt on Lynx's bucket, he added, "Yes. I was saving it."

Not trying to hide the amusement in his voice, Lynx called to Gekko outside. "Gek, it's Lynx. MCR on tower holing grenades down the chute."

"Got them on thermal. Have the new guy stick his head into the stairs and fire a shot up at them."

Lynx motioned to PFC Hiram Wells to level a single trigger pull straight up through the stairwell. The man's bolt flew into the ceiling, terminating its run in a shower of sparks.

"That did it," Gekko called. "Firing."

A shock wave masquerading as a blaster bolt tore through the side of the building straight into the head of the MCR playing grenade toss. His head snapped back and he fell back onto the balcony where the activated weapon in his hand rolled next to the open doorway for the tower. The entire structure above them shuddered from the fragmentation blast as the weapon tore apart its dead handler and most of the landing.

"Top floor is primed. Take it now."

The Legion squad rushed the stairs with multiple weapons each taking a line of fire as their own. Stepping onto the landing, Diggs put a short burst from the SAB into the stumbling MCR flopping toward the stairs with his own rifle. A series of quick trigger taps resulted in them owning the tower.

"Gek, it's Lynx. Hoof it to us." Zombie Squad's team leader changed to the battlenet. "Stinger Lead. Yard is yours. Mow the lawn."

Trent checked his battle board. "Sergeant—still got another AA gun across from us."

Lynx looked to his next objective. "So take it out. Diggs, gimme a line on that mobile unit with the gear you nicked."

"On it, Sergeant." Diggs motioned the junior man over. "Hey Drag, if you can correctly ID this launcher I'll let you shoot it."

"Where do you even get all this stuff?" the PFC asked. "Is that a Mark Two Longbow ADS?"

"You asking me or telling me? C'mon. You got three seconds to impress me."

Sami, Zombie Squad's trail man and infiltrator, pushed his way past them into the room. "That's what your girl said to him last night."

Not waiting for Corporal Digger's reaction to the provocation, Wells went through a fast-paced lineage of the weapon. "The MK-2 is a rocket-fired high-yield surface-to-air missile capable of engaging targets out to ten kilometers with its seventy-millimeter missile launched by its primary control unit."

Diggs pointed out the window to the mobile air defense missile launcher spinning to life between the two airstrips. "So engage that target for me."

"Through the window?"

"Figure it out, Leej!"

The newly minted Legion warrior folded out the control unit and took aim through the holographic sight. Without warning, the kid raced forward, shattering the window with the front of the launcher and relished the reaction of the senior troopers in the hall when they flinched. A series of beeps turned the reticle green and the kid barked, "Back blast area clear!"

Diggs slid the hatch closed on him before he could fire the weapon. The missile flashed from the launcher, filling the stairway and balcony with smoke. Holograms remained visible through the haze using the advanced optical features in Wells's bucket. The missile struck to target with an explosion that transformed the mobile missile launcher set against the runway and the duracrete around it into a fireball. The inferno rose into the air as a mushroom cloud that swept up debris and flung it away like a hurricane.

Lynx tried not to sound angry or amused when he spoke into the L-comm. "Diggs, did you just have that kid fire a missile system through a window in an enclosed space?"

"No. I told him to figure it out."

**Heavy Drop Shuttle *Bulldog Three*
On Approach to Objective Star Deck**

"Stand by!" shouted the lead legionnaire at the side door of the aircraft. He grabbed both sides of the open door to watch the jungle flash beneath him. Leaning out into the thunderous wind, he checked the skin of the aircraft one last time for any sign of damage as well as to see that the engine was solid so that nothing would come from the front to damage his paras as they fell. He did the same toward the sail so that no one could get hung up as they jumped.

The jungle gave way to the sudden drop in elevation as the heavy drop shuttle *Bulldog Three* passed through the smoke of the smoldering wreckage of the MCR air defenses at the top of the mountain. The signal light at the top of his doorway lit green, and the jumpmasters at opposite ends of the bird shouted at the first leejes in the chalk.

"Go! Go! Go!"

A steady stream of legionnaires ran toward the open doors, handing their static line to the jump masters to be pulled away from their body on exit. With each jump-er, the legionnaires working the doors dragged the line away from them to hand back to the flight crewman behind them. When the last legionnaire exited the door, the jumpmasters looked across the expanse of the empty cargo bay, flashed each other a thumbs-up, and leapt into the sky with their brothers.

Victory Company, Zombie Squad
In Support of Fort Blake Airfield Seizure, Objective Star Deck

"Got another Sidewinder down!" Gekko called into the net. "At this rate they're going to splash the squadron. That gun truck crew is also angling on position to lay some hate to the paras."

Sergeant Lynx stripped a field scope from his belt. "Make them understand that kind of behavior will not be tolerated." With his trooper directed, the Zombie Squad NCO returned to the target of interest on the other side of the airstrip. The Q-hut beside the hardened building was unusually busy for a paper-thin structure under assault by an air cavalry strike force. MCR troops were dancing in and out of his scope, just beyond his line of sight into the building.

"Warlock Actual, this is LS-339. I have you on our scope at two hundred meters on two seven degrees from the first air defense tower. Flashing you a ping on the L-comm. If you need a place to hang your hat we are willing to share."

The Warlock CO, Major Chris Sapero, was on comm immediately. "LS-339, this is LS-410A, call sign Sapps. Thanks for the invite, Leej."

"Roger, sir. About to lay down some house rules for the approaching vics on your POS."

"Send it, Leej!"

Monitoring the higher channel, Gekko didn't wait for his squad leader to clear him to fire. "Sending to lead vic." The first blaster bolt cycled nearly half a charge pack of the N-65 variable output rifle. It hit the armored screen right where the driver's head should be, cracking the security glass and causing the driver to panic. The combat sled fishtailed into a halt that sent the vehicles behind it scrambling to avoid.

"LS-339, this is Sapps. Good hit but the shell didn't crack."

Gekko's finger hovered over the trigger. In the high-gain scope, the top hatch for the combat sled slammed open and Kimbrin, dressed in body armor styled with MCR colors, pulled hard on the twins in the perceived direction of the shot. Gekko half paid attention to the trajectory calibration in his HUD at the periphery of his vision. "Firing."

Throttling the power cycler on the N-65 down, Gekko sent a needle-thin bolt flashing through the rebel, splattering the contents of his skull onto the vehicle behind him. His body whipped off the back of the sled and hung there like a fallen pennant. Flash-fried brain matter and blood served as the catalyst for the combat sleds acting as a security element for the L-TAV to scatter. Repulsors screamed as the vehicles broke formation to bee-line their way away from whatever sled wrecker was firing on them.

"Oh, that's not good," Gekko shouted into the squad comm. "Lynx! That tank is going kinetic."

The precision marksman rolled in a scramble for the opposite side of the roof he'd been operating from. He slid down the angled awning onto the observation deck to land in a crouch. The side of the roof he was shooting from sheared off in a whirlwind of energy and debris as the massive twenty-five-millimeter blaster cannon from the L-TAV disintegrated where he'd just been. A shower of flaming timber and roofing tiles, splashed over Gekko's armor. The legionnaire looked up to see the naked impervisteel frame of the building still intact.

"Hey! Are you guys dead?"

"Yeah," Diggs called back. "Are you?"

"Gonna need a new pair of silkies if we go anywhere nice."

"No chance of that," Lynx shouted above the sound of burning roof tumbling around him. "Trent! Hit that thing with the big boy toys."

The squad snapped to, shrugging off the detritus littering the control center for the air defense tower. Trent crawled to the control station where his battle board was still plugged in. "All the kit on these towers is surface-to-air! I'm going to need a minute to work a T-SIG on that armor!"

"Diggs! You got any more of those LADS?" Lynx called to Diggs. "And where the hell is our A-P launcher?"

Before the big legionnaire could answer, the L-comm broke into Lynx's bucket. "LS-339, this is Sapps. Hold what you got, brother. Popping the lids on APMs. Dumping three."

Aero-precision missiles were the heavy workhorse munition for the Legion. Originally intended to knock military-grade shuttles out of the sky or remove tanks from the battlefield, the system had been continually improved and conditioned over the last twenty years to become the premier missile system for legionnaires across a host of conflicts.

Warlock Company launched a salvo of three missiles heading for their target. Semi-autonomous AI targeting worked two of the fire-and-forget weapons in a high arc that brought it well over the ADA tower occupied by Zombie Squad. The third raced along the ground in a lazy arc toward the L-TAV through the still-smoking wreckage of the mobile ADA system Drag had pummeled with his own rocket.

The ground-racing missile stuck first, blowing off the rear wheel that it struck and sent the fifty-ton tank bouncing forward against protesting brakes. The remainders sailed in from above, razing the tank and the duracrete around it as power cell and energy weapon power plants reached a core temperature well above suggested specs. A halo of duracrete and rich dark earth enveloped the mushroom cloud as the missiles tore the vehicle into slag.

"LS-339, this is Sapps. Victor destroyed. Sending ping to your HUD for our stage. Stay frosty and keep us cold until we get into place. I'll see you in a hot minute. Sapps out."

Diggs pulled Sami out from under a layer of scrap that he'd steadily been trying to dig himself free of. "No hurry, Diggs. Just take your time on pulling me out. Any longer and I would have taken a nap."

"Pretty much what you've been doing this whole time anyway," the corporal responded. He brushed off his fellow leej, pulling the smaller man into a bear hug with slaps on his back armor for good measure. "Can't have you dying on me, man. I don't want to have to break out all-new material to harass whoever they give your spot to."

"I'm insulted that you think the Legion could replace me."

"Everyone's replaceable," Sergeant Lynx growled. Then he and Trent went to work pulling the rest of Zombie Squad from the wreckage. Trent brushed off the battle board and positioned it on top of the main control system. "Can't believe you're going to let company come over when the place looks like this."

"What do you want me to do?" Lynx asked. He pointed to the open sky in the control center. "The brooms were over there."

30

Warlock Company
Fort Blake Airfield Seizure, Objective Star Deck

"First Sergeant, I want that weapons squad on the roll five minutes ago," Major Sapero directed through his L-comm.

The first bolt flying their way struck the ground next to him, sending Sapps's legionnaires diving for cover. He hunkered down behind a duracrete pylon housing that runway's holo generator for flight conditions being re-layed to the various craft taking off. An explosion to his right sent bits of sod and runway tumbling past him. He and his fellow leejes ducked for cover again as the scraps of landscape rained down around them.

"Stinger Lead, this is Warlock Actual. I have enemy armor coming down that hill behind the Q-huts. SIG-ID confirms they are LM-3 Red Foot light armor vehicles, and we have a single AD-21 Mastodon running free from that hangar. If they run free we're going to get pinched."

The battlenet squelched as the new Stinger Lead took command. "I copy all on armored vehicles, Warlock Actual. Deploying assets to make runs on that loc."

"Negative, Stinger Lead. You are safe to engage the LM-3s, but stay away from that Mastodon. It has a PDC mounted on the outside."

"Roger, Warlock Actual. Going for the LM-3s."

Switching to the L-comm, Sapps waded through the traffic like walking through downtown on Victory Day. The platoon leaders were passing their various movements through the net while they jumped in and out to their platoon freqs. First and Second Platoons had taken position at the beginning of the Q-huts and were clearing their way to the hardened structure at the end of the row. One weapons squad was angling against the second air defense tower to get a flanking shot on the Mastodon. Another had fired an aero-precision missile into the front of the vehicle, only to have the projectile deflected by the shield array.

Sending rooster tails of grassy earth up from its bisected tracks, the main battle tank stormed out onto the airfield straight toward the advancing Legion lines. The Mastodon's twin turret-mounted blaster cannons coughed out a single blast wave of shimmering death in their direction. The offset cannon bolts pummeled the tarmac ahead of them, digging a crater nearly a meter deep and showering them in frag.

Above them, Sidewinder gunships raced to lance the hills with high-cycle blaster fire from their rotary cannons and rocket pods. Entire sections of the forested terrain caught fire as the first of the tank squad ruptured, its shield generators going kinetic and turning the armored platform into a fireworks display.

As the rain of earth and timber spilled onto the airstrip, the MCR pushed their final surprise from the hangar. A platoon of robots walked from beneath the minor cover, plodding at first until they were clear of the structure and had room to accelerate into an all-out run.

"XO! Get me a proper SIG-ID on those war bots and front that to REPO!"

Super-Destroyer *Centurion*
Combat Information Center

The spacer technician seated at the sensor station called across the bullpen. "Lieutenant Apollo! SIG-ID pegs those war bots as HK-37s. House of Reason tried to retcon the old one-oh-eights with all the bells and whistles and came away what we have down there."

Apollo swiveled the Legion communication officer in his chair. "Captain, I need a contact at Legion Intel so I can figure out where in the black hole the MCR is getting all this tech."

The comm officer stared blank-faced at *Centurion's* intelligence officer. What she was asking him to do wasn't his job. He was there to secure the L-comm from anyone other than Legion assets using it. His eyes narrowed for the briefest of moments before he turned back to his station. "Technically, Lieutenant, that is a request that has to be pushed from the general... but as we're working on his behalf, I should be able to whip something together."

"Thank you." Spinning on her heel, she yelled across to *Centurion's* commander. "Captain Aguiar, I need another blackout shot for the leejes downstairs taking that airfield."

"Fox-Con, you heard the LT," Aguiar said.

"Aye, sir. Loading blackout. Thirty seconds to fire."

The technician repeated the order in keeping with tradition that everyone in the chain leading to the one pulling the trigger understands the order and is duty-bound to carry it out. "Blackout in the tube and angry. Fifteen seconds to fire."

Warlock Company
Fort Blake Airfield Seizure, Objective Star Deck

"Ion strike in thirty seconds!" Sapps called into the net. "Hey RTO, get me a quick line on Zombie Squad."

"On it, sir," came the reply from the nearby legionnaire.

Five seconds into the thirty-second wait, the command crew was pelted with dirt and debris as the incoming blaster fire from the tank supported by the war bots turned into a frenzy.

"Sir!" the RTO cried over the din of bolts and blasts. "All PLs report secured for ion strike. Zombie is thumbs-up too."

The Legion command element dropped prone, hugging various parts of the terrain and available structures on that side of the field. Buckets switched off and EMP-protected tech cycled power feeds to give the incoming missile room to do its devastating work.

The Mastodon tank swung wide on its repulsors to give the advancing line of robots a direct shot at the weapon squads and the command element. The war machine formation went from ranks to wedge until a three-bot jumble looking to get its kill on exploded on the move. Walking infernos plodded to a slow stop with each step dropping wreckage in their wakes. Zombie Squad had taken the last few seconds before the blackout to even the odds for the besieged Legion company.

Segments of the forward-facing war machines turned to flank, dumping wrist-mounted N-50 fire into the tower in response to the attack.

Task Force Hornet
Knight Hunter Squadron
Over Objective Star Deck

"All Knight Hunter elements, this is Knight Hunter Lead. Blackout strike on Objective Star Deck confirmed. Localized ion strike over target complete. We are max burn to drop. I say again, all Knight Hunter elements, get over that airstrip and deploy!"

The heavy haulers slammed their throttles, setting their thrusters ablaze over the approach to the Fort Blake airfield. Spreading in their own wedge formation for maximum dispersion, the shuttles dangling various pieces of gear flew five hundred meters above the target when suspension clamps released, dropping their cargoes to the ground. With full deployment indicators lighting up the tracking boards in the cockpits, the pilots pulled hard on the yokes to drive their craft into a near-vertical climb to orbit.

"Warlock Actual, this is Knight Hunter. All assets deployed. Good hunting. Knight Hunter out."

Victory Company, Zombie Squad
Fort Blake Airfield Seizure, Objective Star Deck

"Man! I thought that tank was going to level us."

"Day's not over yet!" Lynx shouted to the squad. "Everyone un-ass this tower! Once that tank spins up again it's going to be like shooting fish in a bucket."

"Isn't it a barrel?" Trent said, winding up the connection cable to his battle board.

"No one asked you, genius," Diggs said, pushing the leej from his spot at the command console.

"How's the kid?" Lynx asked.

The two NCOs looked through the door to see Wells throw them a thumbs-up. His armor was completely covered in soot and ash from the MK-2 LADS he'd fired from inside the stairwell. As the kid raced to run down the stairs of the tower, Lynx took note of the words *Mom says I'm special* traced into the soot on the back of his armor.

"Really?" said Lynx.

"Wasn't me!" Diggs said with his hands up. He raised his enhanced monocular, taking range between the tower and the armored threat about to come to life again. "So what's the play, Sergeant? Hit those war bots and give digits to *Centurion* REPO for a harder hit?"

"Negative. All that air just landed a heavy drop. That stuff is going to burn silk and set this place on fire." Lynx jumped into the higher net in the L-comm. "Sapps, this is LS-339, we're exiting the first tower. Six coming out."

"Roger, Three-Three-Nine. Get behind the tower and stay there if possible. We're coming to you as soon as the heavies get their slam on."

"Three-Three-Nine, Roger out."

Zombie Squad exited the tower, throwing down their assault packs and landing behind them to use them as stable shooting platforms to level fire on whatever target came their way. Sami called out last man as he exited the tower, the call being obscured as their buckets amplified the noise of an energy cycler's rampant whine bringing a tremendous power core online somewhere in the field.

"If that's the tank, we're karked," Sami said, sliding behind his brothers.

Littered between the two runways was a smattering of parachutes covering angular equipment of various sizes. The silk fell away from the largest of them, exposing a mechanized monstrosity in the form of a Hunter-Killer Planet-Pounder mech.

"Some of you skaggs might want to hit the record button," Diggs commented, "because that thing is about to open an expensive can of slam for the MCR to choke on."

The high-cycle whine of the power core came to a fevered pitch as the HK-PP disengaged the retention rings on its suspension lines and took its first volcanic steps. Several other chutes along the battlefield fell away, exposing one other HK-PP and four Hunter-Killer Scout Walkers. The walkers sprinted away, reaching nearly eighty kph in two directions as they broke into pairs. The first ran a tight circle around the war bots while the second raced for the ten-meter-high security wall behind the Q-huts. Jump jets beneath the scout mechs flared, catapulting the two-legged war machines over the barrier and into the woods at the base of the mountain.

"See that, Drag?" said Diggs. "They're splitting up the team. The two heavies are going after the tank, team two is taking the bots, and those jumpers just went after the remaining LM-3s on the hill."

The plodding mechs accelerated into a trot, pushing the machines to just past sixty kilometers per hour. The leader of the two unleashed a Hell Bat missile from one of its launchers, and it sailed easily to the target with its trademark double slam, putting the AD-21 Mastodon at the center of an explosion that sent a mushroom cloud sailing over fifty meters into the air. As the lighter mechs laid waste to the awakening war bots, the twin HK-PPs circled the devastation of the tank like sharks waiting to see the carcass through the chum.

To everyone's surprise, the tank flew from the debris cloud pulling along a trail of dust in its wake. The sandy particulates hanging in the air were more than enough to show that the Mastodon's protective energy shield had held against the onslaught, but it was in critical danger of failing.

The second HK-PP left the ground nearly a meter on a set of repulsors. Powerful engines behind it fired to life in a burst of violent thrust that sent it rushing into the tank's path. The two collided with a deafening clang that rang out across the airfield and sent the AD-21 careening away from its rush toward the Legion.

Diggs nudged Wells. "You got a designator on that weapon? Fire it up. If that tank outruns those mechs and gets a bead on them, we'll have to improvise."

"What's my spot laser going to do, Corporal?"

"We lase the target and let the Sidewinders slam it with a couple of missiles—or if we're lucky, we get Raptors to tap dance over the top of it with something ultra-violent."

"Why can't *Centurion* just hit it with a real airstrike?"

It was Lynx who answered. "The task force commander wants the airfield intact so we can run and stage the follow-on missions from here. If we're forced to bring in engineers to patch a hole deeper than a skyscraper is tall, that's going to make things difficult, because this is probably the most defendable airfield we have this close to the next objective."

"The MCR sure isn't doing a good job defending it," Wells commented.

The twin HK-PP mechs flashed away from each other, leveling destructive cannon fire from their main blaster turrets with an explosive force equivalent to that of an artillery piece. The tank's twin blaster cannons roared out a volley of its own, striking the second of the mechs in a shower of sparks that spun it toward the tarmac. Self-righting technology went to work to put the mech back on its feet as the lead heavy went to work on the Mastodon.

Another volley lashed out from the AD-21 to scream over the heads of the ducking legionnaires.

"Boss, I don't want to be a Drusic Downer, but that mess is heading right for us!" Sami said.

Lynx pointed his fingers toward his bucket and then past Sami. The group turned to see a Legion squad advancing on them behind a robotic combat support mech. The barrel-shaped, bull-sized robot had become a staple for those areas where the Legion had to operate in the open. They were the perfect mule for carrying heavy gear, resupply, and provisions while also providing an armored fighting platform to fight from should the leejes need it.

The R-CSM positioned itself behind Zombie Squad at an angle to the building, providing a perfect wagon-train fighting position to conduct operations from. It then dropped down into soil to deploy its heavy armored shields to defend the crew against incoming blaster fire and flak.

"LS-339, I presume?" Major Sapps said, offering his fist to his fellow legionnaire.

"Yes, sir. Call sign Lynx, Major. Thanks for the assist."

"You too. Nice hit on those war bots with a reconfigured ADA tower."

Lynx nodded. "Thank you, sir. Trent there is a genius when it comes to getting tech to do what he wants. I wanted to rain some hate on that AD-21, but the thing is too mobile and that shield is making life difficult for systems too used to firing up."

"Might not have to worry about it in a sec," Sapps said.

The tank whirled around in a tight drift that brought it in a loop around the mobile HK-PP so that it had a clear shot on the mech that was down. Just as the cannons tilted to fire on its victim, the target fired its thrusters. The downed mech shot off along the ground, digging a trench nearly half a meter deep as it skipped across the grass.

The remaining heavy fired its own jump jets in a much higher flight than before, terminating the arc to come down on top of the enemy tank. Despite the point defense cannon firing for all it was worth, forty-five tons of armor slamming onto the machine finally ruptured the Mastodon's shield and battered the enemy vehicle into the grass. Another jump freed the tank but also cleared it from friendly forces as the newly righted heavy mech bashed it with another Hell Bat.

The Hell Bat's implosion field, with no shields to contend with, easily cracked the outer shell of the tank's armor. Structural rupture points acted as highways for heat and force as the missile reversed its polarity and exploded. The rupture of the tank's reactor combined with the cooking off of available ammunition decimated the vehicle.

Heavy debris pelted the R-CSM that Zombie Squad had sheltered behind. A shower of duracrete rained down on them as something punched its way through the tower above. As the shower subsided, Lynx looked up at the air defense tower they'd fought so hard to secure. Part of a tank barrel had split in half and was blasted away from the vehicle like a thrown knife. It smashed into the tower above them and embedded itself between the second floor and the observation control deck.

"Lynx!" Diggs shouted over L-comm.

Wells lay behind the R-CSM like the rest of them, but he'd been impaled with a piece of impervisteel rebar flung from the structure by the force of the impact. His heaving gasps were broadcast through the team channel, making the macabre scene all the worse as the kid struggled not to contaminate the net.

"Don't hold it in, kid. Let it out if you need to," Diggs said.

"Sami!" Lynx called.

The Warlock Company commander was quick to send word for his medics. "Lynx, here's my doc!"

The Legion medic came running into a scene that veteran leejes were all too used to. "I got it. You, you, and you. I need you to grab his feet and shoulders. Me and you are going to hold the rod as they lift."

"Can't. Breathe," Wells grunted.

"If you're talking, you're breathing," Diggs assured him. The man had lost his abrasive tone, assuming the role of protector over the wounded man.

"Hey, Leej," the medic said, getting Wells's attention. "What's your name?"

"His call sign is Smoker!" Diggs called out.

"Judging by his armor, I can see why," the medic joked. "Smoker, you need to try and take steady breaths and let the armor do its job. Except for the hole, your armor is functional. Try to breathe normally, bud."

A group of leejes including the Warlock Company commander pulled Smoker from the ground while other leejes held onto the rebar so it wouldn't slide through the wound to cause more damage. Cutting torches were pulled from utility belts in order to shorten the meter of steel sticking through Smoker's chest and make him easier to carry.

"Make sure to cut quick," said the doc. "If that bar heats up from those plasma cutters, the damage it'll cause will make the puncture the least of our worries."

"Lay him on his side for a minute," Sami said. "Smoker. Can you stay on your side while I cut this down for you?"

"Can you do this?" Lynx said. "After the last time, I wouldn't think you'd want to bring that thing out."

Sami stepped past his NCO. "It'll be faster than the torches. Besides, no time to be squeamish."

"What's he going to do?" Sapps asked.

"It's a family heirloom, sir. Straight-up nightmare cutter," Lynx answered.

Sami looked to the doc, whose body language demanded speed even if his face couldn't behind the Legion bucket. Sami's armor stretched as he took a cleansing breath, centering himself in training that was definitely not according to Legion doctrine. In a flash of motion, a black silk-wrapped handle with white diamond patterns sailed from his belt. The silvery blade became ghostly as it flashed through the rebar on one side of the kid, and then with another stroke did the same to the other side, mere centimeters from Smoker's armor.

In moments the doc had Smoker loaded onto a repulsor sled brought out from the R-CSM. "We'll evac him as soon as we secure the field. I just coded his armor to drug him and lock him in place so he can't move. Bio-signs show that he's stable for the moment, although I'm going to keep an eye on him as the armor already ran a spike when he started bleeding into that lung."

"Thanks, Doc. Can you keep me in the loop?"

"Will do, Sergeant Lynx," the medic said, descending into his battle board to begin setting up a casualty collection point for the operation.

Lynx approached the company commander. "Pardon me, sir. I have a tasking from my CO that when you're done with us, we're supposed to rejoin the company."

Sapps took the sergeant by the wrist. "The leash is off, Leej. Do what you have to. But before you go, are you the same legionnaires that slagged the hidden arty site up on that hill and then rolled up the security tower on the gate breaking into the base?"

"Yes, sir. Apparently we're Victory Company's flavor of the month."

"Right on. And what's up with your boy's knife?"

"Old Sinasian vibro-tech. It's a wave knife, sir."

"That's definitely not Legion issue. Those things are dangerous. The Savages used to cut into ship's hulls with those."

"Yes, sir. But my man Samurai just used his to save our brother without causing further injury. So if anyone is going to take the hit over him carrying it, it'll be me, sir."

Sapps motioned for a GMV to be brought over to them. "After the day you've had, Sergeant, the only thing anyone should be saying to you is KTF."

31

Bear stepped out of the armored utility sled onto the sidewalk, buttoning a jacket that protested being forced around his overly wide shoulders. A squad of angry Kimbrin dressed in local finery rushed the three-vehicle convoy.

"You there. Marine! You stop."

Being called a marine stopped Bear, along with his two Zaan security detail. They didn't step in front of the big leej. They knew better. But that didn't prevent them from readying the submachine blasters hidden under their jackets.

"What can I do for you gentlemen?" Bear asked.

"Who do you think you are?" the Kimbrin snapped. "The general has put a lockdown on the whole city!" An explosion in the distance from Fort Blake confirmed the need for such a lockdown. The MCR security soldier raised his off hand and poked a finger at Bear's chest almost close enough to touch him, but never making contact. "You're not supposed to be here!"

"We have permission from Grelin to move about the city," Bear said with his hands out to the sides.

"Do I look like a criminal thug that would be swayed by that?"

Bear couldn't decide if the man was being facetious or wanted a real answer. "I am here at the request of a legitimate businessman in this building. He does work with the chiefs all the time." He held up a paper. "I have this."

The patrol leader slapped the paper out of Bear's hand and into the street. He pressed toward the suit-dressed mammoth and stuck an old X-4 Intec blaster pistol into the covert legionnaire's jaw. "I am no thug. I am Kam Het. Do you know this?"

"Yeah, I know this." Bear nodded. "But I'm not that guy."

Confusion twisted the jaw spikes on the patrol leader's face. He pushed into the pistol, letting the barrel move Bear's jaw to the side. Further confusion appeared in his expression when Bear started laughing.

"First up, Kam Het, look me in the face and decide if this is a fight that you want." Bear tapped the rim of his glasses, drawing the man's attention.

For a moment, the MCR fighter snarled contempt—until he noticed his reflection in Bear's mirrored glasses. Specifically, he saw the red dot hovering between his eyes.

Bear stepped to the side to allow for Jaela's clean line to the target. "And second, now that I have your attention, we don't have to be enemies. I'm just here to make some money and to make sure the chiefs get a taste. I *could* cut you in on a piece of the action."

"No bribe is worth the lives of my men," the Kimbrin said.

And there it was. The chink in his armor that Bear was waiting for. During his time as a line legionnaire, he would have already given the order for his security detail to dump a floodlight worth of blaster bolts into these kelhorns. But that was before he took command of a kill team where nuance was everything. "Doda: Twenty-one Yao Sun Street, Lock Four. Drail: Six Freel Road."

Before Bear could list the third name and address, the patrol leader shouted. "Stop! Stop or I will shoot you in the face!"

"Do it!" Bear growled, deciding to hover over the man for the first time since the interaction began. "Do it, Vryssek. Two-Sixteen Kumo Street. One partner and two children, one of whom is currently playing with his friends across from the Haldo Building in the next district over. Now, I didn't come here for you or your families. I have the approval of the city chiefs, whom your bosses supposedly work for. But if you continue this tough guy act, I'm going to burn everything you care about and leave you with nothing. And if you are stupid enough to pull that trigger, my men here will make you watch as they slaughter everyone under your command but you."

The Kimbrin responded with nothing but the intense breathing of a man deep into his own anger. Bear flicked a finger behind him. The trail AUS-V disgorged four more Zaan fighters, each in a business suit with a submachine blaster trained on the affair. They sprinted in a half-moon formation, easily having line of sight on the Kimbrin patrol.

Bear's micro-comm beeped in his ear. "Bear, this is Jaela. This is taking too long and another squad is driving up the street in a technical. They got a light repeating blaster mounted to the back and an additional six fighters on board. Unlike the ones you're facing, they look like MCR regulars."

Bear factored how much time he had to get into the building. "What's it going to be, Kam Het?"

"Go about your business," Patrol Leader Vyrssek said. "I am going to check with my chain of command, and if this is not legitimate, I will be here when you come out."

Another flick from Bear's fingers dispersed his extra security back into the waiting security vehicle. He waited until the Kam Het team took a few steps away to continue their patrol of the block before he made the trek up the building stairs and into the entrance.

"What is Kam Het?" asked his right-facing security Zaan.

"They're MCR loyalists who turned against their militia units to join the rebellion. While they're typically not as proficient as our friends in the Second Free Rifles, they do have standard combat training and decent gear. Both of you stay tight to me when we walk in here."

Bear pulled open the outer door and stepped into the foyer. Both Kimbrin with him skipped a step when they looked to their flanks to see twin Mechasaga 22 security mechs towering over them. The two-legged armored bots each sported a slug-throwing chain gun on one side and a pulse beamer on the other. The beamer was like a laser pointer with a thousand times the power. It cut through flesh and soft armor like butter while leaving stone structures moderately intact.

Bear held a black card above his head. The simple motion caused the mechs to take a step back while a Kimbrin walked forward with his hands clasped in front of him.

"Welcome to Vai-Kasa Corporation. I see that you have a platinum access card for our facility. What is the nature of your visit?"

"I'm here for Mr. Kein. My name is Barlo."

The Kimbrin wavered in Bear's HUD specs. He had the system run a light dispersion algorithm, confirming that the person in front of him was actually a holo-shrouded bot. That was smart. In the event of an MCR takeover of the city, all the actual living people were locked away in the upper floors, away from the easily accessed lobby.

"Ah, yes," the bot said. "Mr. Kein is expecting you. Please follow the lights to the elevator and Mr. Kein will attend you shortly."

A holographic beam formed at Bear's feet, leading him around the corner. He tapped his brow to the bot in thanks for the help and followed the light to a wall of three sliding lift doors. The centermost one opened before he had a chance to call for an elevator. "I guess we're expected."

The doors sealed once they'd entered, and with a shimmering effect the walls changed to a wrap-around display showing the various products made by the Vai-Kasa Corporation. Along one wall, a series of pixels were out, leaving a streaking, fluttering scar on the display. The company reminded Bear of the Republic. For all their credits, they still had trouble keeping things as neat and as shiny as they would like.

The ding of the elevator doors opening brought up the rifles of a ten-man security team waiting on the other side of the lift. Bear put his hands up, his fingers spread wide to show that he wasn't a threat.

"Name's Barlo. Grelin sent me. I'm here to escort Mr. Kein to safety."

"Boys and girls," said a voice, "lower those guns. Mr. Barlo is here at my behest." The man walking through the double column of security was gray in the temples but fit and strong. He extended a hand that took Bear's in a firm shake.

"Mr. Kein," Bear said. "It's nice to finally meet you."

"And you as well, Mr. Barlo. Thank you for coming on such short notice. I have to confess, I haven't been on this side of one of these planetary insurrections before. Definitely never had to be extracted before. Do I pay you now, or do we wait? What's the protocol?"

"Grelin took a deposit on our behalf once I took the assignment, sir. The rest of the funds are being held in receivership pending your extraction."

"Seems that's in order then. Mr. Barlo, the reason I have you pulling me out instead of my own security is that our mutual acquaintances have made it clear you have the resources to get us past the Legion blockade overhead."

"That is correct," Bear said flatly. He directed his men down the hall into the executive's palatial office.

Kein looked uncertainly after the men. "Um, Mr. Barlo. What are they doing?"

"Checking your office for evidence of espionage or betrayal. I can't move you until I'm sure that no one knows of our plans."

Kein looked suspicious. "That is very bold of you to presume, Mr. Barlo. Shall I search your people for such indications as well? This is, after all, the first time we've talked."

Bear waved his finger in a resounding negative. "Sir, I've flown from one end of the galaxy to the other, and if there's one thing I know, it's that no matter how good the person, there's always someone out there who's sick of their nonsense—and who wants them dead. But feel free to search every dark place the sun don't shine on my team. Point is, we aren't leaving until we can all be sure no one's following us."

One of Bear's security team walked back with a set of forceps in his hand. He said something in the local dialect, prompting Bear to take out his handheld. "Mr. Kein, do you have a comm on you?"

The man held up his wrist to reveal an elegant watch wrapped around it. If Bear had to guess, the thing was worth his salary for the year.

Bear held out his palm. The member of his team with the forceps dropped a small data pin in the waiting hand. "Found it under his chair, sir," the security team member said.

Bear looked at the small device in his hand, then looked up at Kein. "See this? It's a problem. Whoever placed it under your chair has been fed everything you've been doing."

"That's impossible," Kein sputtered. "My people do regular security sweeps."

"Which tells us that it was put there *by* your people. Whoever's ultimately behind this knows everything you know and everywhere you go."

"I am the head of this facility. No one here fails to meet my security standards. My team is *not* compromised. They will do whatever I ask of them."

"I'm not Humanoid Resources," Bear growled. "Don't care who you hire and who you fire. But this commlink you've got on your wrist is compromised. If someone is slicing it via that data pin under your seat—and they were—they surely got a lock on it and can track you wherever you go. Your team will do whatever you ask them to? Great. Have one of them wear it for the time being."

"This is ridiculous," Kein said. "We're wasting time."

Bear shrugged. "It's your call. I had a situation like this once before though. Three-hour ride, changed sleds four times. Got out at the docking pad and—*boom!*—client's head gets vaped. Tracked the comm. First and easiest trick in the book." Bear leaned in close and whispered in Kein's ear, taking advantage of the sudden doubt and nervousness that had come over the Kimbrin. "How much do you trust these kelhorns compared to how much you trust Grelin? Grelin didn't send you these guys. He sent you *me*. And I say we should leave them behind."

Kein's face beaded with perspiration and he looked around nervously.

"C'mon. Get in the lift so we can get out of here," Bear said.

Kein meekly stepped into the lift with Bear, and the only guards who accompanied them were Bear's. Kein's face looked grim, as though he'd just been force-fed a spoonful of medicine he didn't know he had to take.

Bear's HUD specs flashed a message from the INSEC agent posing as his security. "Slice initiated. Initial findings indicate Nether code traces. The source system is unknown but Kein's machines have all been heavily sliced."

"Mr. Barlo," said Kein. "I know that our initial arrangement was to get me off Kima. However, if I doubled your fee, would you be amenable to assisting some of my employees as well?"

"What did you have in mind? You got a local *girl* that you want to come with?" Bear asked. "Happens a lot."

"If we have indeed been sliced, then some of my company's assets in the labs have been sorely compromised. There is a doctor who has to come with us."

"Has to," Bear parroted. While not a question, his comment had the intended effect of loosening the executive's tongue.

"My colleague, Dr. Rantanen, is a vital part of what we do here. Certain shareholders would certainly want her extracted."

"Of course they would." Bear let his view hover over a waiting prompt in his HUD specs. Retinal tracking brought up the message on the display:

Two flagged search terms located on Kein's system. Weaponized and Legionnaire.

32

Chhun slapped his armored bracer against MakRaven's hard enough to rattle his own fillings, then gave the man a hug and a slap on the back armor to welcome him back to the TOC. "Good work out there, Sergeant Major."

MakRaven nodded after he'd removed his bucket and chucked it into the cargo net seating of the assault shuttle. "Yeah. I mean, yes sir. Mids were looking to get hired for fertilizer so we obliged them."

Chhun heard the pain in the man's voice. Losing a man to blasters or blowouts, hell, even accidents was one thing. What had happened to Bouncer was something else. There were some lines that you didn't cross, even in war, and the MCR had not only stepped over it, they'd kicked dirt on top of the grave so the boundary wasn't visible anymore.

"I'm sorry, Mak."

MakRaven rocked his head from shoulder to shoulder. "You watch it?"

"I did. Through Hammer's bucket. He okay?"

"He'll be good until we get off this rock. Though I pity anyone in his way."

Chhun nodded at something behind the sergeant major. "He with you?"

MakRaven looked back to see Bubbles waiting for them on the shuttle's ramp with a torn pack in his mouth. The canine leej gingerly crept forward, aware that he was now the topic of discussion, and looked from Chhun to MakRaven.

"I dunno." MakRaven felt the dog's pain emanating off him in waves, and for a moment it was all he could do to hold himself together. "Hey, pup. Glad you're okay there, uh... ah, dammit. Guess I have to say it now. Bubbles."

The dog set down his package. The small assault pack looked like it had blood and mud from every conflict leejes had been fighting in for the past few years. Bubbles waved his tongue from the back of his mouth to the front several times to dislodge some taste or fiber, then ran from the bay to the bottom of the ramp, barking and growling at something the men couldn't see.

Finn walked onto the ramp carrying a man in en-er-chains with a sensory deprivation hood over his head. He put the man roughly into the cargo netting, pinning his ener-chains to the cargo cable above his head. The leej removed his bucket, holding it under his arm and snapping to attention.

"General. Sergeant Major. LS-4177 reporting with prisoner taken from the advancing Kimbrin company."

"Stand easy", Chhun said. "You good, Leej?"

"Ready to get back after it, sir."

Chhun noted the tears streaking the grime on the man's face. He also noted that the dog was latching his teeth around the prisoner's leg every time the man tried to get comfortable.

"Is the dog with you, now?"

"No sir," Finn said. "None of us are rated for him, sir. And even if we were, well, I um..."

"Spit it out, Leej," MakRaven said.

"Bubbles is a bit of a special case among the STB, Sar'nt Major. He chooses the handler. Not the other way around."

Chhun's brow furrowed. "Come again, Sergeant?"

Finn searched for the right words to use with a former Legion commander turned plain old general officer. The normally snarky leej decided on just following the sergeant major's advice rather than end up being ordered to spill everything anyways.

"Sir, I'm only passing on what Bouncer told me. But before he was Bubbles, that dog was Dozer. Giggs or something before that. There's even some scallywag among the handlers that he might even be Padlock."

That name got the sergeant major's attention. "Padlock? That dog was with us at Ankalor. How is it possible that he's still serving?"

Finn shrugged. "Sergeant Major, I'm just telling you what Bouncer told me. This dog has been in the thick of every nasty conflict we've been in lately. He somehow is in just the right place to be in the worst possible moments for us so he can save every leej that he can. But in each case, his handler never makes it."

"Are you saying this dog is cursed?" Mak asked. "More likely Bouncer was just havin' fun with you."

"Maybe that's it, Sergeant Major, but I don't think so. Bouncer isn't—" Finn caught himself. "*Wasn't* like that. Bouncer would say that this dog only chooses the best of us. Superior fighters and the best character."

Bubbles barked several times while pushing the bag he'd brought in. MakRaven took the cue and reached into the disheveled ruck. Inside were several leashes, toys— of both the squeaky and non-squeaky variety—and a latched pocket. Inside the separate compartment was a ruined drone.

"I'll be karked," MakRaven said. He handed the machine to Chaz. "Can we see what's on this?"

"Of course, Sergeant Major."

Chaz projected the drone's holorecording, replaying the events up to and including Bouncer's death. It was definitely gruesome. Not the way anyone would want to go. Chhun watched the whole affair tucked into his folded arms.

"It is interesting," Chaz said, "that Hammer did not suffer the same fate as Bouncer. The wildlife in his vicinity all succumbed to a quick death."

"Bot's right," said Finn. "We thought at first he was just far enough away, but he ran in before the gas was completely gone, and he didn't suffer so much as a hiccup. Even Bouncer only got it on his arms. It looks like the gas was completely blocked by Legion armor."

Chhun halted in his tracks. "Chaz, run a patch through *Centurion*'s Legion communication's officer. I need Legion Command, now."

Super-Destroyer *Centurion*
Engaged in Orbital Security

Marines on either side of the door leading to the CIC snapped to attention as the portal slid open. Deynolds was on the move. "Thank you, Marines."

She swept from the room, cutting a sharp corner down the passage toward her private quarters. Spacers and marines darted to the side allowing her to pass, some so new that any sight of the old girl sent them into a rigid position of attention while rendering the greeting of the day. She returned their greetings the same way she moved through the passage: with purpose. When a command staff level officer is in a hurry, it's best for everyone to just move out of the way.

A speedlift opened at her advance, its impervisteel doors, painted with the symbol of the Republic over the *Centurion* logo, slamming into their housings as if trying to accommodate her haste. As the lift got underway, she tapped out a series of instructions on her battle board to one of several security elements on the ship. The ride to her private quarters would be brief, so she'd want everything to be in place when she got there.

The lift bounded on its repulsor field, and the doors opened to armed marines. "Thank you for meeting me, Marines."

The senior of the two merely nodded, and both of them fell in step behind her as she continued her trek through the ship. At the end of the passage was a wall bearing her nameplate just beside the blast door that served as the entrance to her quarters.

"Ma'am, do you need a security sweep of the room?"

"It couldn't hurt. Thank you, Sergeant."

One marine waited in the passage while the other moved through the room with a digital distress meter, looking for errant signals or any functioning AI trying to broadcast outside of *Centurion* communication protocols.

"Ma'am, your quarters are clear. We can detect no errant signals. For the duration of the communication, we will monitor your feed for any signal irregularities or protocol masking."

"Thank you, Sergeant."

Deynolds rolled into her cabin, securing the door behind her. Tossing her data slate on the desk, she switched to the secure unit built into it.

Messaging secured. Engaging message protocol Deynolds-Kappa-343-Alpha.

"This had better be good, because I'm in the middle of two boarding actions on capital-class ships."

And then the admiral saw the names of those already holoed into the meeting. Chhun she'd expected. Delegate Asa Berlin and Legion Commander Oosten... not so much.

It looked as though this would be good after all.

Harvester Command Element
Temporary Ops Center
Bulldog Four

"What is the situation there, General?" Legion Commander Oosten asked. He had a slight draw in his left eye from scarring left untreated for too long, and it made the man look like he was ready to go knuckles up at all times if he faced the video capture device a certain way.

"Ladies and gentlemen," Chhun began, "we're in the middle of a lot of moving parts so I'll be brief. One of our casualties on the ground was due to a corrosive, vapor-based neurotoxin with limited range on dispersion. While all manner of germ warfare has been directed at the Legion, something about this particular formula stands out: namely, that it has no effect on those in full Legion armor.

"Our legionnaire had his arms exposed when the toxin was released, which caused extreme corrosion to the exposed tissue, as well as instantaneous pulmonary distress and extreme damage to the central nervous system. We have a Valkyrie team recovering the scene now, and the sample they've analyzed shows nanites dispersed through the vector. These nanites cycle the acid so the pH and the spread affect a predetermined area. Recovered drones show control modes and topographic dispersion formula for the attack."

The three holographic people in Chhun's field of view went from mildly annoyed at being summoned to worried in the span of a heartbeat. Deynolds looked like she'd gone from simmer to boil.

"Are you saying that this is a Legion weapon being used against us, General?" Deynolds asked.

Oosten sighed, not in annoyance at the question but over the gravity of what he had just heard from General Chhun. "No, Admiral," he said. "What the general just described is a substance called VBX-13. It started as a pesticide against celestial-accustomed creatures that live deep inside of mined asteroids. As most of these creatures do not breathe as we do, the company contracted for its development created a nerve agent with a nanite called thiophosphonate. It promotes entry into creatures that have natural exoskeletal plating to protect them from the limited atmosphere and harsh conditions where they dwell. In essence, the compound corrodes the outer layer of the shell to get the neurotoxin into the animal's nervous system."

That sounded bad enough to those on the meeting. What Oosten followed with sounded worse. "In going over classified House of Reason documents after Article Nineteen, we found that Nether Ops contracted several black bag operations to research what the toxin would do in a conventional atmosphere to terrestrial animals and, of course, people. This led to its use on certain prison colonies, as well as several other deployment zones until certain extreme elements in the organization banned its use due to its extremely identifiable signature."

"So what's it doing on Kima?" Representative Berlin asked. "Do we have evidence that Nether Ops is still functioning at sufficient capacity to coordinate with the MCR? I was under the impression all the departments had been brought to heel, their directors dead or awaiting trial."

"That is correct, ma'am. And as to your question, there is no *direct* evidence, beyond a loose string of intel more closely associated with loyalists to the House of Reason. But if you want my gut feeling... they're involved somehow."

"Navy intelligence has uncovered evidence of former Nether agents working on the black market," said Deynolds. "Perhaps they sold supplies to the MCR."

"It was already on planet," Chhun said. "Vai-Kasa on Kima holds the patent and the formula for creating VBX-13 in its original formula as a pesticide. I'm in contact with my kill team asset in Kam Dho City working to extract the on-site supervisor as well as the senior medical specialist for the site. He'll find out if Vai-Kasa weaponized existing supplies of the pesticide for the MCR."

Deynolds shifted at her desk. "General Chhun, pre-combat docs you provided indicated the kill teams had been on fact-finding missions to track Nether links in other sectors. Could we have Nether operators on the ground here, impeding our efforts?"

"Anything's possible, Admiral. The data we sliced from the Nether intel stations had no indicators of any interest or involvement with Kima, but that's hardly definitive. Regardless, my people are in place and working to shut the Vai-Kasa operation down. We also are investigating concerns that deployment of the toxin was the actual purpose for the mobile artillery platforms the MCR was furnished with. I have my legionnaires combing through the munitions to see if we have any loaded with VBX-13."

Berlin took a step back from the image, nearly disappearing until someone in her staff reminded her to stay in the projector's field of view. It was one thing to read or watch about the horrors of war on the holos, it was another thing to be this close to it as it was happening. "To what end?" she asked. "Surely the MCR would know that it would be the Legion who would secure the planet and return it to its people. Why, then, use a weapon that is useless against armored legionnaires?"

Chhun took the question. "It's not for us, Delegate Berlin. It's for the Kimbrin."

Shock and horror fell upon her face. "Their own people."

"It's an old sniper's trick, ma'am," Chhun continued. "We move in to take the cities and then they dump a bunch of this gas to cause chaos. While we're distracted trying to save the population—the only ones able to do so because our armor is immune to the effects—they can make it look like our invulnerability to the gas is a planned event, and suddenly our entire operation looks like a plot for the Republic to take Kima for themselves. While it makes no sense when you say it out loud, they only need to plant the seeds of doubt for the damage to be done. It would hardly be the first time such a tactic was used, and it has been successful in the past, sad to say."

"Tell me you have a counter-agent for this gas," Berlin pleaded.

Chhun crossed his arms. "I have a team on the ground working it now, ma'am."

33

Kam Dho City
Vai-Kasa Corporate Building

"Jaela, it's B! I need you and the combat applications team to make entry!"

"You sound a little flustered, Papa Bear. Sitrep, over."

Bear huffed into the comm as blaster bolts zinged past him. "I have Kein. We just tried to pick up his witch doctor when a hit team started sending bolts up range. We're holding the hall outside the lift but I have no way to secure the rest of the floor."

Hitters, mostly Hools with a few Kimbrin, worked to flank and maneuver their way toward Bear, the cowering Kein, and Bear's two-man security detail—the Kimbrin Roolo and the human Neuschwanger.

Bear's comm bead beeped, indicating a switch on the net. "Bear, this is Zier. We have squads of those patrols from earlier watching us from across the street. If we abandon the AUS-Vs for the building, they might scrap our rides."

"That's a chance we'll have to take, Zier. I need that doctor and we have to eliminate anything that team is carrying."

"We're on it. Jaela?"

"I have you," Jaela said. "I'll distract the patrols. You go team light and have one person from each team behind the wheel to drive those AUS-Vs somewhere they can hole up until this plays out."

"Good call, J," Bear said. "Signal me when you go and I'll work some mayhem on my end to keep these guys under wraps until the team gets here."

More blaster bolts raced toward Bear and his team.

"Where did these guys come from?" Roolo asked. The Kimbrin agent poked out of the lift just long enough to send a flurry of blaster bolts down the hall leading to the labs. "I have to give them credit. They're holding us here while they have their buddies looking for another way out."

Bear checked his battle board. "Kein, do you have access to the building controls?"

The Vai-Kasa administrator held his hand over his ears as he huddled in the back of the lift. "I wouldn't know where to begin. I usually ask one of my techs for building protocols."

"Great," Bear growled. A blaster bolt skimmed past, slicing out a piece of the carbon-fabricated wall to splatter ionized dust in his face. "Damn it. Neuschwanger, can you gain access to the building?"

"Working it, boss."

Bear shifted his blaster pistol to his other hand. Pulling a disc from his belt, he depressed the center to create a glowing blue dot. "Heads down, boys!" He slid the puck down the hall toward the gunfire. The centimeter-thick disc slid along the flooring in an easy glide that brought it to the feet of the Kimbrin and Hool fighters. With a pop, it vented an explosion of acrid, electrified smoke.

"Specs up, gents," Bear said.

The particle-infused smoke stuck to the enemy in the hallway, highlighting them in the HUD specs worn by his team. Two Kimbrin wearing plate carriers and fielding PK-9s were laying down gunfire by alternating their shots between them. The technique, not uncommon among machine gunners, was a good way to save ammunition as well as keep the hallway suppressed from two points.

"Boss, I'm in the system," Neuschwanger said. "I have a team of eight working the other side of the hall on this level. Roolo's HUD shows two in the hall through the smoke. Building surveillance shows two making their way to the stairs."

"Where are the other four, Tyler?" Bear asked.

"Lab Two. They have the doctor and what appear to be four researchers or Vai-Kasa staff. One security guard is dead. Bolts to the chest and neck. Two are looking out the window to the street. The other two are covering the doctor and her staff. They're all armed with PK-9s except the one working the glass. He has a slung surge gun and a pistol on his hip."

"Good spot, Neuschwanger. Can we shut it down?"

Kein looked up from his hiding spot in the lift. "You people aren't smugglers."

"Never said we were, Mr. Kein. I used to be in the military till I shaved my legs." Bear pulled up his pant leg to show complex bionic carbide plating over synthetic muscle strands. "Dealt with the kind of stuff I bet you're fabricating in that lab down there. No one wants to hold up the germ guy, which means it'll be easy to get you off-planet."

"Am I being arrested?"

"Do I look like a cop? Listen, Captain Paranoid. We came down here to nab this doc on your say-so and now we have to shoot it out with these kelhorns in order to make that happen. You wanna get what you paid for, then shut up so I can focus my full attention on the problems at hand."

Roolo plastered one of the far shooters with a bolt to the head, but he took a hit to the shin for his effort. The round sent him to the floor, and Bear yanked him out of the line of fire.

"How bad?" Bear asked.

The Kimbrin agent pulled the backing off a skinpack and slapped it hard against his calf. "Missed the bone." He slammed an auto-injector into his thigh, slapped a fresh charge pack into his submachine blaster, and stood with a nod.

"You Zaan are some tough mothers," Bear said, slapping him on the back.

"Hey, we got it!" Neuschwanger shouted.

Light faded from the end of the hallway as armored shutters closed over the windows on the entire floor. Crisp-sounding *ka-thunk*s echoed down the hallway from magnetic locks slamming into place.

As the smoke dissipated from Bear's sliding disc, a fragger bounced their way. Roolo pushed Bear into the lift with Kein while he tackled Neuschwanger toward the opposing corner. The fragger popped into hyper-accelerated shards of metal and explosive force that shattered the marble wall just outside the lift. A low rumbling boom vibrated the stone floor for a full five seconds before its echo began to die, taking the associated smoke of the weapon and the fragmented bits of plaster with it.

"Sitrep!" Bear coughed.

"I don't think they appreciated your trick and tried to one-up you," Roolo groaned, rolling over onto his back armor littered with charred bits of plaster.

"I bit my tongue when Roolo tackled me," Neuschwanger reported. "Boss, I have the two that tried to clear the exit into the stairs locked in the stairwell. Zier and his team just made entry. I've bounced them the link and they're heading to wrap them up. So we have one in the hall with grenades and four in the lab with the hostages."

"No one coming through the office side?"

"Negative," Neuschwanger confirmed. "But with Zier making entry and the AUS-Vs bugging out, those thugs across the street are trying to smash their way into the building. I just dropped the shutters on them so they can't just smash their way in, but a bunch of those MCR regular technicals just rolled up and they have black-and-gray-clad MCR squad bosses looking at things with their hands on their hips."

"Hands on their hips, oh no," Bear mocked.

"Listen, you cave troll, if they're looking at it like a Hool trying to turn on a holoset versus actually trying to make their way inside, then it means they have no clue what to do."

"Which means they're going to call for help to get it open," Bear said, finishing his agent's thought. "Well that's not good. You and Roolo stay here. Send bolts at that fool down the hall. I'm going the other way and taking the offices. Are any of them occupied?"

Neuschwanger nodded. "Yeah, boss. Got a small gaggle barricaded behind the second door. Looks like the fresher for the floor."

"Good. Let 'em stay in there. I'm going to roll up on that mukka from the back."

"What about me?" Kein barked.

"Don't worry, precious. My boys got you. Just sit tight and let me work."

Bear ran from the lift with his blaster pistol leading the way. Neuschwanger fed info from his control of the building into an overlay inside Bear's HUD specs, showing him the outlines of the offices and what was inside. The halls formed a square around the edges of the building, and it should be a simple matter to go around and come up behind the still-firing Kimbrin, but Bear was taking no chances. At each corner he removed his glasses, held one of the lenses around the corner at knee height, and proceeded only when he saw that the space was clear.

When he reached the final corner, he pulled another of the charged particle smoke bombs from his belt, priming it to instantly detonate when he released the trigger. He tossed the device, and it erupted with a belch of smoke that filled the hall with electrostatic discharge. Bear pulled back only a hair's breadth before two bolts from the Kimbrin's PK-9 split the air where his shoulder had been.

The algorithms running his HUD specs updated their matrix. To his surprise, the shooter wasn't there. A hard light projector was running somewhere in the hall, sending a hologram with enough suspended energized particles to fool the cameras, building sensors, and even Bear's optics. Bear recalled that Ford, working as Keel, had once had an AI co-pilot with a broadcast emitter that would render him as a hard light hologram. A handy trick if the AI could fight, and Ford's could. Or at least that's how Ford had explained it.

A new wave of combat information washed into his HUD, showing where the shooter really was. In the time it had taken Bear to leave the lift and come around the corridors, the Kimbrin shooter had re-positioned himself, tucked into the alcove for the fresher on this side of the structure. Unlucky for him, he couldn't get through the door as Neuschwanger had it locked up tight.

Bear primed two more discs from his belt. He bounced the first one around the corner to zing it into the holographic threat. The micro-popper exploded, shorting out the lights in the hall and, more importantly, the projector drone hovering near the ceiling. The fist-sized bot fell unceremoniously to the floor with a dull *thunk*. Bear then sent the second popper into the passage. He turned away, holding his breath and clapping his paws over his ears so as to block out the noise. A half-second whine was the only warning from the device as it exploded into a screaming shock wave of force and light.

Bear rushed around the corner. The Kimbrin wasn't visible, but the leej knew he was there. He dumped two shots into where the man's lungs should be followed by another into where his skull should be. The Kimbrin's mimetic camouflage poncho shorted out on its way to the ground in the grip of the smoking, falling corpse.

"Clear," Bear said into the comms. Panting, he put an extra round into the skull of each shooter, just to be sure, then watched the stairwell door and the door to the labs. Neuschwanger had locked them both, but that didn't mean this hit team, whoever they were, couldn't try some digital voodoo of their own.

"Bear, it's Jaela, come in."

Bear tapped his comm bead. "Go ahead, J."

"I tagged two SLICs running a suspicious orbit around the district until a minute ago when they changed course and made a beeline for your building. Looks like they're going for the docking pad at the top."

Bear huffed. "Great. You're just full of good news. What are they carrying?"

"First one is carrying troops. The second is empty except for the pilots."

"Troops land on the pad and breach from the top down. The second bird hovers on the outside of the lab and breaches the shutters somehow and then pulls the doc and her kidnappers that way."

"Probably. If you're in the mood, I got more news."

"Good or bad?"

"Both. The patrol group downstairs trying to get in weren't having any luck, so they pulled back across the street. Unfortunately, an MCR regular showed up and directed the gaggle to hook up a bunch of tow vehicles and chains so they can rip the shutters off the entrance."

Neuschwanger fed Bear the view from the cameras inside the labs. The techs and the doctor were still safe, but surge-gun guy was pacing and talking to himself. Never a good sign when a bad guy had hostages. The man rolled his hand, and the doctor stood up with her hands to her sides.

Bear tapped the bead to signal back to Jaela. "They having any luck with ripping the door?"

"Not so far."

Neuschwanger pushed an inventory list he'd found for the lab to Bear's HUD specs. The big man scanned through the list quickly, skimming it until he saw what he'd expected to see. He turned on Kein.

"Mr. Kein. Are you producing a neurotoxin or some kind of anti-personnel gas on the premises? Is that why this doctor needs to be extracted?"

"Why would you—" Kein began.

Bear cut him off. "From what I'm seeing here, the team trying to stop us is having the doctor put something together in the lab. Perhaps something that might help them get past us?"

And there it was. The reaction that Bear was looking for. Abject terror. Kein had no doubt expected to be long gone before anything like this level of nightmare had a chance to manifest itself on the planet, much less in his own building. He looked from one side to the other, as if an escape route would be enough to get him clear of whatever apocalypse they were having his doctor brew up in there.

"I'll take the look of horror on your face as a yes," Bear said. "I don't know about you, but I'd rather survive whatever they're planning on dumping on me. This place got a counter-agent?"

Beads of sweat streamed from the Kimbrin executive's brow like he was a condemned man who'd just finished his last meal. "I was just following orders. They don't tell me what the stuff is for, I'm just here to confirm the orders were filled. But if they release what's in that room, I mean... that stuff is not supposed to be used in an atmosphere. The... the political fallout alone from such a thing would be..."

Bear pressed the man to the wall and took up a handful of his suit jacket in hands that were meant for crushing real opponents. While Kein might have been a good exec, he was out of his depth. "Coun—ter—a—gent."

"Y-yes," Kein stammered. "There's a counter-agent for the batches. Enough to inoculate us."

Kein's concern for himself was truly inspiring. And utterly predictable. "Neuschwanger. I need a way into that room that might save the hostages and that doc, if she is who I think she is."

"Yeah, boss," the human agent said. "Dr. Rantanen is head of the molecular biology and virology lab here at Vai-Kasa. I'll get something going, but if it looks like they'll get to her before we do?"

Bear didn't let the man's dangling question dangle for long. "You know what to do."

34

Reaper One
Kam Dho City
On Approach to Business District

Dax Danns had barely had time to land his Raptor and re-arm from supporting Kill Team Victory when his new best friend General Chhun tasked him with another ad hoc mission—this one in support of another Dark Ops agent on the ground. It was time to see some action over Kham Dho City, and well before any of the other featherheads in support of the *Centurion* or the Legion's operations near Fort Blake could even think of such a flyover.

Danns smiled. He had all the luck.

"Victory One, this is Reaper One. I am running sun to you on hot guns. Do you have a sensor track for those bandits?"

Bear's voice broke through the comm. "Reaper One, this is Victory One. Single target on docking pad; my POS. Target is lased. Second target possibly hovering over third-floor window. Target mark in two mikes, how copy."

According to the playbook Danns had prepared before the op, Victory One was Kill Team Victory's commander. This guy had been on Utopion when the Black Fleet tried to deal it in.

Combat overlays worked their way onto Danns's HUD, showing the distance and direction to the target. Victory One's comm signal acted as the flight track to get him close while the laser worked as a finger point to the bad guy. If they had to get a second laser on target, it would mean the enemy flight had broken into distinct elements to multitask. No worries. The Kilo-model Raptor had speed to burn and weapons for days. Laying the hurt on multiple targets wouldn't be a problem.

Terrain vanished beneath the fighter as Danns locked the craft into attack position. "Lucky. Prime the blasters for a wide spread and low yield. Friendlies on vertical target, and I don't want to punch this all the way to the ground."

The Wizzo bot dutifully supplied weapons trajectory overlays and added them to the swarm of combat data already buzzing in Danns's HUD. "Why do you need this?"

"Because we're not making a straight run on this joker. Hold on back there."

The starfighter came up fast, making a beeline to the cloud cover over the Vai-Kasa Building.

The run was interrupted with a new transmission from Victory One. "Abort run. Requesting change of mission. Say again, abort run."

"What does he mean, change of mission?" Danns complained to his Wizzo.

The fighter altered his trajectory, changing the diagonal diving run he was making into a low orbit. "Run aborted, Victory One. Awaiting instructions."

Warning indicators flared in his HUD as Lucky tracked multiple locks on the fighter.

"Yeah, I see it. I'll worry when they scramble something with enough teeth to deal with me!"

Almost in response to his statement, alarms warning of large drone launches near the civilian star port rang with a repeating tone that accompanied the HUD indicator. "I see it. Two XD Seven-Seven-Eights. Who the hell has military-grade cyber planes over a city?"

Lucky announced that the new attack plan had just been received from Victory One, but Danns's mind was still on the XD-778s. "That is kind of smart to move them from the Fort Blake airfield. Making the run."

Lucky could sense where his pilot's intentions were drifting. "You have a flight plan to follow. Don't abort the run."

"I'm not aborting the run. Just tryin' to run up the score a bit."

The Raptor screamed into the confines of the city along one of its longest avenues. Laser tracking indicators changed their vectors from one target at an elevation of fifty meters to another at ground level. Glancing at the rear-facing camera, Danns watched his jet wash slam the exterior of the buildings and made windows shudder in his wake.

"Hot on two," Danns called to his Wizzo. "Send a note to that leej to keep his head down."

Another glance at the rear camera and he caught sight of the XD-778 Vulture security drone chasing after him.

"Sending love note. Letting Mr. M out the front door. Fox two." Danns launched a medium-range missile as he jerked on the stick to bring his fighter into a frantic climb away from the chasing drone. The projectile raced into the scene where multiple tow trucks with chains, cables, and mechanized support were actively engaged in an effort to rip the security shutters and blast doors from the front of the building to gain entry. The explosive warhead detonated center mass of their gathering, turning the street into a rolling fireball as the initial explosion ruptured the power batteries on the vehicles.

Danns watched the destruction in his rearview. "That might have been too much."

He brought the ship in a spinning arc to put him in a dive straight for the second SLIC on target. True to his word, Victory One had found a way to lase the SLIC as it hovered outside the third-floor window. Lancing blaster fire from the Raptor's outboard cannons shredded the vehicle into flaming scrap all the way down to the hard street.

Danns hugged the stick to bring his Raptor out of its dive and sail through the buildings. Passing between the skyscrapers on his way back into the clouds, the fighter took multiple bolts from the second Vulture drone hovering in place.

"If this is the spot where you tell me 'I told you so,' use that processor power for something else, Lucky."

"Like telling you the Vulture on our tail is going high in an attempt to dive us?"

"Nope! Definitely don't want to hear that."

Danns rolled his plane along a different vector in an effort to escape the newly chasing second drone while running from the dive path of the first. Missile warnings flared in his HUD as the Republic Vulture drone launched a multitude of guided weapons into his path. Streaming flares trailed away along smoky paths as anti-lock countermeasures attempted to defeat the missiles. A single burner streaked through the distraction, nearly exploding into his wing. While the detonation missed, the concussion blanked out his shields.

"Lucky! Work your magic! We're gettin' outta here!"

Kam Dho City
Vai-Kasa Corporate Building

The change of plans that had Commander Danns destroy only one of the two SLICs had occurred while Bear was linking up with more of his security team. Roolo and Neuschwanger were with him. Zier, a Kimbrin who had been watching the lower levels, was making his way back up through the building now that it was obvious there'd be no escape through the front door.

"We got the exec. Zier, where are you?" Bear asked. Left unspoken was the fact that they still needed to recover the scientist.

"Just rolled two E-KIA in the stairs, boss. Coming to you now."

Bear flicked through several screens on his board. "Neuschwanger, crack the shades on this window."

The INSEC slicer looked up in annoyance. "C'mon, boss. They got a guy in that lab trying to break through my firewalls like a fat kid late for a buffet. I can't risk it."

Bear laughed at the reference before showing his own board to the slicer. "I have never seen a fat Kimbrin."

"Oh," Neuschwanger said in surprise.

"Zier," Bear called into the net. "We're unlocking office 206 on the second floor. Window is open. I need you to lase the incoming SLIC."

"Wait," Zier protested. "I thought the plan was we use the SLIC to get out of here. I didn't learn to fly just so I could die in an office building."

"Not that SLIC," Bear clarified. "We're gettin' out on the bird on the roof. This one needs to be scrapped."

"That I can handle, boss!"

Not long after, the building rattled as the Republic Raptor shot its way toward the target, downing the SLIC and leaving the one depositing troops on the rooftop intact, just as ordered.

"Okay," Bear said. "Easy part's over. Let's kill whatever mids got dumped into the upper floor and take their ride."

The fight up the stairs and to the roof took all of five minutes. With Kein in tow, Bear and his security team tore through the roof access door and moved toward the humming SLIC still waiting on the landing pad for a strike team that was never coming back.

"Pilot," called Bear.

"Co-pilot," called Neuschwanger.

The two men encircled the SLIC and put one blaster bolt each through the flight helmets of the waiting Kimbrin featherheads. While they worked, Roolo and Zier made sure to clear the back of the bird of any crew, but there was none; the gun had been left unmanned. They hurried on board, Zier trading places with Bear so he could pilot the ship. Bear closed the ship's side doors and prepared for takeoff by strapping the executive into a jump seat still warm from its previous occupant.

"Nice of the mids to pick us up," Neuschwanger quipped.

"We're in," Bear called to Zier. "Take us up!"

The SLIC angled off the roof of the Vai-Kasa Building, its thumping engines shaking the bird enough to put an expression of discomfort on Roolo's face.

"What's your problem?" Bear asked.

"I hate these things. They crash."

"These things are older than your parents. How would you even know? Besides, we ain't goin' far."

The vehicle settled onto the next building over, hovering with the personnel door reopened just long enough for Jaela to jump into the back. "You boys miss me that much?"

"Who's this?" Kein shouted, struggling to be heard above the din of noise.

"Part of the team," Bear shouted back. "We're going to get your VIP now."

"I don't see how," Kein spat.

"You will."

The SLIC vibrated back up to speed as the military surplus vehicle's repulsors bounced them from the roof and just as quickly took them descending down the back side of the building on an elevator ride to the lab.

"Get ready, we're not going to have a lot of time for this," Bear said to his shooters.

The ship drifted on its repulsors sideways, showing its nose to the open lab window. The windows had already been shot out by the MCR hit team that had entered the building by a SLIC that had subsequently fallen prey to Reaper One's air raid. That hit team now waited inside the lab, and as the new SLIC arrived on scene, the Kimbrin faces of Zier and Roolo waving to the operators must have looked enough like friendly pilots, because the MCR hit team started gathering up the huddled scientists.

Bear's SLIC turned its tail so that the open troop bay faced the lab. The first person to notice something was off was one of the scientists, who ducked when she saw the blaster barrels. The MCR operators reacted an instant later. One spun to the floor to take his upper body out of the line of fire just before Jaela splattered the rebel behind him, shooting the trooper through his open-face helmet.

The surge-gun leader of the group already had his pistol out and had it presented for a shot when Bear hit him with a stolen PK-9 taken from the combatants he'd faced in the hallway. Roolo then unleashed the fury of the medium squad blaster mounted to the door gunner's pintle. The heavy rat-tat-tat of the weapon sounded above the thumping repulsors in a concert of hovering violence that took out the last two men.

Bear tapped his micro-comm, linking him to the building's speaker system. "We're here to extract you," he said to the scientists. "We have Kein aboard. Get in."

The clueless executive laughed and waved his arms. "Get in! Get in!"

35

Kill Team Victory
Fort Blake

Sergeant Pina activated his L-comm. "Bassa, it's Pina. I have a Victory Company squad who just walked in the door to relieve us." He nodded to the legionnaire filling the doorway as the rest of the new blood filtered in.

"Copy," Bombassa rumbled. "Your team is to proceed with Deep Space. Link up with Zombie Squad for support—Major Riggs is aware of the plan."

"On it, Top."

Pina clicked off and pulled the battle board from his wrist to exchange it with the one from the waiting trooper. "Mine has all the target reference points already laid in. This one up on the op so far?"

"Yes, Sergeant. *Centurion* REPO also hot-loaded it so when it meshes to your armor it will unlock all the kill team hacks for you."

Pina wrist-bumped him in appreciation. "KTF, Leej."

The other man nodded in return. "Make 'em pay."

The Kill Team Victory sergeant gave a whistle before donning his helmet. Toots was first to the party. "We rolling?"

"They just hit the airfield."

"That leaves us to do the hard shot on Deep Space. We goin' to Top or is he comin' to us?"

"Top isn't comin'," Pina said. "They're stuck digging out some malicious worms that're keeping us from getting the big guns back up and barking. We're to link up with Zombie Squad, Vic-Co."

Doc Chance slapped a medical rig onto everyone's assault pack. "Goodie bag for you Marvins once we hit Deep Space. There's gonna be a lot of hurt feelings that need their essential oils and sprig juice."

Pina walked the line of leejes, tugging each rig to satisfy an NCO's ingrained need to double-check the double-check so the room for error was hard for Murphy's Law to work through. "Hopefully that's all we find. All right, these guys have control of the guns so it's time for us to bounce."

Objective Deep Space was the designation for a stadium within Fort Blake, long a fixture for the soldiers and spacers housed there. When most civilians thought of a military forward operating base, they didn't think of the many amenities that the Republic put in so that the personnel would feel less alienated from their lives in whatever home they hailed from—things like coffee shops, fast food shops, entertainment facilities, and, in this case, a full-service stadium. The arena had a complete turf field, running track, and replaceable goalposts so that a variety of sports could be played. While the regular military mostly used the space for PT sessions, it wasn't unheard of to convert it for seamball or any other sport favored by the forces.

"I have a group of twelve in the entrance to the stadium," Wello said over L-comm. "I have eight in the upper bleachers on patrol, and eight more on the lower deck. I'm tracking four moving in and out of the tents. Sending the layout to you now."

Pina looked over the display.

The space he examined had been repurposed yet again, this time by the MCR to facilitate the holding of the base's military complement. Multiple large tents had been erected on the field, repulsor train style, to house the various Repub military prisoners. Kill Team Victory's objective was to conduct a combat raid on the POW camp, freeing the prisoners and employing them in defense of the stadium until a QRF in the form of Second Platoon, Victory Company, could arrive.

Centurion REPO, with the help of Republic internal security on the ground, had combed through the various dark nets and pirated video feeds gained from Bear's meeting with the criminal chieftain, Grelin, and had uncovered a basic layout for the prison camp. The outer rings of tents had Repub military personnel packed into them like sardines, and the two inner shelters acted as the MCR command tent and cover for something that the various troops called "the plug" on the radio and net channels. Brit, the sensor analyst for Bear's assigned INSEC team, had determined that the plug was either some sort of weapon of last resort or a method for holding the soldiers hostage.

Brit had been highlighting and tagging the MCR troops moving around the camp when the various Legion eyes on her feed had noticed something peculiar. The MCR moved squad-sized elements of prisoners at a time under a front- and rear-facing guard for things like bathroom breaks and daily walks around the track. During those situations, the prisoners had drones hovering over them while shining a broad-beam red light on them. It didn't take long to string observations together to figure out how such a small guard force could control over a thousand trained Republic fighters.

"Do you have LOS to the guns?" Pina asked.

"I got 'em. Marking them now," Wello answered. "I have DK-630s on the perimeter of the structure. I have four on the top, and six at the bottom of the bleachers."

While mobile AI-driven gun emplacements were another wrinkle in the plan to free the prisoners, Pina had had enough forethought to plan for just in case. He looked to the edge of his HUD, where a message request hovered so as not to affect his vision but also to be annoying enough where he wouldn't ignore it for long. "Wello, hold that thought. Break. LS-339, this is Pina. I'm folding you into our squad net. What's your status?"

The Zombie Squad NCO answered, "Pina, we just approached through the back wall on Star Deck and are waiting at the facilities maintenance building less than a quarter klick from Deep Space. We have twelve assorted at the front gate if that's how you want us to roll in."

"They have a whole company of violence out there," Toots noted. "And all Victory Company could spare was a squad?"

"All Kill Team Victory could spare was us," noted Wello.

Pina laid any concerns his team members had to rest. "The rest of the company is on sweep and clear for the base. Plus, from the net traffic Bombassa has been feeding me, these guys are real knuckle-dusters." He switched over to the net. "Sergeant Lynx, have you looked at the layout I sent you on the way over?"

"Roger that. We were thinking we could make entry and deal with the dozen troops on the gate, but then we set up on this maintenance building. They staged two combat sleds with a squad of Kimbrin in each. Must have stood them up when we hit the gate."

Pina growled. This was yet another example of the current flavor of MCR acting in a manner that showed real military training and tactical forethought versus the usual collection of angry people with guns that the MCR had long been. It was one thing to take an abandoned military base, or a base with a reduced presence, but Blake had been a fully staffed and functional Republic army base, and yet it was taken by force overnight. And now valuable assets like tanks, war bots, and other military surplus had been put to good use by the mids all around the battlefield.

"Lynx, I have three other buildings that probably have close to the same, but I can't wait to hit Deep Space any longer. Chatter we're hearing over the MCR net indicates they're going to hit the middle tent for something called *the plug* if the Legion continues its burn through their forces on the base."

"Yeah," Lynx replied, the hate in his voice palpable. "Major Riggs almost has the situation rolled up, so you're probably right. I could split my team. Put half through the gate and then a team running a combat sled to hold off anything that comes from the buildings."

Pina didn't have the time to mull the situation over for a better plan. He just needed one that wasn't going to have him standing in front of the V-Co commander trying to explain how he turned their Zombies into corpses.

Victory Company, Zombie Squad
Objective Deep Space

Sami pulled Lynx and Diggs aside for a quick jam session once they were clear of the vehicle. "Sar'nt, I know we were supposed to ditch the driver as soon as we could scrape our boots, but we're a man down so we could use him for this."

"And we don't have the time to get creative," Diggs reminded Lynx. "We need to go now."

Lynx's bucket was aimed toward the ground in an attempt to look at nothing that would distract him from forming his plan of attack. "Pina, it's Lynx. If we can get to one of the prisoner tents, we could have all the support we need to make this work."

"I see what you're putting down. I just sent you an updated map of the AO. Can you go low and we'll take high?"

Lynx showed his battle board to the leejes standing with him. "This doable?"

"Damn skippy, Sar'nt. Let's work it," Diggs confirmed.

"Hey, Breaker? You want to make up for that choppy ride over and loan us some skill driving that rig straight over an MCR's fourth point of contact?"

LS-814, PFC Charles Hood, cracked his knuckles and harnessed himself back into his seat. "You don't gotta ask me twice, Sergeant. I was cooped up in that dropship for a long minute. Any chance to smash a gas pedal or win a chest full of metal, I'm all about it."

"Diggs!"

"On it, Lynx!" The rock-steady team leader ran into one of the waiting combat sleds, racing through the back where they'd blown up the Kimbrin squad with an ear-popper before dousing the hatch with suppressed weapons. The hard part had been to lob a smoke grenade into the open driver's hatch so the two rebels working from the cockpit of the sled would stick their mugs into a space where they could be conveniently shot with the rest of their friends.

The corporal held up his hand to show that the chalky purple residue of the smoke was all over the cabin. When he got Lynx's hand counting down instead of an apology for getting Diggs's armor dirty, he simply grabbed the wheel and waited.

Lynx pointed to his fellow leej, who jammed on the throttle to send the standard army combat sled into a frenetic jump off the line. The Legion NCO pulled open the slider just enough to have the sled scrape against it, nearly knocking off the door and making a ton of noise.

When the sled reached the halfway mark between the maintenance building and the stadium, Diggs grabbed one of the dead Kimbrin in the cabin with him and slumped him against the stick. With no hand guiding the throttle, the sled trundled along on a slow glide toward the entrance. The dead body leaned against the controls in such a way that the sled listed to one side and the glide track was exposing more and more of its side to the gate as it traveled.

Lynx ran over to the TC seat in the GMV. "Get ready for a sprint, Breaker. When I tell you to go, you run this beast through that entrance like it's Legion Appreciation Day and the drinks are free."

"Is that a thing, Sar'nt?" Breaker asked.

"Kid, if we pull this off, there's an entire base worth of grateful on the other side of that gate that won't let you pay for a drink ever again."

The best magicians know that a successful trick is one part skill, one part dedication, and three parts distraction. As far as the galaxy was concerned, the Legion was made up of some of the best combat prestidigitators on any stage. You could ask anyone who's ever been in the audience—if they weren't all dead.

The combat sled full of dead MCR regulars drifted toward the entrance of the stadium where a twelve-man MCR squad was waiting to see what in the back end of the galaxy the driver was doing. When they caught sight of the deployed ramp and the stack of bodies inside, six of the twelve-man element ran out to meet the vehicle. A single Kimbrin sat just outside the entrance with a radio in hand, probably calling it in to the support troops in the other buildings.

Lynx watched it all go down until the rebel troopers got to the sled. "Punch it."

The GMV driver gave his best Legion effort to kick the accelerator through the floor, jumping the vehicle into the street. There was a fishtail moment where the driver fought for control and the leejes in the back struggled to stay glued to the vehicle. Gekko rode behind the heavy blaster machine gun while the other leejes had their rifles pointed out from their seats.

"Got four on deck. Break." Lynx barely finished his call before two bolts flew from the leejes in the seats beside. The shots punched through the flimsy armor the MCR were wearing while a burst from Gekko fanned across two more to splatter them into the street. "Diggs, two coming at you."

Echoes of blaster fire drew the attention of the two rebels inside the passenger compartment of the combat sled. They hugged the walls of the vehicle in a crouch they had obviously practiced as they spun into their kneeling positions using a combination of sling tension and proper arm placement to build a stable shooting platform out of nothing. Diggs couldn't help but be impressed that someone had put in the time to teach these guys some basic rifle marksmanship. He almost felt bad about putting a round from his suppressed pistol into both men's skulls.

Shooting from beneath a slumped body in the cockpit, the concealed legionnaire fired a round into the base of each man's skull where their helmets hadn't covered. The angle of the shot splattered the men's brains through their nasal cavities in a spray of blood and bone matter. They had barely slapped the deck when Diggs hit the throttle again on the combat sled and followed the GMV into the entrance.

The remaining Kimbrin watching the affair ran into position and tried to level enough blaster fire on the approaching vehicle to stop the assault dead in its tracks. Unfortunately for him, he didn't have a Gekko. While Diggs might be the squad's resident huckster, Gekko was its artist.

He'd worked a high-risk mining colony where the gravity was twice that of the average Repub world. A massive cave-in trapped his crew under the surface until a rescue team could be dispatched to recover them. The story of their rescue garnered interplanetary attention as well as personal notice for Gekko, as it was his calm decisions under intense pressure that saw them all through. The Legion knows their own even if their own don't know it themselves yet.

Gekko worked the machine gun like a master painter toiling over his next masterpiece. Two men in the door succumbed to the heavy bolts, nearly flipping in place when he hit them. A near hit from inside the archway zinged off the hood of the vehicle to fly into the sky at a weird angle. Breaker fishtailed the GMV again, putting them in perfect position to take the lucky shooter. Gekko worked the gun in broad strokes, decimating the crates and plaster the rebel fighter tried to use for cover. A blaster bolt slapped into the side of the crate and spun it partially around, dropping the man away from his cover. Gekko dusted him with a concentrated burst.

Breaker drifted the truck the other way, putting them back in line with the opening. "One on your right, one left."

Lynx and Sami jumped from the truck as Gekko continued to pour it on through the entrance.

36

Kill Team Victory
Objective Deep Space

"Put two over. Let me know when it's green," Pina said into the squad channel.

"Roger out," Doc responded.

Twin kaff-can-looking objects sailed over the top of the stadium. Despite their tumbling trajectory, the cans managed to make it past the bottom of the bleachers onto the running track. Just before bouncing on the rubberized surface, they extended spikes that planted them firmly into the running track. An electric hum accompanied a wavering flash along the skin of the objects.

The Kimbrin guards at the top of the stadium, now alerted by the sound of blaster fire at the front entrance, hung past the railing to see who or what had thrown the object over. They were greeted by legionnaires hanging on suspension lines just below the lip at the top of the structure. Even as the mimetic features of the armor blended them into their surroundings, the guards faced the all-too-famous combat lens of the Legion bucket.

Wello and Toots planted rounds center mass into each man's skull, leaving them lifeless against the railing.

"I got good tone on the ELMAD. We're green," Pina said.

"Up and over!" Wello called.

Half of Kill Team Victory hoisted themselves over the railing at the top of the bleachers. Frightened MCR fighters raised their rifles or turned to run. In both cases, the battlefield demons shot them where they stood. Mimetic camo fell away into the jet-black nightmare that was Legion armor. Tan accents ran down the length of the arms and chest rigs, a call back to the Victory Company that formed them.

Eight rebel corpses flopping down the bleachers toward their counterparts below caused a panic in the security detail. Some frantically fired up toward the leejes while the others scrambled to find shelter in the passage beneath the bleachers.

"Keep an eye on that tent in the center," Pina said. "Dust anything that makes a run for it."

**Victory Company, Zombie Squad
Objective Deep Space**

The GMV raced into the stadium on a drift and gunned it right into the passage beneath the structure. The knobby tires echoed through the concourse with Gekko and Trent riding the weapons systems left with the vehicle.

The two remaining Kimbrin walked from their cover firing at the erratically driven vehicle in hopes of striking one of the armored crew in the back. The legionnaires returned the favor. Sami and Lynx swept in behind them, launching double-taps that punched through their armor and sent them tumbling to the duracrete.

"Shoulda had a guy on rear-sec and one doing the shooting," Sami commented.

"Preach, brother." Lynx jumped into the L-comm. "Pina, it's Lynx. We got a trio of leej heartbreakers in the concourse moving to the other side of the stadium. We're going in from the main entrance."

"This is Pina, roger out."

Lynx leaned out to watch Diggs sliding the combat sled into the entryway, fully closing it off from the outside.

"I'll watch the outside," Diggs said. "I can already see angry MCR spinning up their sleds in that other building. If I had to guess, the sleds are there to hem in the company when they come for the prisoners. Then they pull this plug and dust the leejes and the Repub personnel in one shot."

Lynx nodded. "Right. Probably pull *the* plug like Pina was talking about. We'll be right back with your replacements."

The Legion sergeant and his combat partner raced into the stadium. They chose to spin left as Gekko and Trent had come out from the concourse into the bleachers and had already started smoking MCR troopers on their side. When two of the lower security had been dusted, Lynx slithered from the bleachers and began ghosting through the tents.

He zipped around the corner of a tent into a squad of four men who immediately opened fire on him. Ducking back behind the tent on his own side into a kneeling position presented the best option for Lynx to get out of their line of sight. The lone leej switched to thermals in his bucket, firmly highlighting the Kimbrin fire team through the fabric.

"Sami?" Lynx asked.

"Do it."

Lynx fired through the tent, striking the first shooter in the face. Teeth and gray matter splashed off the tent into the man behind him, scaring him enough to drop his rifle. The two behind him were lanced in the back by alternating shots from Sami on the raised walkway to the bleachers. The terrified rebel tried to run from the gunfire dropping his friends only to run into a muzzle thump from the Legion NCO on the ground.

"Moving," Sami said.

Lynx stopped at the flap to one of the tents. "Republic legionnaires! One coming in."

"Bring it!" came an elated shout from inside.

Lynx smiled at the tone in the man's voice. Whoever he was, the fire hadn't left him. He ducked into the flap to the expectant faces of a host of Republic personnel who were practically standing room only. The Legion sergeant was glad for his bucket as he was sure this place smelled like plastic-wrapped bacon and body odor.

The enthusiastic prisoner introduced himself. "I'm Staff Sergeant Kevin Gilchrist. How'd you get past the sentry guns?"

"Electromag disruptors," Lynx said through the bucket's external speakers. He didn't want to use the grisly tone of the Legion bucket among friends, but his battle buddy was outside and he'd rather spend the time getting after it. "What unit, Staff Sergeant?"

"Triple Killers. Three-Three FSR."

"Forward strike regiment? You got a squad you can put together on the bounce?"

"You map it, we'll slap it," Gilchrist responded.

"Cut right out of the tent, you'll find four dead MCR and their gear. Scoop and continue straight to the exit where you'll find another leej in a combat sled. He's waiting for you to take over, Staff Sergeant."

Gilchrist slapped his forearm against Lynx's. "Thanks, Leej."

"Before you go, you got MPs in this mess?"

"Roger that. Next tent across. What do you need them for?"

Exiting the tent, Lynx called over his shoulder. "I have unpaid parking tickets I have to settle before they'll let me back in the PX."

"Lynx, this is Pina. We have multiple MCR fire teams sheltering in place. If they move we'll try to drill 'em, but we can't see 'em all."

"Roger that. We just liberated a platoon of Three-Three FSR who are linking up with that combat sled. I have another squad with us to clear the MCR from the tents. Thirty-Fifth Military Police are pulling the folks from the tents and shuffling them out of the stadium into the concourse. We can't risk dumping people outside while we're about to get into a gunfight on some combat sleds."

"Good call, Leej. Pina out."

Trent burst into the L-comm. "Lynx! I got a squirter on thermal moving through the tents. Kimbrin by the looks of him. Going straight at those center huts."

"I can't see him! I'm too low."

"I got him," Sami called. "I'm on it. Looks like he's going for the CP tent first."

"I'm switching places with you."

"Lynx, it's Wello from Pina's team. We have the nest and can see everything. We'll cover. Go back up your leej."

Sami vaulted from the bleachers onto the running track. Sprinting across the field toward the tent, he caught sight of Lynx ventilating an MCR regular looking to do harm to the ELMAD on their side. The disruptors jammed all signals throughout the battlespace that weren't the L-comm. Radio receivers couldn't blow bombs, video cams and audio mics didn't work, and basically anything trying to broadcast was karked. The MCR were all wearing a wristband with emitters that told the turrets not to shoot them. The drones that they called to shine a red light over the prisoners served the same purpose. In essence, *don't shoot here.*

The Legion trail man slid into the back of the tent right as the MCR trooper did. The inside of the tent was covered in maps and a camp layout along with movement plans and a radio base station on a table. Sami shot under the table. The fighter rolled clear and fired at Sami's shins, forcing him to jump from the tent. The MCR scrambled across the floor in a bear crawl, not bothering to get up as he planned to move under the partition of the tent anyway and into the next room.

He gained the main tent in the center—into the waiting rifle of Sergeant Lynx.

"I need you to drop that pistol and come out of there," Lynx said. "That's it. Stand up. Interlace your fingers and put your hands on top of your head." As he spoke to the Kimbrin, his bucket translated his voice into the native language a second after his regular speech.

"Okay, this officially sucks," Sami said. He tapped his finger on a machine the size of a building HVAC system. Surrounding the outside of the control housing were twelve glass canisters with what looked like a black metal silo in the center. "It's a two-stage munition. According to what I pulled off the wall when I dove from the tent, the central housing is a rocket deployment system for eight high-explosive bomblets. It's a FAHEE bomb. Fuel air high-energy explosive. Basically turns the atmosphere into fire and then rolls it out along the detonation. This would launch the bomblets outside the stadium while this, this would disperse this throughout the inside."

"What is that?" Lynx asked.

Sami plinked the glass canisters set into the device. "If I had to guess, it's the stuff Harvester bounced the entire Legion on. VBX-13. Enough to kill everyone in the stadium. Not really lookin' to open it and find out, y'know?"

"That's a big karkin' statement. I got him."

Lynx walked up to the MCR fighter now that Sami had his rifle trained on him from the flank. He grabbed the man's fingers to crush them together so he couldn't untie them. As he pulled back on him to search his pockets, the Kimbrin let his feet drop out from under him, nearly going horizontal so that he was no longer standing in front of Lynx. He spun as he dropped, yanking his hand from the Legion NCO's grip and tripping him toward Sami.

Sami caught Lynx, passing him behind so he could get a clear shot at the rebel. The MCR fighter reached into his jacket to produce a trigger mechanism. He flung the device toward the dispersion system and it latched onto the front console with a metallic slap, magnetized to the surface. A digital chime warned that the connection between the two parts was active.

The rebel dove to the floor and hoisted a nearby table with the hopes of blocking the blaster bolts of the legionnaire trying to take him apart. The bolts splintered the wood of the dense table several times, lancing into the Kimbrin on the other side. Beyond the table, a hand reached out for a device on the ground. The trigger cover on it left no doubt in Sami's mind that it was a remote detonator.

Sami hurried up close, dropping his blaster and pulling his family sword. There was no longer time to hope for a blaster bolt to strike home. He had to see what he was doing and know that he'd finished this kelhorn.

The sword flashed across the table, causing it to split in half and fall away, revealing the man's hand reaching dangerously close to the trigger. But he didn't press it. He couldn't. All the MCR rebel could do was look confusedly at his now-severed arm, as if wondering why he could no longer move it.

Only then did the Kimbrin soldier seemed to notice the blood from his wound. He inspected his stump, still confused, then rolled over onto his back to expire.

Sami disassembled the trigger as Lynx put another round into the man for good measure.

"Pina, this is Lynx. We have the field."

37

"LS-339?"

"You can call me, Lynx, ma'am."

The woman's bruised face managed a smile, showing that she had cracked teeth with an empty socket where a tooth should have been. From the look of things, the Kimbrin that pummeled her were mostly right-handed. But there was still fire there. She was bent but not broken. "Thank you, Sergeant. I mean Lynx. We are fifty percent free from the tents and my tech monkey is working on the sentry guns with some of your legionnaires to repurpose them to work for us."

"Thank you, Captain." Lynx held up his fist, accepting a knuckle bump from his number two leej approaching them.

"Hey, Sar'nt. Ma'am." Diggs seemed unsure what the prison camp protocol was for approaching a regular army officer they'd just pulled out of the suck, so he just nodded. "We got that Triple Killer and his crew in the combat sled, Sar'nt. That outgoing gunfire you hear is them. What's up with us?"

"Gekko and Sami just went up top to gun with Wello. We have to stay here to secure the device until Legion EOD shows up."

The captain held up a hand to insert herself into the conversation. "Sergeant. I have an SRT on station here. They're pretty beat up, but they can still do their job. One of the specialties of a military police special reaction team is high-risk energy source protection. Think reactors that power cities. My guys can secure this while you and the infantry send those kelhorns packing."

"Can we keep her?" Diggs asked.

Lynx pushed the leej from the tent. "Thank you, Captain Anwar."

Leaving the doomsday device in the care of the detachment officer, the two leejes sprinted toward the front of the stadium. "Seems like you have an admirer," Diggs said.

"Couldn't work."

"Because she's an officer and a basic?" Digg asked.

"Too many unpaid parking tickets."

The duo got to the bracketed entrance for the stadium awash with incoming fire from twin combat sleds firing at an angle into the structure. Diggs pointed to a wall on the brink of failure. "These walls ain't going to last, boss."

Lynx watched the first combat sled shooting at them take a pummeling from the one they had under infantry control. The paras found and deployed road shields in front of the sled and dropped the vehicle in its lowest setting on the repulsors, leaving it a mere centimeter from the ground to enjoy the protection of the barriers. While they were meant for traffic control, the road shields absorbed the heavy impact of the twin-fired N-50s on top of the enemy sleds.

Staff Sergeant Gilchrist was barking orders. "Get those guys to that partition. I want a squad with rifles up and laying down fire. You don't have to punch through that armor, you just have to make it difficult for them to see us. You and you, take fire at the twins on those vics. The armor is thickest center mass, but the old House of

Reason sleds didn't armor the connection harness for the CROWS. It's a thin plate. Shoot to the left side of the gun and maybe we can short it out. No, your military left!"

"That staff sergeant is killing it," Diggs commented.

"He is."

Lynx switched the view in his HUD to show him a feed from Gekko. The leej obviously had the same plan as the para. He pummeled the plate on the outlying sled, sending up a wave of sparks.

"Good hit," Wello said through the net. "Following your shot."

"Take it," Gekko agreed.

The heavy report of the N-18 barked over the sound of cycling blaster fire from the twins. The vehicle's wire harness plate shattered under the anti-materiel blaster, sending one of the pieces of the armor spinning off the top of the vehicle.

"Seesaw to you," Wello said.

"Sending," Gekko replied. He dialed up the gain on the N-65 variable output rifle, focusing the bolt for maximum kinetic impact. The rifle rattled in the pit of the leej's shoulder, sending the heavy bolt into the maneuvering sled. It immediately sent up another wave of sparks as the prelude to a flash fire in the center of the housing. Gun barrels twitched as the mount on the truck spasmed under the sled's attempts to avoid much of the blaster fire coming from the stadium. "CROWS control harness hit. If they want to fire that gun, they're going to have to come from the hatch and do it themselves."

Kill Team Victory
Assault on Fort Blake
Defense of Stadium POW Camp

"Pina, it's Toots. I'm on the back side shooting over the kid on the GMV. Any idea when we're going to have those runner turrets up and at 'em?"

Pina wished he could wipe the sweat from his brow. It was bad enough that they'd just dodged a blaster bolt from defusing a mass casualty device, but they were still in the middle of suck central with the heavy that was Victory Company still fighting door to door to clear out the MCR. A good portion of those rats escaping the exterminator were flooding into the surrounding buildings and leveling shots at them. "Working it now. The MPs had a cyber jockey attached to them. He's right next to me working the interface while I'm rigging the algo to accept our targeting lasers."

Echoes of outgoing fire and the quieter report of a machine blaster somewhere distant to him joined Toots in the call. "I'm hearing a lot of whine and I smell no cheese."

Leave it to Toots to bring out one of the oldest digs in the military.

"System's up. Toots, I'm finalizing the algo. Tell our friends down below not to shoot at the turret drones."

Victory Company
Advancing Through Fort Blake

"Lieutenant Chopper!" Riggs called into the L-comm.

The lieutenant snapped immediately into the HUD. "Yes, sir."

"Are you still outside the gate?"

Blaster bolts and near misses sounded over the return fire from the LT. "Yes, sir. I'm here with my platoon. We have an MCR force trapped between us and the advancing Yawds from the Second Free Rifles. It's a meat grinder the rebels can't win, but they're content to slog it out with us anyway, sir. We should be free of this mess to turn the gate over to the militia guys in short order."

Riggs moved items around on his battle board. When the altered pieces were highlighted with a check mark, he knew his orders had been received. "Drop the hammer and have the Second Free Rifles take the gate supported by the Rhino Zero Two. I got an inbound Ram-Wing with your name on it. We're rigging a combat sled for sling load, now. Throw in some goodies, get over to Objective Deep Space, and pick up your wayward squad."

"On the roll, sir."

Victory Company, Zombie Squad
Assault on Fort Blake
Defense of Stadium POW Camp

Cyclic blaster fire from mobile gun turrets sent their thumping rhythm across the expanse into the combat sleds. Moving on four crab-like appendages, the turret drones were basically a heavy blaster with a high rate of fire set onto a giant battery. Add a little armor and the guns could set themselves anywhere and shift as needed.

The first of the skittering heavy blasters sent a bevy of shots into the lead combat sled only to be slagged a moment later when the twins dumped their own version of a blaster tornado straight into it. The gun battery arced and flashed from the impact of heavy bolts slamming into its lightly armored structure. With the battery sizzling, the machine was nothing but a twitching mass of legs. The paras of the Three-Three hauled it away and placed the gun barrel facing out through one of the many blaster holes in the outer wall. They didn't want to risk a surge firing a shot from the downed bot hitting one of the defenders.

Lynx and Diggs were working beside a squad of Three-Three infantry that had managed to collect enough PK-9s and Miif-7s to get them all into the fight. The outgoing fire was frenetic. Shooting in spurts, the infantrymen were selecting targets in the far buildings to drop at their leisure while teamed shooters were keeping fire directed at the CROWS system and the driver's screen to keep them obscured from the vehicles. If they wanted to shoot accurately, they'd have to get gunners into the cupola.

A rocket sailed across the expanse to detonate against the outer wall. Bits of duracrete and rebar rained down on the infantry squad, blowing the team off their feet.

"What was that?" Diggs shouted. He pried off a thick section of wall from his leg so he could get to his knees.

Lynx pointed at the side of the building. A K-19 automated Korodon infantry support mech crawled backwards after making the shot. The legionnaires from Victory Company proper were decimating the vehicles with bot-poppers in both rifled and standard grenade flavors on the other side of the base. Whoever was the operator on this side, they didn't want the legionnaires taking out combat sleds with rifles to get anywhere near their expensive toy. "Trent, it's Lynx. Got a K-19 beside the building I'm pinging."

"I got it, boss. What's the play?"

"How many ionic grenades do you have?"

Trent laughed into the L-comm. "It's not a magic button, boss. I have enough to flip the switch for a minute until it resets. We'd have to blow it in place to kick it off for good. And I'm looking through a drone right now, there are three other ones about to bust us up from the other angles."

"Lynx to Pina. You got any bot-poppers or bangers left?"

"This is Pina. Yes, and I see the Korodon tanks. We need to do something about those or we're about to have a bad day. Don't worry about the grenades, Sergeant. I may have an ace up our sleeve."

"Break, break, break," Lynx said over the L-comm. "Just got word from my higher that they're inserting a combat sled with a squad full of boom. They know about the K-19s and are rigging to take them down. Do we have anything that can hold 'em for a hot minute?"

Toots broke into the call. "I got a basic here that was just bragging he was captain of the seamball team back in the day. He says he can make those throws if we cover him."

Diggs and Lynx looked at each other, not believing what the other was hearing. "Cannon like that for an arm, you figure they'd've put him in artillery."

In front of the entrance, the para on the twins sent an angry typhoon of blaster bolts into the side of the building where the K-19 was hiding. He took two bolts to the head for his efforts, slamming him into the cupola until he fell into the vehicle. His squad pulled him from the sled toward the stack of casualties that was growing by the minute. A new soldier replaced him and was instantly shot through the shoulder. The blaster bolt seared through him, tearing his arm from the socket and splattering blood on the ground in a sizzling mess.

"Dammit! Stay eyeball defilade when you get on that gun!" shouted SSG Gilchrist. "Leejes! If you're going to do something, we need it now. My guys are black on ammo and the barrels on the twins are glowing. We have the same condition on the other side where that gun truck of yours is covering our back side. We're set to fix bayonets and get after it, but I am really hoping you have a better plan than mine."

A mini-swarm of blaster bolts struck the wall over their heads, showering the legionnaires in duracrete powder. "Go for Lynx."

"Sar'nt, we have the turret drones laying the law down on the concourse side to keep all that armor at bay. I just handed all my crackle bangers to the guy Toots just recommended. Boy are you in for a surprise."

A Drusic soldier hopped over a blown-out wall, landing beside the stunned legionnaires. Shouts of "Rigby" went up around the line from Repub Army soldiers who apparently knew the big alien. The simian monster was equal to a war bot in size if not in bulk.

"I hear you guys want me to throw these bot-poppers at someone," Rigby boomed. "Is that a thing or did that leej running the drones just pull me for delivery service?"

Lynx almost laughed. "Hell no, Sergeant. You got the arm, you throw the harm. I need you to peg that corner."

The Drusic smiled, exposing fangs that made Lynx wonder if a Drusic even needed those big muscular arms and legs. "I ain't wearing armor, little leej. You got something for me to keep from getting shot after the first throw?"

"I'm your cover," Diggs said. The expansive legionnaire stood to take an additional shot out from the holes in the wall.

"Lynx to Pina. We have that ball player ready to throw on the K-19 giving us hell. Can you and yours lay some thunder on this side to let him work?"

"Thunder coming. Start your run when you feel the burn. Pina out."

Thunderclaps rumbling the structure above them at a rate of five hundred rounds per minute rattled from the top of the bleachers in the form of five gun drones. Heavy blaster bolts sailed into the building corner, suppressing the shooters and the K-19. Rigby hopped up and put his free hand on Diggs's shoulder to let the leej know it was go time.

The duo moved into position and the Drusic primed the first grenade. He let it fly with a throw that carried it over the expanse between the two structures. It bounced along the ground and sank into a hole bored through the duracrete by outgoing army and Legion blasters. A second toss went farther than the first, but this throw was paid for with a blaster bolt to Diggs's chest as he covered the combat athlete.

The second grenade caused an immense energy bubble that shorted out the weapons hub on the top of the Korodon tank drone. A third throw sent one bouncing underneath, shorting out the repulsors and bricking the vehicle for a total system kill.

"Let's hit the other side!" Diggs shouted.

"But you're hit," Rigby said.

"Move it, Army!"

Lynx followed behind the pair, calling into the L-comm. "Pina, send covering drones to position two for second toss."

"Drones sent, Pina out."

The trio weaved between a group of soldiers shooting with kidnapped blasters and a turret drone laying down suppressing fire to make up for the lack of rifles on this side. The MCR forces supported by their combat sleds and K-19s were making a concentrated push for the stadium. If they could get even one gun team to the inside, there was still a very real chance they could trigger the device and kill a lot of Republic citizens in a very public display.

"Launch it, Sergeant Rigby!" Lynx called.

The two legionnaires went shoulder to shoulder this time to cover the titanic regular army soldier from the incoming wave of fire being leveled at them. The enemy blasters quieted a bit when the gun drones above them went kinetic. The rattle of heavy bolts leaving the chamber and destroying the building on the opposite side became the go button for the titanic NCO. He primed the first grenade and threw.

The K-19 on this side had an offset weapons system. One side contained the large-bore blaster cannon like the model they'd just deadlined. The other side of the turret housed a rotary blaster cannon capable of dumping medium blaster fire at a rate of two thousand bolts per minute. The tank lased the flying popper and brought up its weapon system, sending a spray of energy hornets buzzing from the barrel, destroying the projectile.

The K-19 then reoriented its gun to land its targeting system right on the trio of attackers looking to end its run-time.

Lynx tackled Rigby and Diggs behind what remained of the duracrete wall, grimacing as some of the stone gave way to a free shot at his back armor. The medium blaster bolt rolled him over, leaving trails of smoke venting up from behind him.

"Go!" demanded Rigby. He grabbed the drag handle behind Lynx's neck and carried off the stunned legionnaire in a chaos-induced scramble to a bigger piece of cover. "Everyone get back inside the stadium. Get on the bleachers. We can defend the concourse exits. Use them as chokepoints."

Diggs followed behind the soldier, checking his squad leader's vitals in the L-comm. "I take it you're just faking being hit so that Papa Rigby will carry you?"

"He's doing such a good job leading the way, I don't want to harsh his jam," Lynx said through gritted teeth.

38

Kill Team Victory
Assault on Fort Blake
Defense of Stadium POW Camp

Blaster bolts sent powdered duracrete over Pina as he ducked down behind the bleachers of the stadium. It was nice to have the properly spaced gunfire assaulting his position rather than the bolt tornado that had been laid down by the variant K-19. "All Victory Elements, this is Victory One-Seven. Cover in place. I say again, cover in place for attack run. Victory One-Seven, out."

Screaming overhead, Sidewinder aircraft flashed along their attack run. Blaring rotary cannons and missile pods sent a vortex of destruction onto the targeted drone tanks. One missile detonated in a wide enough ion dispersal that it sent a nearby combat sled tumbling end over end when its repulsors failed.

A Ram-Wing combat transport shuttle climbed into view, carrying a Legion-variant combat sled on a sling line beneath the craft. With the ramp open, legionnaires ran into the expanse, firing jump thrusters on their armor. Jump jets sailed them to the top of a building beside the stadium. They throttled their jets back to crash through high side windows or skylights to get at the MCR fighters cowering inside.

The vehicle's ramp closed a second before the Ram-Wing cut the cable. Firing its repulsors to max, the combat sled crashed into the roof on the next building over. It fell through two floors to crush a good number of the rebels or blast them with the energy wave of its repulsors. CROWS-enabled machine blasters on top of the vehicle laid down covering fire and decimated the remaining rebel troops. An aerial combat drone detached from its securing plate at the back of the vehicle as the robotic infantry assault bot uncoiled from its position behind the gunner's cupola.

Across the yard in the stadium, Lynx growled as he got to his feet, ignoring the looks he was getting from leej and basic alike staring at his back plate. "All Victory elements, this is Lynx. We have friendlies in the target buildings. Shift fire to outside of target buildings. I say again. Shift fire. Redirect fire to the enemy sleds."

Those that still had ammunition fired into the sleds, confusing the drivers and confounding the guns. Legionnaires appeared with AP missiles, dumping them one by one into the MCR-controlled combat sleds. The projectiles turned the mobile gun platforms into slowly hovering burn pits. Vehicular wreckage glided along dying repulsors just waiting for the fire to reach this crucial system or that so it could sputter and die. Legion forces worked the scene, gathering up MCR stragglers and those trying to rabbit.

A lone leej sprinted toward the stadium's main entrance, jumping past the ruined vehicle Diggs had shoved into the archway. MCR forces had done a number on the old girl, but a combination of the road shields and relentless gunning from the twins had kept it mostly intact. A haggard-looking staff sergeant nodded to the leej, then nearly snapped to attention when he saw the rank on the man's armor. The leej just patted him on the shoulder as he walked by. Acknowledgment from the Legion for a job well done.

Lynx gritted his teeth and shot up at the man's approach. "Good to see you, sir."

Chopper knuckle-bumped his NCO. "Good to see you're not dead. Although that back plate is karked."

"It looks better than his back, sir," quipped Doc Chance.

The Legion medic was working on Lynx's back, working over the nasty burns with what he had in his kit until the Zombie Squad leader could be seen by an actual field trauma team. Lynx's synthprene shirt was off, and the skin was inflamed and raw. Blisters were already forming from the blaster burns that had nearly cooked their way through the Legion plate. With a practiced hand, Doc Chance used a spray can to layer a white foam onto the burns. He then carefully applied skinpacks along the burn track to ease some of the pain and promote healing. But when he thrust a pill pack in front of Lynx's face, the leej waved him away.

The medic bounded off for his next patient, and Lynx looked up at his CO.

"What's next, sir?"

Chopper scanned the scene. The stadium would probably have to be condemned, torn down, and rebuilt. The twins mounted to the Repub combat sleds had decimated the outer walls. Military police working in tandem with the Civil Affairs unit were ferrying personnel out from the structure in the event it suddenly gave up the ghost and collapsed on a load of people. And the fighting hadn't stopped. This was only the beginning.

"Hit the airfield," he said. "They're setting up one of the shuttles as a med unit until the real hospital here gets the green light to open the doors again. Fix anything that's broken. Try to get some real food and sleep into you, because the sergeant major wants a word with you jokers."

"Which sergeant major, sir?" Lynx asked.

"MakRaven."

39

Chhun didn't bother waiting for the drop shuttle to hit the ground. He heaved the command element out of the bird and motioned for Chaz to follow. The landing struts had barely had time to take the weight of the craft from the repulsors before Chhun was already on the move.

A medic and his team carried several leejes on stretchers and R-CSMs toward the craft. Chhun motioned them forward. The doc sent Chhun a bounce to speak to him over the sound of the craft's repulsors.

"Sir, are you sure you want us to take your bird?"

The general looked back at *Bulldog Four*. "It's got more than enough space for your wounded, Doc. Once you get to *Centurion*, transfer all these guys to medical and have them hot-load this thing into a med unit. Ride it back down and park it next to that spot over there. That's going to be our ops building."

"On it, sir. KTF!"

Chhun punched the leej's shoulder plate and ran for the far building carrying the hard case that weighed a lot more than he was used to lugging by himself lately.

"Are you sure you don't want me to carry that one, General?" Chaz asked. The robot carried two cases of equal size and made it look like they were just a couple of bags from the shops downtown.

"I got it."

Chhun entered the blaster-riddled hangar bay that had previously housed the tanks and the war bots. Major Sapero walked out with a table for Chhun to put his gear on.

"Any idea where they're getting any of this stuff?"

Sapps shrugged as he set the legs. "No, sir. You need a hand setting this up?"

"Negative." Chhun glanced over to Chaz. "The bot's going to rig it. Should be about two minutes."

"Understood, General. Airfield is yours. Warlock will remain in place to secure. We took some hits getting it for you but we're straight now. HK-PP and the scout walkers are also going to stay on station. Third Platoon is up on patrol to link up with Kalo Company and stalk the woods."

"Roger. This part is set and we have comms with *Centurion*." Chhun took a micro-comm from his equipment belt. "*Centurion* REPO, this is Harvester. We have Harvester Base up and ready to receive traffic."

"Roger, Harvester. Stand by for Harvester Two."

"Chhun, it's Deynolds. Did you get my bounce about that drop carrier?"

"I got it. Are you going to try and board it?"

"I dunno. I'm running out of marines. We knew they had a small flotilla, but this is getting ridiculous."

"Can you get those boats out of orbit so they can't send or do anything on planet?" Chhun asked.

"Not a bad idea. We have a cruiser specifically set up for cyber warfare. We can board the enemy ships and slave them to the *Estoc*. That will keep the crew on their own ships and make it so we don't need a whole complement on each boat."

"Roger. Looks like some of those dropships made it through."

"Yes, General. Three made it. The biggest problem now is that we have one descending on Kam Dho City. We can't get a scan through the armor on those things, so we have no idea what's on them or what their purpose is."

"I'm sure we'll find out soon enough, Admiral."

Super-Destroyer *Centurion*
Combat Information Center

"Give me the digits on that boat!" Aguiar shouted.

"The dropship carrier has significant defenses. *Espada* hit them with several of her torpedoes and big guns, sir," Apollo replied. "The ship's shields were close to failing when they hit back. They hit our destroyer along the flank. We lost thirteen crew from a directed energy weapon tearing open part of the hull. *Espada* has the burn under control and they're returning fire. *Falchion* hit its engines when the shield went down, and now they're hammering on the rest of them. That thing won't be able to jump, sir."

"Status on the dropships?" Deynolds asked.

"All away, ma'am. They also have defensive capabilities so that our fighters and gunships are only able to engage them long-range. The *Raleigh* managed to hit one out of the six with long-range guided missiles. The SSMs cracked the shields and did in the engine. It's just floating in space, Admiral. The other five are away and are heading for major cities across the planet."

"REPO, warn Harvester Command Element they have incoming. If they can deploy assets on their side of the clouds to bring down those ships, I want them to try it. Then get word to the orbital defense station. Have the marines knock those pods out of the sky if they can. The sooner the better so that entire cities aren't wiped out by a falling ship the size of a meteor hitting the ground."

"Aye, Admiral," Apollo said, turning to her station.

Peregrine Company
Orbital Defense Station

Lieutenant Vinesh Narayan was now the Peregrines' CO following the death of Captain Mazzara. "Lance Corporal Hodges," he shouted, "I want a flight track on those beach balls, yesterday!"

"Aye, Lieutenant," replied the embattled corporal to his company CO. As the combat systems controller for the Peregrines, he sliced what she told him to slice and secured what she told him to secure. "First target locked, sir."

Narayan growled as he leaned over the control station. "Send it."

The power core poured massive waves of energy into the firing array for use in the station's main gun. Maneuver thrusters angled the ship in line with the first of the falling spheres turning a bright orange as the friction from atmospheric re-entry built into a firestorm across the shields. The marines on the station growled and groaned under the strain of g-forces as the station rapidly changed position to be in line for its shot on the first dropships.

"Any station this net, any station this net, this is Peregrine Actual. Secure dark out lenses and brace for weapon's shock." Lieutenant Narayan braced himself against the desk, which was bolted to the floor.

Hodges waited for the targeting chains to line up to affect a single box-reticle, and a rhythmic chime harassed him to depress the trigger. The entire station shuddered as the firing battery dumped its power load into the focusing chamber. There was a moment of absolute silence where the weapon molded the energy into a destructive bolt the size of a seamball stadium. The turbulence across the station raged from a shudder to violent tremors when the bolt left the nearly kilometer-long barrel.

The shock wave of golden force struck out from the station toward the falling dropships. A teardrop-shaped vehicle was struck by the titanic fire lance, rupturing its reactor into an explosion that mushroomed from the point of impact to spread across the horizon. Two ships had been neatly lined up for the shot, although the second took a more nominal hit as the bolt deflected slightly off the first target.

Narayan's brows were knitted together in concentration. "Lance Corporal. How fast can you prime the gun for another hit?"

"Ninety seconds, sir. For a shot with a quarter of the power."

"Fire it up, son. I want that second drop bubble ruined when it hits atmo."

"Priming chamber for second deployment. Weapon charge in sixty seconds. Target selected. Maneuvering station to align for target."

"Can ya get 'em all in a straight line, kid?" Gunny Losey asked.

The lance corporal shook his head. "No can do, Gunnery Sergeant. I'd have to shoot toward the ground, and if they're angling over populated areas, this beam could destroy half a city with a single bolt."

Losey shrugged. "Never hurts to ask."

Hodges watched as the power indicator rose to sufficient levels for the middling shot, then hammered down the trigger. The station went through its firing cycle again until the thundering bolt shot from the barrel. It slammed into the target, tearing down its shields and shredding the top of the teardrop. The force of the strike sent the dropship tumbling into the atmosphere as tons of equipment broke free from its rigging and was sucked out through the hull. The flotsam left the ship as flaming tears before explosions inside the craft blew off tremendous chunks of armor plating, sending the shuttle into a tumultuous spin. Less than a minute after being struck, the ship was a meteor storm over the planet.

"*Centurion* REPO, this is Peregrine Actual. Splash two dropships. If you want to greenlight the okay to aim at the planet, we might be able to get some more."

"Negative, Peregrine. Harvester has the ball. Good shooting. *Centurion* REPO out."

40

Harvester Command Element
Temporary Ops Center
Fort Blake, Hangar 2105

"General, you have an incoming call from Harvester Two. Shall I prepare a space for you or a vehicle so you can take the call?"

Chhun looked up from the laminated map spread out on the table. The MCR had gone low-tech in their build-up to take Kima, and now the general was looking at their intelligence hands-on. "No thank you, Chaz. I have my bucket." He swept along the map, the image becoming digital and moving along with his finger until he got to the city. A targeting reticle flashed over a point north of Kam Dho where the river bent. Sho Ven Star Port. Removing his finger from the laminate turned the digital image back into analog, with the reticle still displayed.

The task force commander replaced his bucket and waited for the hiss of the helmet sealing to the rest of his armor. "Deynolds, it's Chhun."

A video stream of the busy CIC behind Admiral Deynolds populated a window inside the HUD. "I'm flashing a data burst to you of all available intel on those drop-ships that entered atmo."

"Does your REPO have a working theory about our gaps in intel on this? I mean, I'm not asking for a crystal ball here, Admiral, but a mining carrier repurposed with military-grade armor for a deployment like this is a pretty big deal."

"You're not wrong, General. We're working it."

"Any word from Bear?" Chhun was asking out of concern more than anything else. He knew that if the operator had something crucial, it would have been reported to him by now.

"He just sent a burst. We're decrypting and running it now. I know your original hope in sending him to Kam Dho was to provide on-site intel for when you hit the cities, but damn if he didn't step into the mummy-bee hive. Having the VBX-13 as an element in this fight is pretty grim, especially when they try to use it against us. What's the play here?"

Chhun tapped twice on the map in front of him, turning the image digital again. He swiped it to display a chemical signature of VBX-13, then leaned on the table. "The MCR had a similar device centered in the POW camp. If they're not using it for chaos, then the purpose is fear. The Mid-Core Rebellion wants the people on Kima to be afraid to side with the Republic. Work beside the Legion and you'll die. They want the populace to believe there's nothing we can do about it. A majority of Kimbrin don't support what the MCR are doing, but it's not that *much* of a majority."

Deynolds was silent at that.

"How long until the dropships make landfall?" Chhun asked.

"Within the next two minutes."

"Can you hot-load some blackout OSMs and hit all three?"

There was no reply. Chhun assumed that she was calling for the strike order as he waited. Deynolds confirmed it a moment later when he heard the fire control officer and the *Centurion* Republic intelligence officer re-laying her commands in the background.

"Firing now."

Sho Ven Star Port

The glow on the hull against the teardrop-shaped MCR drop shuttle faded in the cool atmosphere on the descent to the star port. Buffeting winds sailed around the aerody-namic vehicle as the flight suspension field continued to guide it along its flight path. The ship fell to an altitude of forty-five hundred meters and took up an orbit around the city as though it was a king surveying newly conquered lands. Angling thrusters changed the attitude of the craft so that its largest part aimed at the surface while its top, adorned with various antennas and sensory equipment, faced the sky.

The main engines retracted stabilizer struts, allowing the repulsor pods to rotate in place, arresting the fall of the titanic dropship. The struts re-engaged into a locking position above the engines so the strain of whatever load the dropship was carrying wouldn't shear off the engines as they tried to keep the ship aloft. Tremendous shudders buffeted the craft as the engines, becoming retro thrust-ers, brought the controlled fall into a hover.

The upright dropship continued its orbit around Sho Ven Star Port. It adjusted its trajectory in ticking course corrections as it continued to make its way toward an in-evitable touchdown. Periodic flares of the angling thrusters vented across the ship, keeping everything in order for the drop. Landing struts the size of buildings deployed from the housings to slap in place with titanic slams.

A missile flashed out of the clouds, descending on the orbital deployment ship like a falcon after a fish. It dodged PDC fire streaking out from the descending craft, juking in erratic flight paths that confounded whatever fire control was running the point defense cannons. It struck the shields and exploded with a white, arcing flash that spread a kilometer in all directions.

The engines abruptly stopped.

Groaning metal twisted against a frame no longer supported by a structural integrity field or complex motorized stabilizers. The craft increased speed with the outright failure of the power of four mammoth drive repulsors. Hard creaking sounds echoed off the skyscrapers for which Kam Dho City was known.

The teardrop collided with the ground from a fall of five hundred meters. It fell into the air traffic control tower, shattering the structure and causing an explosion of fire. Shrieking metal snapped and armored plating sheared off, skidding along the tarmac before striking the hangars. One armored plate flipped end over end before hitting a fuel depot, detonating the structure into a fireball nearly as tall as the fallen ship.

Gelatinous fuel sprayed in multiple directions from the blast, coating other structures. Metal caught fire as the fuel burning at two thousand degrees Celsius rendered roofs into slag. Molten bits of scrap and flaming jet jelly fell into the space below, further igniting aircraft until they, too, exploded.

Sliding and rolling across the duracrete, the dropship lost most of its shape. Huge gouts of metallic slag continued to transform into fragmentation that smashed hangars and support buildings alike. The entire affair came to a screeching halt at the end of Sho Ven's second main runway. In its wake was a kilometer-and-a-half-long impact trail littered with fire, broken buildings, and ancillary explosions.

41

Republic Safe House
Kam Dho City

"Man, it's like a ghost town out there. You'd think there was a war on somewhere," Bear commented as he walked into the INSEC safe house.

"But did you wipe your feet?" Brit asked. "Never mind. I already know the answer. We got intel from our scouts on the ground. Three, like, stupidly huge dropships made it past the Republic blockade over Kima."

"What were they carrying? Are they down yet?" Jaela asked, walking in the rest of the team after the extraction of the Vai-Kasa exec.

"Don't know, but whatever it was, it's all over Sho Ven. Your boy Cha-hoon knocked all three of them out of the sky with blackout orbit-to-surface missiles."

"That'll do it," Jaela said.

Brit adjusted the micro-comm in her ear. Somewhere in between when Bear had left and come back, she'd managed to change the color of her hair to jet black with an orange frost at the tips while growing it to shoulder length.

Bear tugged at her hair, trying to figure the trick. "What is this, nanites?"

She slapped the hand away. Bear shrugged. "Never ask a woman her beauty secrets. How are we looking on Fort Blake?"

"Legion has it. Chhun is setting up on RIAS now."

"Funny how you can tell how long a person has been deployed to Kima by what they call that strip," Bear commented. "Been here a little while and it's Fort Blake Airstrip. Been here a longer while and it's the Republic Interplanetary Air Station. What else you got for me, Brit?"

"Since you're the only one who noticed my hair, I think I'll tell you. We've been mob-logging the intel hack on Vai-Kasa. There are some very strange work requests coming in from the corporate offices, though there's a lot of paper shuffling to mask where the requests actually originated from."

"What are the requests?" Bear asked.

"A lot of them center around VBX-13. They had a huge influx of credits and a work order to fabricate the stuff. The thing is, Vai-Kasa is rated to make things like solvents and cleaners and stuff. And while they have a patent on the underlying pesticide, they're not rated for Class One restricted neurotoxins."

"Especially not one with a nanite-cycled thiophosphonate that amplifies its use as a weapon."

Brit looked over her wire-rimmed glasses at the smug leej. "Look who's been practicing all day to say that word."

"Hopefully I got it right and I only have to say it once," Bear replied. He flashed her a two-finger mock salute and then spun his hand as though it were a spinning wheel. "I got a bounce from Chhun's buddy-bot on the way over. Same stuff was recovered at the artillery sites by Venom Company, the ones on Blake, and the canisters on the doom machine my kill team shut down. Do we have the amount of gas Vai-Kasa was contracted for if we factor in the stuff that was already used to kill that legionnaire?"

Brit looked over the numbers between two screens at her station. "Not even close."

Bear set his face to a hard and worried frown. "Jaela, let me know when we're set."

The Zaan Kimbrin spoke softly to her teammate. "We're set."

Bear nodded. "Brit, when I get in, make contact with Harvester TOC and run our feed to Chhun."

The INSEC slicer whistled at the retreating legionnaire. "Give me sixty seconds and you're good."

"Thanks, Brit."

Jaela followed him through the maze that was the safe house. Twists and turns where formerly open rooms were bisected by corrugated metal sheeting flowed along walkway planks that kept their feet from plunging into the water under the floor. The side of Kam Dho they'd been working in was near the river district, and part of a section of warehouses that no longer saw use after they started sinking into the river. The buildings now formed a shantytown where those with no better options could at least put a roof over their head for next to nothing, leaving them enough credits to eke out whatever existence they made for themselves. Since most of the apartments were on the second floor and higher to stay above the waterline, most bottom floors were abandoned and available for use by criminals, Mid-Core Rebels, and the occasional covert Legion outfit.

Bear lifted the hasp on the wrinkled metal door and stepped inside. "Dr. Rantanen. Thank you for speaking with us today."

The woman's poise spoke of a good upbringing in the best of Republic society. Her speech was tinged with a slight accent. She spoke well, although her voice had a hint of the exotic. "It wasn't as if I had much of a choice. It was either be pulled into an aircraft by one thug or another. You just happened to ask rather than demand."

"I'm sorry about that, Doctor. I'll try to keep my thuggish nature to myself during our conversation. Can you tell me why Vai-Kasa needed a viral bio-technical engineer, seeing as they're pretty much a high-end soap company?"

"I would love to answer your question, but according to the Republic constitution if I ask you to declare yourself, you are bound by law to do so. Who am I speaking with, please?"

Bear nodded. "Let me just get my credentials. I have them right here." He placed his blaster pistol on the table between them after removing the charge pack. The Asogram D-31 medium blaster pistol was a mid-range thumper favored by all the creepy black bag operators who liked to put holes in their enemies and not have stray bolts fly through flimsy walls into innocent people. "I guess that withdrawal of my thuggishness doesn't extend to doctors plotting mass murder on a Republic population center."

Bear's indictment slapped the doctor as surely as if he'd dragged his mitts across her face at a high rate of speed. "What are you talking about, Mister—I'm sorry, I don't know your name."

"It's right there on my credentials. Right next to the part where I have every right to end you if you don't cooperate, considering what you've done."

She folded her arms against a dirty ruffled shirt that normally would have been the height of high fashion business attire. "And what do you think I've done?"

"You've fabricated a Class One restricted neurotoxin for use on a population center or against soldiers in a military action, both of which carry a death sentence according to Republic law."

Rantanen looked to Jaela. "And who is she?"

Jaela let her eyes rest on the doctor but remained silent.

"She's the one that's going to dump your corpse in the river if you don't stop it with the attitude," Bear said, pushing his battle board toward the woman. The video feed from Hammer's bucket showed the last minutes of Bouncer's life.

Bear was pretty good at judging reactions. Classes in psychology, training from top-tier poker players, and simply being an operator in Dark Ops for so long had transformed the brutish legionnaire into a first-class dung detector. He knew that people could fake quite a lot of reactions. Sniffles, tears, even some responses like blushing could all be faked by someone with enough practice. But there were certain tells a person had when distressed. Those little quirks such as a tic in the face, a tapping of a finger, or even the choice of wording in the way someone talked all spoke volumes.

The doctor's reaction told Bear one thing. She was horrified.

"How?" she managed to croak.

"It was deployed against a legionnaire who was escorting a captured Mid-Core Rebel. Another ambushed him and activated a suicide vest. Killed every living thing in a thirty-meter radius."

The doctor swept her hand across her cheek to clear the tears from her eyes. "But if he was a legionnaire, then the vector should have ignored him. His armor, even the synthprene suits that are worn underneath, all contain a polymer that the nanite controllers inside the compound are programmed to ignore. They could swim in it and as long as they were in their armor, nothing would happen to them."

"Look closer."

She replayed the video, zooming in on his torso. "His sleeves were off."

"Yeah. Dog handler. Needs skin-to-skin contact. So once again, Doctor, why did you fabricate huge batches of this neurotoxin for use against Republic citizens?"

"I... I didn't. I created it as a batch order to process ship hulls coming from mining colonies on the edge. I was given after-mission briefs about an aggressive simple organism, retrieved from an asteroid belt, that was doing considerable damage to ship hulls. The toxin was supposed to be for scraping the hulls clean before the ships made it into dock on populated worlds. VBX-13 had an invoice and a release label from the government or I never would have touched it."

Brit came online in Bear's earpiece. "I scrubbed that database for a rights-of-usage writ that Vai-Kasa would have needed to get their hands on the formula, much less the actual compound. There is no writ on the local server or the public one on file with the corporate office."

"Dr. Rantanen, do you have a copy of the rights-of-usage writ that would have gone along with the VBX-13 formula?"

"Agent, this isn't the first time I've been asked to handle a sensitive substance. And while the money for doing so is keeping my daughter in school and me out of debt, I've learned enough from my co-workers getting burned by other facilities that I take snaps of everything."

"Ask her about the NDA she signed."

"By telling me this, does this violate your NDA?" Bear asked.

The doctor snorted, the first sign of relief in her posture. "I'm pretty sure being prosecuted for war crimes and crimes against humanity allows me to breach confidential information clauses from a criminal enterprise. Though I'm a doctor, not a lawyer. Still, when I take a high-risk contract like this, I wear a set of snap lenses so I can record everything. That way I don't end up in a room with a murder agent where even if I live, I'm probably going to get aspergillus."

"I've opened the link to that board. Load me up, Doc," Bear said softly.

The woman did as requested. When she was finished, Jaela circled around her. She roughly snatched the woman's head backwards, eliciting a scream of surprise. Jaela rubbed the doctor's eyelid and opened it, and then repeated the procedure with the other eye.

"No lenses."

"You could have asked," Rantanen barked as she shrugged out of Jaela's grip.

"No offense, Doc, but until we can verify everything you've given us, we trust you as much as you trust the fungus in this room to respect your boundaries and not get you sick."

"Bear, I found the paperwork they showed her," Brit sounded in his ear. "They also claimed to put the documentation in a server location where she could supposedly access it at any time. There's no file associated with the reference number."

As Bear pushed away from the table and started out of the room, Rantanen spoke behind him. "Agent? What's going to happen to me?"

"We're going to hold you until we can verify your story. We're also looking into the counter-agent you were told by Kein to retrieve from the lab. If it works, then you may have just been hired for the most important job of your life: saving the planet from your screw-up."

Bear walked from the makeshift interrogation room into a flurry of activity. "Brit? I don't like walking into a room where everyone is panicking, running, or both."

"Outside alarms just got triggered. We're bouncing to site two."

Bear was instantly on the comm. "Jaela, did you search the doc?"

"Yes," came the garbled reply. "She had no active or passive tracking and she isn't chipped."

"What about the case?" Bear said. He hurried back down the corridor to rip open the door to the room. "One coming in."

Jaela was behind the doctor, whose head was pressed against the table. The INSEC agent had a pistol aimed at the door. "The case was clean as well. Same for the lab techs."

"C'mon, we're getting out of here. I don't get it though. If we're clean and we didn't take the AUS-Vs back here because we stole their SLIC, how did they find us when we ditched the bird out of bounds?"

"Zier, it's Jaela. Did your drivers just get back to base?"

"Roger. We're loading the trucks up now."

"They were tracking the trucks," Jaela and Bear said in concert.

"Zier, ditch the AUS-Vs. Run all gear down to the alternate egress," Jaela ordered.

"C'mon, Doc," said Bear. "You just earned a ride and a job, as they're either coming to kill you or steal you back."

Kam Dho River District

Bear pulled the conical hat low over his eyes as the covered longboat glided across the water. The staff had switched into the local attire favored by the river folk in Kam Dho City, and now made their way across the largest floating market in the sector. They passed a river taxi ferrying a few passengers clutching bags as the boat motored by.

"This is the largest open-air river market on this or any world in the sector, and everything is closed," Jaela noted. "Things have got to be pretty bad if it's this quiet."

Brit huffed. "People took off after Bear's buddy crashed three huge honkin' dropships into the city. Things get real when you have a super-destroyer overhead dropping death from space!"

"It was only the one ship. I mean, you can hardly see the smoke from the star port from here," Bear said weakly.

"Yeah," teased Brit. "You hardly notice it with all the smoke coming out of Fort Blake, anyway. I guess I give up on why it's so quiet."

The boat sidled into the dock of a fish warehouse. They quietly crept from the junk, along the dock into the facility. Rows of hooks and conveyors littered the space, creating a stink of rust and rotting fish. Normally the place would likely be packed with real-world workers interspersed with INSEC agents keeping on the lookout for anyone who didn't belong. The firebombing of an entire street in the business district and the crashing of a heavy cargo carrier into the star port was enough to warrant a mental health day for an entire city.

They proceeded through a series of hanging plastic flaps keeping the temperature from one part of the facility separate from another, and made their way to a nondescript door with ultramodern biometric security. It led to a room where the lights winked on at their arrival, revealing inert computer equipment, large blank sheets of laminated paper, and the occasional holo telling them there was no BIOS detected.

Brit inserted several data stacks into the machines and was rewarded with power indicators telling them that the systems would be up momentarily. Bear held up his battle board, and the micro-sheets flared to life with maps of the area. Minutes ticked by as the team went about powering up this device or that to check the process of what was happening outside the room.

As her hood came off, Dr. Rantanen saw her picture and a dossier of her work populate the laminate. "Who are you people?"

Bear handed her a battle board and hit the *play* icon. "Since we have a minute, I want you to watch the feed from this board. It will show you faces that you've interacted with. When it prompts you, type in their name as best as you can remember it."

"What will that accomplish?"

"If nothing else it will keep you quiet," Brit said. "Hey boss, Zier is below prepping the rooms. Also got word on that guy. He was just moved to the big C."

Bear nodded. He'd been waiting on word that Kein had been moved to *Centurion* for interrogation. While the man probably didn't know anything, Vai-Kasa at large had thought him important enough to pay the fee for his extraction from Kima.

"One more thing. Our system has still been on the hunt for that actor you like," Brit said. "We may have a way to find out what venue he's playing."

Masters.

42

It was the flashing, winking lights of ships entering atmosphere that finally convinced Masters it was time to turn back around and reunite with the missionary bot, J-316. The ships' shields, taking the burn of reentry, were especially visible in the early dark that came with being on the eastern slope of the mountain, in dead lands where only one type of tree grew up to the heavens, further blocking out the sun. In marshes and swamps that teemed with life while reeking of death.

"That's either an invasion force, or enough reinforcements that I'm karked," Masters muttered as his eyes followed the streaking glow of dropships.

He had taken to talking to himself. Even more so than usual. And though he tried to keep all the words in his head, he knew that they were formed by his mouth far too often than was wise. He had been like that during Legion selection as well. Long ago.

The time out in this forsaken land, hunting zhee but never finding more than a small three-donk patrol, had been difficult. It had felt like he was in selection again. Which proved the Legion instructors correct: they really were preparing him for the worst the galaxy could dish out. It just took a while for things to ever feel as bad as they did back when he was a boot.

Calorie-dense rations kept him alive, but he could feel his physical strength waning. And he looked like hell.

Which, he often reminded himself, was an incredibly difficult feat for him to achieve. The grime and filth he found himself covered in went beyond field exercises and into the realm of wild survival. Everything was dirty. His hair was caked with oil and mud. The lines of his face were filled with dirt that wouldn't be flushed out with sweat.

That wasn't so bad, though. The grimy layer made him as one with the bog. The bugs no longer paid him any mind.

Sleeping without a helmet had been a torturous invitation to the insect population the first few days in the swamps. Every night, a new swath of bites welled up on his face. Luckily the battery of auto-injections he was subjected to by the camp's med bot kept him from experiencing any of the ravaging diseases those insects carried with them. All he had to endure for that first stretch was the bite pain.

He had come across a dead zhee, left by its compatriots, and stripped of all its gear and clothing. The little kel-horned bugs that populated the swamp had so thoroughly chewed on the donk that large pink and red pustules crowded out the gray and brown fur across most of its face, neck, and belly as well as on the tender spots inside the arms and legs. Masters guessed that the thing had contracted some illness and was left to die. Its clawed hooves were red with its own blood and matted fur and big, self-inflicted gouges from what had to have been the furious scratches of madness.

Masters had hoped the dead zhee would lead him to a base of operations, but all he'd encountered thus far were scattered patrols or listening/observation outposts.

Overhead, as the dropships reduced altitude toward Fort Blake and the surrounding cities, Masters could see the air around the ships burst and explode with targeted anti-air fire. Fast movers raced through the air, leaving vapor trails in their wake.

"Hey, it's us," Masters muttered, and then moved to a spot between two monolithic *Ceentar* trees to find a better view between towering canopies.

All he saw was glimpses, flashes of light, but they told a story to eyes honed and trained by war and combat. It was the spectacle of invasion as seen from the ground, a planet being infiltrated from the perspective of one too far away to hear any of the cracks and booms of the ordnance used.

Everything was far from where Masters now was. There was simply nothing in this dead and forsaken land he had escaped to that was worth fighting against or fighting for. Or at least, nothing that Masters had encountered. Or that the Legion was aware of. Because prior to invasion, Dark Ops would have been on the ground, along with Republic Intel, and the fact that they hadn't found Masters, or zhee, or done anything to leave any trace of themselves on this side of the mountains, showed that their focus was entirely on the lost Repub Army bases and population centers.

Masters straightened himself out and let out a sigh. Nearby, above a still and fetid pool of brackish water, blue and green glowing bugs circled over the surface lazily.

"Might be easier to go find the Legion than it has been the zhee," he whispered.

Overhead, the streaking comets that were the dropships increased in number, a growing rain that would soon punish any MCR forces on the ground.

Masters reoriented himself and moved to find the bot. And then... the Legion.

"Hey," Masters called into the darkness. Without a bucket, he was no longer the all-seeing predator he had become accustomed to being while in Dark Ops, but his natural night vision had improved dramatically from regular use. He'd forgotten just how good the human eye could naturally see in the dark in blackout conditions.

It was because of that night vision that Masters risked calling for the bot. He was sure this was the place he'd left the curious proselytizing machine.

"Hey. Jay-Three."

There was no answer. Masters moved back to the fallen log where he'd left the bot, got down onto a knee, and checked to see if the hobbled machine had dug itself underneath. As he searched, he heard a clink somewhere behind him.

Masters turned slowly, not wanting to draw attention to himself with an abrupt and loud movement. The clink was followed by a thump from somewhere overhead. Masters looked up and saw a pair of glowing eyes looking down at him.

"Jay-Three? That you up there?"

The glowing eyes moved up and down in a nod.

"Well, get down here. We've got to move."

All at once, the bot stepped off its branch and plummeted to the ground with a resounding metallic thud. The bot helped itself up by its crutch and then spoke in a loud voice.

"Your return is most welcome. Staying up there, I was reminded of the spiritual attunement believed to be received by the moktaar when mating high in—"

That was all J-316 got out before Masters closed the ground to the bot, tackled him, and shoved his gloved hand over J-3's mouth.

"Quiet down," Masters hissed.

"I apologize," the bot answered, his voice muffled but still louder than Masters would like. "The salve you applied washed away during the rains six days, eight hours, and twelve minutes ago. I attempted to maintain your application but was unable to do so."

"It's fine," Masters said, helping the bot up but keeping its mouth covered. "Now what were you saying about the moktaar's mating habits—actually never mind. Why were you up there?"

"Evasion."

"Evasion? From what?" Masters was hopeful that perhaps a troop of zhee had come through. With a fresher lead, he might be able to track them to whatever deeper hide they occupied.

"Armed bands of Kimbrin. I opted to hide given your situation, although typically my programming suggests that I reason with them according to the preferred faith of those I shepherd. In this case, the worship of Oba as so studiously practiced by you."

"Not as studious as you hope," Masters said, looking about for any signs of the MCR. Them following him down the other side of the mountain had been a possibility from the moment he'd jumped off the edge, but it had been a while since that fight, and Masters had almost convinced himself that they wouldn't be coming.

"Well. Now that we are reunited, perhaps we can begin a study? I have pondered several new revelations received from Oba. I believe his coming is imminent."

"That a good thing or a bad thing?"

J-316 tilted its head to the side with a mechanical whir of old gears that stubbornly continued to function. "That depends on the individual. Will they accept calories, or will they become calories?"

"If I've got a choice, I'll go ahead and accept them."

"In that case, you should be fine."

"Good to know. These Kimbrin you saw—how long ago and which direction?"

"I witnessed the first patrol move through the vicinity thirty-six planetary hours ago." J-316 pointed toward the underbrush. "The most recent patrol moved in that direction only two planetary hours ago."

"How many?"

"I counted four Kimbrin. A much smaller patrol than the thirty I initially viewed."

Masters nodded. "Okay. Let's go find them."

"Do you intend to share with them the deep and lasting faith of Oba?"

"No, I intend to turn them into calories for whatever's hungry."

J-316 paused and considered this. "I suppose Oba will be accepting of that as well."

43

It was a three-man patrol of Kimbrin MCR regulars that Masters first tracked down, and it was evident that they were doing their best to track *him*. Or if not him, someone else. Their every movement was a searching one. Their patrol was rambling and inquisitive. They weren't trying to get anywhere in particular, they were trying to see who else was out here.

They had food and fresh charge packs. At least one of them used an old-model radio that probably couldn't get over the mountain and its dead and lifeless back side, but could potentially be used to reach the Legion on the other side. If nothing else, he might be able to keep abreast on what the MCR were doing on this side of the mountain.

But first, he had to eliminate the patrol and take what he wanted. And he had to do it quietly enough not to draw the others before he had a chance to disappear into the wilderness again.

Masters followed the patrol for that chance, stalking them quietly. Patiently.

Evening drew long shadows as the sun dipped behind the mountain. The sun's glow cast a shining blaze behind the high peak's crown, giving enough light for the glow-bugs and other end-of-day creatures to come out to feed. Fish flopped from the slow swamps where the MCR patrol began to settle in.

That was odd—a patrol so small planning to stay in the back country overnight instead of reuniting with the main body. Masters wondered if they were lost. He had been close enough to hear them speak in their native tongue, but without his bucket or a functioning micro-comm to do on-the-fly translation, he didn't know what they were saying beyond a few words. Masters had learned a decent amount of the Kimbrin language from the Yawds, but the accent here was different, and the cadence of speech was entirely too quick to keep up.

J-316 could tell Masters what was being said, if he dared bring the bot this close. The bot had gotten better about being quiet when commanded—in fact, when it came to moving stealthily, it had done an admirable job.

It was the speaking voice that was a concern. J-316 was incapable of whispering.

Masters, lying concealed in tall grass, waved for the bot to join him. A pair of low, glowing eyes appeared in a bush some fifty meters back, and as the bot approached, it was perfectly noiseless. Masters wondered if that skill-set was learned or simply something that those serving with a missionary bot required of the unit. It was a universal constant that most species hated being told their gods were false and their way of life in need of changing. Being able to shut up and hide was probably invaluable for missionaries and new converts alike from time to time.

The MCR patrol started a small fire by over-charging their blaster packs. That worked fine in a pinch but would ruin the packs eventually. There were secondary pieces of kit that could easily start a fire without compromising your weapon system, but the mids didn't seem to have them.

"I need to know what they're saying," Masters whispered to J-316, "but you're not allowed to talk or we'll get found out."

The bot nodded to say it understood and then held out its palms and shrugged to say it didn't know how that would be possible.

Masters frowned. He hadn't quite figured that out either. They could try writing in the mud, but in the low light he doubted that would work and he didn't want to leave so obvious a track to be followed, either.

"Just listen to them," Masters whispered. "I'll ask you some yes or no questions. Nod for yes, shake for no. Understand?"

J-316 nodded, and then set to listening.

The three Kimbrin spoke at length, and when Masters decided there might have been enough discussion to get some sort of useful intelligence, he began his questions.

"Did they say if they're expecting more to join them?"

J-316 shook its head no.

"Are they lost?"

The bot shrugged.

"What are they looking for?"

The bot shrugged.

"Are they staying here all night?"

The bot shrugged.

His frustration rising, Masters asked, "Well what in the nine hells were they going on about?" He quickly held up a hand. "Don't answer. Stick to the plan. Yes or no. Has the Legion landed on Kima?"

Another shrug.

Now immensely frustrated over the spectacular failure of this plan, Masters turned back to face the Kimbrins. One of the men motioned toward the water's edge a ways, said something, and then sauntered off with his rifle slung to his back.

"That guy say he's going to go take a leak?"

The bot shook its head.

"Dump?"

The bot nodded.

"Alone?"

Another nod.

"Yeah, dumb question." Masters nodded as well. "Guess that's where I'll start. You stay here."

The legionnaire began to slide through the mud and saw one of the blue fireflies buzz across his face. It gave him an idea. He turned back to J-316. "Hey, the blue ones are the ones you don't want to swallow, right?"

The bot nodded affirmative.

Masters winked. "This is gonna go in my screenplay."

He trapped the insect between his hands and then crept away, taking a route that let him silently sink into the water. After swimming to the opposite bank where the Kimbrin now squatted, he checked to be sure the bug was still intact, being careful not to let it fly from his hand. The glowing blue light bug stretched its wings and attempted to take off before Masters closed his fist around it again.

Ignoring the smell, Masters crept behind the Kimbrin attending to its business. Then, all at once, the legionnaire threw one arm around the MCR soldier's neck while slamming the blue glow-bug into his mouth and clamping it inside. A small, muffled yell sounded against Masters's gloves as the Kimbrin struggled.

Masters used his other hand to force the Kimbrin's jaw to crush the insect. He didn't pull his hand away until the MCR began to make a gagging noise. He pushed himself off of the soldier's body just as a swarm of the blue insects set upon the dazed Kimbrin's open mouth and neck, biting furiously.

The Kimbrin let out a shriek of terror and pain as he forgot all about his attacker. He thrashed and slapped at his face, which only drew more of the terrible swarm. Masters had seen what these insects could do to a fish—gutting it in a moment and leaving only bones—but what they were now doing to a full-grown Kimbrin was far more horrific. Already it seemed the man's lips were eaten away and a hole was forming through his neck and into his throat that strained his desperate screams for help.

The other two Kimbrin came running and Masters, hidden from sight, watched as they tried to make sense of what had happened to their friend. The soldiers sprang into a sort of tentative dance on the edge of taking action. They wanted to help but were afraid of sharing their friend's fate. Finally one of them knelt at the victim's side and tried to shoo away the bugs, to no avail.

None saw Masters re-emerge from his hiding place. He plunged his knife into the neck of the Kimbrin who stood back from the affair, driving the blade down to the collar bone and then fishing it out with a gout of blood that sent the soldier into darkness. The one who knelt to render aid was next, dying as quickly as the first and in the same manner.

The first Kimbrin was already dead by that time, as the flies continued to gorge themselves.

Masters barely felt his heart rate increase. He looked at the bodies. "Second thought... this might be a little too much for the script."

Masters had only managed to search two of the bodies before the first shouts reached him. A bark of clipped orders organizing maneuvers from a force too large to worry about being heard as they moved rapidly through the swamps. Masters had only minutes to put distance between himself and the patrol he'd just permanently ended.

Charge packs were the one thing he wouldn't leave without. Somewhere there was a radio and rations, likely back at the site of their initial setup. There was no time to check. Weapons and ammunition would have to do. Masters took as spoils from the dead a well-used KMA-8G assault rifle, six charge packs, and two fragmentation grenades.

"Okay, Pastor, we're going," Masters called to the bot, still waiting hidden amid the reeds and scrubby bushes that grew in the muddy soil beyond bog and swampy pool.

"It pleases me to hear you call me that," J-316 said as the bot stood and then hobbled toward Masters. The legionnaire pointed to reorient the bot and then the two moved hastily along an old, dilapidated fence that was petrified where not rotted away. The very fact that it was out here was a mystery now forever lost to the galaxy.

"If we get away without getting shot at, we can both be happy," Masters answered.

They moved along the fence line, finding that the footing was surer than the wilds around it and less yielding, which might help to hide their tracks, though Masters doubted it given the pace at which they were traveling. The bot, despite needing its makeshift walking stick, made impressive time as it hobbled along. And the tracks it left behind would likely confound even the most experienced trackers.

They moved close to a kilometer along the fence. Sometimes it would disappear completely into the land, other times it was marked only by boot-high remains of posts more like stone than wood. Eventually it was back and mostly intact, though no two split rails managed to exist parallel—one was always dislodged and lying diagonally on the ground, occasionally in line with the posts, but more often twisted to one side or another, an obstacle for the pair to jump over or around.

Behind them, a blaster bolt sounded, far enough away that Masters only turned to get a better sense of where precisely it had been fired.

"We are being shot at!" J-316 declared. "Kneel, my son, and receive a prayer of purification in the event of death."

The bot attempted to reach up and grab Masters's shoulders to force him down into the muck. The legionnaire swatted away the attempt. "They're shooting at ghosts, Jay-Three. That sounded like it was all the way back at the camp."

Masters let the explanation hang in silence, listening for any signs that they were being pursued before giving the order to move again. "Let's keep putting distance between us."

"I thought your intention was to provide calories for the galaxy," J-316 noted. "Would that not be easier by moving toward the sound of the blaster rifle?"

"I already killed three of 'em, you little psychopath. Besides—"

Masters dropped to his stomach and hushed himself. J-316 looked down curiously, only to be pulled into the muck by its congregant.

"Someone's coming," Masters explained with a whisper.

The pair lay covered in mud amid a scrubby grass that rose just a little higher than they did. The sounds of soldiers moving through the brush soon grew louder. Gone this time were the careless conversations of MCR rebels who believed themselves to be the only humanoids in the area. They expected that Masters was nearby.

The legionnaire waited, sucking in small, even breaths, not seeing the bot but trusting it to keep quiet and stay hidden. The moments went by and then the fence shook and the peculiar wood groaned as someone climbed over it. Another soldier followed, stepping through the split-rail beams before stopping to look back at something in the direction from which he had come.

Masters could see the MCR soldier plainly, and all the enemy would need to do to see the legionnaire was turn his head and look at the ground a few meters in front of him. Trusting in fate to keep that from happening was all fine and well, but Masters trusted more in his ability to shoot the kelhorn first if it came down to it. He imperceptibly shifted the rifle from the ready at his chest so the barrel was now facing down toward his toes—the same direction as the MCR soldier.

The tense waiting game was over almost before it started. The soldier turned his head and his eyes flashed. Masters had put two blaster bolts into the man's head and neck before the mid even had a chance to bring his weapon to bear.

The legionnaire rolled onto his stomach in the direction of the first MCR who'd hopped the fence. He quickly found the Kimbrin, light repeating blaster rifle up and searching for a target. Masters dropped the soldier with three shots to the chest. It was then that blaster bolts from the other side of the fence began burning their way into the muck near his position.

Masters threw himself against a fence post and watched for targets. The terrain was thick, and navigation was hard. A Kimbrin in a khaki uniform emerged from chest-high scrub and did his best to hurry toward the fence. His boots made a distinct *sluck* noise in the mire that stood out to Masters in the moments before he killed the man.

With two scouts and now one regular dead, Masters watched the flash of blaster bolts that erupted from beyond. It gave him an indicator of where to send one of his grenades and how many hostiles he was dealing with.

"Too many," he mumbled to himself as he primed the grenade from behind another post.

Thus far, the poor visibility and bad terrain were keeping the regulars back. But once he timed the fragger and sent it back to the mids who'd brought it out this way, that would change. Their blood would be up at the loss of six of their own plus whoever got stung by the shrapnel and explosion.

Masters would have to withdraw into the swamps— the opposite direction he had hoped to travel.

Most of the MCR were spread out, but a group of five close-knit muzzle flashes told him that at least one squad must love each other too much to space themselves and had opted to fire together. He threw the grenade into the brush nearby and heard their moans and screams for help after the ordnance erupted with a single *boom* that seemed to be swallowed up by the swamp almost as soon as it sounded. A *Legion* fragger, with its double explosion, would have killed them outright. Oh well, no sense sulking about what one didn't have. Masters was going without so much, it would be all he had time to do.

He scampered back toward the swamp, heading for the MCR with the light repeater he'd killed early on. Masters couldn't recall if he called for the missionary bot to follow him, but the machine did so all the same.

Masters took the light repeater. Unlike the Republic's SAB model, this one was fed by a single, oversized charge pack instead of being powered by a wearable pack. Even worse, the pack was a single unit. A SAB pack could be recharged by inserting several smaller packs into the individual charge cells.

It didn't matter. Masters only intended to use it briefly and for a diversion. He hoisted the weapon onto his shoulder and ran pell-mell for the swamps. There he would find more natural dangers, but also an opportunity to escape.

He pushed through thigh-high waters, resisting the urge to swim as he checked his six. J-316 was dutifully trudging along, but the bot would need to be carried before much longer, unless it wasn't kidding about its ability to simply walk along the bottom.

At least Masters found what he was looking for: a strand of heavy vines looped like hanging sashes between two massive black trees, their roots forming a cage of sorts that rose up out of the brackish water.

Most legionnaires carried combat knives; Masters's preference was for the Legion N-95 Combat Survival Knife. What it lacked in thrusting ability, it made up for in sheer durability. And he'd had the opportunity to plunge the weapon into a Gomarii slaver once upon a time, proving it worked just fine as a killing tool. But it was better now as he sliced and spliced his way through the tangle of vines, always checking his six for the MCR he knew were struggling through the terrain to reach him.

When he was done with his work, he had the light repeater hung on a vine, with another vine pared down and tied in a knot inside the trigger well, depressing the trigger into a state of fully automatic blaster fire. The weapon clicked as its internal ignitor searched for a charge pack to work with, but Masters held that heavy device in his hand.

He got a glimpse at the first intrepid MCR soldier to reach the far edge of the swamp and killed the man with his blaster rifle. That would bring the others.

Masters stepped behind his rigged auto-turret and dialed up the charge pack for the maximum number of available shots. Killing MCR with the weapon would be nice, and a higher charge rate would help with that, but keeping them back was his ultimate goal.

As soon as he inserted the pack into the well, the weapon began to spit a steady stream of blaster bolts in the direction of the dead MCR. Masters gave the weapon a slight wobbly push, and the bolts began to eat up the territory to the left and right of the dead soldier in lazy, back-and-forth swings.

With his diversion set, Masters pushed his way deeper into the swamp, intent on putting as much distance between himself and his MCR followers as possible. His best chance now was to disappear—and avoid at all costs what would otherwise become a running firefight with no help of relief or support to be found.

44

River District
Kam Dho City

Bear, Roolo, and Neuschwanger floated along the river toward the market. After the dust had settled from the dropship crashing into the star port, Bear had taken his team onto the water to see how the city was going to react. Only a few stubborn merchants on the river market had pulled up their coverings to hawk their wares for anyone brave enough to venture out on the water. A smattering of sampan-styled craft similar to their own drifted up and down the waterway, lazily avoiding the smaller dory boats as they paddled, pushed, or motored by.

"I'm going in," Bear said.

Roolo, who sat beneath the prow, looked back long enough to nod his affirmation before returning his attention to the river.

Bear entered the covered cabin in the center of their lengthy riverboat on his knees. The squat cabin would double as shelter to fishermen during flash storms, and also served to keep a catch out of the sun and refrigerated for those boats that had power batteries to run a cooler. Inside he found Zier, Jaela, and Brit hovered over a multitude of holographic screens. A server rack had been built on the bottom of the boat allowing those with HUD specs keyed to the system the use of gear networked back to the safe house. The three worked the feeds in their own augmented reality displays with none of them looking up to acknowledge the kill team leader's presence.

"What's on the holo for tonight?" Bear asked.

Brit dropped her glasses to her nose to look at the leej without the filter of ten open-tiered displays getting in the way. "We got tons of Kimbrin in a hurry to get to this place or that all over the city. It's causing all sorts of sled accidents, service backups, and a ton of nonsense that no one needs right now. Most of the boaters are staying off the river though, probably because these shacks on their sampans wouldn't stop a strong breeze, much less a blaster bolt."

"Do we have anything on ATAC?"

"Nothing in the air, boss," Zier said.

"Do you even know what ATAC is?" Brit chided.

"Yes. It's the airspace between your ears."

Bear snorted at his own joke, which bought him a scornful look from Brit. "Listen, sizzle toes, I get paid to catch a hard time from my team. *You* want to give me a hard time, you got to pay."

Bear rolled his eyes. "I have to listen to that music you like. Trust me, I've paid my dues. Any news over the airfield?"

"Yeah, we're streaming the drone feeds to *Centurion* REPO. Believe it or not, a good number of those drop jockeys survived getting splashed by a not-so-subtle ion strike cutting their engines at half a klick from the ground. They're pulling themselves from the wreckage now."

"Why doesn't the Legion just drop the units into the city now?" Jaela asked. "The fight at Blake has to be pretty much over."

"Well, ya see princess," said Bear, "the MCR have proven they've been hiding all the best stuff for this one. Legion needs folks on the ground like us to find all the battle rattle so a plane full of legionnaires doesn't get barbecued on the way into the objective."

Jaela motioned for Bear to put on his glasses. An overhead feed of the crash site on Sho Ven filled his display. Still-burning auxiliary fuel bathed the scene in a chalky black smoke as painted corrugated buildings melted into ruin. At the center of the destruction, the formerly teardrop-shaped ship now resembled a hard-boiled egg crushed into the dirt.

"Damn," Bear said. "Do we have a read on the number of troops filing out of that thing?"

"There's at least two hundred on the ground," Zier said.

Tremors shook the wreckage from an armored plate slapping against the hull. If the ship was still intact, this would have been one of the twenty-five-meter-high ramps that was positioned in between the engines on the ship. It slapped once, then twice, and came to rest against the hull as sparks flew out from the lower portions.

"Look at that," Jaela said. "Something on the inside is looking to cut the door hinges for the ramp."

A localized explosion at the corners where the hatch connected to the ship blew out both. The ramp fell with a cheer from the swarm of MCR fighters next to the ship. Something stirred in what was left of the ship that forced the drone pilot to alter the flight path and zoom in.

Bear squinted at the image. "Oh, that sucks."

Super-Destroyer *Centurion*
Combat Information Center

"Mechs!" Deynolds shouted. "Where did these kelhorns get mechs? Chhun, it's Deynolds. Are you seeing this?"

Chhun appeared in her HUD. "Roger, Admiral. I see it. We have the RIAS for large-scale evacuations and equipment drops if we need it. Knight Hunter Actual is on station to move supplies when the need arises."

"So what I'm hearing is, we don't need that particular runway on Sho Ven Star Port."

"Runway number two is my least favorite Sho Ven runway," Chhun agreed.

The crew in the CIC took a moment to laugh at the exchange. Even the normally stoic Legion L-comm officer couldn't help but crack a smile. Across the bullpen, Lieutenant Deven Marinkovich, the fire control officer, shouted, "Fox-Con ready for target package, Captain Aguiar."

The next station over, Lieutenant Apollo shouted over the din. "*Centurion* REPO has negative contact for civilians on target, Captain."

Aguiar pushed his board into Deynolds's field of view. The board had a pre-made strike profile for all three dropships that had come down hard on Kima star ports across several continents. "He wants us to hit all three, and he wants us to use these," the Endurian captain noted.

Admiral Deynolds furrowed her brow at the choice of weapon until something clicked in the back of her mind. "Fox-Con, assemble strike package on targets of opportunity. Secondary hits on all three targets."

"Loading Shockfall OSMs for secondary hits on target objectives. OSMs are set."

The target and weapon type scrolled across the admiral's mind as she called back to the planning stages of the operation. General Chhun's first target was the Kimbrin Citizens Defense Airfields holding the area's stockpile of SLIC aircraft. That strike severely limited the MCR's mobility through the battlespace, forcing them to slowly navigate the jungle. Hitting Fort Blake with blackout OSMs brought down the advanced tactical air control system, allowing the Legion to seize the strip while negotiating minor surprises by way of tanks and bots.

All that had gone as planned. But the drop carrier and the pods hadn't been in the planning. No one had suspected the MCR could field something to carry a force of this size. Targeting them with ship-based ion munitions dropped them into the ground but left the ships mostly intact. Chhun was now doubling down on having the sky belong to the navy. The ordnance they were deploying now would detonate any energy storage units like weapon batteries or small-craft power cells, which would in turn set off the reactors. The general wasn't looking to simply destroy the ships, he wanted to ruin the star ports they'd crashed into. When it was all said and done, the only readily accessible places for large transport ships to land and wage war from on Kima would be controlled by Republic forces.

"Send it," Deynolds said.

Aguiar expanded on her order. "Fox-Con, execute target package Delta Three."

"Executing Delta Three!"

Deynolds watched a feed transmitted from one of the many Legion Vindicator observation bots piloted by legionnaires across the battlespace. She wanted to see first-hand the damage this strike would do.

The feed sparked into a multitude of screens for the command element to watch. The armored shell on the outside of the Sho Ven airfield wreck shivered again, dislodging a titanic plate to clang to the ground. Easily weighing several tons, the impervisteel barrier slammed into the broken tarmac with enough force to stand it on end.

Free from the debris keeping it in the ship, a mechanized war machine trundled forward a few steps. The top of the machine appeared as an amalgam of a robot's shoulders with a cockpit where a head should be. Bringing in its focus to expose more details, the Vindicator captured the top of the antenna array where several spines reached for the sky pushing whatever format it broadcasted in. On the opposite shoulder was a fixed rocket pod.

The drone tracked the zoom in the video feed to give it maximum resolution for the operation. Seven heavy utility sleds drove away from the star port cargo facility. They worked over the ruined terrain until getting to the main access road for the port. Making their way onto the undamaged road, the vehicles picked up speed. Indicator markings in the display marked the second vehicle as the primary target for tracking back to the enemy locations.

An explosion that nearly shorted out the feed sent a shock wave across the previously decimated runway. Bodies littered throughout chunks of impervisteel and terrain rained down on the crater. Before the debris had a chance to land, a brilliant white flash erupted from the center of the dropship. The Vindicator drone tracked the expansion of the blast at a rate of five kilometers per second across Sho Ven Star Port. The detritus of the previous crash caught fire in the whiteout as superheated air ignited to create a mushroom cloud that climbed toward the sky. The video feed over the vehicles shuddered and whited out until forward- and flank-facing cameras all went black and read:

No input detected.

Thirty seconds passed and the sensor systems completed their reboot. The Vindicator was still flying and still tracking the convoy. The third driver in the convoy lost control in the blast wave that swept over them. It was one the drone pilot was going to allow out of the kill box, but ignoring a target of opportunity like that would cast doubt on what Harvester wanted for the op.

The first weapon struck the rolled-over third truck. The utility sled reached critical temperature and ignited into a fireball when its power core went nova. The trucks in front of and behind it were lanced with shrapnel that decimated the troops and drivers within and caused both to come to a meandering stop as their drivers lost their grip on the accelerators. The repulsors failed and dumped the bodies of the dead and dying onto the road.

The second missile struck the lead vehicle, which had accelerated to avoid the mayhem happening behind it. It exploded in a flash of fire that bounced it several times along its intended direction when the power cell finally released its payload to mimic the death of the trail vehicles. Fragments of metal and meat flayed the road, leaving a crater nearly as wide as it was deep.

Three of the vehicles veered around the flaming wreckage, scattering to different directions to keep from being caught in another missile-induced funeral pyre.

45

Harvester Command Element
Temporary Ops Center
Fort Blake, Hangar 2105

"How we doin', sir?" MakRaven asked.

"I was always good with pulling the trigger and dusting a guy I could see," said Chhun. "Guess I haven't gotten used to having destroyers willing to actually use those death-from-above weapons for us. Not sure how I feel about it, if I'm being honest. Spent my whole career being denied those assets by the points in the sky."

MakRaven chuckled. He chewed something around in his mouth and then spit outside of the building. "How many civilians did you save with that little drop pod stunt, sir? How many leejes?"

"Just sayin', Mak."

"That being said, eat this or I'll make you, sir." MakRaven tossed a ration gel to his commander.

"Sergeant Major, this is the veggie omelet gel. It's the worst one in the pack."

"Then maybe you should step away from that desk and get some real food and sleep. I know you deleted the getsum prompts from Chaz. I know because I asked him if you *getsum* sleep or *getsum* food and he said he didn't have that prompt logged into his memory doo-hickey thing."

"Guilty as charged."

"Yep. Now before I task a crew to knock your ass into that cot over there, the one I set up with my own two arthritic hands, at great personal expense I might add, I have some people that want to talk to you."

Chhun laughed. "Great personal expense?"

"Thousands of years of military tech and the two greatest inventions ever devised by military minds, the green military cot and the poncho woobie, are also still the source of greatest frustration. I mean, that synth-fab cot could hold up a tyrannasquid, but man if it ain't a chore getting that last support bar in place. Know what I mean?"

"Too bad the repulsor models are so loud. They require no setup at all. What's wrong with the woobie?" Chhun asked. Waiting for the answer gave him just enough time to gag down the omelet gel and play the game of keeping it from coming back up.

"Story for another time, sir. Looks like it's time for you to meet Colonel Novo, Major Jinaar, and Captain Reevee from the Second Free Rifles Regiment."

The trio of officers had just walked into the hangar, all three carrying what looked to Chhun to be wreaths made of orchids or other exotic flowers. Of the three, the captain drew his attention most. He was still in his armor, which was littered with score marks that should have done him in, and he was field filthy, with not a spot anywhere on him that wasn't coated in ash or grit. His face was the most telling of all. Like the other two, he had tears streaking through the grime.

"*Zeen kho,*" Chhun said. "I've been following your missions. Your people owe you a tremendous debt, and so do we."

Reevee placed a ring of flowers on the general's neck and handed him a piece of paper. The paper was expansive, almost as long as Chhun's torso. MakRaven whistled when he took in the significance of the markings smeared on the page. In one corner was the Legion crest, a sword and wreath, drawn in ink. Below it was a raven holding a thunderbolt, the symbol of Kalo Company. In neat lines up and down the paper were the dried bloody thumbprints of over a hundred fighters.

The colonel stepped forward to MakRaven. He placed another lei around the sergeant major's neck.

"I don't know what to say," said Chhun. He glanced at the grim scroll, again, noting each bloody print as a promise to fight for the Legion. "Thank you."

Colonel Novo bowed. "Nothing must be said. Blood, tears, and promises have been exchanged. Time to get back to work."

Kill Team Victory
Kam Dho City, River District

Lanterns bobbed up and down on the river leading to the markets, making the waterway reminiscent of the many-hued fireflies on Sinasia. The lanterns were made of paper, but to save on the need for oil or other combustibles, the light sources were small holo-projectors that mimicked flames. For a single credit, you could buy a mock flame that would last a lifetime. It seemed everything made on Kima wasn't expensive but tended to last.

The same was true of the MCR. Kimbrin were fiercely loyal once they'd thrown in with this faction or that, which was why the rebellion against the Republic had simmered, died out, and been reborn here. The Kimbrin had thrown in with the idea that Kima didn't need the Republic and their fancy credits, ships, and luxuries. The planet was fine the way it was. Sparsely populated. Naturally beautiful. The only ones who wanted to change things were the outsiders.

When it all boiled down to it, the Kimbrin were like anyone else. They just wanted to be left alone to live as they saw fit.

That's what Bombassa thought as they bobbed along in the sampan on their way through the river district to meet up with their commander. Nix had wanted to swim into the safe house, using attachable re-breathers and swim fins to move up the river undetected. Other members of the team had offered to let him have his swim while they took the covered boat, which was indistinguishable from all the other covered boats on the river. Why swim when you could ride?

Bombassa couldn't fault the young NCO for his enthusiastic energy. He was young enough to not feel his joints ache every time it rained because he'd never had to stick the landing with a vibro-knife on an escaping Navy cruiser trying to make orbit. His time would come.

The kill team HMFIC—head man first-in-charge—adjusted his HUD specs to key into his battle board. Clear lenses overlaid a series of virtual screens along a heads-up display that allowed the legionnaire to work through various points of attention without walking through a market with a bucket on his head. In the HUD, Bombassa watched their two R-CSM mechs, Harry and Henry, working their way along the bottom of the river while Dave, the robotic mule for the operation, trailed behind. The entirety of their gear had been stowed in waterproof bags and boxes and set atop Dave for the trek up the river, with no one even aware that three robotic bulls were stomping along beneath their boat.

"Bombassa, it's Bear. I see you coming up near the second bazaar. Go another fifty meters and the fish cannery is on your two-o'clock."

"Got you, Cap. Thanks for leaving the light on for us," Bombassa said. He issued a series of hand signals to the Kimbrin piloting the boat. The man accepted the direction with the practiced lazy nod of a Kam Dho ferryman, even though he was one of Bear's INSEC agents. The sampan drifted to the side of the river, moving along the few shops still open in the early evening air despite the calamity of the day. Despite the Legion.

Shopkeepers had emerged from their self-induced exile while the battle had raged. Commerce was a lifeblood. It could only afford to be stopped when absolutely necessary. They called out in the native language to every boat that passed by. "You come here. I got good stuff. Good prices. Best on the river!"

The sampan sauntered up to a taxi dock where passengers looking to exit the river for the hard duracrete streets of the city could do so. Bombassa's HUD specs flashed a warning that the purveyor of the floating stall next to the ferry dock was armed with a scatter blaster under the counter. When the aged Kimbrin took note of the cloak-wearing passenger scoping him instead of the product, the shopkeeper merely nodded before waving his hand twice with two fingers sticking out, and once with his fingers shaped like a gun.

"He's good," the boat driver said from the back. "He's with us."

Bombassa knocked on the top of the raft's cabin. The leejes exited from the craft onto the dock and split into groups of two for a bit of evasion work. Roving packs of MCR littered the streets, along with the natives meandering along the thoroughfares on their way to finish out whatever errand had brought them outside at night.

After a short while signal indicators flowed into Bombassa's HUD, telling him that his men had successfully avoided detection and were taking their party inside. After slipping through the alleys himself, Bombassa and the junior NCO, Nix, found the maintenance hatch to a utility bunker beneath the street.

"You can't expect either one of us to go in *there*," Nix said.

Bombassa shrugged as he slipped under the hatch to step onto the ladder down. "You've been in places that smelled worse than this. But if this is the dealbreaker, turn in your bucket at the counter."

"What counter?"

Bombassa used the HUD specs to see in the near darkness of the tunnel while the augmented reality overlay mapped out their route to the safe house. After roughly a hundred meters of travel through the twisting cistern, he whirled on a splash behind them.

Nix was standing on one foot with his other held up over the sluiceway that kept the water below the walkways that flanked either side of the tunnel. His disgust was evident in his expression. "I don't like rats."

"I have literally seen you eat Xanthar eel eggs on a dare. How can a rat bother you?"

The familiar voice of Bear whispered in the darkness. "You both make enough noise to make setting up the alarm in here not worth the effort."

Bombassa looked up to see the man's massive silhouette standing in a doorway. "Couldn't be helped, sir. You know how these kids get. Are we there yet? Are we there yet?"

Bear patted his friend and senior NCO on the back. "That trip to Kublar gave you a sense of humor. You know that?"

"Don't worry, he's trying to lose it again," Nix said, accepting his CO's crushing version of a handshake.

The new hallway deposited them into a room with little room left over after the holoscreens, makeshift furniture, and the rest of Kill Team Victory mixing with the Republic internal security agents. Bombassa dispatched Nix to find his space as he followed Bear over to a busy workstation where a woman worked the equipment like a conductor working a symphony.

"First Sergeant Bombassa. Have we heard a lot about you." When Bombassa didn't respond, Brit returned to her screen. "Wow, you just can't shut this guy up. Captain, I suppose this is the part where I give the cool briefing now that the team is all here."

"No," Bear said. "They had all the briefings on the ride over. What they need now is the updates since they left the river."

Brit batted her eyelashes as she looked over her shoulder and used a bedroom voice that did not have the desired effect. "Bucket or eyeballs?"

"Brit, just push the holo right here, please."

"Sheesh. I'm trapped in here with Mr. Focus-on-the-Job and a bucket of Kimbrin for the last month. Give a girl a break when she responds to a little testosterone."

After a few tense heartbeats, the leejes broke open like a dam during a storm, laughing and clapping but trying to keep the level low enough that it wouldn't be heard outside in case this safe house wasn't as good as the first one. Brit blushed at the sudden attention of very virile men who were considered the best physical specimens humanity could produce without cheating and going all gene splice like some other races in the Republic. A low whistle from Bombassa brought the ruckus under control.

Bear coughed to bring the attention back to the table. The holo sprang up, showing a three-dimensional render of Kam Dho City. "All right, settle down. As per the change of mission order from General Chhun, Kill Team Victory is the point of contact in Kam Dho City for Second Bat when they make their run on the roof. That's an airborne operation for those in the room who don't speak the language. Let me go into a bit more detail for those of us who'll be working the street. We're breaking into teams to run down intel for when the line leejes start kicking down doors. We track the leads, run them to ground, and then point the Legion proper to the hole. A little pyro in the dirt and it's mission complete. Rinse and repeat.

"Also not covered is this bit of nastiness. VBX-13. We are the primary hunters for this mess inside the city. We have our friends with INSEC working leads right now to find out if and where they have this stuff in the city. Without Legion armor, this stuff will chew through you while you're still breathing and then spit you out deader than Neck's bullitar-riding career."

"It could still happen," said Neck.

Bear snapped several times to regain the room. "If you even suspect this stuff is on scene, especially if we're plain clothes, call in the Legion."

"There was mention of a doctor you extracted," Bombassa noted.

"On the money, Top," Bear said. "We have her here on site. She's working with us for the time being, but the broad strokes are, she has a way to keep this stuff from going full apocalypse, but we don't have the gear or the goo to make enough of what she needs for the entire population. At some point, we're probably going to have to kick her upstairs to *Centurion*. Until that time, we use her for her expertise."

"Questions, gentlemen?" Bombassa asked.

When the room remained silent, Bear continued. "Good. We have until morning for you to clean up, get a little rest, and reorient to the new battlespace. At oh-dark-stupid tomorrow, we kick off the next phase and work on getting Second Bat boots on ground. I have a meeting in five, but after that I'm up to answer any questions you might have."

Nix tilted his head toward Brit. "If you're not available, can *she* answer our questions?"

"You do you, Leej," said Bear, "but that woman is a pencil sharpener. You do the math on that one."

Brit waggled her fingers at him in a flirtatious wave that set the legionnaires laughing again. They filed by, each taking turns slapping Nix on the back and throwing their cloaks over him. By the time the leej got his head free from the fabric, Kill Team Victory had dispersed.

"Really?" he said. "Really?"

Harvester Command Element
Temporary Ops Center
Fort Blake, Hangar 2105

"Please tell me you got something," Bear said over the holotransmission.

Chhun had to look straight at his kill team leader when he spoke or the effect of the HUD specs brought up a weird sense of vertigo. Looking peripherally, he could see through the space between his face and the glasses, and as Bear was only an overlay in the altered reality display of the glasses, having someone's feet suddenly disappear was a bit jarring. He much preferred his bucket.

"Lots of something. We got some serious intel from the Kimbrin we turned over to the Second Free Rifles. Seems our friends in the militia know a thing or two about making people give up the goods. Through interrogation of the various prisoners and an assistant field leader, this kid named Kosh, they've determined that there is a legionnaire alive out there in the jungles outside of Fort Blake. Somewhere in the dead zone beyond the mountains."

"It's him," Bear insisted.

MakRaven leaned against the desk. He broke a piece of his energy bar to give to the dog sulking beneath. The master sergeant wasn't exactly sure how it had happened, but it seemed Bubbles was assigned to him now. "We don't know that," he said. "But... it *might* be him."

An image appeared in the displays. A legionnaire shooting on the move. Body type, the way that the image showed the trooper vaulting over a low wooden fence in tall grass, and the brazen manner in which the man fought, all screamed Masters to anyone who knew him.

"What's he got with him?" Bear asked.

"That," said MakRaven, "is a bot. We can only assume he found it somewhere. Judging from the chassis design and the posture, I'd say the thing's older than Oba. Still, Masters might be using it to navigate or get to some populated area that might be unfriendly to the Kimbrin."

Chhun pointed at the map. "Thing of it is, there's nothing on that side of the mountains to get to. It marks the extreme edge of some biological disaster zone from who knows how long ago that snuffed out all vegetation. There's this one certain type of tree that grows there, and that's it. Beyond that, it's near-impenetrable swamps. Not even the Yawds populate the region."

"He was forced off that mountain," Bear said, his energy growing. "We saw the footage of him jumping."

"We saw someone who looked like a legionnaire jump," Chhun said, working hard not to let himself get too excited over the prospect of finding their friend. He found himself wishing that Ford was here somehow. The man seemed made for these sorts of impossible missions.

He traced a line on the map. "This is our best understanding of his route. Each of these highlighted points is an encounter where the MCR tried to nab or slab him. I'm talking recently. And these marked waypoints are three destinations we believe he may be headed toward. But like I said, there's not much out there. The Yawds we've talked to say that this area is cursed and their ancestors avoided it. There are stories of everything from vengeful ghosts to land that curses with infertility anyone who tries to cultivate it."

"I knew a Tennar girl who would've loved to set up shop in a place like that," said MakRaven.

Bear didn't laugh. "Sir, I'd like to be transferred from command of Kill Team Victory and allowed to lead the recovery."

Chhun had anticipated this moment. The dread in the pit of his stomach had been gnawing at him in anticipation of the call. And given his own kinship to Masters, it made what came next all the more difficult.

"I cannot take you out of your role right now, Bear. I need you there and leading that team. You've laid the groundwork; you know all the players. With you and Bombassa there leading that team, we have the best shot of retaking the city and minimizing casualties. As much as I really want you leading the recovery team, I need you leading the one you have."

Bear didn't back down. "Sir, Masters and me are tight. You know that. What we've been through. What we've *all* been through. I owe him." The distance between the general and his team leader did nothing to quell the pain in the man's voice. "Sir. Cohen... we're all that's left from back then."

When Chhun didn't immediately respond, MakRaven spoke up. "Captain. I've recently found myself stuck with a puppy. LWD 2060, call sign Bubbles. I'm tryin' to get him to answer to somethin' a bit more respectable, though. Not a lot of leejes get to work beside dogs, especially not like the ones they got over at the STB. But this hound here is a bona fide hard-rock leej. Don't let the cute cold nose and those eyes fool you, sir. Stone-cold killer operator, this one. He'll be on the hunt for your buddy."

"Message received, Sergeant Major," Bear said.

MakRaven smiled. "Sir, we have a hard-nosed team ready to bring that boy back, and we have the support of the Legion and the task force commander to do it. I'd say that gives us a pretty high chance of success."

"Who's leading the team?" Bear asked.

"Bubbles," MakRaven answered. When the joke fell flat, MakRaven added, "I'm leading the team, sir."

"You're the senior enlisted adviser to the task force," Bear noted.

"Fixed that problem once already. I know a few tricks. Anyway, that might be a problem in the regular army, maybe, but a force made up of leejes don't need some relic telling them war stories from back before the Legion commander started shaving or making sure they wear the right footwear with their PTs. I'm goin' out there to get your boy back, Captain, General. Make no mistake about it. It's going to be me, my kankari knife, some Legion pipe-hitters, and the dog. We're going to kill our way across the country until the MCR begs me to take him back. Straight-up KTF."

The dog barked at the mention of the Legion motto.

Chhun held a tight, wan smile across his face. "Sounds like your 'puppy' is ready to get it on."

"Thank you, Sergeant Major MakRaven," Bear said. "I owe you one."

"Nah, sir. It's the leej I go and rescue who'll owe me. You just show up to the bar to make sure he pays."

"Deal. Bear out."

Chhun eyed his sergeant major. "When were you going to fill me in on this plan?"

"Well, I got to thinking. Best thing I never had was a dog. Killed a few doros, but never owned a dog. Don't seem right. Always wanted one when I retired, but couldn't bring myself to do it while I was in, sir. I'd never be home to spend any time with it, and that'd be a shame. Saw how that went with a few of my ex-wives, anyway."

"I'm not going to convince you to stay," Chhun said.

"Have to kill me first."

"Thank you, Mak. I mean it."

"Hell, General. Let's not have a moment."

"Fair enough. Who are you taking with?"

MakRaven smiled. "I got some prospects."

Super-Destroyer *Centurion*
Combat Information Center

"Status on things in orbit?" Chhun asked.

Deynolds leaned on her desk. She had just taken her boots off and was using the desk as a support to stretch when Chhun called in. "We've slaved some of the first MCR ships we've captured to *Estoc*, which is our cyber warfare boat. Our next play is to take the drop carrier, but if they have as much crew as a ship that size demands, we're going to need more than a boarding squad. We might have to redeploy the SOAR to take it."

"Would it help if you had Legion assistance?"

Deynolds sent the general a dour frown. "How about you worry about the business of saving Kima and let me worry about all the floaty stuff up here in orbit. We basics have been doing the whole zero-g combat thing since before there was a Legion, ya know."

Chhun held his hands up in the holo. "True enough. And for the record, we call the army basics."

"Still, I might need your help on something. I got an MCR dropship floating out here in orbit that's just disabled. It's too big for us to bring into the hangar on *Centurion*. I also don't want to board it without significant backup."

"Contact the BC at Third Bat. They're batting cleanup on this so his boys will be itching to get their fight on. You add in the bit that they get to show up the marines in zero-g, you'll have them trying to get out the airlocks with cutting torches because you can't open them fast enough."

"I'll open the airlocks before I ask," Deynolds shot back. After a minute in her own head, she noted, "There's a lot here that doesn't make sense. Some of this MCR gear is twenty or thirty years old. Some even older. That mech we saw almost crawl out of the crashed ship was old when my dad was in the navy."

"You ever hear about Tyrus Rechs—the bounty hunter—going ballistic on some leejes out on the edge right before the war with the empire?"

"I really can't say that I did," Deynolds said hesitantly, not sure where Chhun was going with this.

"He had this gun. It was a slug thrower connected to a feeding device on the armor. Big bullet. Savage Wars-era or older. Anyway, he dusted a whole field of leejes on this one planet. The House of Reason sent them there for tax enforcement. Lots of points, lots of non-Legion activity going on. And they got in the way of Tyrus Rechs, so he shot them down through their committee-approved shiny armor."

"Sounds criminal."

"My point is, he was using old weapons that were so perfectly suited to killing people in their time that they transcended the era in which they were made. All of this gear the MCR is using is surplus. It's all outdated because some delegate awarded a contract to a buddy for better gear. Then another for more better gear to replace the better gear. The new gear doesn't invalidate the old gear unless it's so advanced that it borders on the obscene. And yet all this old stuff was put out to market and sold for pennies on the dollar because the government wanted to recoup some of its investment."

"So even though it's old, it'll still do the job. Well that's encouraging. Maybe I should just shoot down everything out there that isn't flying our colors."

"Admiral, with what we've seen over the past few days, that's not the worst plan I've heard."

Harvester Command Element
Temporary Ops Center
Fort Blake, Hangar 2105

"Straighten your boots. Here he comes," Lynx said to his men.

"Sergeant Lynx? I'm Sergeant Major MakRaven. Thanks for coming by."

The entirety of Zombie Squad stood at parade rest, with the exception of Gekko, who couldn't help but eye the dog carrying a backpack.

"You boys stand easy. I got an op on the burner and I hear you guys are the go-to for when Victory Company wants to punch a kelhorn in the eye."

"Yes, Sergeant Major," Lynx said.

"C'mon now, Sergeant. I said earlier to stand easy. So give it to me Legion style."

The corner of Lynx's mouth curled at the reference. "We do eyes, bloody or broken noses too, depending on your preference. We'll even knock out some teeth if that's your thing, Sergeant Major."

MakRaven clapped his hands. "Now that's what I'm looking for. See here, I got this leej that got blown off a mountain in the artillery attack when the MCR took Blake and the kid made it through. The MCR's been trying to dust him for a hot minute now, but the stubborn kelhorn just won't die."

"Sergeant Major," said Diggs, "this guy's been dusting MCR for the better part of a week on his own, with no backup and in the middle of the suck, to boot? Sounds like a vacation to me."

"See, now that's what I thought," MakRaven agreed. "But when you give it a hard minute of thought, what's a vacation without a handful of your best buds to hang out with? Now, this vacation is going to be anything but easy. There's more than a good chance I'm walking into a meat grinder on this. But I've been hearing all day about this Zombie Squad. So I thought to myself, 'Self, you'd probably not die in the first five if you, too, had a Zombie Squad.'"

"He's not wrong," said Trent.

"Look, I got me, a dog, and a seriously bad attitude against whatever MCR is in the way of me getting back my leej. What do you guys say about causing some seriously off-the-books mayhem?"

"You had us at punching kelhorns, Sergeant Major," Gekko said.

"Good. Now you guys grab your gear and meet me at that hangar over there. I just have to run a quick errand before we bounce. Some intel jockey said they recovered a Wizzo bot from a downed Raptor, says he's seen our guy and can give us a place to start lookin'. Hope you boys like cursed wastelands. What am I sayin', of course you do."

EPILOGUE

Masters evaded the MCR for two days. During that time he and the bot developed a running argument over how many he'd killed. Masters said it was fifteen. J-316 counted twelve.

However many it was, it had been enough to drive the Kimbrin hostiles into something resembling a crusade. Deeper and deeper Masters moved through the swamps, and deeper and deeper the MCR followed.

They caught up to him in a rainforest comprising tall black trees that didn't mind the water, their branches thick with hanging moss and vines. Here the ground alternated between hardpack, with roots gnarling their way up to trip passersby, and large swaths of inch-deep mud. The MCR made up ground on the hardpack and verified that they were on the right trail thanks to the tracks left in the mud.

J-316 had never been this far in and had no knowledge it could provide to help in navigation.

Masters desperately wanted to find the thick brush or expansive swamps he'd found earlier, but those were all behind him. He tried to double back several times, but could never find a hole in what had to be a company-sized element attempting to hunt him down.

The fighting started when scouts caught up with him near a massive fallen tree, partly hollow, with disc-like mushrooms jutting out from either side.

Masters indisputably got four of the scouts. Of that he and the missionary bot were in agreement. And then the rest arrived and the firepower grew intense enough that the legionnaire was forced to keep down. The MCR were determined to win their prize. They began to ensnare him, leaving no avenue of escape—none other than running straight back, which would expose him to enough blaster fire that he might as well stand up and slug it out, which he was just about to do when the inexplicable happened.

A furious counter-fire exploded from the woods behind him. MCR fell but would not fall back. Perplexed and suddenly hopeful, Masters wondered if somehow, some way, the Legion had come for him.

He stood, taking advantage of the serendipitous change in circumstances. "C'mon, Jay-Three, we gotta go!"

Masters led the charge as blaster bolts skipped behind him, going just wide or short of the mark, but only a few from those so determined to catch their prize that they ignored the new firefight they found themselves in.

Farther into the woods the legionnaire moved, searching for who might be supporting his retreat. If indeed that was what they were doing. He could see no one and didn't dare shout or make his presence known.

The blaster bolts being sent weren't from N-4s, but they sounded close. Something in the same family. Perhaps a new model advanced to another Dark Ops team? Masters himself was often given the opportunity to test out new arms while serving with the teams. If that was so, then perhaps rescue—

The thought left Masters's mind in a blinding flash of pain as something struck him behind the ear—hard—and turned off his lights.

Masters awoke feeling nauseated. His vision was blurred, and the smell of a rotting stable floor assaulted his nose and forced him to vomit up what little rations were in his stomach. As he retched, he could feel an intense pain in his ear on the side of the head where he...

He what?

Had he somehow stumbled into an unseen branch? From where his head throbbed that seemed unlikely. Someone had hit him. His body bore the memory of the uncontrolled fall that followed. His shoulder was tender and sore, and when he tried to roll it to loosen it up, he realized at once that his arms were bound behind his back.

Clarity followed quickly. The smell. The sounds...

J-316 was at his side. Or rather, some of him. He looked as though he'd been shot to pieces and dumped next to Masters while the legionnaire was unconscious. Remarkably, as Masters stared at the head and upper torso of the machine, its optical sensors flicked back to life.

"I am still functioning. I am disappointed to see that you are as well. We have been captured by the zhee."

"Sorry to disappoint you." Masters spit the last of the bile from his mouth. "But you're right about the zhee. I know the smell, yeah."

"It is all very confusing," said J-316. "The four gods of the zhee are reconciled with the overgod Oba. I have received this revelation while in my trance."

Masters squinted and looked for any sign of the zhee. He could only smell their odor and faintly hear their braying farther into what must be a camp, as tiny orange glows from small fires scattered about broke up the blanket of nightfall.

He tried to get up, and found that his legs were bound by rope. That meant his arms and wrists were likely tied up by the same. Rope was good. It was a hell of a lot easier to get loose from than ener-chains.

But it would still take time.

"So if the donk gods and Oba are all buddy-buddy now... they should let us go, right?"

"I attempted to argue such before I was shot," J-316 said solemnly. "They do not appear to share my view of doctrine."

Masters tested the ropes on his arms. They were strong, and while he was hardly a waif, the time in country had him at something less than his usual peak physical conditioning. "So what's that gonna mean for me? You hear anything?"

J-316 stayed silent.

"Jay-Three. You hear anything?"

"You are to receive death by a thousand cuts. I was praying you would simply die while unconscious to spare yourself the torment. My prayers were not answered. You will receive the judgment once the zhee realize you are awake."

Masters stared at the bot and blinked. "Think I'll pass."

He began working furiously at his restraints.

The zhee came shortly after. Finding Masters awake, they finished stripping away his armor. They brayed in laughter at seeing that the bot still somehow functioned. To allow the missionary bot to watch the show, they impaled J-316's head on a crude spike made from a fallen tree limb.

And Masters...

By the hundredth cut, he finally screamed.

ABOUT THE MAKERS

Jason Anspach is the co-creator of Galaxy's Edge. He lives in the Pacific Northwest.

Nick Cole is the other co-creator of Galaxy's Edge. He lives in southern California with his wife, Nicole.

Explore over 30+ Galaxy's Edge books and counting from the minds of Jason Anspach, Nick Cole, Doc Spears, Jonathan Yanez, Karen Traviss, and more.

LAST BATTLE OF THE REPUBLIC

REBIRTH OF THE LEGION

JOIN THE LEGION

Honor Roll

We would like to give our most sincere thanks and recognition to those who supported the creation of *Galaxy's Edge: Remains* by supporting us at GalaxysEdge.us.

Cody Aalberg
Artis Aboltins
Sam Abraham
Guido Abreu
Chancellor Adams
Myron Adams
Garion Adkins
Ryan Adwers
Kyle Aguiar
Elias Aguilar
Neal Albritton
Jonathan Allain
Bill Allen
Justin Allred
Jake Altman
Justin Altman
Tony Alvarez
Joachim Andersen
Jarad Anderson
Galen Anderson
Pat Andrews

Robert Anspach
Melanie Apollo
Britton Archer
Benjamin Arguello
Thomas Armona
Daniel Armous
Linda Artman
Jonathan Auerbach
Fritz Ausman
Sean Averill
Albert Avilla
Matthew Bagwell
Marvin Bailey
Sallie Baliunas
Nathan Ball
Kevin Bangert
John Barber
Logan Barker
John Barley
Brian Barrows-Striker
Richard Bartle

Austin Bartlett
Robert Battles
Eric Batzdorfer
John Baudoin
Adam Bear
Nahum Beard
Antonio Becerra
Mike Beeker
Randall Beem
Matt Beers
John Bell
Daniel Bendele
Royce Benford
Mark Bennett
Edward Benson
Cody Bente
Matthew Bergklint
Carl Berglund
Brian Berkley
Corey Berman
David Bernatski
Tim Berube
Michael Betz
Shannon Biggs
Brien Birge
Nathan Birt
Trevor Blasius
WJ Blood
David Blount
Evan Boldt
Rodney Bonner
Rodney Bonner
Thomas Seth Bouchard
William Boucher

Brandon Bowles
Alex Bowling
Chester Brads
Logan Brandon
Jordan Brann
Ernest Brant
Daniel Bratton
Dennis Bray
Christopher Brewster
Jacob Brinkman
Geoff Brisco
Wayne Brite
Spencer Bromley
Paul Brookins
Raymond Brooks
Zack Brown
Marion Buehring
Johncarlo Buitrago
Sean Bulman
Jim Burkhardt
Tyler Burnworth
Tyler Burnworth
Matthew Buzek
Noel Caddell
Daniel Cadwell
Brian Callahan
Joseph Calvey
Van Cammack
Chris Campbell
Danny Cannon
Zachary Cantwell
Brett Carden
Robert Cathey
Brian Cave

Shawn Cavitt
Brad Chenoweth
David Chor
Cooper Clark
Casey Clarkson
Ethan Clayton
Jonathan Clews
Beau Clifton
Sean Clifton
Jerremy Cobb
Morgan Cobb
William Coble
Robert Collins Sr.
Alex Collins-Gauweiler
Jerry Conard
Gayler Conlin
Michael Conn
James Connolly
Ryan Connolly
James Conyers
Brian Cook
Michael Corbin
Robert Cosler
Ryan Coulston
Seth Coussens
Andrew Craig
Adam Craig
Christopher Crowder
Phil Culpepper
Ben Curcio
Tommy Cutler
Thomas Cutler
Christopher Da Pra
John Dames

David Danz
Matthew Dare
Chad David
Alister Davidson
Peter Davies
Walter Davila
Ashton Davis
Brian Davis
Nathan Davis
Ivy Davis
Ben Davis
Joseph Dawson
Ron Deage
Anthony Del Villar
Tod Delaricheliere
Anerio (Wyatt)
Deorma (Dent)
Isaac Diamond
Alexander Dickson
Nicholas Dieter
Christopher DiNote
Matthew Dippel
Gregory Divis
Ellis Dobbins
Brian Dobson
Samuel Dodes
Graham Doering
Gerald Donovan
Dustyn Down
John Dryden
Josh DuBois
Garrett Dubois
Ray Duck
Marc-André Dufor

Trent Duncan
Christopher Durrant
Cami Dutton
Chris Dwyer
Virgil Dwyer
Brian Dye
Nick Edwards
Justin Eilenberger
William Ely
Michael Emes
Brian England
Andrew English
Stephane Escrig
Dakota Estepp
Benjamin Eugster
Jaeger Falco
Nicholas Fasanella
Christian Faulds
Steven Feily
Julie Fenimore
Meagan Ference
Brad Ferguson
Adolfo Fernandez
Rich Ferrante
Ashley Finnigan
Matthew Fiveson
Waren Fleming
Kath Flohrs
Daniel Flores
William Foley
Steve Forrester
Skyla Forster
Kenneth Foster
Timothy Foster

Chad Fox
Bryant Fox
Doug Foxford
Mark Franceschini
Greg Franz
Griffin Frendsdorff
Bob Fulsang
Jonathan Furney
Elizabeth Gafford
David Gaither
Seth Galarneau
Christopher Gallo
Richard Gallo
Kyle Gannon
Joshua Gardner
Michael Gardner
Alphonso Garner
Mackenzey Garrison
Cordell Gary
Brad Gatter
Tyler Gault
Angelo Gentile
Stephen George
Nick Gerlach
Eli Geroux
Christopher Gesell
Kevin Gilchrist
Dylan Giles
Oscar Gillott-Cain
Nathan Gioconda
John Giorgis
Johnny Glazebrooks
Martin Gleaton
James Glendenning

William Frank Godbold IV
Justin Godfrey
Luis Gomez
John Gooch
Tyler Goodman
Zack Gotsch
Justin Gottwaltz
George Gowland
Mitch Greathouse
Gordon Green
Matt Green
Shawn Greene
John Greenfield Jr.
Eric Griffin
Ronald Grisham
Paul Griz
Preston Groogan
Kyle Gudmundson
Harry Gurney
Levi Haas
Tyler Hagood
Tyler Hagood
Michael Hale
Brandon Handy
Erik Hansen
Greg Hanson
Jeffrey Hardy
Tyler Hardy
Adam Hargest
Ian Harper
Revan Harris
Jordan Harris
Brett Harrison
Brandon Hart

Matthew Hartmann
Adam Hartswick
Mohamed Hashem
Ronald Haulman
Joshua Hayes
Ryan Hays
Adam Hazen
Richard Heard
Colin Heavens
Jon Hedrick
Jesse Heidenreich
Brenton Held
Kyler Helker
Jason Henderson
Jason Henderson
John Henkel
Jonathan Herbst
Daniel Heron
Bradley Herren
Kyle Hetzer
Korrey Heyder
Matthew Hicks
Samuel Hillman
Victor Hipolito
Jonathan Hoehn
Aaron Holden
Clint Holmes
Jacob Honeter
Charles Hood
Garrett Hopkins
Tyson Hopkins
William Hopsicker
Jefferson Hotchkiss
Fred Houinato

Ian House	Jason Jones
Jack House	David Jorgenson
Ken Houseal	John Josendale
Nathan Housley	Sunil Kakar
Jeff Howard	Ryan Kalle
Nicholas Howser	Chris Karabats
Mark Hoy	Ron Karroll
Kirstie Hudson	Timothy Keane
Mike Hull	Cody Keaton
Donald Humpal	Brian Keeter
Bradley Huntoon	Noah Kelly
Bobby Hurn	George Kelly
Charles Hurst	Jacob Kelly
James Hurtado	Caleb Kenner
Michael Hutchison	Daniel Kimm
Wayne Hutton	Kennith King
Gaetano Inglima	Zachary Kinsman
Antonio Iozzo	Rhet Klaahsen
Wendy Jacobson	Jesse Klein
Paul Jarman	William Knapp
James Jeffers	Marc Knapp
Tedman Jess	Robert Knox
Eric Jett	Andreas Kolb
Anthony Johnson	Steven Konecni
Josh Johnson	Ethan Koska
Eric Johnson	Evan Kowalski
James Johnson	Byl Kravetz
Cobra Johnson	John Kukovich
Nick Johnson	Mitchell Kusterer
Randolph Johnson	Brian Lambert
Nick Johnson	Clay Lambert
Tyler Jones	Jeremy Lambert
Tyler Jones	Andrew Langler
Paul Jones	Mikey Lanning

Dave Lawrence
Alexander Le
Jacob Leake
David Leal
Andy Ledford
Nicholas Lee
Joseph Legacy
Ruel Lindsay
Eric Lindsey
Eron Lindsey
Paul Lizer
Kenneth Lizotte
Andre Locker
Maxwell Lombardi
Richard Long
Oliver Longchamps
Joseph Lopez
David Lopez
Kyle Lorenzi
David Losey
Doug Lower
Steven Ludtke
Andrew Luong
Jesse Lyon
Brooke Lyons
Taylo Lywood
David MacAlpine
Patrick Maclary
Daniel Magano
Richard Maier
Chris Malone
Adam Manlove
Andrew Mann
John Mannion

Brian Mansur
Brent Manzel
Robert Marchi
Jacob Margheim
Deven Marincovich
Cory Marko
Quinn Marquard
Logan Martin
Edward Martin
Jason Martin
Lucas Martin
Pawel Martin
Trevor Martin
Christopher P. Martin
Bill Martin
Alexander Martin
Tim Martindale
Joshua Martinez
Joseph Martinez
Phillip Martinez
Cory Masierowski
Tao Mason
Wills Masterson
Ashley Mateo
Michael Matsko
Justin Matsuoko
Ezekiel Matze
Mark Maurice
Simon Mayeski
Joseph Mazzara
Sean McCafferty
Logan McCallister
Kyle McCarley
Quinn McCusker

Alan McDonald
Caleb McDonald
Jeremy McElroy
Dennis McGriff
Hans McIlveen
Rachel McIntosh
Ryan McIntosh
Richard McKercher
Ryan McKracken
Jason McMarrow
Colin McPherson
Christopher Menkhaus
Jim Mern
Robert Mertz
Jacob Meushaw
Brady Meyer
Pete Micale
Christopher Miel
Mike Mieszcak
Ted Milker
Daniel Miller
Corrigan Miller
Patrick Millon
Reimar Moeller
Ryan Mongeau
Jacob Montagne
Ramon Montijo
Mitchell Moore
Matteo Morelli
Joe Morgan
Todd Moriarty
Matthew Morley
Daniel Morris
William Morris

Christian Morrison
Alex Morstadt
Nicholas Mukanos
Bob Murray
Jeff Murri
Joseph Nahas
Vinesh Narayan
Colby Neal
James Needham
Ray Neel
Merle Neer
Adam Nelson
Tyler Neuschwanger
Travis Nichols
Bennett Nickels
Trevor Nielsen
Andrew Niesent
Sean Noble
Otto (Mario) Noda
Greg Nugent
Christina Nymeyer
Brian O'Connor
Matthew O'Connor
Timothy O'Connor
Sean O'Hara
Colin O'neill
Ryan O'neill
Patrick O'Rourke
Jacob Odell
Grant Odom
Conor Oehler
Quinn Oehler
Nolan Oglesby
Tyler Ornelas

Gareth Ortiz-Timpson
James Owens
Will Page
John Park
David Parker
Matthew Parker
Shawn Parrish
Eric Pastorek
Andrew Patterson
Wesley Patteson
Joshua Pena
Thomas Pennington
Kevin Perkins
Zac Petersen
Trevor Petersen
Marcus Peterson
Chad Peyton
Jon Phillips
Dupres Pina
Jared Plathe
Luke Plummer
Paul Polanski
Matthew Pommerening
Stephen Pompeo
Jason Pond
Nathan Poplawski
Chancey Porter
Rodney Posey
Brian Potts
Jonathaon Poulter
Chris Pourteau
Daniel Powderly
Chris Prats
Matt Prescott

Thomas Preston
Matthew Print
Aleksander Purcell
Joshua Purvis
Max Quezada
Scott Raff
Joe Ralston
Frederick Ramlow
Jason Randolph
Aindriu Ratliff
Beverly Raymond
T.J. Recio
Ryan Aguiar
Cannon Renfro
John Resch
Nathaniel Reyes
Jacob Reynolds
Cody Richards
Dalton Richards
Eric Ritenour
John Robertson
Walt Robillard
Brian Robinson
Joshua Robinson
Daniel Robitaille
John Roche
Paul Roder
Zack Roeleveld
Thomas Rogneby
Thomas Roman
Elias Rostad
Joyce Roth
Rob Rudkin
Arthur Ruiz

Jim Rumford

John RunningWolf

John Runyan

Chad Rushing

Sterling Rutherford

RW

Mark Ryan

Justin Ryan

Greg S

Lawrence Sanchez

Dustin Sanders

David Sanford

Chris Sapero

Jaysn Schaener

Shayne Schettler

Jason Schilling

Andrew Schmidt

Brian Schmidt

Ray Schmidt

Thomas Schmidt

Kurt Schneider

Peter Scholtes

Theodore Schott

Kevin Schroeder

William Schweisthal

Anthony Scimeca

Cullen Scism

Connor Scott

Preston Scott

Robert Sealey

Aaron Seaman

Dan Searle

Phillip Seek

Kevin Serpa

Dylan Sexton

Austin Shafer

Mitch Shami

Timothy Sharkey

Christopher Shaw

Charles Sheehan

Wendell Shelton

Lawrence Shewark

Ian Short

Glenn Shotton

Emaleigh Shriver

Dave Simmons

Joshua Sipin

Chris Sizelove

Andrew Skaines

Scott Sloan

Steven Smead

Anthony Smith

Daniel Smith

Lawrence Smith

Sharroll Smith

Tyler Smith

Michael Smith

Michael Smith

Timothy Smith

Neal Smith

Ian Smith

Tom Snapp

David Snowden

Alexander Snyder

Robert Speanburgh

John Spears

Thomas Spencer

Troy Spencer

Peter Spitzer	Lawrence Tate
Dustin Sprick	Kyler Tatsch
George Srutkowski	Justin Taylor
Cooper Stafford	Robert Taylor
Travis Stair	Tim Taylor
Graham Stanton	Jonathan Terry
Paul Starck	Stavros Theohary
Ethan Step	Vernetta Thomas
John Stephenson	Marc Thomas
Thomas Stewardson	David P. Thomas
Tanner Stewart	Chris Thompson
Maggie Stewart-Grant	Steven Thompson
John Stockley	Jonathan Thompson
Rob Strachan	William Joseph Thorpe
James Street	Beverly Tierney
Joshua Strickland	Daniel Torres
William Strickler	Matthew Townsend
Shayla Striffler	Jameson Trauger
John Stuhl	Dimitrios Tsaousis
Brad Stumpp	Scott Tucker
Kevin Summers	Oliver Tunnicliffe
Ernest Sumner	Eric Turnbull
Randall Surles	Ryan Turner
Sonny Suttles	Brandon Turton
Andrew Suy	John Tuttle
David Swantek	Dylan Tuxhorn
Aaron Sweeney	Nerissa Umanzor
Shayne Sweetland	Jalen Underwood
Tiffany Swindle	Barrett Utz
Lloyd Swistara	Paul Van Dop
Carol Szpara	Andrew Van Winkle
Travis TadeWaldt	Patrick Van Winkle
Daniel Tanner	Paden VanBuskirk
Blake Tate	Patrick Varrassi

Daniel Vatamaniuck
Jason Vaughn
Jose Vazquez
Stephen Vea
Brian Veit
Daniel Venema
Marshall Verkler
Cole Vineyard
Ralph Vloemans
Anthony Wagnon
Wes "Gingy" Wahl
Humberto Waldheim
Christopher Walker
David Wall
Joshua Wallace
Justin Wang
Andrew Ward
Wedge Warford
Scot Washam
Tyler Washburn
Quentin Washington
Christopher Waters
Zachary Waters
John Watson
William Webb
Bill Webb
Hiram Wells
Jack Weston

William Westphal
Ben Wheeler
Paul White
Paul Wierzchowski
Grant Wiggins
Jack Williams
Justin Wilson
Scott Winters
Evan Wisniewski
Matthew Wittmann
Reese Wood
Tripp Wood
Robert Woodward
John Wooten
John Work
Bonnie Wright
Jason Wright
Ethan Yerigan
Matthew Young
John Zack
Phillip Zaragoza
Brandt Zeeh
Kevin Zhang
David Zimmerman
Jordan Ziroli
Nathan Zoss